THE FIRST
LAW

*Also by John Lescroart
in Large Print:*

The Oath
The Hearing
The Mercy Rule
The 13th Juror

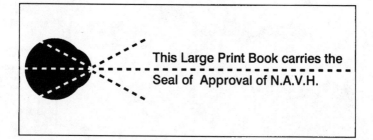

THE FIRST LAW

John Lescroart

Thorndike Press • Waterville, Maine

Published in 2003 by arrangement with Dutton, a member of Penguin Group (USA) Inc.

Thorndike Press® Large Print Americana Series.

The tree indicium is a trademark of Thorndike Press.

The text of this Large Print edition is unabridged.
Other aspects of the book may vary from the original edition.

Set in 16 pt. Plantin. *T 29613   4/2003*

Printed in the United States on permanent paper.

Library of Congress Cataloging-in-Publication Data

Lescroart, John T.
    The first law / John Lescroart.
      p. cm.
    ISBN 0-7862-5187-5 (lg. print : hc : alk. paper)
    1. Hardy, Dismas (Fictitious character) — Fiction.
2. Police — California — San Francisco — Fiction.   3. San Francisco (Calif.) — Fiction.   4. Fugitives from justice — Fiction.   5. Large type books.   I. Title.
PS3562.E78F5 2003b
    813'.54—dc21   2002044749

To Lisa

Nunc et Semper

ACKNOWLEDGMENTS

I'd like to thank my publisher and editor, Carole Baron, not only for her encouragement and support over so much of my career, but for her truly extraordinary interest and efforts from the earliest outlining stages of this book, which is in some ways so different in structure from my other novels. Mitch Hoffman's intelligence and insights likewise contributed importantly to the finished product; beyond that, his good humor and accessibility are as much appreciated as they are rare.

My friend and agent, Barney Karpfinger, remains an incredible source that I turn to whenever I need an injection of calm, wisdom, or good taste. His receptivity to the idea for this book and his early enthusiasm for it contributed mightily to its creation.

In San Francisco, the peerless Al Giannini was a great help, as always, from the original concept through the eventual execution. His knowledge of the law world within San Francisco has been a cornerstone of the entire Hardy/Glitsky series of books, and this one is no exception. In the police department, Shawn Ryan shared with me his considerable expertise with a variety of firearms; much more importantly, his description of what it's like to be under fire provided a crucial perspective. Assistant District Attorney Jerry Norman provided some choice nuggets as well.

Peter J. Diedrich provided much of the background for the very real San Francisco Diamond Center scandals of the late nineties. Peter S. Dietrich, M.D., M.P.H., still makes the best martini in the universe.

Closer to home, my assistant, Anita Boone, aside from being a creative genius in her own right, is simply terrific. Combining a wonderful personality with superhuman efficiency, she is truly one of a kind. I couldn't do what I do without her. The excellent novelist Max Byrd is a great friend and careful reader who was a help many times and at many stages during the writing of this book. Barbara Vohryzek's "good karma" plays a big role in my daily writing environment, and I want to thank her for thinking to include me in such a positive work space.

My children, Jack and Justine, continue to inspire and hopefully to inform these books, and this one particularly, with a welcome nonadult perspective. Rebecca and Vincent they are not, but Dismas Hardy's children could not exist as fully formed characters without them.

Finally, I'd like to acknowledge the work of two excellent writers for providing much of the inspiration for this book. Loren Estleman's *Bloody Season* tells the story of the gunfight at the OK Corral better than it's ever been told. I've read the book five times now, and it just keeps getting better. Carsten Stroud's *Black Water Transit*, though unique in execution, plot, and tone, could nevertheless serve as a primer for the construction of the modern thriller, and in fact did in the creation of this work. The use of language in both of these books reminded this writer again of the power of the unexpected, the original, the inspired word. Thanks, guys. You write terrific stuff.

And we are here as on a darkling plain
Swept by confused alarums of struggle
  and flight
Where ignorant armies clash by night.

— Matthew Arnold
"Dover Beach"

Part One

Part One

At a little before two o'clock on a chill and over-cast Wednesday afternoon, Moses McGuire pulled his old Ford pickup to a grating stop in front of his sister Frannie's house and honked the horn twice.

He waited, blowing on his hands, which he couldn't get to stay warm. The heater in the truck didn't work worth a damn and the driver-side window was stuck halfway down, but he knew it wasn't the weather. It was nerves. He blew into the cup of his hands again, lay on the horn another time.

The door opened. His brother-in-law, Dismas Hardy, walked briskly, businesslike, down his porch steps and the path that bisected his small lawn. Normally he was good for a smile or some wiseass greeting, but today his face was set, his eyes cast down. He carried a rope-wrapped package under one arm, wore jeans and hiking boots and a heavy coat into the pockets of which he'd stuffed his hands.

13

The coat, McGuire thought, was a good idea, not so much for the cold as to disguise the fact that he was wearing Kevlar, and packing.

Hardy, at fifty-two, was two years younger than McGuire. The two men had known each other for over thirty years, since they'd been in Vietnam. Over there, Hardy had pulled McGuire to cover and safety in the midst of an intense firefight — both of the men had been hit, both awarded the Purple Heart. But Hardy had saved McGuire's life and that bond had held, would always hold.

When Hardy's first pass at adult life fell apart, he'd worked for years at the bar Moses owned, the Little Shamrock, and eventually, when Hardy was ready to risk life and commitment again, he became a quarter partner in the bar. He'd married McGuire's sister, was godfather to one of McGuire's daughters, as Moses was to his.

Family.

Hardy slid in and dumped the package onto the seat between them. "There's your vest. I did have the extra." Saying it aloud seemed to cost him some energy. He drew a deep breath and took a last look back at his house as the truck moved into gear. Turning back to his brother-in-law, he asked, "What are you carrying?"

McGuire motioned over his shoulder, indi-

cating the truck bed. "I got fifty shells and my over and under wrapped in the tarp back there."

"Twelve gauge?"

"Yeah, and in there" — McGuire pointed to the glove box — "I got my Sig."

"Automatic?"

He caught Hardy's tone of disapproval. "They don't always jam," he said.

"Only takes once."

"I expect I'll be using the shotgun anyway."

The truck turned a couple of corners, the men riding in silence until they were rolling on Geary. McGuire blew on his hands again. Finally, Hardy spoke. "You okay with this?"

McGuire looked across the seat, his dark eyes flat. "Completely. You not?"

Hardy worked his mouth, shook his head. "I don't see another choice."

"That's 'cause there isn't one."

"I know. I know. It's just . . ."

"There's always another choice?"

"Usually."

"Not this time." McGuire bit it off, impatient. He accelerated angrily through a yellow light. "You already tried all of them."

"Maybe not all. That's what I worry about. This would be a bad time to get pulled over, don't you think?"

McGuire touched the brake, slowed a hair.

He slammed his hand on the dashboard. "Come on, heater, kick in. Fuck."

Hardy ignored the outburst. "I just think," he said, "we do this, then what?"

"Then we're alive, how about that? We don't, we're not. It's that simple." The next light was red and he had to stop, took the moment to make eye contact. "How many people do these guys have to kill, Diz? How many have they already killed?"

"Allegedly . . ."

"Don't give me that. You have any doubt at all, reasonable or otherwise?"

"No."

"So don't give me 'allegedly.' You don't believe it yourself."

"Okay, but maybe Abe could bring in the feds. Him going in alone to arrest these guys now . . ."

"He's not going to be alone. We're backing him up."

Hardy chewed at his cheek. "We're not the cops."

"Truer words were never said. There's no time to call in the feds, Diz. There's no time to convince any bureaucracy to move. You of all people should know that."

"I'm just saying if we had a little more time . . ."

McGuire shook his head. "Time's up, Diz.

They decide you're next — the good money bet by the way — they pull up to you maybe today, maybe tomorrow; they're not going to care if Frannie's in the car with you, or the kids. You're just gone. Like the others."

"I know. I know you're right."

"Damn straight." The light changed. McGuire hit the gas and lurched ahead. "Listen, you think I want to be here? I don't want to be here."

"I keep thinking the law . . ."

McGuire snorted. "The law. Your precious fucking law. It's gonna protect you, right? Like it has everybody else?"

"It's my life, Mose. I've pretty much got to believe that, don't I?"

"The law's not your life. It's your job. Your life is something else entirely. The first law is you protect your life and the people you love."

Hardy stared out the window.

McGuire was riding his adrenaline. "These guys don't give a shit, Diz. Isn't that pretty clear by now? They've got the law — the cops in this town anyway — in their pocket. It's unfair and unlikely, okay, but that's what's happened. So now all that's left is they take out you and your meddling friend Abe and it's all over. They win. Life goes back to normal. Except you guys are both dead, and maybe my sister with you, and I'm not willing to take that chance." His eyes ticked across the seat. "You're telling me after all that's gone down, you don't see this? You don't know for a fact this can happen? Is going to happen?"

"No. I see it all right, Mose. I don't know how we got here, that's all. It's so unreal."

"Yeah, well, remember 'Nam. It was unreal, too, until the bullets started flying. The World Trade Center was pretty unreal, too, if you think about it. You think people are reason-able, you think there are rules. But then, guess what? Suddenly there aren't."

"All right. But we're not going in shooting, Mose. We're backing up Abe, and that's all we're doing."

"If you say so."

"Unless something goes wrong."

McGuire threw him another look, couldn't tell if he was serious or not. Hardy would crack wise at his own execution. The truck turned onto the freeway, going south. Hardy pulled a box from his jacket pocket and set it on his lap, then pulled off the lid. Reaching under his arm, he pulled out the massive, blue steel Colt's Police Special that he'd carried when he'd been a cop years before. He snapped open the cylinder, spun it, and began pulling .357 copper-jacketed hollow-points from the box one at a time, dropping them into their slots.

When the six bullets were in place, he closed up and reholstered the gun, then pulled a second cylinder from his other pocket. Methodically — click, click, click as they fell into the cylinder — he sat filling the speed loader.

1

Ten o'clock, a Wednesday morning in the beginning of July.

John Holiday extended one arm over the back of the couch at his lawyer's Sutter Street office. Today he was comfortably dressed in stonewashed blue jeans, hiking boots, and a white, high-collared shirt so heavily starched that it had creaked when he lowered himself into his slouch. His other hand had come to rest on an oversize silver-and-turquoise belt buckle. His long legs stretched out all the way to the floor, his ankles crossed. Nothing about his posture much suggested his possession of a backbone.

Women had liked him since he'd outgrown his acne. His deep-set eyes seemed the window to a poet's soul, with the stained glass of that window the odd whitish blue of glacier water. Now, close up, those eyes revealed subtle traces of dissolution and loss. There was complexity here, even mystery. With an easy style and pale features — his jaw had the clean definition of a blade — he'd been making female hearts go pitter-patter for so long now that he took it for granted. He didn't much understand it. To him, the prettiness of his face had finally put him off enough that he'd grown a mustache. Full, drooping, and yellow as corn silk, it was two or three shades lighter than the hair on his head and had only made him more handsome. When his face was at rest, Holiday still didn't look thirty, but when he laughed, the lines added a decade, got him up to where he belonged. He still enjoyed a good laugh, though he smiled less than he used to.

He was smiling now, though, at his lawyer, Dismas Hardy, over by the sink throwing water on his face for the third time in ten minutes.

"As though that's gonna help." Holiday's voice carried traces of his father's Tennessee accent and the edges of it caressed like a soft Southern breeze.

"It would help if I could dry off."

"Didn't the first two times."

Hardy had used up the last of the paper towels and now stood facing his cupboards in his business suit, his face dripping over the sink. Holiday shrugged himself up from the couch, dug in the wastebasket by the desk, and came up with a handful of used paper, which he handed over. "Never let it be said I can't be helpful."

"It would never cross my mind." Hardy dried his face. "So where were we?"

"You're due in court in forty-five minutes and you're so hungover you don't remember where we were? If you'd behaved this way when you were my lawyer, I'd have fired you."

Hardy fell into one of his chairs. "I couldn't have behaved this way when I was your lawyer because I didn't know you well enough yet to go out drinking with you. Thank God."

"You're just out of practice. It's like riding a horse. You've got to get right back on when it tosses you."

"I did that last night. Twice."

"Don't look at me. If memory serves, nobody held a gun to your head. Why don't you call and tell them you're sick? Get a what-do-you-call-it . . ."

"Continuance." Hardy shook his head. "Can't. This is a big case."

"All the more reason if you can't think.

But you said it was just dope and some hooker."

"But with elements," Hardy said.

In fact, he hadn't done a hooker case for nearly a decade. In his days as an assistant DA, the occasional prostitution case would cross his desk. Hardy mostly found these morally questionable, politically suspect, and in any case a waste of taxpayer money. Prostitutes, he thought, while rarely saint-like, were mostly victims themselves, so as a prosecutor, he would often try to use the girls' arrests as some kind of leverage to go after their dope connections or pimps, the true predators. Occasionally, it worked. Since he'd been in private practice, because there was little money in defending working girls, he never saw these cases anymore. As a matter of course, the court appointed the public defender's office or private counsel if that office had a conflict.

In this way, Aretha LaBonte's case had been assigned to Gina Roake, a mid-forties career defense attorney. But Gina's case-load had suddenly grown so large it was compromising her ability to handle it effectively. If she wanted to do well by the rest, she had to dump some clients, including Aretha. By chance she mentioned the case to her boyfriend, Hardy's landlord, David Freeman, who'd had a good listen and smelled money. With his ear always to the ground, Freeman had run across some similar cases.

Aretha's arrest had been months ago now. Her case was interesting and from Freeman's perspective potentially lucrative because her arresting officer wasn't a regular San Francisco policeman. Instead, he had been working for a company called WGP, Inc., which provided security services to businesses under a jurisdictional anomaly in San Francisco. In its vigilante heyday a century ago, the city found that its police department couldn't adequately protect the people who did business within its limits. Those folks asked the PD for more patrols, but there was neither budget nor personnel to accommodate them. So the city came up with a unique solution — it created and sold patrol "beats" to individuals who became private security guards for those beats. These beat holders, or Patrol Specials, then and now, were appointed by the police commissioner, trained and licensed by the city. The beat holders could, and did, hire assistants to help them patrol, and in time most Patrol Specials came to control their own autonomous armed force in the middle of the city.

On his beat, a Patrol Special tended to be a law unto himself, subject only to the haphazard and indifferent supervision of the San Francisco Police Department. They and their assistants wore uniforms and badges almost exactly like those of the city police; they carried weapons and, like any other citizen, could make arrests.

Aretha LaBonte's arrest had occurred within the twelve-square-block area just south of Union Square known as Beat Thirty-two, or simply Thirty-two. It was one of six beats in the city owned by WGP, the corporate identity of a philanthropic businessman named Wade Panos. He had a total of perhaps ninety assistants on his payroll, and this, along with the amount of physical territory he patrolled, made him a powerful presence in the city.

Aretha's case was not the first misconduct that Freeman had run across in Panos's beats. In fact, Freeman's preliminary and cursory legwork, his "sniff test," revealed widespread allegations of assistant patrol specials' use of excessive force, planting of incriminating evidence, general bullying. If Hardy could get Aretha off on this one assistant patrol special's misconduct, and several of the other "sniff test" cases could be developed and drafted into legal causes of action, he and Freeman could put together a zillion dollar lawsuit against Panos. They could also include the regular police department as a named defendant for allowing these abuses to continue.

But at the moment, Hardy didn't exactly feel primed for the good fight. He brought his hand up and squeezed his temples, then exhaled slowly and completely. "It's not just a hooker case. It's going to get bigger, and delay doesn't help us. There's potentially huge money down the line, but first I've got to rip this witness a new one. If he goes down, we move forward. That's the plan."

"Which gang aft agley, especially if your brain's mush."

"It'll firm up. Pain concentrates the mind wonderfully. And I really want this guy."

"What guy?"

"The prosecution's chief witness. The arresting cop. Nick Sephia."

Suddenly Holiday sat upright. "Nick the Prick?"

"Sounds right."

"What'd he do wrong this time?"

"Planted dope on my girl."

"Let me guess. She wasn't putting out

for him or paying for protection, so he set her up."

"You've heard the song before?"

"It's an oldie but goodie, Diz. Everybody knows it."

"Who's everybody?"

A shrug. "The neighborhood. Everybody."

Suddenly Hardy was all business. He knew that Holiday owned a bar, the Ark, smack in the middle of Thirty-two. Knew it, hell, he'd closed the place the night before. But somehow he'd never considered Holiday as any kind of real source for potential complainants in the Panos matter. Now, suddenly, he did. "You got names, John? People who might talk to me? I've talked to a lot of folks in the neighborhood in the last couple of months. People might be unhappy, but nobody's saying anything too specific."

A little snort. "Pussies. They're scared."

"Scared of Wade Panos?"

Holiday pulled at the side of his mustache, and nodded slowly. "Yeah, sure, who else?"

"That's what I'm asking you." Hardy hesitated. "Look, John, this is what Freeman and I have been looking for. We need witnesses who'll say that things like this Sephia bust I'm doing today are part of a pattern that the city's known about and been tolerating for years. If you know some names, I'd love to hear them."

Holiday nodded thoughtfully. "I could get some, maybe a lot," he said. "They're out there, I'll tell you that." His eyes narrowed. "You know Nick's his nephew, don't you? Wade's."

"Panos's? So his own uncle fired him?"

"Moved him out of harm's way is more like it. Now he's working for the Diamond Center."

"And you're keeping tabs on him?"

"We've been known to sit at a table together. Poker."

"Which as your lawyer I must remind you is illegal. You beat him?"

A shrug. "I don't play to lose."

The Wednesday night game had been going on for years now in the back room of Sam Silverman's pawnshop on O'Farrell, a block from Union Square. There were maybe twenty regulars. You reserved your chair by noon Tuesday and Silverman held it to six players on any one night. Nobody pretended that it was casual entertainment among friends. Table stakes makes easy enemies, especially when the buy-in is a thousand dollars. Twenty white chips at ten bucks each, fifteen reds at twenty, and ten blues at fifty made four or five small piles that could go away in a hurry. Sometimes in one hand.

With his neat bourbon in a heavy bar glass, John Holiday sat in the first chair, to Silverman's left, and two chairs beyond him Nick Sephia now smoldered. He'd come in late an hour ago and had taken a seat between his regular companions, Wade's little brother, Roy Panos, and another Diamond Center employee named Julio Rez. The other two players at the table tonight were Fred Waring, a mid-forties black stockbroker, and Mel Fischer, who used to own four Nosh Shop locations around downtown, but was now retired.

At thirty or so, Sephia was the youngest player there. He was also, by far, the biggest — six-three, maybe 220, all of it muscle. While Silverman took the young Greek's money and counted out his chips, Sephia carefully hung the coat of his exquisitely tailored light green suit over the back of his chair. The blood was up in his face, the color in his cheeks raw beef, the scowl a fixture. He'd shaved that morning but his jawline was already blue with shadow. After he sat, he snugged his gold silk tie up under his Adam's apple, rage flowing off him in an aura.

The usual banter dried up. After a few hands during which no one said a word, Roy Panos pushed a cigar over in front of the late arrival. Holiday sipped his bourbon. Eventually Silverman, maybe hoping to ease the tension, called a bathroom break for himself, and Sephia lit up, blowing the smoke out through his nose. Waring and Fischer stood to stretch and pour themselves drinks. Holiday, quietly enjoying Sephia's pain, had a good idea of what was bothering him. Maybe the whiskey was affecting his judgment — it often did — but he couldn't resist. "Bad day, Nick?"

Sephia took a minute deciding whether he was going to talk about it. Finally, he shook his head in disgust. "Fucking lawyers. I spent half the day in court."

"Why? What'd you do?"

"What'd *I* do?" He blew smoke angrily. "I didn't do dick."

Roy Panos helped him with the explanation. "They suppressed his evidence on some hooker he brought in for dope a couple of months ago. Said he planted it on her."

"So?" Holiday was all sweet reason. "If

you didn't, what's the problem?"

Sephia's dark eyes went to slits, his temper ready to flare at any indication that Holiday was having fun at his expense, but he saw no sign of it. "Guy made me look like a fucking liar, is the problem. Like I'm supposed to remember exactly what I did with this one whore? She's got junk in her purse; another one's got it in her handbag. Who gives a shit where it was? Or how it got there? It's there, she's guilty, end of story. Am I right?"

"Fuckin' A." Julio Rez, a medium-built Latino, spoke without any accent. All wires and nerves, he'd probably been a good base stealer in his youth. He'd lost the lower half of his left ear somewhere, but it didn't bother him enough to try to cover it with his hair, which was cropped short. "She goes down."

"But not today. Today they let her go." Panos spoke to Holiday. "They suppress the dope, there's no case."

"Were you down at court, too?"

Panos shook his head. "No, but Wade was. My brother? He is pissed off."

"Not at me, I hope," Sephia said.

Panos patted him on the arm. "No, no. The lawyers. Bastards."

"Why would your brother be mad at

Nick?" Holiday sipped again at his tumbler of bourbon.

"He was working for him at the time, that's why. It makes Wade look bad. I mean, Nick's doing patrol for Christ sake. He busts a hooker, she ought to stay busted at least. Now maybe they start looking at the rest of the shop."

"Judge reamed my ass," Sephia said. "This prick lawyer — he had the judge talking perjury, being snotty on the record. 'I find the arresting officer's testimony not credible as to the circumstances surrounding the arrest.' Yeah, well, Mr. Hardy, you can bite me."

Holiday feigned surprise. "Hardy's *my* lawyer's name. *Dismas* Hardy?"

Now Sephia's glare was full on. "The fuck I know? But whatever it is, I see him again, he's going to wish I didn't."

"So he must have convinced them you did plant her?"

Rez shot a quick glance at Sephia. But Sephia held Holiday's eyes for a long beat, as though he was figuring something out. "She wasn't paying," he finally said, his voice filled with a calm menace. "Wade wanted her out of the beat. Most of the time that's intensive care. I figured I was doing the bitch a favor."

Dismas Hardy's wife, Frannie, cocked her head in surprise. They'd just sat down at a small Spanish place on Clement, not far from their house on Thirty-fourth Avenue. "You're not having wine?" she asked.

"Not tonight."

"Nothing to drink at all?"

"Just water. Water's good."

"You feel all right?"

"Fine. Sometimes I don't feel like drinking, that's all."

"Oh, that's right. I remember there was that time right after Vincent was born." Their son, Vincent, was now thirteen. She reached her hand across the table and put it over one of his. "Did you hurt yourself last night?"

Half a grin flickered then died out. "I didn't think so at the time. I'm out of shape pounding myself with alcohol."

Frannie squeezed his hand. "Out of shape could be a good thing, you know." But she softened her tone. "How was John?"

"Entertaining, charming, drunk. The usual. Though he came by the office this morning fresh as a daisy. He must have been pouring his drinks in the flowerpots."

"So what time did you finally get in?"

"One-ish? That's a guess. You were asleep, though. I think."

"Aren't you glad you decided to take a cab when you went out?"

"Thrilled. I guess I must have taken a cab back home then, huh?"

"If John didn't drive you."

Hardy pressed two fingers into his temple. "No. I think we can rule that out."

A look of concern. "You really don't remember?"

"No. I remember. I didn't even think I'd hurt myself until this morning when that moose in my mouth wouldn't stop kicking at my brains." He shrugged. "But you know, with John . . ."

"Maybe you don't have to keep up with him."

"That's what they all say. But then you do."

The waiter came by with a basket of freshly baked bread, some olives, a hard pungent cheese. Frannie ordered her usual Chardonnay. As advertised, Hardy stayed with water. They kept holding hands over the table. The waiter vanished and Hardy picked up where they'd been. "He's more fun than a lot of people," he said, "and more interesting than almost everybody except you."

"What a sweet thing to say. And so sincere." She squeezed his hand. "I don't have a problem with him. Really. Or with you. I don't know if I understand the attraction — if you were a woman, okay — but I don't like to see you hurting."

"I'm not so wild about it either. But you hang out with John Holiday, there's a chance you'll drink too much sometimes. And in spite of all this, by the way, today wasn't a total loss. Maybe I should have a drink, after all. Celebrate."

"What?"

"You know that motion to suppress . . ."

He told her about his afternoon in the courtroom, getting Nick Sephia's evidence kicked out, which led to Aretha LaBonte's case being dismissed. "Not that it's going to change her life in any meaningful way. She's probably back on the street even as we speak, although if she's smart she's not working one of Wade Panos's beats. But it was nice to serve notice that this stuff isn't flying anymore. When it was over, David even had a little moment of actual drama right there in the Hall of Justice."

The curmudgeonly and unkempt seventy-four-year-old legal powerhouse that was David Freeman wouldn't give Wade

Panos or his hired thug Nick Sephia the satisfaction. Further, he did not believe in revealing pain or weakness under any conditions, but most especially in a professional setting. So even Dismas Hardy, who'd been there, wasn't aware of how badly he'd been hurt. How badly he still hurt.

At first, he even tried to fake it with Roake. On her sixth full day of automatic redial, she had finally succeeded in getting dinner reservations for them both at the legendarily swank restaurant, Gary Danko. Freeman wasn't going to whine and ruin the special night she'd so painstakingly orchestrated. So after the successful hearing and the little problem he'd had with Sephia and Panos, he'd forgone any celebration with Hardy and instead had beelined home from the Hall of Justice, hailing a cab as soon as he was out of sight around the corner. In his apartment, he popped a handful of aspirin with a hefty shot of Calvados. Then he ran a hot bath and soaked in it before dragging himself into bed, where he slept for three and a half hours until his alarm jarred his aching body into a disoriented awareness.

It cost him a half hour, laboring mightily through the pain, to get himself dressed.

Freeman held fast to a lifelong core belief that juries didn't trust nice clothes, and so of the seven business suits he owned, six were brown and straight off the rack. But the last one was a khaki Canali that Roake had bought him last Christmas. He was wearing that one tonight, with a red silk tie over a rich, ivory, custom-made shirt. His scuffed cordovan wingtips were the only sign of the usual Freeman.

By the time Roake had come by to pick him up at seven o'clock, he had steeled himself and thought he was ready. But then she surprised him, or perhaps his flashy clothes surprised her. In any event, she hung back in the doorway and whistled appreciatively, frankly admiring him for a moment, then took a little skip forward and threw her arms around him, squeezing hard.

A cry escaped before he could stop it.

"What is it? David? Are you all right? What's the matter?"

He was fighting for control, his jaw set, brow contracted, blowing quick, short little breaths from his mouth.

Now, two hours later, he awoke again from his third brief doze. He was back in bed, in his pajamas, and Roake was sitting at his side, holding his hand. "You really ought to see a doctor," she said.

But he shook his head. "If it ain't broke, don't fix it. And nothing's broke."

"But you're hurt."

He started to shrug, then grimaced. "Tomorrow I'll be dancing. You wait." He put a hand to his neck and turned his head slowly from side to side a couple of times, then stopped and fixed her with a sheepish gaze. "I feel like such a fool."

"What for? You didn't ask for this."

"No. But I knew who I was dealing with. I should have been prepared. In the old days, I would have been."

"Prepared for Nick Sephia to knock you over?"

The old man, looking every year of his age, nodded wearily. "They set me up."

"How did they do that?"

"Child's play with a trusting soul like myself." He sighed in disgust. "I'd already had a few words with the elder Mr. Panos after Dismas beat the hell out of Sephia on the stand."

"What in the world prompted you to do that?"

"Hubris, plain and simple." Another sigh. "I couldn't resist the opportunity to crow a little, though I thought I'd done it subtly enough in the guise of giving him a friendly warning of what was coming."

Roake allowed a small smile. "Hence your nickname, Mr. Subtle."

"In any event, it didn't fool him much. So afterwards a bunch of their guys — Dick Kroll's there, too. You know Dick? Sephia's lawyer? And Panos and his little brother and one of Nick's pals I'd seen in court with him before, some greaser. Anyway, all these guys are having some kind of powwow out in the hall. So Wade sees me come out with Hardy and motions to me over Nick's shoulder. Come on over."

"And you went?"

"What was I gonna do? I tell Diz to wait and give me a minute. I'm thinking no doubt I put the fear of God in Wade and he's talked to Kroll and decided to cave and try to cut some kind of deal right there."

"That hubris thing again."

Freeman raised his shoulders an inch, acknowledging the truth. "Occupational hazard if you happen to be cursed with genius. Anyway, it's here to stay." Another shrug. "So I'm like two steps away when Nick the Prick suddenly whirls around — whoops, late for a bus — and next thing I know I'm flat on my keister, stretched out on the goddamn floor, and there's Nick leaning over me, all 'Sorry, old man, didn't see you.' " Finally, his eyes got some real fire back into them. "Sorry my ass. Wade gave him some kind of sign and he turned on cue. That was his warning back at me — fuck with me and you'll get hurt." He went to straighten up in the bed, but his bones fought him and won. He gave it up, falling back into his pillow.

Roake put her hand on his chest, brought it up to stroke his cheek. "You guys," she said gently. Then, in a minute, "It could have been an accident, after all, couldn't it?"

"No. No chance."

"So now you need to get back at them, is that it?"

He nodded. "In the words of Ol' Blue Eyes, I'll do it my way, but bet your ass I will." Reading her reaction, he added, "That's the only message they hear."

"And how about you? Which one do you hear?"

"What do you mean by that?"

"I mean, you warn them, they attack you, now it's your turn again, and it all escalates, until somebody really gets hurt. Maybe it doesn't always have to be that way."

"With some people, maybe it does. What

else do you do when they're pulling shit like today? You fight back, is what."

Roake had her hands back in her lap. "Then you're both still fighting. And what's that prove?"

"When somebody wins, it ends. And I intend to win."

"And that's what it's all about, is it? Who wins?"

"Yep." Defiantly. "What else?" he asked. "What else is there?"

Roake sat with it for a beat. She blew out in frustration. Finally, she looked down at him and stood up. "How very male of you."

"There's worse ways to be, Gina. What else do you want?"

She looked down at him. "I want you to be smart. Don't get drawn into playing their games. This doesn't have to continue being personal, especially if they believe in doing things like today, in actually hurting people. That's all I'm saying. File your papers, keep out of it, and let the law do its work."

"That's exactly my intention. What else would I do?" Freeman patted the bed. "Come, sit back down. I'm not self-destructive, you know. I'm not going to fight anybody physically."

Roake lowered herself down next to him again. "That's what I thought you were saying." She took his gnarled hand in both of hers.

"No, no, no. I'm talking what I do. The law. That'll beat up on 'em good enough. But I will tell you one other thing."

"What's that?"

"Whatever else it might look like, it's going to be personal."

Lieutenant Abraham Glitsky, once the powerful head of San Francisco's homicide detail, was half-black and half-Jewish, and in his job he'd groomed himself to exude a threatening mixture of efficient competence and quiet menace. His infrequent smiles would even more rarely get all the way to his piercing blue eyes. A Semitic hatchet of a nose protruded over a generous mouth, rendered unforgettable by the thick scar that bisected both lips.

Now this fearsome figure stood framed in the doorway to his duplex. He wore neither shoes nor socks and his bare legs showed at the bottom of a dirty kitchen apron. He'd draped a diaper over his right shoulder. It was streaked — recently — with the oranges and greens and off-browns of strained baby food. He held his ten-month-old daughter Rachel in the crook of his left arm. She had somehow wriggled out of one of her pink baby booties, and just as Glitsky opened the door, she'd hooked it over his ear.

"Where's a camera when you really need one?" Hardy asked.

Frannie stepped forward. "Here, Abe. Let me hold her."

In what had become a largely unacknowledged weekly ritual, the Hardys' Wednesday Date Night was ending here again. Since Rachel's birth, Frannie couldn't seem to get enough of holding her. She was turning forty soon and their children were both teenagers. Maybe she and Dismas should have another baby. There was still time. Just. If Dismas wanted one, too. Which he did like he wanted cancer.

He couldn't decide if the visits to hold Rachel were a good thing because it satisfied Frannie's need to hold a baby, or a bad thing because it made her want one of her own even more, but either way, they'd been coming by now regularly enough that there was usually some kind of dessert waiting for them when they got there.

Glitsky shrugged the baby over to Frannie, immediately grabbed at the bootie.

"You ought to leave it," Hardy begged. "It's so *you*. And that pink goes just perfect with the puke on the diaper."

Glitsky glanced down at his shoulder. "That's not puke. Puke is eaten, regurgitated, expelled matter. This" — he touched the diaper — "is simply food that didn't quite get to the mouth."

"Guys! Guys!" Frannie whisked the diaper over to her own shoulder. She slipped the bootie over Rachel's foot, then fixed each of the guys with a look. "Fascinating though these distinctions are, maybe we could leave them just for a minute."

She turned into the living room. Hardy, behind her, didn't want to let the topic go. He could score some valuable points here. "You know, Fran, if you really want another baby, you've got to be ready to deal with puke."

"I can deal with it fine," she said over her shoulder. "I just don't want to talk about it, much less conjugate it."

Hardy took the cue. "I puke, you puke, he she or it pukes . . ."

Suddenly Treya came around the corner from the kitchen. "Who wants another baby?"

Ten minutes later, they were arranged —

coffee for the Hardys, tea for the Glitskys — around the large square table that took up nearly all the space in the tiny kitchen. Rachel was dozing, ready to be laid down in her crib, although neither Frannie nor Treya seemed inclined to move in that direction. The treat tonight was a plate of homemade macaroon cookies, still hot from the oven, all coconut and stick-to-the-teeth sweetness. "These," Hardy said to Treya after his first bite, "are incredible. I didn't know normal people could make macaroons."

"Abe can. Not that he's a normal person exactly."

"Or even approximately," Hardy said. "But if he can make these things, maybe there's still some use for him."

"You're both too kind." Glitsky turned to Hardy. "So where did you think they came from? Macaroons."

"I thought they dropped straight out of heaven, like manna in the desert. In fact, I always imagined that manna had kind of a macaroon flavor. Didn't any of you guys? I'm serious." His face lit up with an idea. "Hey, Manna Macaroons. That wouldn't be a bad brand name. We could market them like Mrs. Fields. Abe's Manna Macaroons. We could all get rich. . . ."

Frannie spoke. "Somebody please stop him."

Glitsky jumped in. "It's a good idea, Diz, but I couldn't do it anyway. I'm going back to work next week. Monday."

Treya gave him a wary look. "You hope."

"All right," he conceded, "I hope."

"Why wouldn't you be?" Hardy asked. "How long's it been, anyway?"

"On Monday, it'll have been thirteen months, two weeks and three days."

"Roughly," Treya added pointedly. "Not that he's been counting."

Glitsky was coming off a bad year, one that had begun with a point-blank gunshot wound to his abdomen. For the first month or so after the initial cleanup, he'd been recovering according to schedule — getting around in a wheelchair, taking things easy — when the first of several medical complications had developed. A secondary infection that finally got diagnosed as peritonitis put him back in the hospital, where he then developed pneumonia. The double whammy had nearly killed him for a second time, and left him weakened and depleted through Rachel's birth last August until late in the fall. Then, suddenly the initial wound itself wouldn't completely heal. It wasn't until

February of this year that he'd even been walking regularly at all, and a couple of months after that before he began trying to get back into shape. At the end of May, his doctors finally declared him fit to return to work, but Glitsky's bosses had told him that homicide's interim head — the lieutenant who'd taken Glitsky's place — would need to be reassigned and there wasn't an immediately suitable job befitting his rank and experience.

So Glitsky had waited some more.

Now they were in July and evidently something had finally materialized, but obviously with a wrinkle. "So what's to hope about getting back on Monday?" Hardy asked. "How could it *not* happen? You walk in, say hi to your troops, go back to your desk and break out the peanuts." The lieutenant's desk in homicide was famous for its unending stash of goobers in the shell.

Glitsky made a face.

"Apparently," Treya said, "it's not that simple."

Hardy finished a macaroon, sipped some coffee. "What?" he asked. "Somebody from the office saw you in the apron? I bet that's it. We can sue them for discrimination. You should be allowed to wear an apron if you want."

"Dismas, shut up," Frannie said. "What, Abe?"

"Well, the PD will of course welcome me back, but maybe at a different job."

"What job?" Hardy asked. "Maybe they're promoting you."

"I didn't get that impression. They're talking payroll."

"Head of payroll's a sergeant," Hardy said. "Isn't he?"

"Used to be anyway." Glitsky hesitated. "Seems there's been some concern that I was excessively close to my work in homicide."

"Evidently this is a bad thing," Treya added.

"As opposed to what?" Frannie asked. "Bored with it?"

"You haven't even gone to work for a year," Hardy said. "How does that put you excessively close to it?"

Glitsky nodded. "I raised some of the same points myself."

"And?" Hardy asked.

"And in the past few years, as we all know, my daughter was killed, I had a heart attack, and I got shot in the line of duty."

"One of which actually happened because of the job." Treya was frowning deeply. "He also got married and had a baby, as if there's some connection there, too."

Glitsky shrugged. "It's just an excuse. It's really because my extended disability made them put a new guy in homicide for the duration. . . ."

"Gerson, right?" Hardy said.

"That's him. They probably told him it was his permanent gig when they moved him up. And now that I've had the bad grace to get better, they're embarrassed."

"So transfer *him*," Hardy said. "What does the union say?"

"They say Gerson's been doing okay so far, and it wouldn't be fair to transfer him before he's even really gotten his feet wet. It might look bad for him later. Whereas I've already proved myself."

"And so as a reward, they're moving you out?" Frannie asked. "And down?"

"Not down," Treya said. "He's going to be *lieutenant* of payroll."

"I don't even know where payroll is," Glitsky said, "much less what they do."

"That's perfect," Hardy said. "You wouldn't want too many people working at jobs they know about."

"God forbid," Glitsky said. "And the

great thing, as they so graciously explained to me, is that this is not a punishment. It's an opportunity to improve my résumé. I spend maybe a year in payroll; then they promote me to captain at one of the stations. Couple of years there, next thing you know I'm a deputy chief."

"His lifelong dream," Treya added with heavy sarcasm.

Hardy knew what Treya meant. Glitsky had worked fourteen years in the department before he got to inspector sergeant at homicide, and then another eight before they promoted him to lieutenant of the detail. Abe didn't crave varied administrative experience. He wanted to catch murderers.

"Have you talked to Batiste?" Hardy asked. This was Frank Batiste, recently promoted to deputy chief. For many years, as Captain of Inspectors, he had been Glitsky's mentor within the department. "Maybe he could throw some juice."

But Glitsky shook his head. "Who do you think I talked to?"

Hardy frowned. "I thought he was your guy."

"Well . . ." Glitsky made a face.

Treya knew that her husband wasn't comfortable complaining about a colleague, so she helped him with it. "It seems like Frank's going through some changes himself."

"Like what?" Frannie asked.

"It's not Frank," Glitsky said. He wasn't going to let people bad-mouth another cop, even if there might be something behind it. "He's stuck, too. His wife hasn't sold a house in a year. They got kids in college. Times are not sweet."

"So he makes them bad for you, too? What's that about?"

Again, Glitsky wouldn't rise. "I can't really blame him, Diz. He can't afford to lose his own job to make me happy."

"That wouldn't happen," Treya argued. "He's too connected."

"People might have said the same thing about me last year," Glitsky said. "It's a different world down there lately." He shrugged. "Frank got the word from above; then he got to be the messenger. If he didn't want to deliver it, they'd find somebody else, and then he's not a team player anymore. He had no choice."

But Treya shook her head. "He didn't have to tell you good cops don't go where they choose, they go where they're ordered. That doesn't sound like a friend."

"I could hear me telling one of my troops the same thing." Clearly uncomfortable with the discussion, Glitsky looked around the table. "As for being friends, Frank's my superior officer. He's doing his job."

"So you're really going to payroll?" Frannie asked. "I can't really see you crunching numbers all day long."

The edge of Glitsky's mouth turned up. "I'm sure there'll be lots of hidden satisfactions. In any event, I'll find out on Monday."

"You got a backup plan?" Hardy asked.

Glitsky looked at Treya, tried a smile that didn't quite work. "We've got a new baby," he said. "What else am I going to do?"

2

It was a Thursday evening in early November. Daylight Saving Time had ended on the previous weekend, and consequently it was full night by six o'clock. It was darker even than it might have been because the streetlights on O'Farrell Street between Stockton and Powell had not come on — perhaps they hadn't been set back for the time change.

A fifteen-knot wind was biting and blowing up from off the Bay, pushing before it the occasional large drop of what was to be the first real rainstorm of the season. Although Sam Silverman's pawnshop was located only one block south of the always-congested Union Square neighborhood, tonight — with the awful weather and deep blackness — the street out front was all but deserted.

Silverman had already locked the front door and pulled both sides of the antitheft bars on their tracks. Now all he had to do when he was ready to leave was to unlock the door again for a moment, step outside, and pull the bars so that he could padlock them together. He stood at the door inside an extra second and frowned — that hour of lost daylight always depressed him for the first week or so.

Sighing, he turned and walked back through the center aisle of his shop, reaching out and touching the treasures of other people's lives against which he'd loaned them money — guitars and saxophones and drum kits, silverware, cutlery, fine porcelain china sets, doll collections, televisions, radios, microwave ovens. Much of it bought new in a spirit of hope for the future, now most of it abandoned forever, secondhand junk without a trace of dream left in it.

At the back counter, he stopped again, struck by the display. Jewelry was by far his biggest stock item, and the watches and rings, the necklaces and earrings, though lovely, tonight seemed to hold even more pathos than the other goods. These were mostly gifts — at one time they'd been the carefully chosen expressions of love, of vows taken and lives shared. Now they were locked under the glass in a pawnshop, to be sold for a fraction of their cost, with all the human value in them lost to time and need.

He shook his head to rid himself of these somber thoughts. The start of winter always did this to him, and he'd be damned if he'd give in to it. Maybe he was getting that sickness where you got sad all the time when the weather sucked. But no. He'd lived in San Francisco his whole life, and God knew there had been enough opportunity that he would have caught it before now.

It was just the early darkness.

He glanced back at the front door and saw himself reflected in the glass — a small, somewhat stooped, decently dressed old Jewish man. It was *black* out there. Time passed during which he didn't move a muscle. When he heard the wind gust, then fade, and drops of rain just beginning to sound slowly onto the skylight overhead, he started, coming suddenly back to where he was. He looked up at the source of the noise — the skylight, covered with bars, was just a dark hole in the ceiling.

The thought crossed his mind that he wished he'd kept up his contract with Wade Panos. It would be nice on a miserable night like tonight to have one of his big and armed assistant patrol specials walk with him the two blocks around the corner to the night deposit box at Bank of America. But he and Sadie had gone over it and decided they couldn't justify the prices anymore, especially since Wade was raising them again.

While it was somewhat comforting to have the private patrol watching out for you — especially on your walks to the bank — it wasn't as though this part of the city was a magnet for violent crime anymore. Nothing like it used to be. The shop hadn't even had a window broken in over twenty years. No, the Patrol Special was a luxury he really didn't need and couldn't afford anymore. And it wasn't as though the city police didn't patrol here, too. Maybe just not as often.

Still, though, he considered calling the station and requesting an officer to walk over to the bank with him. But even if they could spare anyone, he'd have to wait here another hour or so. Maybe he just shouldn't do the errand tonight. But Thursday, after the poker game, was always his deposit night. And last night he'd made one of his biggest hauls.

He flicked on the small night-light in the jewelry cabinet. Enough with maudlin.

He'd better get finished here or he'd get soaked on the way to the bank. Working the combination to his safe, he considered that maybe this should be the year he and Sadie pack up and buy a condo like the ones they'd looked at last summer in Palm Springs. Maybe even Scottsdale.

Although when they'd gone there in the summer a few years back, it had been way too hot. And leaving his friends here, and his synagogue — did they really want to do that? What did he think he was going to do in Palm Springs without the company of Nat Glitsky, a brother to him all these years? And Nat, with a new baby grandchild, wasn't going anywhere. Sam loved Sadie, but she was a reader — a very solitary and passionate reader — not a games person. Nat, on the other hand, loved all kinds of games — backgammon, dominoes, Scrabble, anything to do with cards. They had *tournaments*, for God's sake, with trophies. No, Sam didn't really want to move. He just wanted the days to be longer again.

"Fart-knocker," he said aloud to himself, shaking his head. In the back room, he went to a knee, worked the combination, swung open the door to the safe. Lifting out the old maroon leather pouch, he was struck again by the thickness of it. He unzipped the top and ran his thumb over the top edges of the bills, nearly twenty-two thousand dollars in all, more than two months' worth of the shop's earnings, even if he included what he made on his poker fees. It would be the largest deposit he'd made in years.

He zipped it back up and placed it in the inside pocket of his jacket. A last check of the shop, then he grabbed his fedora off the hat rack, pushing it down hard over his crown against the wind he'd encounter when he got outside. He turned out the lights and retraced his steps down the center aisle. Stopping a last time, he looked both ways up the street and saw nothing suspicious.

He reached for the door and pulled it open.

The plan was a simple one. Speed and efficiency. They wore heavy coats, latex gloves, and ski masks to thwart identification. None of them was to say one word before they knocked Silverman out.

The old man was holding his hat down securely on his head with one hand, pulling the door to behind him when the three men came out of hiding in the doorways on either side of his shop windows and, pulling their masks down over their faces, fell upon him. The biggest guy got the door while the other two grabbed him by the arms, covered his mouth, and manhandled him inside and back up the aisle.

In the back room, they turned the light on. But the old man had gotten his mouth free and was starting to make noise now, yelling at them, maybe getting up the nerve to give them some kind of fight, as though he had any kind of chance. But delay would mean a hassle.

And since hassle wasn't part of the plan, the big man pulled a revolver from his pocket. The old geezer was actually making a decent show of resistance, struggling, manipulating his shoulders from side to side, grunting and swearing with the exertion. Because of all the lateral movement, the first swing with the gun glanced off the side of the man's head, but it was enough to stop him, stunned by the blow. The instant was long enough.

The next swing connected with Silverman's skull and dropped him cold. He slumped into dead weight and they lowered him to the ground, where he lay unmoving.

The big man knew just what he was

looking for and where it would be. In two seconds, he'd unplugged the surveillance video mounted over the office door. Five seconds later, he had the maroon leather pouch in his hands and was back on his feet. He pulled his ski mask off and threw it to the floor. His accomplices removed theirs and put them in their coat pockets. "Okay," the big man said. *"Vámonos."*

Leading the way, he doused the shop lights again. He was at the front door, halfway out. Somebody called out, "Guys, wait up."

The gunman stopped and turned. Waiting up wasn't in the plan. The idea was to get the money and then get out, closing the dark shop behind them. When Silverman came to, if he ever did, they'd be long gone.

"The fuck are you doing?"

Their third partner remained in the back of the shop, over the jewelry case, still glowing under its soft night-light. "He's got great stuff here. We can't just leave it."

"Yeah we can. Let's go."

The big man had the door open and was checking the street. He turned back and whispered urgently. "We don't need it. We gotta move move move."

The man in the back moved all right, but

in the wrong direction. Now he was behind the counter, pulling at the glass, trying to lift it up. "He's gotta have a key somewhere. Maybe it's on him."

At the door. *"Fuck it! Come on, come on."*

His partner pulled again at the countertop.

A noise in the street. *"Shit. People."*

The two men up front ducked to the side below the windows as two couples walked past the shop. Directly in front of the door, they stopped. Their voices filled the shop. Would they never move on? Sweat broke on the big man's forehead and he wiped it with the back of his hand.

He pulled the revolver from his pocket.

Other people joined up with the first group and they all started walking again, laughing.

The big man looked out. The street seemed clear. But at the back counter, his partner was holding something up now — a key? — and fitting it to a lock.

"Jesus Christ! There's no time for —"

When suddenly he was proven right. Whatever it might have been, there wasn't going to be time for it.

Silverman must have come to and had a button he could push in the back room. The whole world lit up with light and the awful, continuous screaming ring of the shop's alarm.

Wide-eyed in the sudden daylike brightness, the big man threw the door all the way open, yelling, *"Go, go, go!"* This time — the jewelry forgotten in the mad rush out — both his partners went. He was turning himself, breaking for the street, when he caught a movement off to his left. One hand to his head, blood running down his face, Silverman was on his feet, holding the side of the doorway for support.

The big man saw the shock of unmistakable recognition in the pawnbroker's face. "I, I can't believe . . ." Silverman stammered, then ran out of words.

Shaking his head in frustration and disgust — their good plan was all in tatters now — he stood up slowly and took three steps toward the old man, as though he planned to have a conversation with him. He did speak, but only to say, "Ah, shit, Sam."

Then he raised the gun and shot him twice. The second bullet went through his heart.

The streetlights on O'Farrell came on as assistant patrol special Matt Creed, working Thirty-two, came around the corner a long block down on Market. Though Creed had been on the beat less than a year, when he heard the squeal of the burglar alarm and saw the two men breaking out of a storefront ahead of him on a dead run, he knew what he was seeing.

"Hey! Hold on!" he yelled into a gust, over the alarm and the wind. To his surprise, the men actually stopped long enough to look back at him. Creed yelled again and, moving forward now, reached down to clear his jacket and unholster his weapon. But he hadn't gone five steps when —

Crack!

Unmistakably, a gunshot. Brickwork shattered by his head, rained down over him. Creed ducked against the front of the nearest building. Another man broke from the door of Silverman's shop. Less than a half block separated them now, and Creed stood, stepped away from the building into the lamplight, and called again. "Hold it! Stay where you are!"

The figure stopped, whirled toward him and without any hesitation extended his arm. Creed caught a quick glint of shining steel and heard the massive report and another simultaneous ricochet. It was the first time he'd been fired at and for that moment, during which his assailant broke into a run, he half ducked again and froze.

By the time he'd recovered, raised his own weapon, and tried to level it with both shaking hands, the third man had disappeared with the other two, and there was no real opportunity to shoot. Creed broke into a full run and reached the corner in time to get a last glimpse of what seemed to be a lone fleeing shadow turning right at the next corner. Vaguely aware of pedestrians hugging the buildings on both sides of the street, he sprinted the length of the block along the cable car tracks, past the trees that incongruously sprang from the pavement near the end of the Powell Street line.

By the time he got down to the cable car turnaround at Market, it was over. There was no sign of any of them. They'd probably split up and gone in separate directions. But even if they had stayed together, which Creed would have no way of knowing, they could go in any one of six or seven directions from this intersection — streets and alleys within a half block in every direction, each a potential avenue of escape. The turnaround also marked the entrance to the subterranean BART station.

And since Creed hadn't gotten close enough to get a good look at any of them, as soon as his three men stopped running, they would look like anyone else. He had a sense that the man who'd fired at him was bigger than the other two, but that was about it.

A fresh gust of wind brought on its front edge a wall of water as the drizzle became a downpour. Creed heard the insistent keening, still, of Silverman's alarm. He took a last look down Market, but saw nothing worth pursuing. He looked down at his gun, still clenched tight in his right hand. Unexpectedly, all at once, his legs went rubbery under him.

He got to the nearest building and leaned against it. He got his gun back into its holster, buttoned the slicker over his jacket against the rain, began to jog back to Silverman's. It didn't take him a minute.

Still, the alarm pealed; the door yawned open. The shop's interior lights illuminated the street out front. Creed drew his gun again and stood to the side of the door. Raising his voice over the alarm, he called into the shop. "Is anybody in there?" He waited. Then, even louder, "Mr. Silverman?"

Remembering at last, he pulled his radio

off his belt and told the dispatcher to get the regular police out here. With his gun drawn, he stepped into the light and noise of the shop. But he saw or heard nothing after catching sight of the body.

The victim might have been napping on the floor, except that the arms were splayed unnaturally out on either side of him. And a stream of brownish-red liquid flowed from under his back and pooled in a depression in the hardwood floor.

The skin on Sergeant Inspector Dan Cuneo's face had an unusual puffiness — almost as though he'd once been very fat — and it gave his features a kind of bloated, empty quality, not exactly enhanced by an undefined, wispy brown mustache that hovered under a blunt thumbprint of a nose. But his jaw was strong, his chin deeply cleft, and he had a marquee smile with perfect teeth. Tonight he wore a black ribbed turtleneck and black dress slacks. He was a professional and experienced investigator with an unfortunate arsenal of nervous habits that were not harmful either to his own or to anyone else's health. They weren't criminal or even, in most cases, socially inappropriate. Yet his partner, Lincoln Russell — a tall, lean African-American professional himself — was finding it increasingly difficult to tolerate them.

Russell worried about it. It reminded him of how he'd gotten to feel about his first wife Monica before he decided he was going to have to divorce her if he wasn't going to be forced to kill her first. She wasn't a bad person or an unsatisfactory mate, but she had this highly pitched laugh that, finally, he simply couldn't endure any longer. She'd end every sentence, every phrase almost, with a little "hee-hee," sometimes "hee-hee-*hee*," regardless of the topic, as though she was embarrassed at every word, every thought, every goddamned *impulse* to say anything that passed through her brain.

By the last few weeks of their cohabitation, Russell would often find himself in a high rage before he even got to their front door, merely in anticipation of "Hi, honey, hee-hee," and the chaste little kiss. His fists would clench.

He knew it wasn't fair of him, wasn't right. It wasn't Monica's fault. He'd even told her about how much it bothered him, asked her politely more than several times if she could maybe try to become aware of when she did it, which was *all the time*. And perhaps try to stop.

"I'll try, Lincoln; I really will. Hee-hee. Oh, I'm sorry. Hee . . ."

One of the things he loved most about Dierdre, his wife now of eleven years, was that she never laughed at anything.

And now his partner of six years, a damn good cop, a nice guy and the other most intimate relationship in his life, was starting to bother him the way Monica had. He thought it possible that this time it could truly drive him to violence if he couldn't get Dan to stop.

Here, on this miserable night, for example, they had been called to a homicide scene just outside the Tenderloin, some poor old bastard beaten up and shot dead. And for what? A few hundred bucks? No sign of forced entry to his shop. Nobody even tampered with the safe. Botched robbery, was Russell's initial take on it. Probably doped-up junkers too loaded to take the stuff they came for. But a tragic scene. It's looking like the guy's married forever — an old lady's picture on the desk. Kids and grandkids on the wall. Awful. Stupid, pointless and awful.

And here's his partner humming "Volare" to beat the band: humming while the young beat guy, Creed, all traumatized, is giving his statement to them; humming as he follows the crime scene photographer around snapping pictures of everything in the store; humming while the coroner's assistant is going over body damage, occasionally breaking into words in both Italian and English. "Volare, whoa-oh, cantare, oh, oh, oh, oh . . ."

Now it's ten-thirty. They've been here three hours. Somebody is knocking at the door and Cuneo's going over to open it, suddenly breaking into song: "Just like birds of a feather, a rainbow together we'll find."

Suddenly Russell decides he's had enough. "Dan."

"What?" Completely oblivious.

Russell holds out a flat palm, shakes his head. "Background music. Ixnay."

Cuneo looks a question, checks the figure at the door, then gets the message, nods, mercifully shuts up. The sudden silence hits Russell like a vacuum. The rain tattoos the skylight overhead.

"I'm Wade Panos, Patrol Special for this beat."

And no pussycat. Heavyset, an anvil where most people have a forehead, eyebrows like the business side of a barbecue brush. Pure black pupils in his eyes, almost like he's wearing contacts for the effect. "Mind if I come in?"

Under his trenchcoat, Panos was in uniform. In theory, Patrol Specials were supposed to personally walk their beats in uniform every day. Then again, in theory, bumblebees can't fly. But obviously Panos at least went so far as to don the garb. He looked every inch the working cop, and Cuneo opened the door all the way. "Sure."

Panos grunted some kind of thanks. He brushed directly past Cuneo and back to where Silverman's body lay zipped up in a body bag. The coroner's van was out front and in a few more moments they'd be taking the body away, but Panos went and stood by the bag, went down to a knee. "You mind if I . . . ?"

The coroner's assistant looked the question over to Cuneo, who'd followed Panos back to the doorway. The inspector nodded okay, and the assistant zipped the thing open. Panos reached over, pulled the material for a clearer view of Silverman's face. A deep sigh escaped, and he hung his head, shaking it heavily from side to side.

"Did you know him?" Cuneo asked.

Panos didn't answer right away. He

sighed again, then pulled himself up. When he turned around, the Patrol Special met Cuneo's gaze with a pained one of his own. "Long time."

To a great degree, Cuneo's nervous habits were a function of his concentration, which was intense. His mind, preoccupied with the immediate details of a crime scene or interview situation, would shift into some other trancelike state and the rest of his behavior would become literally unconscious. And the humming, or whistling, or finger-tapping, would begin.

Now Panos took up space next to Russell in the front of the shop, neither man saying much of anything, although they were standing next to one another. The body had been taken away and the crime scene people were all but finished up, packing away whatever they'd brought. Cuneo was back in the office, doing snippets of Pachelbel's Canon in D while he took another careful look around — he'd already discovered the unplugged video camera, located one of the bullet holes in the wall and extracted the slug, lifted some of his own fingerprints.

Matt Creed had finished his regular beat shift after the preliminary interview he'd had with the inspectors at Silverman's, and now he appeared again in the doorway, this time carrying a cardboard tray of paper coffee cups he'd picked up at an all-night place on Market. He paused at the sight of his boss. "Mr. Panos," he said. "Is everything all right?"

"I'd say not."

"No. I know. That's not how I meant it."

"That's all right, Creed. That coffee up for grabs?"

Creed looked down at his hands. "Yes, sir."

A couple of minutes later, the last of the crime scene people were just gone and Panos, Creed and Russell had gathered at the door to the office, in which Cuneo was now rummaging through the drawers in Silverman's desk, bagging in Ziploc as possible evidence whatever struck his fancy. He had stopped humming, though now at regular intervals he slurped his hot coffee through the hole in the top of the plastic lid, loud and annoying as a kid's last sip of milkshake through a straw.

Suddenly he looked up, the sight of other humans a mild shock. But he recovered, slurped, spoke to Panos. "You said he wasn't your client anymore?"

"No. But he'd been for a long time."

Panos boosted himself onto Silverman's desk and blew at his own brew. "I had to raise my rates last summer and he couldn't hack them anymore. But ask Mr. Creed here, we still kept a lookout."

Creed nodded. "Every pass."

Cuneo moved and his folding chair creaked. "Every pass what?"

"Every pass I'd shine a light in."

"No charge," Panos put in. "Just watching out."

"But he — Silverman — wasn't paying you anymore?"

"Right."

"So then" — Cuneo came forward, his elbows on his knees — "why are you here again?"

The question perplexed and perhaps annoyed Panos. He threw his black eyes over and up to Lincoln Russell, who stood with his arms crossed against the doorsill. But Russell just shrugged.

"The incident occurred on Mr. Creed's shift, so he was obviously involved, and he was one of my men. Plus, as I say, I knew Sam, the deceased."

"But this place isn't technically in your beat? Thirty-two, isn't it?" Cuneo sucked again at his coffee.

Panos straightened up his torso and

crossed his arms. "Yeah, it's Thirty-two. So what?"

Cuneo sat back in his chair. "So since the deceased is your friend and ex-client, you might know something more about this shop than your average joe off the street, isn't that right? And if you do, what do you think might have happened here?"

Panos grunted. "Let me ask you one. Did either of you or any of the crime scene people find a red leather pouch here? Maybe on Sam?"

"What leather pouch?"

Panos held his hands about eight inches apart. "About this big. Real old, maroon maybe more than red."

Cuneo glanced up and over at Russell, who shook his head. Cuneo spoke. "No pouch. What about it?"

"No pouch makes it open and shut. What this was about, I mean."

Russell spoke from the doorsill. "And what is that?"

"We're listening," Cuneo said.

Panos shifted his weight on the desk. "All right," he said. "First you should know that Thursdays was when Sam took his deposit to the bank."

"Every Thursday?" Russell asked.

Panos nodded. "Clockwork. Everybody who knew him knew that. I used to walk with him myself over to the B of A. He put the cash in this pouch. It's not here now."

"So," Cuneo butted in, "he was going to the bank tonight, and somebody who knew him decided to take the pouch?"

"Three guys," Creed corrected. "One of 'em pretty big."

"Okay, three." Cuneo hummed a long, unwavering note. "Must have been a lot of money, they were going to split it three ways."

"Might have been," Panos said. "I wouldn't know."

Cuneo indicated the surroundings. "This little place did that well?"

Panos shrugged. "Wednesday nights they played poker here."

The two inspectors shared a glance. "Who did?" Russell asked.

"Bunch of guys. It was a regular game for a lot of years. Sam took out ten bucks a hand for himself, except when he played blackjack, when he was the house."

Russell whistled softly. "Every hand?"

Panos nodded. "That was the ante. Per guy. Per hand. Ten bucks."

A silence settled while they did the math. Cuneo hummed another long note. "Big game," he said, pointing. "That's the table then."

"Right."

"We're going to need the players," Russell said. "Did he keep a list?"

"I doubt it," Panos replied. "Knowing Sam, he kept them in his head. But I might be able to find out, and you can take it from there."

"We'd appreciate that." Cuneo was making some notes on his pocket pad. "So they came in masked . . ."

"They weren't masked," Creed said. "Not when they came out."

"They were when they came in," Cuneo said. "Because Silverman knew them. They knew him and the setup here." He pointed to the hidden video up above. "They knew about that, for example."

Panos stopped him. "How do you know about the masks?"

Cuneo reached into his pocket and pulled out a gallon Ziploc bag into which he'd placed the one ski mask that had fallen to the floor.

"Sons of bitches," Panos said.

"Who?" Cuneo asked.

Panos's jaw was tight, his heavy brow drawn in. "It'd be a better guess once we know who was at the game."

"All right," Cuneo said, "but this is a homicide investigation. What you'll do is give us a list of players at the game and we'll work from that."

Panos nodded. "All right, but I'd appreciate it if you'd keep me in the loop. Whoever killed Sam, any way I can help you, count me in."

3

For several years after the death of his first wife Flo, Glitsky had a live-in housekeeper — a woman born in Jalisco, Mexico, with the German name of Rita Schultz. She had slept in the living room of his duplex behind a shoji screen and had come, in her own way, to be almost one of the family. After the marriage, when Treya and her then sixteen-year-old daughter Raney had come to live with Glitsky and his sixteen-year-old son Orel, Rita wasn't needed anymore and Glitsky, regretfully, had had to let her go.

Now and for the past eight months since Treya had gone back to work at the DA's office, Rita, no longer living in, was again at the Glitskys' five days a week, taking care of the baby. Two months ago, the big kids had both gone off to college — Orel to his dad's alma mater of San Jose State, and Raney all the way across the country to Johns Hopkins, where she'd gotten a full academic scholarship and planned to major in pre-med. The baby Rachel moved out of Abe and Treya's bedroom and into Raney's old room behind the kitchen.

Over the summer, he and Treya had actually fixed up the place a bit. They tore out the old, battle-worn gray berber wall-to-wall carpet in the living room and discovered the original blond hardwood underneath. Over one weekend, they stripped the seventies wallpaper and repainted the walls a soft Tuscan yellow. Then with the fresh new look, they got motivated to go out and buy a modern brown leather couch and matching love seat, some colorful throw rugs, Mission-style coffee and end tables. They put plantation shutters over the front windows.

It wasn't a large place by any means, and Glitsky had lived in it for more than twenty years, but with all the recent changes, he would sometimes come out into the new living room holding Rachel in the dimly lit predawn and wonder where he was. He knew it wasn't just the room. In reality, everything seemed different. The whole world since the terrorist attacks, the new reality perhaps more psychic than physical, but all the more real for that. All his boys now moved out, his old job gone, a new marriage with a young woman, and for the past fourteen months, their baby girl.

At such times — now was one of them — he would stand by the front windows with Rachel in his arms and together they would look out at the familiar street. He'd done the same thing dozens of times with Isaac, Jacob and Orel when they were babies, but now he did it to try and convince himself that he was the same person with Rachel that he'd been to his sons, and that his home was not foreign soil.

He opened the shutters and looked down the street toward its intersection with Lake. The rain had kept up throughout the night, but the wind had finally abated with the first sign of light. Now outside it was all heavy mist under high clouds that would hang on all day if not longer. Glitsky stared out through it, holding his daughter up against him, patting her back gently.

A pedestrian appeared at the intersection and turned into his street. Though he wore a heavy raincoat that hid the shape of his body and had pulled a brimmed hat down over his face, Glitsky knew who it was as soon as he saw him.

"What's grandpa doing here?" he asked his daughter. His own brow clouding — this could only be bad news — he watched his father plod slowly up the street, hands in his pockets, head down. When he was out front, Glitsky moved to the front door and opened it. Nat was already coming up the stairs, the dripping hat in one hand, lifting his feet, one heavy step after the other.

"What?" Glitsky asked.

His father stopped before he got to the landing. He raised his eyes, but something went out of his shoulders. "Abraham." The way he said his son's name made it sound as if just getting to him had been his destination. He let out a breath. "Sam Silverman," he said, shaking his head. "Somebody shot him."

Nat walked the last few steps up and Abe stood aside to let him pass. While Nat hung his coat on the rack by the door, his son went in to wake Treya and give her the baby. When he came back out, his father was sitting forward on the edge of the new love seat, his hands clasped between his knees. He looked feeble, a very old man.

In fact, he was eighty years old, but on a normal day, no one would guess it. Abe went down on a knee in front of him.

"Did you get any sleep, Dad?"

Nat shook his head no. "Sadie called me about midnight. I went over there."

"How's she holding up?"

His father lifted his shoulders and let them drop. A complete answer. Treya was holding the baby and came up beside them. "How are you holding up, Nat? You want some tea?"

He looked up at her, managed a small smile. "Tea would be good," he said.

Treya moved around her husband and sat down next to Nat. Rachel reached out a tiny hand to touch his face, said "Gapa," and got a small smile out of him. Treya put an arm across his shoulders and rested her head against him for a beat, then kissed the side of his head and stood up again. "We'll be right back."

The men watched them leave. Nat turned to Abe. "Why would somebody do this? To Sam of all people. Sam who wouldn't hurt a fly."

Glitsky had heard the refrain hundreds of times when he'd been in homicide, and the answer was always the same. There was no answer, no why. So Abe didn't try to supply one. Instead, as though knowledge could undo any of it, he asked, "Do you know how it happened?"

"I don't know what you want me to do. I'm not in homicide anymore."

"What, nobody remembers you over there?"

The two men were at the kitchen table. Rita had arrived and could be heard reading a children's book in Spanish to Rachel in the living room. Treya was getting dressed for work. Abe had no intention of snapping at his father, but it took some effort. Even after four months on the new job, the topic of his employment with the police department still tended to rile him up. He forced an even tone. "People remember me fine, Dad, but I don't work there. It'll look like I'm meddling."

"So meddle."

"In what way exactly?"

"Just let people know this one is important. People care who shot Sam."

Abe turned his mug. "They're all important, Dad. Most people who get shot have somebody who cares about it."

With his index finger, Nat tapped the table smartly three times. "Don't give me with everybody cares, Abraham. I've heard your stories. Most are what do you call, no humans involved. I know how it is down there. I'm saying go make a difference. What could it hurt?"

"What could it hurt."

"That's what I said."

"I heard you." Abe sighed. "You want me to what exactly?"

"Just keep up on it. Keep *them* on it." Nat put a hand on his son's arm. "Abraham, listen to me. If they see it's family . . ."

Abe knew that wouldn't help, not in any meaningful way. The inspectors on the case — and he didn't know who they were yet — were either good at their jobs or they weren't, and that more than anything else would determine whether they succeeded in identifying and arresting Sam Silverman's killer. "Then what?" he asked. "They look harder?" He shook his head. "They'll look as hard as they look, Dad. They'll either find him or not. That's what will happen, period. Me butting in won't make any difference. It might, in fact, actually hurt."

Nat's eyes flared suddenly, with impatience and anger. "So what, then? You can't even try? You let the animals who shot Sam walk away?"

Abe couldn't completely check his own rush of frustration. He bit off the words sharply. "It's not up to me. It's not my job anymore."

"I'm not talking job. I don't care from *job!* I'm talking what's right." He drew a deep breath, again rested his hand on Abe's arm. "Just so they know. That's all. This one matters."

Abe glanced down at his father's hand. Since he'd started with payroll, he hadn't even shown his face once in homicide, even for a social visit. He realized now that his reluctance with his dad was probably more about his own demons than whether he could actually have any effect in turning the heat up on any given investigation. It might not hurt after all. He put his own hand down over his dad's. "All right," he said. "But no promises."

"No, of course not. Heaven forfend."

The Payroll Detail had four entire rooms, each twelve feet square. Glitsky was the sole occupant of his. He had a standard, city-issue green desk, four wooden chairs, a computer and his own printer (which also served the rest of the detail), and natural light through the windows that made up the back wall. These overlooked the ever-scenic Bryant Street and the rest of the industrial neighborhood to the south. All the free space around the other three walls was taken up with mismatched black, gray, or green filing cabinets, except for one metal floor-to-ceiling bookshelf filled to overflowing with bound computer payroll reports going back four years.

An hour after he got to work, he was talking to Jerry Stiles in his office. Stiles was the lieutenant in charge of narcotics. Before that, he had been in many people's opinion the absolute best narc in the city. Certainly his arrest record backed that up, his seizures of illegal substances. Three years ago, before his promotion, he'd been named "Police Officer of the Year." Stiles was thirty-eight years old.

In spite of his administrative role, he often found an excuse to get back on the street, and today he wore a ratty beard and looked as though he hadn't combed his greasy brown locks since the World Series. In fact, currently he could have been mistaken pretty much exactly for a typical street drunk, but that came with the territory.

Making Glitsky's small, airless office a less than optimal spot to talk to him.

That office was one floor up from homicide, on the fifth floor of the Hall of Justice. Glitsky's normal staff in his new role in payroll included five civil service secretaries, two half-time sergeants of police, and one rotating patrolman-grade gofer. This morning, he'd been planning to check in at his desk, then zip on down to homicide while the motivation held, but instead he found a note from Frank Batiste on his chair telling him to expect Stiles within the hour. Glitsky and Batiste had already discussed Stiles's situation with some heat.

Luckily for Glitsky's peace of mind, since he had no other duties at the present moment, within the hour turned out to be about ten minutes.

He and Stiles made small talk, catching up for a while. They'd worked together on cases before and gotten along. Beyond that, they'd both caught lead in the line of duty, and that put them in the same club. Stiles made a few profane remarks that made it clear he thought Glitsky's latest career move was unjust. Abe didn't comment, though the sentiment did his heart good.

Finally, though, the air got a little ripe and Glitsky decided to get to the point. He went around his desk, tried the windows — both hermetically sealed, no chance — and sat down. "So," he began, "sorry to pull you in after your shift."

"Hey." A shrug. "It's overtime. I'm here anyway. I'm not complaining. What's it about?"

"Well, funny you should mention."

"OT? Is somebody bitchin' about OT again?" Stiles straightened up in his chair, his eyes getting some life in them. "They can kiss my ass."

"Yeah, well . . ." He let it hang. Of everything Glitsky hated about this new job, this kind of bureaucratic nonsense was first. "I'm just delivering the message, Jerry, and only because I've been requested to. Informally. I'm not keeping any record of this meeting."

"Fuck that. As if I care. Who requested, if you don't mind my asking? Just curious."

"It doesn't matter."

"Right. What do you think's got into Frank lately?"

"I don't know. He must be getting mature." But Glitsky didn't want to discuss Batiste. He pulled a printout from a file in front of him, glanced at it, then turned it around and slid it across the desk.

Stiles, all belligerence now, came forward and snatched it. He raised his voice in the small room. "So what's the message? Tell my guys to go out and risk their lives every night, live with these scum, smell like a sewer, and do it all for free?"

Glitsky had his elbows on the desk. He templed his fingers at his mouth for a moment, then pointed at the paper. "Your unit's OT is about twenty percent over department guidelines." He raised his eyes, met those of his colleague. "I've been asked to bring the matter to your attention." Glitsky tried to avoid profanity, but this was so much bullshit and nothing else that the temptation was almost too great. Instead, he said, "Now I've done that."

"All right. So what?" Stiles stared at the paper for another couple of seconds. "Narcotics works *nights*, Abe. We catch bad guys and the DA takes them to court during the *day*. Quite often on a day after a night shift. You know why? We get subpoenaed to show up, that's why. We're the fucking key witnesses. Without us there's no case. Get it? So what do they want us to do?" But Stiles didn't want an answer. He wanted to vent. "The reason we work nights is because that's when these lowlifes crawl out from under their rocks. It's when they buy their shit and make their deals and have their fights. It's when it *works!*" Stiles turned on his chair, stood up, sat back down, glared across the desk.

Glitsky did his Buddha imitation.

Stiles started again, even louder. "They don't want to pay the guys extra, maybe they can have night court. 'Course then nobody's out on the street doing the *job*.

Or maybe we could just ask these scumbags if maybe they could do all their business between eight and five? Business hours." He half turned again on his chair, ran a hand over his forehead, finally settled a little, shook his head back and forth. "I don't believe this shit."

Glitsky came forward an inch. "You might want to take it up with the chief, Jerry. Either that, or tell your guys they can only work days."

"We'd never bag a soul."

"But your detail would be under budget, and that's the important thing, right? Who cares about crime?" Glitsky gave no sign he was joking.

Stiles sat still a moment. "Abe, we're the *police department*. What are these clowns thinking?"

When Stiles left, Glitsky didn't give himself any more time to think about it. He stood up, came around his desk, and looked in at the room next door. There, two of his secretaries — Mercedes and Jacqueline — were engrossed at their respective desks in front of their computers. Jacqueline didn't look up when he cleared his throat at the door — she must have been at a really juicy part of her romance novel — but Mercedes, in the middle of her daily crossword puzzle, brightened at the sight of Glitsky's face. "Lieutenant. Nine letters, 'Jackson A.K.A.' Ends in 'L.'"

It took him less than ten seconds. "Stonewall."

"That's it! Stonewall. I was thinking something about Michael, if there was another way to spell it, but normally that's only seven letters. But Stonewall. Andrew, right? You're great, Lieutenant." She looked over to Jacqueline. "Stonewall," she said.

The other woman nodded. "Umm."

Glitsky pointed down the hallway. "I've got an errand. You women okay holding the fort?"

But Mercedes was leaning over her newspaper, carefully filling in her boxes, and didn't respond, or notice as he left.

Down a flight on the internal stairs and in a few more steps he was back where he'd lived for all those years. It brought him up short how physically close the homicide detail was to his current office, where nothing important had or ever would happen. It was probably no more than sixty feet, although the spiritual distance was incalculable.

Standing in the middle of the familiar room, he was surprised by how little it had changed in the near year-and-a-half since he'd been here. As usual on a weekday morning, the place was deserted — some inspectors were out working cases, others might be in court or, increasingly, had not come in at all because of vacation, alleged sickness, special training, or any of a dozen other reasons. Somebody had moved the full-size working stoplight off of Bracco's desk and it now hung from the ceiling. A floor-to-ceiling picture of the World Trade Center at the moment of the second impact was attached to the pillar behind Marcel Lanier's desk, and the old bulletin board on it — formerly reserved only for the grossest, most explicit crime scene photographs — had been done over with an Osama bin Laden motif, mostly email printouts of the terrorist being sexually abused by a variety of weapons and animals.

Otherwise, the decor was the same. So was the smell, but at least Glitsky knew what that was. As usual, the last one out had left the coffee cooking and it had turned to carbon at the bottom of the pot. He automatically walked over, leaned down to make sure, and turned it off.

"Can I help you?"

He straightened up and turned at the voice. The lieutenant had silently come out of his office. Or maybe Glitsky's senses were taken up with his impressions. In any event, for a heartbeat he felt somewhat bushwhacked, although there was no indication that that had been the man's intention.

It was Barry Gerson. Glitsky recognized the face immediately from the newspaper pics, which he'd had occasion to notice when they'd announced the appointment. Ten years Glitsky's junior, but no kid himself, Gerson had gone a bit to paunch and jowl, though he didn't come across as soft or flabby in any way.

Here on his turf, he appeared relaxed and in complete control. The smile was perfunctory, but there wasn't any threat in it. "You're Abe Glitsky."

"Guilty."

"I didn't realize you were back at work."

"Four months now." Glitsky kept it low-key. He pointed at the ceiling, put some humor in his tone. "Payroll, the throbbing pulse of the department."

Gerson, to his credit in Glitsky's view, clucked sympathetically. "They give you that 'varied administrative experience' crap?"

A nod. "It's making me a better cop. I can feel it every day."

"Me, too," he said, then, more seriously. "Sorry I turned out to be the guy."

Glitsky shrugged. "Somebody had to be. Not your fault." He added. "I'm not hearing any complaints, though I can't say I've been in touch."

Gerson cocked his head, as though the comment surprised him. His next smile might have been a bit more genuine. "Not even Lanier?"

This question wasn't a great surprise. Marcel Lanier was a long-time homicide veteran inspector who'd passed the lieutenant's exam well over two years before. It was no secret that he'd craved the appointment to head the detail after Glitsky. He'd even turned down a couple other of the varied administrative experiences he'd been offered, waiting for the homicide plum, only to be disappointed at Gerson's appointment. Like Glitsky, Lanier was homicide through and through. His refusal to take what they offered before he'd even made his bones as a lieutenant had, at least for the time being, doomed him with the brass. But Glitsky hadn't talked to him in six months or more.

"Not a word," he told Gerson. "He

94

making trouble here?"

The lieutenant seemed to consider what he would say for a minute. Then he shook his head. "Naw, he's all right." And suddenly the preliminaries were over. "So how can I help you?"

Three hours after concluding his meeting with Gerson, Glitsky was in another of the payroll rooms, this one internal and hence windowless, and more crowded since it held not only as much paper and other junk, but also two desks to accommodate its two workers. In practice, because the two office residents rarely worked the same days, one desk probably would have sufficed, but nobody ever brought this up, or suggested that the second desk be removed to make more room. That, of course, would mean that neither person working there would have his own desk, and wouldn't that be just an unbearable slight? In any event, pride of desk was typical of a number of similar crucial issues facing the detail.

At this moment, Glitsky was behind the closed door of this office with Deacon Fallon, who it appeared was having continuing problems with Jacqueline, the romance novel fanatic from the office across the hallway. As a sergeant with the police department, Fallon made more money per hour than Jacqueline did. In spite of his part-time status, he had conceived the notion that he somehow outranked her, a mere clerk originally hired from the civil service pool, though by now she'd been working full-time for five years, three more than Fallon.

Fallon was in his early forties. His wife had some honcho job in what he called the private sector. Between the two of them and the police union, they'd brokered a deal with the city whereby Deacon could stay home a lot with the kids. He'd been in the department for twenty years and could have already retired on pension, but the department had a few of these part-time positions, and Deacon could increase his retirement base one year for every two he worked, which he considered a good deal.

Glitsky, propped on the corner of one of the desks, sat back with his arms crossed. His concentration had been wavering in the tedium and now he realized that Fallon — pacing in front of him while he'd been talking — expected some sort of response. "I'm sorry, what?"

Fallon sighed. "Jacqueline. She says she's always taken her lunch between noon and one, though we know that isn't true, and she doesn't have to change now if she doesn't want to. But Cathy and I . . ."

"Cathy?"

"My wife."

"Okay, right."

"Cathy and I signed up for this incredible six-week course on Website design. I know, I know, but it's the new wave of this net stuff, believe me. It's going to explode. It really is a great business, Abe; you might even want to look into it yourself. The opportunities are just . . ." Perhaps sensing Glitsky's lack of enthusiasm for the project, he wound down. "Anyway, it's twice a week, Tuesdays and Thursdays, at noon."

"Which happens to be when you're supposed to be here."

"Right. I mean, I get the hour lunch, which is enough time. Each lesson is forty-five minutes." Glitsky knew that what Fallon meant was that by leaving twenty minutes early and getting back half an hour late, then eating lunch at his desk, he could squeeze the class into his "hour" lunch. Nobody would ever say a word about an abuse of free time like this. These were the little perks enjoyed by those ready to lay down their lives for their fellow citizens. "But it's got to be the noon hour, and

Jacqueline won't trade."

He looked expectantly at Glitsky, who hadn't moved. His posture was relaxed, his arms still crossed over his chest. He might have appeared to be thinking hard.

"Abe?" No response. "I mean, I don't want to have to go to the union about this." He tried another tack. "Maybe we could both get off at the same time, me and Jacqueline. It's only for six weeks."

Finally, Glitsky took a deep breath. His eyes came into focus. "When I came on here, didn't I read in your file that you decided that you'd like to have lunch from one to two? And didn't Jacqueline agree back then to change to noon so the office would be covered?"

"Yeah." Her earlier scheduling flexibility didn't seem to have made much of an impact on Fallon. "But that was before this class, and I'm the sergeant here after all. Besides, she's not doing anything special, just meeting her regular friends. And hell, it's only six weeks. . . ."

Glitsky later told Treya that the knock at the door probably saved him from at least a charge of aggravated mayhem if not homicide. It was Mercedes, telling him Frank Batiste was on the line and wanted to talk to him immediately. He thanked her, slid off the edge of the desk, and without so much as a glance at Fallon, hurried from the room.

The rain continued unabated, a fine slow drizzle that only seemed heavy to Glitsky because he hadn't supposed he'd be leaving the building and so was in his shirt-sleeves. Batiste had been standing, waiting at the head of the hallway that led to his office. When Glitsky got off the elevator, he'd fallen in beside him and without much preamble led the way out the Hall's front entrance to the street.

"Where are we going?" Glitsky asked on the outer steps.

"I thought Lou's. Sound good?" Batiste broke into a jog and Abe had no choice but to follow across Bryant and down to the floor below the bailbondsman's place, where Lou the Greek's had operated continuously as the legal community's primary watering hole for nearly thirty years. The last of the lunch crowd was finishing up and they had no trouble finding a booth under one of the small, elevated windows that, because Lou's was below ground level, opened at about gutter height to the alley outside.

Lou was a hands-on and voluble proprietor who knew everybody who worked at the Hall of Justice by first name. He came by before they'd gotten settled and offered them a once-in-a-lifetime deal on the last couple of servings of one of his wife's inspired culinary inventions, Athenian Special Rice. "Minced pork, scrambled eggs, I think some soy sauce, cucumber and taramosalata. Everybody's raving about it."

"Taramosalata," Glitsky said. "That would be fish roe dip?"

Lou grinned. "I know. I told Chui the same thing, but that's why she's the genius. The taramosalata is like anchovies, just included for flavor. You don't even taste it."

"I bet I would," Glitsky said.

"It sounds terrific, Lou," Batiste said, "but I don't think we're eating. Thanks."

Lou wasn't five steps away, putting in their orders for tea and coffee, when Glitsky spoke. "So this isn't about Jerry Stiles and his department's overtime."

Batiste checked the surrounding area. No one was in earshot, and still he leaned in across the table between them. "I thought it'd be helpful if we had a talk, Abe. Just you and me, man to man, friends like I think we've always been."

Glitsky thought that the friendship they'd always shared would not have allowed one to peremptorily summon the other for a serious discussion of issues during work hours, but he only nodded. "No *think* about it, Frank."

"Good." Batiste folded his hands on the table between them. "I know you haven't been exactly thrilled with the new job. I sympathize. I spent a year before I got homicide in personnel records, so I know. It's been what now, a couple of months?"

"Four, but the time's just flying by."

A pained look. "That long?" Batiste sighed. "Well, I'm aware of you up there. The rest of the administration is, too. It's not going to last forever."

"I thought it already had." But the corners of Glitsky's mouth turned up, for him a broad smile. He was keeping it light and friendly.

"Well, I'm sure it does seem that way, but I've got my eye out for a chance to get you out of there. Lateral or up, either way. Getting back to homicide isn't even out of the question."

"That's good news, Frank. Thank you."

Lou returned at that moment with their drinks, and it broke their rhythm. When Lou walked away again, a silence fell. At the window by their ear, the rain picked up. Batiste put some sugar into his mug and stirred thoughtfully. Glitsky blew over the surface of his tea.

Finally, Batiste found the thread again. "I guess what I'm trying to say is that it would be well worth your while if you could just hang in there a little while longer. You've got great support across the board, Abe. You've been a hero and now you're putting up with this . . . this waste of your talents for the good of the team. Don't think people don't recognize this. Don't think it doesn't matter."

"Well, that's gratifying," Glitsky said.

"I mean it. It should be."

"It is." Glitsky put his mug down, leveled his eyes across the table. "So why am I hearing a 'but'?"

Now Batiste broke a small and formal smile. "Could it be that finely honed and well-deserved reputation for cynicism?"

Glitsky allowed his own expression to match Batiste's. "It could be that, but I'm thinking maybe it's also that Gerson talked to you."

A slight pause, then a nod. "Maybe some of that."

Glitsky let out a heavy breath, turned his mug around on the table. He hated to explain, to be on the defensive, and his jaw went tight. Still, he kept his voice tightly controlled. "Silverman, the victim, was my father's closest friend, Frank. I asked Barry if he could just keep me informed. No press at all."

"That's what I heard, too." Batiste spread his hands, all innocence. "He didn't come to me with it as any kind of complaint. We were just having lunch and it came up."

Glitsky nodded, perhaps somewhat mollified. "All right. But what?"

"I'm talking as your friend. What I said when we got here. This is the kind of thing that's nothing in itself. Hey, one time. Your dad's friend. You want to be inside. Who wouldn't understand?"

"That's all it was. One time. Four months back and I finally stop by homicide once. . . ."

Batiste reached out his hand over the table and touched Glitsky's. "You're listening to me, Abe, but you're not hearing. It wasn't a problem. Really. Not with Barry, not with me." He drew his hand back. "I'm talking about the future, just that you be a little careful, you don't want to have people — and not only Barry — misinterpreting. That's all. People are touchy. You know what I'm talking about."

"I told my dad the same thing this morning."

"There. See?"

"Okay. But then I figured what could it hurt to go to the horse's mouth? I was completely up-front with Barry. I'm not horning in on him or anybody else."

"Nobody's saying you were."

"Lanier, Thieu, Evans" — all homicide inspectors — "any of them would have found out anything I wanted, but I didn't want to go behind Barry's back." The explaining was wearing him out. "I thought if I could, I'd give my dad a little more peace of mind, that's all."

"I hear you, Abe. I do. I also know how badly you want homicide back. And I wouldn't be a friend if I didn't make it crystal clear that this wouldn't be the way to go about getting it."

"That never occurred to me."

"I didn't think it would. But I wanted the air clear between us. I'm trying to fast-track you and it wouldn't help if it looked like you were trying some end run."

Glitsky shook his head. "Not even a double inside reverse, Frank. But just for the record, I truly am ready for another assignment."

"I'm trying, Abe, I really am." He finished his coffee. "Think you can make it another couple of months?"

Glitsky put his own cup down. "If a couple doesn't mean a whole lot more than four," he said.

4

Inspectors Dan Cuneo and Lincoln Russell had pulled a long night that ended near dawn, so they didn't come back to work the next morning until after 10:00 a.m. When they finally checked in, they found they'd miraculously, after only six weeks, received a positive DNA match on one of their outstanding cases — a rape and murder — so their first stop was the video store where Shawon worked and where they put a pair of handcuffs on him. By the time they finished the arresting folderol and were ready to get back to Wade Panos, less than an hour of daylight remained. Though with the continuing and steady rain, what daylight there was didn't amount to much.

The administrative offices for all of Panos's operations weren't downtown in Thirty-two, but a couple of miles south in a no-man's-land of underutilized piers and semiabandoned warehouses lining the Bay below China Basin. This neighborhood comprised another beat — Sixty-three. It was light years from the high-end marinas such as McCovey Cove that had sprung up by the Bay Bridge with the Embarcadero upgrades and the draw of PacBell Park.

Cuneo parked at the curb directly in front of the one-story, flat-roofed stucco box and double-checked the address. "I admire a man who doesn't waste his money on overhead," he said. Neither the single glass door nor the large picture window afforded a hint about what was inside — both were tinted black with fitted blinds. On the wall next to the door, gone-to-green brass lettering identified the building as the home of WGP Ente_p_ises, Inc. Cuneo looked across at his partner. "Maybe Roto-Rooter needed the 'r's and stole 'em."

Russell had no idea what he was talking about and wasn't going to ask. He got out of the car and was a step behind Cuneo when they walked in. Inside, the place was much deeper than it looked from without. Several offices opened off the hallway back behind the well-appointed reception area. A pretty, dark-eyed young woman in a heavy cowl-neck white sweater stopped working on her computer and smiled a greeting at them. "Can I help you?"

"Absolutely." Cuneo flashed all his teeth.

All business, Russell stepped around his partner. He had his identification out and showed it to her. "We're with homicide. We talked to Mr. Panos last night at Mr. Silverman's pawnshop. He's expecting us."

"Oh yes. You're the gentlemen who called earlier?"

"Well, one of us is," Cuneo said, then clarified, "a gentleman."

"That's nice to hear. They're getting to be in terribly short supply."

He extended his hand. "Inspector Dan Cuneo. And this is Inspector Russell. First name unnecessary."

She took his hand. "Liz Ballmer. Nice to meet you" — her eyes went to Russell — "both." The smile disappeared and she swallowed nervously. "I'll tell him you're here."

It was an impressive, albeit industrial, office. Glass block served as opaque windows just under the ceiling, and found an echo in the large coffee table in front of the long leather couch against one wall. The rest of the furniture — several chairs and another smaller couch — was all chrome and leather. Framed and mounted photos of Panos with various luminaries — San Francisco's mayor, the police commissioner, both U.S. senators, rock stars and other celebrities — covered most of one entire wall.

"That's who was there," Panos was saying. "All of them."

Cuneo studied the list of the poker players from Silverman's game. He was sitting sideways from Panos's expansive desk drumming the theme from *Bonanza* with two fingers on the coffee table in front of him. "With addresses yet," he said. "Very nice."

Panos nodded. "I thought I'd save you guys some legwork." As he had last night, he wore his uniform. Steam curled from a large mug of coffee at his right hand. "One of the guys in the game — Nick Sephia?" He pointed. "You'll see him there — he's my nephew. Used to work for me, in fact."

"Since when has poker gotten legal?" Russell asked.

"You know anybody in vice wants to hassle with it?" Panos asked. "When so many of them play themselves? Anyway, it turns out Nick knows all the guys from Wednesday. Those five, six including him. Which makes this your lucky day."

Cuneo stopped his drumming. "In what way?"

Panos sipped coffee. "In the way that you won't even need to talk to all of them."

Russell came forward to the edge of the couch. "How would we avoid that?"

"You start with John Holiday. You ever heard of him?"

Cuneo raised his head. "Not much since Tombstone. I heard he died." Then, "Why would we have heard of him?"

"He had some legal troubles not too long ago. They made it into the news-papers."

"What'd he do?" Russell asked.

"What he *used* to do," Panos said, "was run a pharmacy, Holiday Drugs. Ring any bells?"

Cuneo looked the question to Russell, shrugged. "Nada," he said. "So, what?"

"So he got into the habit of filling pre-scriptions without worrying too much about whether or not they had a doctor's signature on them. When they stung him, they had guys on videotape writing their own scrips at the counter right in front of him."

"When was this exactly?" Russell asked. "I think I did see something about it."

Panos considered briefly. "Year, year and a half ago."

"And he's not still in jail?" Cuneo asked.

"He never went to jail. He got himself a hotshot lawyer who cut some deal with the DA, got the thing reduced to a Business and Professions Code beef. He got some community hours and they took his license, but that's it. Basically, he walked."

Cuneo's fingers started moving again. The *William Tell* Overture — ta da dum, ta da dum, ta da dum dum dum. "So you think Holiday's the shooter?"

"I'm saying you might save yourselves some trouble if you talk to him first. If you can find him sober." He sipped some coffee. "My brother Roy is working up in Thirty-two now. Maybe he could help you."

"You keep wanting to help us," Cuneo said.

If Cuneo was trying to get some kind of rise out of Panos, he wasn't successful. The Patrol Special took no offense, turned his palms up. "I liked Sam Silverman, Inspector. I liked him a lot. If I've got resources that might help you find his killer, I'm just telling you you're welcome to them. If you're not so inclined, of course that's your decision."

"What's your brother do," Russell asked, "that he might help us?"

"Roy? He's an assistant patroller, same as Mr. Creed last night. He works the beat. He'll know the players."

"In the game, you mean?" Russell asked.

"That, too," Panos said. "But I was talking more generally. The connections."

"Always Thirty-two?"

Panos nodded at Cuneo. "Mostly. He likes the action downtown." A shrug. "He might be able to save you some trouble, that's all. He'll know where you can find Holiday anyway, without a bunch of running around."

Cuneo flicked at the player list. "Why him? Holiday. Other than the old pharmacy beef."

"He lost six thousand dollars at Sam's the night before."

The number jerked Russell's head up. "Six *thousand?*"

"That's the number Nick gave me."

Cuneo whistled. "He came to this game with six grand in his pocket?"

Russell was on the same page. "Where'd he get that kind of money?"

"He owns a bar, the Ark." He pointed northward. "Again, up in Thirty-two. A real dump, but they must move some booze. Whatever it was, he had the money on Wednesday, and lost it all."

"I know the Ark," Cuneo said. "Maybe your brother could meet us outside, give us what he can. Say a half hour?"

"I'll call him right away," Panos said. "Set it up."

"Six grand?" Russell asked again.

"Yeah, well," Panos said. "The point is he'd be motivated to get it back. Wouldn't you think?"

They were driving back downtown through the dark drizzle. Cuneo was forcing air rapidly back and forth through the gap in his front teeth, keeping a rhythm, tapping the steering wheel to the same beat. After ten blocks of this, Russell finally had to say something. "You ever get tested for like hyperactivity or anything, Dan?"

His partner looked over. "No. Why?"

"Because maybe you don't know it, but you never stop."

"Stop what?"

"Making noise. Humming songs, keeping a beat, whatever."

"I do?" A pause. "Are you kidding me?"

"No. You do. Like right now, you were doing this." Russell showed him. "And hitting the steering wheel to the same beat."

"I was? I was just thinking about these poker guys."

"And last night it was 'Volare.' And back in the office just now with Panos, you were doing the *Lone Ranger* or *Bonanza* or something with your fingers." Russell played the beat on the dashboard. "I mean, I don't want to complain, but you've always got something going and I just wondered if it was something you could control."

Cuneo accelerated through an intersection. He looked across at his partner. "All the time?"

Russell considered. "Pretty much."

Cuneo made a face.

"I think, as you say, it's mostly when your mind's on something else," Russell said. "When it's just you and me it's one thing. But around witnesses . . ."

"Yeah, I hear you." They drove on another few blocks in silence. Finally, Cuneo turned in his seat again. "Maybe we could get some signal, where you tell me when I'm doing it. You pull at your ear or something."

"I could do that."

"And when it's you and me alone, just tell me."

"I don't want to be on your case all the time."

"Hey, be on my case. You're doing me a favor."

"Well, we'll see."

They had gone a few more blocks and were stuck in rain-soaked Friday rush hour gridlock a couple of blocks south of Market when Russell spoke again. "Dan. You're doing it again. 'California Girls.' "

Clint Terry knew trouble when he saw it, and this time he recognized it right away. Roy Panos, all by himself, was usually good for some kind of problem, and tonight he had reinforcements. Cops, without a doubt, the smell all over them. Cops were always trouble.

In the bar's mirror, he saw them enter, stop in the doorway, look the room over. They stayed by the front for a moment, talking. Checking out the place, the one good window with its view of the Parisian Touch massage parlor across the street. Plywood over the other one. The stools were bolted to the floor. The bar was pitted and overlacquered.

Clint Terry went about six feet four, 280. He had been almost famous once as a young man, when his life had breathed with great promise. An All-American linebacker at Michigan State, he then had gone on to play half a season with the Packers before a couple of guys had clipped him, one from each side, and had broken all three major bones in his right leg, which Bob Costas on national TV had conceded was a damn good trick. They still replayed the tape of his last moment in pro ball a couple of times a year, on shows with titles like "Football's Ugliest Moments."

By the time he was twenty-four, his football career over, he came out to the left coast, where nobody knew him, to explore his sexuality. He'd heard there was more tolerance for alternative lifestyles in San Francisco than anywhere else, and that turned out to be true. To support himself, he got a job as a bouncer at the Condor, a strip club in North Beach. For almost three years he did okay, until in a misplaced burst of enthusiasm he bounced one tourist too hard and got charged with manslaughter.

Now, thirty years old and a convicted felon, he'd served his four years at Folsom. He'd had sixteen months to get reaccustomed to living outside of prison walls, and he liked it way better than in. He had a partner he loved, and didn't need much more. This bartending gig was about as good as he thought it was ever going to get, and he didn't want to lose it.

The cops finally made it to an open spot at the rail.

Terry swiped at the bar with his towel, threw down some coasters. As always, when he spoke to law officers, his stomach fluttered high up under his ribs, but he ignored that as best he could and offered up a smile. "Hey, Roy. Help you gentlemen?"

The badges, the flat no-nonsense faces, one black and one white. Homicide inspectors. Then the black guy saying, "We're looking for John Holiday. You know where he is?"

"No, sir. I haven't seen him. He hasn't been in today."

"When's the last time you saw him?" the white guy asked. He'd picked up his coaster, holding it in one hand and flicking it with the fingers of the other.

"Yesterday, I think. He opened up. What's this about?"

Roy Panos moved forward, put his elbows on the bar. "Let's see if you can guess, Clint. We'll make it a quiz. What do you think homicide inspectors would be interested in?"

Terry wiped his hands on his towel, shifted his eyes up and down the bar. He had maybe a dozen drinkers for the twenty stools, and none of them looked ready for a refill.

"You nervous, Clint?" The white guy again, still flicking the damn coaster. He seemed pretty high-strung, maybe nervous himself.

"No." He wiped his bar rag across the gutter. "It's just I'm working . . ."

"That was the other thing," the black guy said. "We were hoping you could give us a minute, maybe go to the office. You got a room in the back here I assume?"

"Yeah, but as I said." He motioned ambiguously around him. "I mean, look."

The white guy sighed heavily and finally put the coaster back down. "So you won't talk to us?"

Terry wasn't too successful keeping the fear and worry out of his voice. "I'm not saying that. I'm talking to you right now. Tell me what it is you want to know."

"He wants to help, Dan," the black cop said. "We can tell his parole officer he wants to cooperate."

"That's an intelligent response," the cop named Dan replied in a cheery and suddenly frightening tone. "And especially

118

coming from an ex-convict. It gives me confidence that the prisons are doing a good job after all." His eyes never left his partner. "Ask him where he was last night."

"Last night? I was here. The whole night, six to two."

"And I didn't even ask him yet," the black guy said. "See? He's just volunteering everything. Mr. Cooperation."

"Yeah," Dan said, "but you notice he happened to know what hours we'd be asking about?" He came back to Terry. "What about that, Clint?"

"I don't know what you're saying. You asked where I was last night and I told you. I was here."

"So then you couldn't have been up at Silverman's pawnshop?" Dan flashed some teeth at him. "Did you hear about that?"

Terry felt sweat breaking on his forehead. "Yeah. Sure. But I heard that was like a gang."

"No. Just three guys," Dan smiled across at him. "But let me get this straight. You didn't know what we wanted to talk about when we came in here tonight. Even hearing we were from homicide? But you knew about Silverman?"

"I just didn't put that together," Terry

said. "And that couldn't have been John." He shook his head, wiped down the gutter again. "John wouldn't have done anything like that."

"That would be the same John Holiday who got arrested last year?" Dan asked.

"That was different," Terry said. "And he got off on that. Besides, that wasn't violent. John wouldn't do anything violent."

"Actually," the black cop said, "it's interesting you brought up Holiday again and mentioned violence, because as it turns out we don't think he was the shooter. He just thought up the idea, is what we hear. Kind of like a white-collar idea that went south."

"Yeah," Dan agreed, jumping right in, giving Terry no time to process this stuff as it came out. "In fact, our best witness was one of Roy's partners here, walking his beat last night. What's his name again, Roy?"

Panos appeared to be enjoying every minute. "Matt Creed. You remember Matt, don't you, Clint?"

He nodded.

"This place used to be one of the beat's clients," Roy explained.

Dan nodded, apparently fascinated with the history lesson. "Well," he said, "Matt says no question it was the big guy of the three who shot Silverman. He was the last one out, the big guy. Big like a football player."

Terry put his hands on the gutter for support. His legs were going to give out under him. "I was here," he said.

"I *love* a consistent story," Dan announced happily to his two companions. "He's said the same thing three times now, you guys notice that? No deviation at all. Always a sign a guy's telling the truth." Suddenly, he started whistling the theme song from *Bridge on the River Kwai*. He stopped in midphrase. "Who worked till six?"

One of the customers slammed his glass down on the bar. "Bartend! You sleepin' down there? I need another drink!"

Terry worked the orders for the next few minutes, finally made it back to where the cops sat. They hadn't budged.

"You know, on second thought, I could use a glass of water," Dan said. Then, as Terry was filling it. "So who worked till six last night?"

"Didn't I say that? I told you John opened up."

"So he was here with you when you changed shifts?"

"For a few minutes, yeah. But he had a date."

"A date? With who?"

"I don't know. You've got to ask him that."

"I will when I meet him." Dan drank some water, did another bar or two of *River Kwai*. He'd taken over the interview now, moved it into high gear. "So was Randy here, too?"

Terry gave Roy a bad look. "What did *he* tell you?"

"Nothing. Just that you and Randy were an item. You're together a lot."

"That's right."

"You seem a little defensive."

"I'm not defensive. Randy's got nothing to do with this."

"With what?"

"What we're talking about here. Silverman."

"I didn't say anything about Silverman. I asked if Randy was here last night."

"He's got nothing to do with it."

"As opposed to you and Holiday?"

"No. I didn't mean that." Terry ran his whole hand through his hair. "But listen, whatever . . . it's not Randy."

"But he *was* here?" Again, the young white guy came quickly forward, pouncing.

"Don't be dumb, Clint. If he was here, he's your alibi. Think about it."

"I already told you he was here."

"As a matter of fact, no you didn't. But now you do say he was?"

Terry nodded. "We were alone here after John left for, I don't know, an hour or two. It was a slow night."

As quickly as he'd come forward, Dan leaned back, smiled triumphantly, spread his arms out. "There! Beautiful! That's all we wanted. You, Randy and Holiday here together at six o'clock last night. That wasn't so hard, now, was it?"

"He lives with you, doesn't he? Randy?" The black cop got back in the game. "Is he there now, do you know? Maybe you could give us the address?"

When they came out of the Ark, the two inspectors stopped and stood on the sidewalk in front of the place. Roy Panos had gone to the bathroom, and they were waiting for him to finish up and come outside. "I like this guy Roy," Cuneo said. "His brother was right. He knows the players."

Russell cocked his head back toward the bar. "You think Terry was part of it?"

"I'll tell you one thing — Roy thinks he was."

"That would be pretty easy, wouldn't it? The first guy we talk to?"

Cuneo shrugged. "I've heard it happens."

"Not to us generally."

A grin. "Maybe not yet. First time for everything, right?" The bar door swung open. "Hey, Roy, that went pretty well. Thanks."

"My pleasure. I've got to tell you, it was awesome watching you guys work. Another minute, he would have been crying."

"He did seem a little nervous," Cuneo said.

"I would have been, too."

"Why's that, Roy? You think he did it?" Russell asked. "Terry?"

Roy gave it a second. "Was it true what you guys said about the shooter being a big guy? You didn't just make that up to spook him?"

Russell nodded. "That's what Mr. Creed said. Three of them. One of them big."

Roy looked back and forth at the two inspectors. "Clint's not little," he said.

"No, he's not." Cuneo shot his partner a glance, came back to Roy. "What about this Randy? Clint's boyfriend. He with Holiday, too?"

"They're all buds," Roy said. "Lowlife."

"Would Mr. Creed know Terry?" Cuneo asked.

"On sight. Sure."

"I'm wondering if he could ID him as the shooter. Get him in front of a lineup."

"It'd be worth checking out," Russell said.

"We could find out pretty quick," Roy said. He looked at his watch. "He's on the beat in ten minutes. He'll be at the station checking in now. You want to walk down, I'm on my way there anyhow, to check out. It's like four blocks."

Matt Creed was in fact at the station, signing in to come on for his night's work with the Patrol Special liaison. He greeted Roy perfunctorily, then glanced at the men with him and recognition hit. He spoke first to Roy. "This is Silverman, then, isn't it?" Then to Cuneo, "Are you inspectors having any luck yet?"

"Getting a few ideas," Cuneo said. "Roy here says you might know Clint Terry."

Creed's brow contracted in a question and Roy answered it. "Bartender over at the Ark?"

"Oh, yeah. I got him," Creed said. "Why?"

"You said last night that the shooter was a big man. Mr. Terry's a big man."

The idea played itself across Creed's face. "You think he shot Silverman?"

"We don't know," Russell said. "We're open to the idea. Do you remember seeing Mr. Terry at the Ark last night when you walked your beat?"

Creed shook his head. "I didn't even look in," he said. "They're not on the beat anymore."

"But you passed by the place, right?" Cuneo asked. "Couldn't have been five minutes before you got to Silverman's. Do you remember if it was open?"

The young security guard tried but finally shrugged, frustration all over his face. "The door's closed, the window's boarded up. If they were open, they weren't having a party, but beyond that, I couldn't tell you. I didn't see anybody go in or come out, but I couldn't tell you I really looked." He met Cuneo's eyes. "You really think it might have been Terry?"

"You're the one who chased him. We were hoping maybe you could tell us."

"You said the shooter was big," Russell added. "As big as Terry?"

Creed closed his eyes for a moment. "Maybe. But it happened fast and it was dark. Plus, I was shitting in my pants at the time. I don't think I could pick him out of

126

a lineup, if that's what you mean."

This was disappointing news, and both inspectors showed it. Cuneo, however, bounced right back. "All right. But you wouldn't eliminate him is the point."

"No. I suppose it could have been him."

"There you go," Cuneo said.

"But who were the other guys?" Creed asked. "You must be thinking Randy Wills and John Holiday?"

Cuneo started making a little clicking sound. "I'm thinking it a little more right now," he said. "What made you think of them?"

"They hang out a lot. You see them around together."

"Holiday was at Silverman's poker game," Russell said.

Roy Panos was nodding through a deep scowl. "He lost six grand."

Cuneo was still making the clicking noise. "Anything about the other two guys you saw make it impossible it was them? Holiday and Wills?"

"No. But they didn't stay around to talk. The other two could have been anybody else."

"But it also could have been them. Am I right?" Cuneo didn't want to lose his focus.

"Yeah. Sure. Or them."

The clicking stopped. "Okay, then."

Dismas Hardy was listening to his wife's voice on the speakerphone in his office and taking notes about what he might want to pick up at the grocery store on his way home if he wanted to be the perfect husband and save her a trip. Ordinarily, she would have just walked over herself. The Safeway was only a couple of blocks down around the corner. But now with the rain, she'd have to drive, which meant finding another parking place possibly even farther from their house than the store was.

"Not possibly, definitely," Hardy said. "I do a little victory dance whenever I get closer than Safeway. So what's on the list?"

He wrote as she finished reciting. "Coffee, cottage cheese, cherries, Claussen's, celery."

"Goods beginning with 'c,' I got it. Anything else?"

A short silence. Then Frannie said, "Oh, and some copper clappers."

"Got it, Clara. See you in an hour."

Hardy hung up. He moved the newly framed picture of his wife to front and center on his desk and gave it a moment.

The planes of his face softened, the edges of his mouth tickling at a smile.

It was a head and shoulders shot he'd taken recently in their home on an Indian summer Saturday morning. For the first time ever, Rebecca and Vincent had both spent the night with separate friends. Frannie was turning away from re-arranging the caravan of glass elephants on the mantel over the fireplace in their front room. In the picture, Frannie's eyes were full of mischief, her own smile about to break. The unseen story was that they'd just finished making love on the living room floor, by no means a daily event. The camera had been sitting next to Hardy's reading chair and he'd grabbed it, called her name, and got her.

"Mooning over your wife again?"

Caught in the act. "We are having a bit of a renaissance."

"Good for you." David Freeman stood in the doorway, a large wineglass in each hand. He schlumped his way across the office, put one of the glasses on Hardy's desk, and pushed it across. "Chateauneuf du Pape, Cuvée des Generations, nineteen ninety. It's just too good not to share and the pups downstairs are all working."

"Maybe I'm working, too."

The old man shook his head. "Not likely this time Friday night. I know you. You're done." He had come around behind Hardy. "New picture? That *is* a good one. Though I'm surprised she's letting you display it in public."

Hardy feigned ignorance. "What are you talking about? Why wouldn't she?"

Freeman gave him a knowing look. "Maybe because under that innocent and pretty face, she's not wearing anything?"

Hardy had long since given up being surprised at Freeman's perspicacity. But even so. "How in the world . . . ?"

"Completely obvious to any serious connoisseur of naked women, one of whom I pride myself on being." Freeman pointed. "Taste the wine. Tell me what you think."

Hardy did as commanded. "It's pretty good and I think you may actually be mythically ugly. And I've only got about five minutes if you're really here on business and the wine is a ploy."

Over at the couch, Freeman lowered himself into a sit. "The wine is genuine largess on my part, but as a matter of fact I did hear from Dick Kroll on the Panos thing."

"I'm starting to love the Panos thing."

"I'm still a little more in the infatuation

stage myself. Especially with your recent input."

"That wasn't through much effort on my part, David," Hardy said. "That was Abe and John Holiday."

Freeman made a face.

"Okay, you don't like him. But you've got to admit he's doing us some good."

This was, and both men knew it, quite an understatement. Holiday had come to believe that some of the WGP guards had played undercover roles in his own sting and arrest, and he was out for vengeance. In the past four months or so, he'd brought in no less than seven disgruntled WGP clients and/or victims to Freeman's offices, out of which four were on board with causes of action ranging from fraud and intentional infliction of emotional distress to assault and battery. Named defendants in the lawsuit included Wade on all the causes of action, of course, but also his brother, Roy, his nephew Nick Sephia, and nine other WGP current and past employees.

By the same token, common scuttlebutt at the Hall had made Glitsky realize back when he was still in homicide that Panos was a bad egg, his organization fairly corrupt. His "rate increase" of the year before had been nothing more than a thinly disguised protection racket. Glitsky knew that several businesses had at first elected to drop out of Thirty-two only to sign back up after windows had been broken or goods stolen. Two men had been mugged. One storefront cat killed. All of them had filed complaints with the PD, only to drop them. Glitsky, up in payroll, found it entertaining to chase these paper trails and identify potential plaintiffs for his friend Diz. Was he doing anything else worthwhile? Eventually, he had turned all of these names over to Hardy, and most had joined the other plaintiffs in the lawsuit.

Hardy thought it was starting to look pretty solid for the good guys. "So what did Mr. Kroll want?" he asked.

"He wants to talk some more before the next round of depositions."

Hardy shrugged. "Did you tell him that that's what depositions are all about, everybody getting to talk?"

"I believe I did. Told him we could talk all we wanted starting Tuesday, but he wants to put it off, maybe till early next year."

"If I were him, I'd want that, too. What'd you tell him?"

"No, of course." Freeman cleaned out

his ear for a minute, his eyes somewhere in the middle distance. He picked up his glass and swirled it, then took a sip. "My gut is he's feeling us out for a separate settlement."

Hardy was about to take a sip himself, but he stopped midway to his mouth, put the glass back down. "We're asking for thirty million dollars, David. Rodney King got six and he was one guy. We've got fourteen plaintiffs. Two million and change each. What could Kroll possibly offer that would get our attention?"

"I think he was having a small problem with that question as well. I got the feeling he'd been chatting with his insurance company, which won't pay for intentional misconduct. To say nothing of punitives, which we'll get to the tune of say six or eight mil, and again there's no coverage. So if we win, Panos is bankrupt."

"Which was the idea."

"And still a good one."

"Did he actually mention a number?"

"Not in so many words."

"But?"

"But he's going to propose we amend the filing so Panos gets named only for negligence, no intentional tort. This leaves his insurance company on the hook for any damages we get awarded."

"And why do we want to do this? To help them out?"

"That's what he wanted to talk about before the depositions. I predict he's going to suggest that he rat out the city, give us chapter and verse on the PD and their criminally negligent supervision of his people, which strengthens our case, and in return he gets insurance coverage on any judgment we get."

"What a sleazeball."

"True. But not stupid," Freeman said. "If we were equally sleazy, it's actually a pretty good trick."

"Let's not be, though. Sleazy. What do you say?"

"I'm with you. But still, it's not bad strategy. And it could be even better if he thinks to suggest settling directly with us for say a quarter mil per plaintiff, which puts three and a half mil in the pot, a third of which comes to you and me, and his insurance pays for all of it. Panos comes out smelling like a rose. We make a bundle. The city's self-insured so they're covered. Everybody wins."

Hardy liked it, but shook his head. "I don't think so, though. His insurance would have to agree, and why would they?"

"Maybe Panos has got it himself. In cash."

"That's not coming out smelling like a rose. That's down three plus mil."

"But at least then he's still in business. We settle, sign a confidentiality statement, he raises his rates, he still wins."

Hardy nodded grimly. "It's so beautiful it almost makes me want to cry. And all we have to do is change a word or two?"

"Correct."

"Just like guilty to not guilty. One word." For a brief instant, Hardy wondered if Freeman were actually considering the proposal, which Kroll had never actually voiced and may not even have thought of. "Are you tempted?" he asked.

Freeman sloshed his wine around, put his nose in the bowl, took it out, and nodded. "Sure. It wouldn't be a worthwhile moral dilemma if I wasn't tempted. But it's half your case and I'm duty bound to admit that I believe it's a solid, pragmatic strategy, and not overtly illegal. If we don't do it, it'll be way harder to win."

Hardy took the cue from Freeman and swirled his own glass for a minute. "So it's my decision, too?"

"Got to be," Freeman admitted.

"Give me a minute," Hardy said. "How

much do I clear?"

"Well, Kroll never gave me a specific number. But if I'm even close to what he's thinking at three and half million, say, and I bet I am, you personally bring in close to a half million before taxes."

Silence gathered in the room. "Couple of years work," Hardy said.

"At least."

Hardy's mouth twitched. He blew out heavily. "For the record, I'm officially tempted." He put his glass down, walked to the window, pulled the blinds apart and stared a minute outside at the street. When he turned again, his face was set. "Okay," he said, "now that that's out of the way, fuck these guys."

5

For a wealthy man, Wade Panos kept a relatively low profile.

He didn't need flashy clothes, since he wore a Patrol Special uniform every day at work. The Toyota 4Runner got him wherever he needed to go. The three-bedroom house on Rivera that he shared with Claire blended with the others in the lower Richmond District. He mowed his own lawn every Saturday, took out the garbage, talked over the fence with his neighbors. To all outward appearances, Wade was a regular guy.

He'd started working as an assistant patrol special in Thirty-two when he was just out of high school. It was his father's beat. George ran a tight ship in those days, providing basic security for his two hundred clients, patrolling the beat on foot.

It didn't take Wade long to realize that his father was missing a substantial opportunity — big money could be made in this field. People wanted protection, especially once they came to understand that without it, bad things could happen. More importantly, Wade was adept at identifying enterprises — prostitution, the drug trade, gambling dens — that operated outside the protection of the law. These businesses couldn't survive in his beats without his protection, and rather than roust them out or turn them over to the regular police, he found most of them willing to enter into partnership with him.

By the time Wade was twenty-five, he'd made enough on his own to buy his first beat from the city. Ten years later, when he inherited Thirty-two after his father's death, he had six of them and a payroll of nearly ninety assistants. He was fortunate that his timing was so good. About five years ago, the city had limited the number of beats to three for any one individual, but his holdings were grandfathered and allowed to stand. His books showed that he was pulling down close to a million dollars a year.

Until relatively recently, the actual figure was about twice that. And in the last three years, the profits had become nearly obscene. Not that he was complaining.

Since so much of his income was in cash, Wade had had to become skilled at laundering it, and to this end he formed a holding company that owned four bars in various parts of the city, each of which pulled down a tidy legitimate profit and substantially more in dirty money. Being a good businessman, Wade always kept his eyes open for run-down watering holes that he could scoop up at bargain prices, then renovate to a veneer of respectability. He'd also found that, once a property appealed to him, his connections, associates and business practices could often help a struggling bar along on its journey to bankruptcy.

He'd wanted the Ark now for a couple of years, and since he'd learned of John Holiday's interference with his business in the past four months, he was more motivated than ever to take control of the place. Put the son of a bitch back on the street where he belonged. Because of its central downtown location, with any kind of attractive atmosphere it would draw heavily from the police, legal and financial communities, so it was a natural fit for his operation. But this lawsuit didn't look like it was going away anytime soon — Dick Kroll wasn't having any luck with Freeman and Hardy

— and anything Wade could do to cut into their enthusiasm was to the good.

Not incidentally, if he could get his hands on the Ark, it might also finally provide a safe and comfortable living for the son of his little sister Rosie. Nick Sephia had become a trial for all of them. He'd proven his loyalty to Wade on several occasions, true, but his judgment often got him into trouble, as it had with the LaBonte girl. Wade was hoping that with seasoning, age and experience, Nick could become an asset as a bar manager, instead of a liability as muscle — he didn't have the self-discipline that muscle called for.

Also, truth be told, Wade felt guilty about Nick, who'd grown up without a father because of him. Twenty-some-odd years ago, when Wade had realized that Sol was hitting Rosie, he had beaten his brother-in-law to within an inch of his life, then given him the option of leaving town or dying. Nick's father had made the smart choice.

Now, near eight o'clock on this Friday night, Wade was in a tuxedo, waiting for Claire to finish dressing and come downstairs. He sat in a folding chair hunched over a large jigsaw puzzle that he was working on at a card table in the enclosed porch at the back of his house. A light rain still fell just outside the windows.

He usually worked on his puzzles for the half hour before dinner after he got home. It took about two weeks to finish one of these big ones, after which Claire would transfer the completed puzzle to a plywood backing and glue it down. She told him she donated the things to shelters or schools or something, but Wade couldn't really imagine anyone really wanting one of them. He thought it possible that Claire simply threw most of them away and told him the story about giving them to charity to spare his feelings.

Wade didn't really care.

The joy was in the doing of them, and this one was particularly challenging. Twelve hundred pieces. The picture on the front showed nothing but the water in a swimming pool — blues and shadows. He had most of the border now, and was about a third done. Suddenly, a five-piece segment fell into place and he sat back, pleased.

"Claire!"

"Two minutes," she chimed from upstairs.

He frowned. Two meant ten. Standing up, he pulled at his bow tie and walked back to the kitchen, where on one of the stools by the counter the paper lay open to the Metro section. And as so much did — except for his jigsaw puzzles — the story brought him back to business. And again, to Nick.

The article was about the new Russian Kamov Ka-32 helicopter that one of Wade's relatively recently acquired clients, Georgia AAA Diamond, had purchased as a gift for the San Francisco Police Department. The deal was that, in return, the jewelers could use the chopper to transport their gem imports, with police guard, directly to and from the corporate jet at the airport in south San Francisco to the city.

Here was a nice picture of Dmitri Solon, the company's thirty-four-year-old CEO. He was posing by the helicopter with Mayor Washington, Police Chief Dan Rigby, some city supervisors, and members of the California legislature. It was amazing, Wade thought with some pride, that he and Solon had been able to create such a substantial *krysha* — Russian for "roof" — as protection for Georgia AAA in such a short time.

Wade knew Solon well by now. He was a smooth operator who spoke nearly perfect English. The protégé of Severain Grotny, head of the Ministry of Precious Metals and Gems in Russia, Solon had ostensibly come to San Francisco with a twofold mission — to open a state-of-the-art diamond cutting and distribution center and, not incidentally, to make inroads into the international monopoly of the De Beers diamond cartel.

Wade couldn't help smiling as he scanned the platitudes in the article, for he knew the truth about Georgia AAA, and this was that Solon and Grotny were using the business as a front to systematically loot nothing less than the national treasury of Russia. He knew this because about eighteen months ago, before Solon had even opened his doors, Wade had signed him up as a client in another of his beats. It hadn't taken him three months to become suspicious of some of the activity he witnessed, some of the questionable personnel on the periphery of things.

So he set up special surveillance teams and about two months later, he and his nephew Nick found a pretext to stop one of Solon's imported Russian employees as he left the building one evening. He was carrying a bag of uncut diamonds worth, Wade later discovered, approximately fourteen million dollars. Rather than report the incident to San Francisco police, Wade brought him first back to Solon.

The ensuing discussion was more than enlightening. It was breathtaking.

Once it became clear that Wade's agenda was cooperation rather than interference, Solon seemed almost relieved to be able to explain. The financing for Georgia AAA, about $170 million, had come directly from the Russian treasury in the form of diamonds, jewelry and silver, but mostly from gold, *five tons* of gold — and most of that investment grade commemorative coins from the 1980 Olympics. This had all come under diplomatic pouch, Grotny's pouch, on Lufthansa Airlines. After it had arrived in this country, Solon arranged for its delivery to Premier Metals, the top gold distributor on the West Coast. Premier then melted down the coins and established the Georgia AAA account, based on ounces of gold on deposit with them.

With his $170 million line of credit, Solon had gone a little wild. Although it was on the market for a mere five million dollars, he paid eleven million for the four-story building that would house his new Diamond Center. At about the same time, he spent three million dollars for his rambling mansion in the hills of Kensington;

$800,000 for two cigarette boats; more than a million for a Rolls-Royce and two Aston Martins; and around eighteen million for a Gulfstream twin-engine corporate jet. There were other acquisitions as well — condos at Lake Tahoe, a small Napa winery, a chain of Bay Area gas stations. All were intended to bolster the image Solon wanted to convey — he had unlimited money and extraordinary connections.

Wade looked down at the newspaper photograph again. The young Russian entrepreneur had certainly done himself proud.

But he couldn't have done it without Wade Panos, who'd helped him build his *krysha,* extended Solon's connections through Wade's own to the political elite of the city and even the state. And it had all begun the night that he and Nick had busted the messenger with the bag of diamonds. Wade had asked Solon this simple question: If Georgia AAA was in the business of cutting and selling diamonds, why was he sending fourteen million dollars' worth of them away? The answer was that only a fraction of the diamonds imported from Russia ever made it to the floor of Georgia AAA's high-tech cutting room

145

showcase. Most were sent to a sister Georgia AAA office in Antwerp, where disguised with false invoices from Angola and Zaire, they were then, ironically, sold to De Beers for cash, which was then wired either back to San Francisco or to Grotny in Moscow.

Essentially, it was a money laundering scheme through which diamonds from the Russian National Treasury could be dumped into the world market and converted to cash. The San Francisco Georgia AAA Diamond Center, for all of its grandeur and visibility, was in fact merely a front to legitimize an immense traffic in unregulated diamonds. And, established in the center of one of his beats, it had fallen into the lap of Wade Panos.

His commission during the past year — essentially to have Nick instead of one of Solon's people carry the diamonds and guard them to and from the airport to the Diamond Center, plus a little muscle and political favor — was a little more than six million dollars, most of which Solon wired directly from the Antwerp office to Wade's account in the Caymans. The rest came back to San Francisco, where Wade used it to keep his own *krysha* in good repair. He loved the term — the roof that protected you. The people you paid off.

But Nick.

Even with his new job, Nick remained a problem. Because he was young, headstrong and prone to violence, he hadn't worked out at all as an assistant patrol special. Wade had thought the simple job at Georgia AAA would serve two purposes. First, it would keep his nephew out of trouble and, second, Wade would have his own man, and a relative at that, on the inside to protect his position with Solon.

But after a little more than a full year at it, neither part was working out too well. Nick had too much free time, no real job to do, and too much money. He was upping his profile all over town — getting into fights, gambling, throwing his weight around — and this was not good. When it was time for his deliveries, he would show up around the Georgia offices, self-important, well-dressed and surly, and alienate everyone from the cutters to Solon himself.

Even more disturbingly, he had somehow ended up with Julio Rez as his partner on these trips. Wade didn't know Rez well, but thought him capable of shooting Nick and stealing the diamonds they were transporting.

147

He needed to get Nick out of there, get him a real grown-up job, maybe at the Ark, then put his brother Ray in with Solon to protect the relationship. Ray was good with people.

But suddenly he straightened up, tugging hard now at his collar, getting it loosened up. He looked at himself in the mirror on the kitchen wall — his skin color was awful, a flushed ochre that made him look both pale and flushed. He thought he could feel his blood pressure pushing on his eardrums. He brought a hand up to his nostrils, checked it for blood.

Look at him. What the hell was he doing?

Here he was, Wade Panos, nobody's idea of a lightweight, brooding over individual strategic moves again — and again and again — when the real issue, the big issue, was that these two goddamned lawyers looked like they were going to try to shut him down. They were threatening the entire foundation of his life's work. Okay, he understood they saw their chance to clear a nice chunk of change here. He assumed that they were just businessmen like he was, looking out for opportunities. He didn't blame them for that. And maybe it was true that Wade had been pushing his

148

luck the last couple of years, throwing his weight around too much in the beats, giving them the opening. So okay, the lawsuit was a wake-up call. Maybe he'd rein things in a little with his troops in the future. His dealings with Solon were bringing in the bulk of his income now anyway. But without the beats and Wade's *presence* in the field as his legitimate power base, even that relationship could erode. And that would be disaster.

So Freeman and Hardy had delivered the message that they were on to him. So he'd tone things down and they'd make a decent pile for their efforts. What more did the greedy bastards want? He'd floated the idea that he was ready to make an offer, settle this thing. He'd even provide evidence to help them fleece the city a bit.

Fuckers.

"What's the matter?" Claire stood in the door to the kitchen. He hadn't heard her come downstairs. "You're frowning," she said. "You look sick. Do you feel all right?"

"Fine." He shook his head. "It's nothing. Just business."

"I thought business was good."

"Business is all right."

"And yet you're frowning."

He shrugged, debating with himself

whether he should burden her with his own worries about the lawsuit. But no. The solution came to him full-blown, all at once. He didn't have to do this Kroll's way, according to Hoyle. He wouldn't even tell Kroll. He could end his troubles with the lawsuit, or at least slow things way down, anytime he wanted. He was being reasonable, and if Freeman and Hardy and their spies and stooges didn't choose to be, then what happened after that wouldn't be Wade's fault. They would have asked for it. All of them.

"Wade?"

He came back to his wife. "I'm afraid I'm going to have to move Nicky again, that's all."

It was her turn to frown. "Maybe you want to move him all the way out."

"I can't," he said. "Rosie —"

She held up a hand, stopping him. "Your poor sister Rosie."

"She's had it rough, Claire."

"Who hasn't? And Nicky's nothing but trouble. He's already cost us and it's going to get worse, you watch."

"He's growing up. He's going to be okay."

She shook her head. "When you were his age you had three beats already, your own business. Trying to help him is just throwing good money after bad. Anyway, where are you going to move him to?"

"I was thinking the Ark."

"Which we don't own, last time I checked."

"Not yet." The seed of an idea had sprung. "But it turns out the owner of the place was with the guys that shot Sam Silverman. After they bring him in, he's going to need all the cash he can get his hands on. I'll pick the place up for a song."

"And then give it to Nicky? There's better people, you know, Wade, even if he's family." She was a short, buxom woman and stared up at him defiantly, her arms crossed over her chest.

After a minute, he leaned down and kissed her, conciliatory, on the cheek. "Nothing's written in stone, Claire." He smiled, took her arm, started to steer her toward the front door. "Now, who are we giving our money to tonight?"

Hardy's daughter Rebecca had at last reached sweet sixteen years old and tonight she was going on her first solo date. She'd been out to the movies and the malls with mixed-gender groups of friends many times before, of course, but this was the homecoming dance and this boy, young man, whatever he was — a seventeen-year-old senior named Darren Scott — had asked her.

Frannie had done herself up somewhat, too, for the occasion. She wasn't exactly Mrs. Cleaver, but she wore a skirt and a light salmon-colored sweater. She'd pulled her red hair back into a tight bun, applied some makeup — mascara and lipstick. Vincent, their fourteen-year-old son, had gone to a football game with some of his friends.

Now Hardy was standing in the kitchen, alone with Frannie, while they awaited the Beck's grand entrance from her bedroom, into which she'd vanished after her shower about a half hour before. He was talking in that half-whisper parents sometimes adopt when their children might be within earshot. "It's just that I'm not exactly thrilled that the sum total of what I know about this guy who's taking out my daughter is his name, Darren Scott. If that's really his name."

Frannie threw a glance back over her shoulder. "Dismas. Of course it's his name. It's all I've been hearing for weeks. Darren Darren Darren."

Hardy was undeterred. "Doesn't mean

he didn't make it up. Maybe he and the Beck are in on it together and are planning to run away. If I was making up a name, it would be Darren Scott. I mean it. If he honks from out on the street, she's not going."

"I'll let you tell her that."

"I will, too. Don't think I won't."

"What?" Rebecca looked unimaginably grown-up in basic black, spaghetti shoulder straps, hemline three inches above the knee. Heels and hose. Sometime in the past year or so, she'd pierced her ears and now gold teardrop earrings hung from them, matched by a thin gold necklace Hardy had bought her. Her red hair, like her mother's, was up off her neck and some kind of glitter graced her cheeks and the bare skin beneath the necklace. "What?" she asked again, worry flitting over her brow.

"Nothing," Frannie said, moving toward her. "Just your father being silly. You look beautiful."

She spun in a pirouette, beaming now with her mother's approval. "What do you think, Daddy?"

He found that he couldn't reply for a second, then cleared his throat. "I think this Darren Scott is one lucky guy. I hope we're going to get to meet him."

Mother and daughter shared an amused look, and then Rebecca skipped across and put her arms around her father. "Of course you will. I'd never go out with anybody my favorite daddy didn't know. He should be here any minute."

And as though on cue, the doorbell rang.

"That's him!" The Beck turned back to her mother. "I look all right?"

"It's not your looks . . ." Frannie began.

"I *know*, Mom. It's who I am inside. But do I look okay? Really?"

Frannie gave up on the mother lecture and hugged her. "You look perfect."

Meanwhile, Hardy walked down the hallway, geared up to be polite and yet somehow firm and even awe-inspiring. He swiped at his eyes, opened the door, and it was Abe Glitsky.

"Not with my daughter, you don't!" His voice was harsh. "Darren!" And he slammed the door in his friend's face.

A couple of seconds later, he opened it again, grinning at his cleverness. He noticed that a lanky young man in a suit was standing behind Glitsky on the stoop, looking tentatively over Glitsky's shoulder. "Excuse me," he began. He appeared to be sufficiently terrorized to last through the evening. "Is this where Rebecca Hardy lives?"

"He seemed like a nice kid," Glitsky said. "I doubt if he's even got a sheet."

"There's a consoling thought if I've ever heard one. My daughter's dating a guy who's never even been arrested."

They were at the dining room table, Abe with his tea and Hardy and Frannie finishing their wine.

"Dismas has been preparing himself for this, so he wouldn't be too harsh," Frannie said. "Imagine if it had just been sprung on him."

"I thought I was downright civil," Hardy said, "considering. That thing with Abe at the door was meant to be a joke. I had no idea Darrel was there."

"Darren," Frannie corrected him.

"Didn't I say that?"

"That was just bad timing," Abe put in deadpan. "Could've happened to anyone."

"Anyway, it'll give him something to think about later," Hardy said. "When he's wondering whether he should keep the Beck out past eleven-thirty or not."

"I don't think that'll be much of a question," Frannie said. "In fact, I don't think it will even cross his mind, especially not after the six reminders."

"Not six," Hardy said. "Not more than two. Abe was here. He heard. No way was it six, was it, Abe?"

Glitsky sipped at his tea, looked up in all innocence. "I'm sorry," he said. "I wasn't paying close attention."

Glitsky and Hardy had a chessboard set up between them on the dining room table. It wasn't much of a contest. Although Glitsky had won the vast majority of the many games they'd played over the years, they both pretended that they were fairly evenly matched.

Hardy explained his poor record by the fact that since he was more excitable than his friend, he tended to see a move and act precipitously. And it was true that Glitsky was more patient, even methodical, in his play. It was also true that Glitsky never drank alcohol and Hardy would have a beer or two and sometimes, as tonight, an after-dinner cognac or two after he'd already had his wine for dinner. Hardy felt that the mere suggestion that this had any effect on his strategy or play was, of course, ridiculous.

But Glitsky was happy to take advantage of whatever mistakes Hardy made, and he'd already made one that would be conclusive. So Glitsky made his next move, then sat back and relaxed a degree or two. He was already tired, as he'd done the wake-up call for their baby Rachel before dawn. She had a low fever and maybe a tooth was coming in as well, and Treya had basically done him the kindness of kicking him out for the night, freeing him to go talk about his father's demands and his job frustrations with his friend Dismas. It was her turn for baby duty. No need for both of them to suffer.

Hardy studied the board, raised his eyes. "You don't look good."

"Neither do you. So what?" Glitsky let out some air. "But I admit I am a little tired."

"Ha! The excuses begin."

"For what?"

"For when I beat you here."

Glitsky kept all expression out of his face. He picked up his mug of tea. "We'll see. I believe it's your move."

"See? He worries." Hardy lifted his snifter and studied the board. He understood that Glitsky thought he had an advantage, but danged if he could see what it was. After a minute, he looked up. "I'd take a teething daughter over a dating one anytime."

"You want," Glitsky said, "I'll bring Rachel over. We can trade."

"No thanks!" Frannie from the front room where she was reading.

"Okay, we'll leave daughters," Hardy said. "So moving in the other direction, what's the problem with your father? Is he all right?"

Glitsky pushed his chair back far enough from the table so that he could cross a leg. He let out a long breath. "You hear about Sam Silverman?"

Hardy shook his head. "Don't know him. What about him?"

"He was Nat's best friend. He ran a pawnshop by Union Square and somebody shot him last night in his store. It's still your move, by the way, if you don't want to concede, which you should. Anyway, Nat doesn't seem to get it that I'm not in homicide anymore. He asked me if I'd look in on the investigation and make sure they're on track. Like that. So, much against my better judgment, I went downstairs and talked to Gerson today. . . ."

"In homicide? How'd that go over?"

"About like you'd expect. After the parade, the welcome kind of wore off pretty quick. Gerson even found a way to mention it to Batiste. Evidently, in one of those strange coincidences you read so much about, the topic just happened to come up while they were having lunch."

"Imagine that," Hardy said.

"Right. But in any event, Frank called me off. Period. Not that I was on. Are you going to move someday?"

"I'm savoring the anticipation," Hardy said. "So what about Nat?"

"Nothing, really. But I've got to tell him and he's not going to like it. He might even decide he's got to go talk to somebody himself which — no matter what — would be a disaster."

In the kitchen, the telephone rang and Frannie, although she was farther away in the living room, jumped up to answer it. "It might be one of the kids," she said by way of explanation as she passed by them. She got to it and after a short, amiable-sounding talk, she was back in the doorway. "It's John Holiday. He says it's important."

"I bet." Hardy pushed his chair back. "Two minutes," he said to Glitsky.

"You want to move first?"

He paused and pushed a pawn up one

square. "You're dead very soon." Then turned toward the kitchen.

Ten minutes later, Hardy came back into the dining room, where Frannie and Abe were sitting side by side at the table. As he'd talked to Holiday, he'd heard the two of them erupt in laughter several times. This, especially from Glitsky, was a rare enough event in itself to warrant comment, but then as soon as Hardy looked, he saw the cause of it and didn't have to ask.

They were going through a stack of birthday cards that Holiday had been randomly sending Hardy now for over a year, whenever he ran across one that was particularly funny or insulting or both. The latest was a lovely, romantically out-of-focus picture of a forest of redwood trees with streams of sunlight shining through them and a gorpy poem extolling their majesty and incredible longevity, "adding to the magnificent beauty of the earth for thousands and thousands of years." When you opened the card, it read "Thanks for planting them."

"These are pretty good," Abe admitted.

Hardy nodded. "I laughed at the first seventeen of them myself."

"I wish I'd thought of this. Hey." He

snapped his fingers. "Maybe it's not too late."

"It's way too late," Hardy said.

"Was it important?" Frannie asked.

Another shrug. "Everything's relative." He moved back up to his chair and hovered a moment over the chessboard, raised his eyes quickly to Glitsky. "You moved something."

"Just one little knight. It was my turn."

"That's all you moved?" He stared back down, saw it, swore under his breath.

"Tut-tut." The lieutenant wagged a finger, then checked his watch and stood up. "But enough of this wild partying. I think I'd better go spell Treya."

"So what did you decide about Nat?" Hardy asked, somewhat unexpectedly, out of context.

The question stopped Glitsky and he considered for a minute. "He'll get used to it, I suppose. I just hate to disappoint him." They'd gotten to the door. Frannie had opened it, and Abe was putting on his jacket.

"You want," Hardy said, "you and I could do a field trip to the crime scene tomorrow. Maybe get a tidbit for your dad, make him feel better, like you're working on it. Maybe we even do some early

Christmas shopping."

"I'll check my social schedule," Glitsky said, "but sounds like a good idea. You'd really do that?"

"Sure. What are friends for? Say ten, eleven?"

"I'll let you know."

When he was gone, Frannie closed the door and turned to him. "Maybe do some early Christmas shopping? Since when?"

"It could happen," Hardy said.

"Okay, but what else?"

"But that call from John? It turns out it was pretty important. The police want to talk to him about this guy Silverman's death. Abe's father's friend."

"What about him?"

"Whether he was involved somehow."

"Involved? How could John be involved? In what way?"

"In the way of whether he had something to do with killing him."

6

The sun broke through while Hardy read the morning paper at his kitchen table, waiting for Glitsky's call, which never came. He finally called Abe's and left a message at around eleven. Next he tried Holiday at home — useless — then at the Ark. Nothing.

His own house had been empty now for an hour and a half. Though for years he'd fantasized about the magic day when he and Frannie's lives weren't ruled by the schedules of his children — the lessons and ballgames, the colds and homework and simple *stuff* that had cluttered his every waking moment for the past sixteen years — now that the time was upon him he wasn't sure how much he liked it.

Frannie was dropping the kids off somewhere and in an ironic turnabout he wasn't sure he fully appreciated, she was seeing one of *her* clients on a weekend morning. Technically still a student, Frannie had gotten hooked up with a psychologist friend of hers, Jillian Neumann, and was working about twenty accredited apprentice hours a week in family counseling.

So with the day looming empty as his house before him, Hardy went into the kitchen and took his black cast-iron pan down from where it hung off a marlin hook behind the stove. He ran his knuckles across its surface — silk.

Automatically, he threw in a big pinch of salt — Frannie had switched to kosher salt and kept a bowl of it open next to the burners — and turned on the gas. He went to check the refrigerator, grabbed a Sierra Nevada Pale Ale from the top shelf, opened it, and drank. In two minutes, he'd cut up garlic and scallions, poured in some olive oil, added leftover rice, a can of sardines, a good shake of red pepper flakes. It occurred to him that he was eating too often at Lou the Greek's if he found himself hankering for this kind of treat, but the smell pushed him onward. Soy sauce, some plain yogurt, and then, finally, an egg to bind it all. When it was done, it looked awful but he almost couldn't wait to get back to the table to dig in. He thought it was even possible that he'd stumbled upon one of Lou's wife Chui's secret recipes such as Athenian Special Rice or even, wonder of wonders, Yeanling Clay Bowl.

First, though, before he sat down to eat, he kept the heat up and threw in more salt. Swiping at the bottom of the pan two or three times with a dish towel, he then dumped the contents into the garbage can. The magic pan was as it had been before he began, gleaming, oiled.

As he ate his masterpiece, his thoughts returned — if in fact they'd ever left — to Holiday. To most outside observers, the failed pharmacist was not typical of Hardy's friends. The serious overdrinking, the gambling, the women. Certainly, bartending and trying to keep the bar he'd inherited afloat, he wasn't working on any kind of career. That alone set him apart. Beyond that, Holiday had ignored his earlier friends until he lost them. He'd burned out his parents and the rest of his solidly suburban family, rejected their values and hopes for him.

This was because John Holiday had no real hopes anymore himself. They'd been dashed six years ago when his wife and eight-month-old baby daughter — Emma and Jolie — had been killed by a hit-and-run driver who'd run the red and never even slowed down.

Hardy, too, had lost a child. In another lifetime, he'd had a son, Michael, who'd lived seven months. A couple of years into his first marriage to Jane Fowler, the child had somehow pulled himself up over the bars of his crib one day, fallen to the hardwood floor. For about ten years after that, his own marriage and fledgling legal career having collapsed under the weight of the grief, Hardy drank Guiness Stout, bartended at the Little Shamrock. Like Holiday, he was glib all the time.

So Hardy knew what made Holiday the way he was. He didn't blame him, wouldn't judge him, didn't expect anybody else to understand the connection. It was what it was.

He was no longer eating. He was considering his friend's life, and wondering if it could now have led him to a murder.

Holiday grew up in a middle-class home in San Mateo. His father, Joseph, ran three independent and successful sporting goods stores until they were bought out by a nationwide chain in the eighties. His mother, Diane, stayed at home with the kids — John, his younger brother Jimmy, and their two sisters, Margie and Mary — until Mary was in kindergarten; then she went back to teaching.

He went to an all-boys Catholic high school, lettered in baseball and track, became the school's "blanket" player — the best all-around athlete whose name went on the blanket that hung in the school's gymnasium. For a time he held the WCAL record in the half mile. Popular with students and faculty alike, he was secretary of the student body his senior year. Academically, he was sixth in his class with a 3.88 GPA, a National Merit and California State Scholarship Finalist, and a lifetime member of the California Scholarship Federation.

These accomplishments were impressive, but said little about Holiday's essence. Evidently between the ages of fifteen, when he lost his virginity, and thirty-one, when he got married, his chief persona was sexual predator. The first time was with Anne Lerner, a neighbor and friend of his mother, who . . .

It was a warm, windy Saturday afternoon in late spring and he was with his three best buds from school buying sodas at the Safeway where they'd been let off by one of the moms after the ballgame. In the checkout line, Anne Lerner — the youngest and always the foxiest of Mom's married friends, with a really cute bobbednose face and a great smile — was her usual friendly self to all of them. Every one of John's pals admitted having the private hots for her — Mrs. Lerner was the only adult who got mentioned when the guys were making one of their frequent lists of the cutest girls, the best breasts, and so on. Today she looked almost like a teenager herself with her long, tan legs, the short white tennis shorts, the ash-blond hair hanging around her shoulders.

She had a cart full of grocery bags and all four of the guys were happy to help her load them into the back of her wagon. Since none of them drove yet and all lived up the hill on her way home, she asked if they wanted a ride and all of them piled in, John in the front where, when she leaned forward to put in the key, he couldn't help but see that the top button on her blouse had come undone. She glanced and caught him looking, gave him a playful, open smile, then buttoned up.

When the last of them but John got out, Mrs. Lerner asked him if he'd mind stopping by her place first — just a few blocks farther up the street — and helping her unload the groceries. Her daughters were both gone on a weekend camping trip with the Girl Scouts and her husband was traveling again and wouldn't be back until midweek. So she was all alone.

He carried the bags inside. It took him four or five trips, and the button came undone again, and then the one under it. Finally, by the time he put the last bag on the counter and turned to face her, only one button remained.

"Thanks, John. Can I offer you something? A glass of water?"

He was mesmerized by the fall of her blouse, but stammered out a no. He had to be getting home.

She took a step toward him. "Are you sure? You can stay a few minutes. Anything?"

He swallowed — his mouth had gone dry — then he looked at her face, which wore a mysterious smile now, an expression unlike any he'd seen before. She closed the gap between them even more; they were so close he smelled the wonderful scent of her — almonds and . . . and something else. She cocked her head up at him. "What?" she asked playfully. "Tell me."

Following his gaze, she looked down. "Oh, these darn buttons." But slowly,

slowly, her eyes never leaving his, her hand went not to any of the open buttons, but to the closed one under them all, which was suddenly open, too. "Oops," she said, laughter in her throat. She took his hands and brought them up to the little snap in the front of her bra, which she helped him open with a practiced ease.

"What a charming story of young love," Hardy said. "She was how old?"

"Thirty-five. Forty. Somewhere in there."

"So if you were fifteen, she raped you."

"Diz, please, rape has such ugly connotations. I infinitely prefer the word seduced. And I promise it did not scar me for life. In fact" — a slow grin lifted Holiday's corn-silk mustache — "I've been known to drop by in the recent past from time to time. And you know what? She is still *hot*."

"I'm happy for you both. Maybe not so much for the husband."

"Long gone, I'm afraid. I believe his prostate gave out." Holiday kept his grin on, knowing he was pushing Hardy's buttons. They were both sitting on folding chairs in sunshine just outside the propped-open front door of the Ark. Holiday was drinking a Bud Lite from the bottle and had his brown denim workshirt unbuttoned halfway. He was supposed to be bartending, but he owned the place and there weren't any customers.

"Well, fascinated though I am with all this history, it's not why I came down. You talk to any cops yet?"

"I haven't had that pleasure."

"They didn't come by your house?"

"They might have." Holiday tipped up some beer, the sloe-gin eyes twinkling. "I don't believe I slept there last night, so I can't be sure. But I did stop by here and Clint told me what was up, which was when I called you."

"And I'm so happy you did." Hardy squinted up at the bright sky. He moved his chair back into the shade of the doorway. "So what do you think?"

"I think I didn't shoot Sam Silverman or anybody else."

"You pretty sure?"

A nod. "Reasonably. It's the kind of thing I'd remember."

"You got an alibi for when it happened?"

Suddenly, all trace of the grin was gone. "This is starting to remind me of when you were my lawyer last time."

"That didn't turn out so bad. Look at

you now. They don't let you drink in prison. Bud Lite or anything else."

"You chumming for business?"

"Hey, you called me. The last thing I want in the world is a murder case. And here's a hint — you don't want one either. If Frannie wasn't working, I'd be having lunch with her right now instead of checking up on your sorry ass. But as you appeared to be seeking advice and counsel — lo, I appear."

"All right." Holiday leaned forward in the folding chair, his elbows on his knees. He had his index finger in the neck of his beer bottle and spun it in little circles near his feet. "So where were we?"

"On your alibi."

Holiday gave an impression of thought. "What night again?"

Hardy came forward and spoke with some sharpness. "Don't give me that, John. It was the night after your poker game, which makes it Thursday. This is Saturday. I'm thinking even you, two days and who knows how many drinks ago, you might remember."

"Okay, between you and me, I had a date," Holiday said. "Dinner and a movie."

Hardy sat back, spread his hands in victory. "There you go. Was that so hard?"

But Holiday's expression was far from relaxed. "What?" Hardy asked.

"Well. Couple of things."

Hardy waited a minute, finally spoke. "Do I guess or are you going to tell me?"

"No. I'm going to tell you." He pulled the bottle off his finger and took another pull at it. "First, the lady in question is married, so she's not going to want to be involved."

"Why am I not surprised? Maybe she's not going to have a choice. So who is she?"

"I can't say. Not even to you. Her husband would . . ." He let it drop.

"Well. There's a ray of good news. Her husband, then, is still alive, I take it."

"Oh yeah. You'd know him."

"I'd know him? How's that?"

"I mean he's well known, a public figure. She can't come out."

"Great. Swell. You're seeing the wife of a famous guy. Do I dare ask if this is a long-term relationship? Between you and her, I mean, not her and her husband."

"We went out a couple of months, but it looks like it's over now anyway." Holiday shrugged. "It ended Thursday, in fact. Before the movie. Before dinner, if you want to get technical."

"Technical's good. Let's go that way." Hardy barked half a laugh. "So you didn't go out with this unnamed married woman for dinner and a movie after all? And hence you don't have an alibi for the time of the murder? Is that what you're saying? And might I add parenthetically, do you have any idea how much fun I'd be having with you already if you were on the stand in court?"

"But I was with her till at least six-thirty, is what I'm telling you, Diz. By which time Silverman was dead."

Hardy was shaking his head, not sure if he was near despair or enjoying himself. There was no question but that he believed Holiday — who else would go to these lengths to make up something so Byzantine and absurd? — but his predicament vis-à-vis the authorities might become very real if these vital facts couldn't be managed. "I think I could use something to drink, John. You carry any nonalcoholic mixers? Club soda? Cranberry juice?"

While Holiday went searching behind the bar, Hardy brought in the folding chairs, then sat at one of the bolted-down stools. "Just out of curiosity, where do you take the wife of a well-known public person out to dinner for a couple of months

174

and never get recognized?"

Holiday shot club soda from the gun over some ice, squeezed in a lime wedge. "Chinatown," he said. "We all look the same to them. Hey, it's true. It's the next best thing to invisible." He handed the drink across. "Anyway, the point is, Silverman was dead by the time we got to dinner, am I right?"

"I don't know. I haven't got the time-table on it. I gathered from Glitsky it was the end of the day, but five-thirty, six-thirty, I don't know. You want to just tell me privately who the woman was?"

"I could tell you, but so what? She'd just deny it. Especially now. She always had a cover story for her husband anyway, where she was. Look, maybe we won't even need it, okay? Weren't there three guys?"

Again, Hardy had no previous connection to the case and he didn't know.

"Well," Holiday said, "I'm telling you, there were. Clint, my night guy, said the cops were trying to scare him putting the three of us together — me, Clint, and Clint's boyfriend Randy. Clint's gay."

"I guessed," Hardy said. "And they've got alibis? Clint and Randy?"

"They were here together the whole time from six. Clint was behind the bar."

"And customers saw them and would swear to it?"

Holiday shrugged. "Somebody must have."

"Very strong, John, very strong. Does Clint remember any of them, these customers?"

"I'm sure he could come up with somebody."

This answer didn't warm Hardy's heart. He sipped at his club soda, wiped his finger along the overlacquered bar. "John, remember our first few interviews when they busted you for the bad scrip? When you just couldn't believe anybody really cared about prescription drugs enough to hassle anybody about them?"

"I still can't believe it. Adults ought to be able to get anything they want. If they kill themselves with whatever it is, hey, they're adults."

"It's really special you believe that, and we can have a debate about it later, but maybe right now we can agree that murder is more serious."

Holiday, on the other side of the bar, was filling the garnish trays. He stopped cutting lemon peel and looked up. "I really didn't kill Sam, Diz. The other thing was different since I actually did it."

"Then why'd you call me last night? About this?"

He went back to cutting. "Clint was freaked out about the cops coming by. It got a little contagious."

"But you're over that now?"

A shrug. "I really didn't do it. Clint and Randy certainly didn't do it. They're not going to nail three of us when none of us were there."

Hardy sipped his club soda, said nothing.

Holiday stopped again. "What? What's that look?"

"No look," Hardy said. "I guess I forgot for a minute that nobody's ever been arrested for a crime they didn't commit."

"They're not going to arrest me. They didn't arrest Clint last night and they were right here with him."

"Okay, I'm convinced. You're in no danger. But do me a favor. The cops come by to talk to you, call me first. Don't say one word."

Holiday made a face. "Surely I should say hello. If I don't return their greeting, they become surly. I've done experiments."

"Sure, say hello. Bake 'em a cake if you want." Hardy drained his glass, stood up and walked out the open door without another word.

After he calmed down a little, he called his home from the cell phone in his car, but nobody answered. At Glitsky's, too, he got the answering machine again. This was turning into a rare day, with no work and no family. He considered going home and doing something physical — they had half a cord of wood that needed to be stacked, or he could take a run — but then he decided screw it. He'd go to his own well-run and pleasant bar and talk to someone with a functioning brain.

"The guy's an idiot," he told McGuire, who'd once, when he cared about different things, earned a Ph.D. in philosophy from Cal Berkeley. They were both waiting for the churning foam in Hardy's Guinness to fall out. "I don't know why I waste my time."

"You like him, that's all. I like him, too. He's a firstborn male, right?"

"And this means something?"

McGuire had his standard Macallan poured into a rocks glass that sat in the Shamrock's gutter. He took a bite of a piroshki he was eating from a place around the corner and washed it down with scotch. "You got any close friends that aren't?"

Hardy quickly filed through the litany — McGuire, Freeman, Glitsky, Pico Morales, even Graham Russo, another ex-client. And now Holiday. "That's interesting."

To McGuire, it was an old, self-evident truth, and he shrugged. "It might be that, but don't mistake it for a character reference. He reminds me of everybody we knew when we went to school. Sex, drugs, rock and roll, party all night. You remember."

"Not as much as you'd think. I didn't go to Berkeley."

"You were *alive* in the sixties, though, if I'm not mistaken."

"Here's an ugly surprise, Mose. I *hated* the sixties. The only good thing in that decade was the Beatles."

"Come on. The Turtles. Herman's Hermits."

Hardy had to smile. "My point exactly. But I give sixty-eight my vote for the worst year of our lifetime. So saying Holiday brings back those good ol' days isn't what I'd call high praise."

"I'll tell you something, though, and no reference to the sixties." Moses leaned over the bar, his broken-nosed face six inches from his brother-in-law's. He spoke quietly, nearly in a whisper, but with some intensity, possibly even rebuke. "He's just like you were when you worked here. You weren't so hot on all the rules before you got with Frannie and decided it was time to grow up."

This brought Hardy up short, threw him back on himself as McGuire straightened back up and turned to check on the other five customers in the bar. Hardy took a slug of his daytime stout and looked at his face in the back bar mirror.

McGuire was right, he realized. Crippled by grief, loss and guilt over his baby's death and the breakup of his marriage in the wake of that, Hardy had walked the boards behind this very bar for most of another decade. A lawyer without a practice, a thinker without a thought, he hadn't been able to commit to much more than waking up every day, and sometimes that was too much.

Now, with a good marriage, a thriving practice, and teenaged children, Hardy had a life filled — sometimes overfilled — with meaning, import, details, routine, relationships and responsibility. Holiday's life, his situation, couldn't be more different and more importantly, it hadn't been of his choosing. Hardy, of all people, should remember that Holiday was living day-today, waiting for that first flicker of meaning or hope to assert itself. Until then, he'd take his solace from whatever source, a woman or a bottle or easy money at the poker table.

McGuire was back in front of him. He poured another half inch of scotch, dropped in one ice cube and stirred with his finger. "So where were we?"

"At the part where I was being a judgmental old dick."

"There's a sixties concept, the famed value judgment." His brother-in-law reached over and good-naturedly patted his arm. "But you can't qualify for true old dickdom for at least a couple of years."

"The sad thing is, though, Mose, I kind of believe in value judgments nowadays."

McGuire clucked. "Yeah. Well, as you say, most of those sixties ideas — value judgments are bad, dope won't hurt you, fidelity's not important — they haven't exactly stood the test of time. But there's still that old nagging tolerance for different lifestyles."

"And the Beatles," Hardy said. "Don't forget the Beatles."

"Only two of 'em left, though, you notice," Moses said.

7

Hardy didn't talk to Glitsky again until he showed up unannounced late Monday afternoon at his office. His baby's fever hadn't been from teething, and by early Saturday morning it had gotten to 104 degrees and he and Treya were with her at the emergency room. Roseola.

"You should have called me," Hardy said. "The Beck had it, too. I could have diagnosed it over the phone."

"Next time she wakes us up screaming at three a.m., I'll call you first."

"I'll look forward to it." For the past couple of hours, Hardy had been reviewing the technical specifications of a supposedly fully automated truck-washing unit. One of his clients had bought it for a million and a half dollars. It hadn't worked even within the ballpark of the manner promised by the company's brochure from day one. The gap between the gallons of recycled clean water the system could actually process and the gallons guaranteed by the brochure was big enough, Hardy thought, to drive an eighteen-wheeler through. He'd studied the numbers enough to master that fact. He was taking the case to trial in a little over a month.

He could spare his friend some time. "So what's up? Did you take today off?"

Glitsky sometimes wasn't much of a sitter. First he'd crossed over to one of the windows and peered out, now was pulling darts from Hardy's board. "Amazingly enough, I finished all my critical work by," he looked at his watch, "about six hours ago."

"You must be underutilized. I hope at least you looked busy."

Glitsky threw a dart. "I sat behind my door and gnashed my teeth."

"For six hours? That must be hell on your molars."

"I don't care about my molars."

"You would if you cracked one with all that gnashing. But then, you're the guy who chews ice all the time. I bet you grind your teeth at night, too."

Glitsky turned to face him. "How'd you like a dart in the eyeball?"

"You'd probably miss." He stood and

came around his desk, strode over to the dartboard, and waited for Glitsky to throw the third dart. "So did you ever get to find out anything else about Silverman?"

"Else implies I found out anything at all." He threw.

"And yet just today you whiled away six perfectly good hours when you could have been detecting."

"Except I'm not a detective anymore."

"Nor much of a dart player." Hardy pulled the darts, walked back to the tape line on the floor. He whirled, paused for an instant setting up, and threw a triple twenty — one of the very difficult shots. "Right now you're probably asking yourself how I can be so good."

"The question fills my every waking moment. Nat tried to find out something, though, about Silverman."

"Without you? How'd he do that?"

Glitsky appeared to be gnashing his teeth again. "When I got busy with Rachel, he told Sadie — Silverman's wife — she might as well go through the normal channels. So she called homicide."

"And?" Hardy's focus was suddenly lost, and his next two darts didn't score at all.

Glitsky pulled the darts for his round. "And nobody called her back all day yesterday or today. Nobody."

"They were probably busy."

"Right. So finally, maybe an hour ago, Nat called me. Again with would I check? So I called Lanier."

"And a fine inspector he is. Are you going to throw or not?"

"Are we playing a game? I'm shooting bull's-eyes, that's all."

"Not too many."

Glitsky pegged a dart, missed his target by three inches. Threw, missed again. Threw the last dart, missed.

"Good round," Hardy said. "So what did Lanier say?"

"He hasn't seen Gerson all day."

"All right. Progress."

Glitsky ignored him, stepped to the side as he came to the line. "But — and you'll love this — the guys working the case, Russell and Cuneo . . ."

"Do I know them?"

"I'd be surprised. Anyway, Lanier checked the sign-in and they hadn't been in over the weekend, or today."

Hardy threw a bull's-eye. "They're not out in the field?"

"Lanier didn't think so. They would have checked in. We're big on paperwork nowadays. They don't sign in, they get a nasty letter from payroll. Ask me how I know."

Hardy threw the last two darts in quick succession, leaving all three clustered in the middle of the board. He eased himself back up onto his desk. "They'll probably get to it someday." He paused. "I probably shouldn't tell you this . . ."

At the dartboard, pulling the darts again, Glitsky turned around, a question.

"They're snooping around one of my ex-clients who, I need hardly add, had nothing to do with it. You remember John Holiday?"

It didn't take Glitsky two seconds. "The drug guy."

"Right. And two of his friends, all of whom have alibis."

The tumblers fell into place. "The call you got Friday night."

Hardy nodded. "It pains me to admit it, but that was why I was willing to go and peruse the crime scene with you on Saturday, and would do the same today if you were so inclined."

For a long moment, Glitsky considered it, then shook his head. "That's what I came by here thinking we might do, to tell you the truth. But what are we going to do there, except get me in trouble? How do we even get in?"

"You're probably right," Hardy said.

"I'll let Gerson call Sadie first, find out for sure what they've got, if anything. At least get some questions of my own I might want to ask. Why do they like your guy?"

"He doesn't know, and in any case he's not worried about it."

"Except that he called you."

Hardy shrugged. "It was early in the process. He's over it. But his bartender's got a sheet and maybe a squishy alibi. John thinks they were just shaking his tree, see if he knew anything at all."

"And did he?"

"He was bartending a couple of blocks away."

Glitsky frowned. "What's squishy about that?"

"It was evidently a slow night. Few if any customers. He and his partner — the other alleged suspect — they alibi each other, but that's about it."

"And what about your guy, Holiday?"

"He was having dinner with a girlfriend. Chinatown," he added.

"So he's out of it."

A tight smile. "Yep."

"Well." Glitsky pursed his lips, thinking. "If they're even shaking this guy's tree, at least they're doing something." He let out a heavy breath. "It's not my job. I keep telling myself. I guess I'm just not so good with being patient."

"You're kidding me," Hardy said. "When did that start?"

Matt Creed had been off the past two nights, but now he was back in the beat, walking with both hands in his pockets. Vapor appeared in front of him with every breath he took. The night, outside the glow of the streetlights, was full dark, as it had been about the same time that things had gotten hairy outside of Silverman's last week. That sequence of events had been an unending tape loop in his mind over the weekend — the first shot and simultaneous ricochet by his ear so much louder than anything he'd ever heard with his earphones on at the range. Even now it re-echoed in his memory.

He turned the corner up from Market and on the other side of the street came abreast of the Ark, noticed this time that a dim light emanated from the doorway. Stopping, he tried to force himself to picture, to remember, *anything* about the previous Thursday. But it was such a nondescript length of street, such an anonymous location, that it had no discrete existence for him at all. There was the plywood in the hole for one window, the tinted blank of the other, the darkened mouth of the doorway. The door itself stood open tonight, but he couldn't for the life of him recall even glancing in the bar's direction when it mattered the most.

Here he was, all dressed up like a cop and really nothing like one. His apparent duty was so far from the reality that it almost made him sick to his stomach. Creed was twenty-two years old and taking courses in criminology at City College during the day. He had taken the assistant patrol special job with WGP Enterprises because it offered decent pay along with the opportunity to attend the Police Academy on, essentially, a Panos scholarship. Creed's plan was to get his AA from City, get training at the PA and experience with Panos, then apply for the regular PD, where he thought he'd have the inside track. His life goal was to become a homicide inspector, and he'd been thinking he was well on his way.

Until last Thursday, when he hadn't seen a damn thing, and of what he'd seen he noticed even less. Although he was the only real witness to any part of the crime, he'd been little enough help, no more than coffee gofer, when Wade Panos — the big boss himself! — had been at Silverman's Thursday night. Even worse, he had a sickening feeling that he'd let himself be manipulated when Roy had come by with the two real-life homicide inspectors. Because he'd so wanted to please them, to be important, he'd picked up the thread of their suspicions and let himself more or less volunteer Randy Wills and Clint Terry as suspects.

Creed had run into Randy Wills a few times in the Ark, but he didn't know him except to nod at. Terry, on the other hand, was a pretty good guy who, back when they'd still been clients in the beat, had often given Creed a free coffee or a Coke when he'd stopped in. In reality, he hadn't seen enough of the two forward runners in his chase last week to say for sure whether or not they were two-headed Martians. And as to the shooter? Sure, he'd seemed like a pretty good-size guy, but again, running away at seventy-five feet in the dark and wearing a heavy coat against the weather, he could have been anybody. Hell, he could have been a she.

But now Creed worried that he might have helped direct the homicide cops to some innocent people. More, because it had been so nonspecific, he didn't know how to undo what he might have done.

Suddenly, he found himself standing inside the Ark. It was Monday night, slow as death, two patrons at the bar, and the huge, really hulking form of Clint Terry stood behind it, right up by him, by the front door. Suddenly, forcefully, it struck him that the shooter surely couldn't have been *that* big. Creed would have retained that as a positive memory rather than a vague sense.

"Hey, Matt. Checking up on us? You cold?"

"It's not warm, Clint."

"I've got some go-cups. You want one? Two sugars and cream, right?"

"That'd be good, thanks. Everything okay in here?"

"Good." A pause. "Roy was in here the other night with a couple of inspectors from homicide."

"Yeah, they told me. The Silverman thing, huh?"

"That's what he said. I was working here, though, just at that time. You might remember."

"I never crossed over, Clint. Never looked in. Sorry."

"Yeah, well, it probably don't matter. The cops haven't been back, but listen, from now on, you want to poke your head in here when you pass, the coffee's on me."

The cup did warm him up, but neither Clint's hospitality nor the steaming brew made him feel much better. By the time he got to Ellis, he'd pretty much decided he would have to talk to Russell and Cuneo, back off from his earlier stance. And this might be his opportunity now. The lights were on at Silverman's.

When abreast of the door, Creed saw an old man sitting on a chair by the counter, an old woman standing in the center aisle facing the shelves, writing on a clipboard. For a few seconds, he watched them. They appeared relaxed if somewhat subdued, and were having some kind of conversation between the woman's notes. When Creed knocked on the glass, it startled both of them, but then they noticed the uniform and the woman came to the door and unlocked it.

"Can I help you?" she asked. To Creed, she looked to be in her late sixties, early seventies. Her face was sharp-featured, birdlike under her wispy white hair. He would be surprised if she weighed more than a hundred pounds. But there wasn't

anything frail or timid about her. Her eyes
— no glasses — narrowed down critically
at him.

"I was going to ask you the same thing,"
Creed said.

"How would you be able to help me?
You're with WGP, aren't you?" She peered
closely at the name tag over his pocket.
"Well, Mr. Creed, I'm Sadie Silverman,
Sam's wife. We're not with the beat any-
more."

"Yes, ma'am, I realize that. I just saw the
light and . . ." He came to an end,
shrugged.

Suddenly the man was up with both of
them. He put a hand on Sadie's shoulder,
pulled the door open, and motioned Creed
inside. "I'm Nat Glitsky," he said, ex-
tending his hand. "A friend of the family.
We thought it would be smart to take an
inventory. Were you here the night it happened?" He closed the door, threw the
deadbolt.

"Yes, sir. I was the . . ." Again, he
stopped. "I discovered the body," he said.

"Do you know if the police took anything?"

"No. I don't think so. From the shelves,
you mean?"

"They haven't told me anything," Sadie

snapped. "I can't get anybody to call me back. I just came down here with Nat and opened up myself."

Nat laid a hand on the woman's arm. "All they told Sadie was that Sam had been killed in a robbery attempt. Three men, apparently. Did you see them?"

Creed temporized. "From a distance. One of them shot at me twice. I chased them but couldn't catch up."

"So if you'd come by just a couple of minutes earlier . . ." Sadie let out a heavy breath. "What about these robbers, these *killers?* Why did they pick *here?* Why was it Sam who . . ."

A small tremor began in her jaw, and Nat put an arm over her shoulders. "It's all right, Sadie; it's all right." He walked her back to the chair he'd been sitting in by the jewelry case, sat her down, then turned and came halfway back down the center aisle, to where Creed was now standing. "It would be nice to know if anybody's interested in what happened here," he said. "That's all. Is anybody looking for who did this?"

"They're looking. The inspectors came by and interviewed me on Friday night."

"And what did you tell them? What did you know?"

"Pretty much what I told you. Three guys. At least one of them with a gun. Mr. Panos thought they probably got away with Mr. Silverman's bank deposit. This old leather pouch he was supposed to be carrying."

"That's what it was," Sadie said. "Thursday was his deposit night."

"Who's Mr. Panos?" Nat asked.

"My boss," Creed said.

Sadie had recovered enough to stand up again. "He owns the security patrol we used to pay. But he raised his rates last summer and we had to drop it."

But Nat wore a confused expression. "Wait a minute. If this guy Panos didn't do security here anymore, why was he here on Thursday?"

"Because I was," Creed said. "The cops asked him the same question. Also, he and Sam knew each other." He turned to Sadie. "He was really upset about this, ma'am. He told the inspectors he'd give them any help he could, and I know he was working with them as of Friday" — he included Nat — "when they interviewed me."

"How do you know that?" Nat asked.

"His brother, Roy — that's Mr. Panos's brother — was with them, interviewing suspects."

"So they have suspects, after all?" Sadie asked.

Creed made a pained face. "They were looking at a few guys who'd been at a poker game. Apparently one of them lost a lot of money the night before, and the thought was he might have come back to get it. Mr. Panos had given the inspectors a list of who'd been there, and that's where they started."

A sharp rapping on the front door made them all turn. A dark, menacing hatchet face scowled through the glass, and Creed reached for his gun. Nat, though, put a hand on his arm, stopping him. "It's my son," he said.

"What are you doing here, Dad?" The intimidating black man took up a lot of room in the cramped aisle. He turned impatiently to Creed and held up a badge. "I'm Glitsky, SFPD. Who are you?"

"I'm assistant patrol special Matt Creed, sir."

But Glitsky had already whirled. "Nat, you shouldn't be here."

The old man was unbowed. "Sadie wanted . . ." He stopped. "We thought it would be a good idea to do an inventory. Nobody's gotten back to her, and she has the key, so we thought we'd let ourselves in, find out what they took. Find out *something* at least, Abraham, since nobody seems to want to tell us anything."

"I got that much from your message." Shaking his head disgustedly, Glitsky looked around. He walked to the entrance to the back room, glanced down at the brownish stain on the floor, then threw a cursory glance over the jewelry case. Then he was back at his father. "I told you I'd talk to Gerson as soon as I could, Dad, find out what I could. He wasn't in today."

He took a deep breath, focused on Sadie. "Mrs. Silverman," he said, "I know it's very hard to wait to learn anything when at the same time you're trying to deal with your grief. My heart goes out to you, but it would be better if my father wasn't here right now. Nat will tell you, I did this homicide stuff for sixteen years — not just did it, *I ran the detail* — so believe me, I know. When the police know something, they will tell you. And I really can't have my father involved in this case in any way."

When Creed realized that he had been in the room with *Lieutenant* Glitsky, formerly head of homicide, he decided that even if it delayed him for a few stops in his rounds, he was going to talk to him after his father and Mrs. Silverman had been sent on their way. Even a low-level connection with someone of Glitsky's rank and experience might translate to a letter of recommendation, or something, later on. He might also get some advice on how to approach Cuneo and Russell about his perhaps-squirrelly identification of Clint Terry.

So as Glitsky left with his father and Silverman's wife, Creed trailed along behind, invisible, while the trio walked down the street and across it into the underground level of the Macy's parking lot.

Hanging back by an overhang until Mrs. Silverman's car had driven away, Creed tried to time his moment. In his best mood, Glitsky didn't exactly invite an easy familiarity, and now — standing with his hands on his hips, looking after the taillights of the Lexus — he positively simmered over a low flame of anger, frustration, maybe fatigue. After a minute, he brought a hand to his forehead and squeezed at his temples.

"Are you all right, sir?"

The return to professional mode was immediate and impressive. "I'm fine, Mr. Creed. I didn't realize you were still with us."

"Yes, sir."

Glitsky was walking and Creed fell into step next to him. "I'm sorry I snapped at you back there at the shop. I was upset with my father. It wasn't your fault."

"Thanks." It seemed to be a chance at an opening. They'd come to the mouth of the garage, up on the street level again. "Crime scene stayed till about four in the morning."

Glitsky stopped and faced him. Between the garage and streetlights, they stood in a pool of visibility. "How do you know that? You stay around, too?"

"I came back after my shift." Creed shrugged. "I'm taking crim courses in school. I'd been the first person on the scene and nobody seemed to mind if I stayed. I wanted to see how it worked in real life."

"And how was that?"

"I thought they were pretty thorough, from what I know, which isn't much."

Glitsky put his hands into his jacket pockets. Several seconds passed. "So what happened that you got there first? Did you get a call?"

"No. Really it was just mostly a coincidence. I was on the block, right over there" — he pointed to a spot across the street — "when the alarm went off at Silverman's. I saw some guys running out the door. So I yelled after them to stop, and one of them shot at me. Twice."

Glitsky's mouth moved, an impulse to smile. "And missed, I see."

"Yes, sir."

"You're lucky." His eyes went to the shop. "Though maybe not so much from that distance. But either way, you don't want to get shot."

"It's never been in my plan."

"Yeah. Well, it was never in mine either. It just goes to show you."

Creed couldn't stop himself. "You got shot?"

It was the wrong question. The lieutenant's face closed up. "Nothing to brag about," he said, clipping the words.

Glitsky was wrestling with himself. He'd only come downtown — fifteen minutes after he'd arrived home — to keep his father from getting him into more trouble. He hadn't even had dinner yet, and knew that Treya would be waiting for him. Rachel was still feverish, and in some low-level but constant way he was worried about that, too. Certainly, he didn't want to stay in any kind of private conversation with this young rent-a-cop, even if he did seem bright, interested and idealistic.

These were not traits Glitsky normally associated with Panos's crew, especially since he'd been reviewing the police reports on behalf of Hardy and his pending lawsuit. He'd had innumerable dealings with WGP on his own as well, and few of them had been pleasant.

On the other hand, this boy had been the first person on the scene, had actually been a witness to the crime in progress. Undoubtedly, he had been interviewed by the case inspectors, and Glitsky had no reason to believe that they were less than adequate. He didn't know Cuneo and Russell at all. They'd been brought up in Gerson's watch and might, for all he knew, be the most competent and committed policemen in San Francisco, although most of his recent experience in the department argued against that.

"Nothing to brag about," he said, and realized that he sounded too harsh. "But . . . so you actually saw these guys?"

"Well, to tell you the truth, Lieutenant, I saw three figures running away from me in the dark. I couldn't identify any of them to save my life."

"That happens. I wouldn't worry too much about it." The open face of the young man took on a troubled look, and

Glitsky said "What?"

Creed blew out heavily, a deep sigh. He seemed suddenly ashamed of himself. "Except maybe I was trying too hard to be helpful."

"Helpful's generally good, son. What's the problem?"

A shrug. "I might have given your guys some bad information."

Glitsky had seen enough confessions to know when somebody wanted to talk. He leaned against a parking meter, crossed his arms, met Creed's eyes, waited.

"I had told them — your inspectors — that the person who'd shot at me seemed like he was kind of big. So then they came back the next day and said they were looking at this other guy who works in the neighborhood, a bartender over at the Ark, do I know him? Do I think it could have been him? And I'm thinking, I don't know what I'm thinking, to tell you the truth, probably just wanting to be important, you know? So I give them the impression that, yeah, maybe it was this guy. I mean, I say it could have been, and then I told the inspectors he's got these two friends he hangs with . . ." The recitation ground down to a stop.

"And now you don't think it was?"

202

Creed shook his head miserably. "I really don't know. I went by there tonight — the Ark — and he was behind the bar. I mean, it *could* have been him, I suppose, maybe, but I was a lot stronger than that when I talked with the inspectors. It was like I gave them the impression that I could positively ID him."

"So call them up and tell them," Glitsky said.

"Just like that?"

"Yep. They're probably working half a dozen leads right now. They'll be glad to know sooner rather than later. Believe me, they'll thank you for it."

"And think I'm an idiot."

Glitsky actually broke a smile. "Possibly, but if you're not an idiot next time nobody will remember. But I'm curious. How'd they get on to this guy, the big guy, in the first place? There must have been something."

"Yeah. There was. It was the Ark. The connection there."

"Which is what?"

"This guy John Holiday owns the place. Evidently he was at Silverman's poker game — you know about the poker game? Wednesday nights? Anyway, Holiday was there the night before and lost a lot of money. Mr. Panos knew about it and told the inspectors and they went by the Ark to talk to him — Holiday. But since he wasn't there, they got Clint. The big guy. The bartender. And after that, of course, they came to me."

"Talk to the inspectors," Glitsky said. "Maybe they've got something else on these guys, too."

"I just wouldn't want them to waste their time because of what I told them. And also, I've got to tell you . . ."

"What's that?"

"These guys. Holiday, Clint and Randy Wills. I think they're pretty harmless. I'd hate to get them in trouble if they had nothing to do with this."

Glitsky chewed on the inside of his cheek, his brain fully engaged. "I wouldn't worry about that," he said. "If they did it, some evidence of it will likely turn up, and that's what they'll get them on. They're not going down on your ID, I promise you that. Meanwhile, I'm keeping you and my wife thinks I'm on my way home." He pointed a finger at Creed. "Call the inspectors, though, all right?"

"Yes, sir."

Forty-five minutes later, Creed was

working the beat south of Market and saw Roy Panos taking a break in a booth at Carr's coffee shop. Like Creed, he was on duty tonight, and in uniform. Roy was engaged in an animated conversation and after Creed was inside, he realized that one of the two men facing away from him was Nick Sephia. Not a big fan of Nick's, whom he'd worked with a few times before he went to the Diamond Center, he considered turning around and walking out, but by then Roy had seen him and motioned him over, sliding over to the wall to make room.

"Hey, Mattie." Creed hated the diminutive, and had committed the cardinal error of mentioning it once to Roy, thereby assuring that he'd forever be Mattie, or Little Matt, or Mataroni. In any event, it was hard to stay mad at Roy, who was always hale fellow well met and tonight so much so that Creed wondered if he'd been drinking. Or maybe he was nervous. "I was just telling the guys here — you know Nick and Julio . . . no? Julio Rez, Matt Creed."

Creed reached across the table and shook hands with a very well-dressed, overshaved, alert and unsmiling Hispanic with a little less than half of his left ear. "Nice," he said as though adding "to meet you" would have been excessive.

Creed had a quick impression of danger, of suppressed energy, maybe of cocaine. He wondered if Nick, who'd moved into the stratosphere of security positions transporting diamonds, now had his own bodyguard. When Rez had leaned across to take Creed's hand, his coat had fallen open, revealing a shoulder holster and the butt of an automatic.

But this was the observation of a split second. Roy was back carrying the conversation. "I was just telling these guys about you. I mean, here I've been doing this work, what, fifteen years, and it's shine the flashlight, see nothing, go to the next window and do it again. Mattie here, he's on less than a year, he comes round the corner — *blam! blam!* — couple of rounds right at him, guys running, him chasing, the fucking Wild West. Awesome action."

"Anytime you want, I'll trade you," Creed said. "I took the job for the flashlight work."

"You don't like gettin' shot at?" Sephia asked. "I love it, you know that, swear to God. Makes me horny as hell."

"Anything *doesn't* make you horny, Nick?" Roy asked.

Sephia considered briefly. "Nothing

206

comes to mind," he said.

But Rez turned to Creed. "Roy said you fingered those assholes at the Ark," he said. It wasn't quite a question. It sounded more like a challenge, but then Rez had made the single word "nice" sound the same way.

"Fingered might be a little strong," he said.

"He's being modest," Roy said. "He set 'em all up to go down. Holiday, Terry, his little girlfriend, what's his name?"

"Randy Wills." Rez didn't have to think. He had it all in his head. He might have been an accountant.

"Wills, Terry, Holiday, all of 'em," Roy repeated. "Not only does the kid get himself shot at a few times, he solves a murder before his first anniversary."

"Not exactly that."

But Roy pushed it. "Hey, it's true, Matoosh. After your ID the other night, those guys are going down for a long time."

"Yeah, well . . ."

"You don't seem so happy about it," Rez said. He leaned in across the table, a tight smile fixed under a glassy cat's-eye stare.

Creed felt a line of sweat forming at the back of his neck. "The thing is, it might not have been them."

Roy snorted, half laughing. "What are you talking about? Of course it was them. You're the one who saw them, didn't you? How could it not be them?"

But now, having gotten it out, Creed continued in a rush. "That's what I wanted to talk to you about. Do you know a Lieutenant Glitsky?"

Roy nodded. "Sure. He used to run homicide. What about him?"

"Well, his father was a friend of Silverman's and they were by there tonight."

"Who was by where?" Rez asked.

"Glitsky and his father. And Silverman's wife. At the shop."

"Doing what?" Sephia's color was suddenly up.

Creed shook his head. "Nothing, really. They never got to it. They were going to do an inventory, but barely got started before Glitsky got there and cleared them out."

"There you go," Roy said, as though he were satisfied with the answer. "So Glitsky's working the case now? What's that about?"

"No. I think he was just there because of his father. But outside, after, I asked him what if I wasn't as sure as I sounded about the three guys with the other inspectors."

"And what'd he say?"

A shrug. "He said just to tell them. Not a big issue. They'd be glad about it."

"Wait wait wait, not if . . ." Sephia said.

But Roy raised a hand — firmly. Made eye contact across the table. "Exactly right!" he said. Then, in a milder tone. "Exactly right." He smiled a shut-up warning at Sephia and Rez. "No way they want to spend all that time chasing the wrong guys." Back to Creed. "But you're sure this time? You seemed pretty certain the other way the other night."

Creed shook his head miserably. "I don't even know that. It still could have been them, I suppose. I just didn't want them — the inspectors — thinking I was positive, basing their case on what I said . . ." He scratched at the tabletop.

Roy nodded in full agreement. "Hey, bottom line is Glitsky's right. You got to tell them. In fact, I'm meeting up with them later tonight down at the Hall." Roy tapped his own pocket. "Wade's little PR moment for our good friends among the police. Forty-niner tickets, fifty yard line. You want, I'll pass the message on for you when I see them."

Creed felt a wash of grateful relief and it

209

showed. Roy Panos was far better with people, especially with city policemen, than he was. Roy could phrase Creed's ambivalence about the ID in such a way as to minimize the idiocy factor, maybe even give it a rosy gloss. Certainly, Creed himself could avoid the embarrassment of having to face the inspectors and admit that in his zeal to be a help, he'd screwed up. "You sure?" he asked Roy. "You'd do that?"

Roy smiled and took a pinch of Creed's cheek. "Hey, anything for my little Matooshka. Huh?"

Creed took this as his cue to leave. He slid out of the booth and said good-bye all around. But he wasn't completely out the door to the coffee shop when Nick leaned across the table. "He can't take back that ID, Roy." He was whispering, but with great intensity. "That's the thing that's keeping the inspectors busy."

Roy picked up his coffee cup, sipped at it. "He's not taking back the ID," he said.

Sephia hit the table for emphasis. "Hello. Roy? He just told us he was."

Roy finished his sip, slowly put the cup down. "I don't know if you heard me, but I said I'd tell the two inspectors. And I'm going to forget."

"Not enough," Rez said.

"It would still screw it all up," Sephia said.

"He still knows." Rez methodically turned his own mug around and around on the table.

Roy shook his head. "Look, guys, Creed doesn't know anything. Don't go all paranoid around this. Even if he somehow gets back himself with Cuneo and Russell and says the ID on Terry isn't positive, so what?"

"Maybe he gets them thinking," Rez said. Still spinning the mug, never looking up.

"It's not going to happen, especially since I'm not passing it on."

"I still don't like it," Sephia said.

Rez nodded in agreement, finally looked over at Sephia. "Creed's a problem," he said.

"Creed's not a problem! He thinks it might not have been Terry. That's all."

"But if he can't talk at all, it doesn't even get to that," Sephia said.

"Don't you guys be stupid," Roy said. "This is under control; I'm telling you."

Rez slowly brought his empty gaze around across the table to Roy. He nodded his head once, a dismissal. "Oh, okay," he said.

8

"Is this the same man who prides himself on living according to John Kennedy's old motto of never explain, never complain? I've only heard you say those words about a hundred and fourteen times now."

"I'm sure I meant them every single time, too."

"Well?"

"Well, this particular fine day" — and it was, the good weather continuing as they drove together into work — "I'm going to have to do some explaining before I can succeed in doing some real good."

"The explaining part will neither be appreciated nor understood. And neither will the real good, if in fact that's what it is."

Glitsky stared at the road ahead of him.

His wife kept it up. "When are you going to learn, Abe? There's no point in trying to live by a motto, even an excellent one, if you can't dredge it up and act on it when you really need it. Which you do today, believe me. You don't want to even start to do this."

He kept his voice civil. "So what do you suggest I do?"

She turned to him. "You *know* that one."

"No. I'm asking."

She sighed. "All right, then. I suggest you do absolutely nothing. You go up to your office and close the door and read a good book."

"And just ignore all this other stuff?"

She glanced over at him. "How can I put this so you understand? It is not your job. You are not responsible for what happens down there. You should not even care."

"How can I not care? Tell me that."

"Easy. You say to yourself, 'Self, I'm at my job because I have a wife and a child and two kids in college and I need the paycheck and benefits. That is why I go to work.' Period."

"And that's how you feel about your job?"

"Actually, no. I love my job, but it's not the same situation."

"How is it different then?"

She rolled her eyes. "I don't believe we're having this discussion. It's different because I care about the job they're paying me to do. *You,* on the other hand, care about a job nobody's paying you for. It's like if you decided you cared about, I don't know, being an astronaut. I'm sure astronauts have problems all the time, but guess what, Abe? *They're not your problems!*" She slapped at the console between them. "And neither are homicide's!"

They rode in silence for a block. Finally Abe said, "So I shouldn't go to Gerson?"

Again, Treya sighed. "You think you know something, call one of your people there. You've still got friends there, right? Marcel, Paul. They make the same argument to Gerson, tell him what you told them — the ID might be funky — then you buy them a hamburger, everybody's happy. What's the problem with that?"

"I don't know," Glitsky said. "I really don't know. It just doesn't seem right, somehow. And it still leaves me having to explain why I was by Silverman's if he finds out, which he will."

"How would he find out? Who's going to tell him? The young rent-a-cop?"

"I don't know, but he's going to find out — that's the way these things go — so given that, it'd be better if he heard it first from me."

They'd gotten to a parking place in one

of the lots under the freeway, a couple of blocks from the Hall of Justice. Glitsky switched off the motor, but made no move to get out. Treya pulled down the visor and carefully, with an exaggerated calm, applied some lipstick. She was breathing heavily through her nose. When she was done, she — again, carefully — closed the lipstick and dropped it back in her purse. At last, she turned to her husband. "Well?"

"I'm thinking about it," he said.

Glitsky was in a booth at Lou's with Marcel Lanier, a long-time colleague in homicide. He was bragging modestly about his wife, who'd convinced him that there was no point in having a motto if you were going to jettison it at a real opportunity to have it work for you. It would be like being a Boy Scout and just before a rafting trip in Class V rapids forgetting to put on your life vest. "So what good would all that earlier 'Be Prepared' stuff have done you?"

Lanier squinted in the dim light. "I know you don't drink, Abe, especially this early. Otherwise I'd be worried. What the hell are you talking about?"

Glitsky blew on his tea. "Not explaining to Gerson about why I'm interested in this Silverman thing."

"And this has to do with the Boy Scouts somehow?"

The tea was too hot and Glitsky put it down. "Never mind, Marcel. Let's leave it. What I really want to talk about is Wade Panos."

Lanier made the face of a chronic heart-burn sufferer. "Do we have to?"

At a few minutes after eleven o'clock, about two hours after Glitsky had told Lanier about Creed's perhaps bogus iden-tification, there was one sharp rap at his door. Glitsky took his feet off his desk, snapped shut his latest Patrick O'Brian novel — *Desolation Island*. He opened his drawer, deposited the book, pulled some paperwork over in front of him. "It's open," he said.

Glitsky wasn't altogether stunned to see Barry Gerson. He came to his feet with what he hoped was a warm greeting, in-vited the lieutenant in, shook his hand, told him to take a chair. "Returning the courtesy visit?" he finally asked.

Gerson, polite as an undertaker, inclined his head an inch. "Something like that."

"But not exactly?"

"No, frankly, Abe. Not."

"All right." He squared himself, linked his fingers on the desktop in front of him. "How can I help you?"

"Actually, I came here to ask you the same thing. I thought I'd made it clear yesterday when you came down to the detail that my door was open to you. You needed anything, all you had to do was ask."

"That's true. I appreciated that, too, Barry, I really did. I still do."

"But?"

"But then I had a talk with" — he almost named Batiste, stopped himself — "with some colleagues, who didn't think it would be smart of me to abuse the privilege. It might look like I was trying to insinuate myself back into the detail."

"Which you're not."

"No. Of course not." Glitsky pushed his chair back, crossed his arms behind his head. "I'm minding my own business up here, keeping an eye out for payroll irregularities."

But Gerson didn't smile at the witticism. "So you're denying that you went down to Silverman's last night?"

Glitsky repressed his own rare urge to smile. Of course, as he'd told Treya, Gerson would have to find out. He was almost pleased that he'd predicted it. "No-

217

body's asked me. If they did, if you're asking me now, I admit it."

Gerson nodded. "You mind if I ask you why?"

"Not at all. My father went down there with Mrs. Silverman and I didn't think it was a good idea. I wasn't there ten minutes."

"You expect me to believe that?"

Glitsky let out a weary breath. "As I told you yesterday, my father was Silverman's best friend."

"You mentioned that. I remember." Gerson straightened to his full length in the chair. "And as I believe I told you yesterday, I would inform you as soon as we unearthed anything that moved the case forward."

"Of course. I appreciate that. It's just that my dad and the wife hadn't heard from your department and thought they'd take an inventory. I told my father it wasn't a good idea for him to be involved because of the discussion I had with you. That's what happened."

"I was out yesterday. Cuneo and Russell both had personal time off. That's why nobody called the wife." At Glitsky's look, he added, "Hey, it happens."

"Yes it does." Good, Glitsky thought,

I've got him explaining, too.

"So you just went down to Silverman's and found them there?"

"He called me and left a message. And I don't need to answer these questions. I've got no interest."

Gerson displayed a small air of triumph. "And because you've got no interest, you didn't talk to Lanier this morning?"

"So what?" Glitsky pushed his chair back far enough to allow him to cross a leg. "You want to know the truth, Lieutenant, I was trying to do you a favor."

"Goodness of your heart, huh?"

"Believe it or not, I actually have some understanding of the job you've got. I thought I could save you some misery."

"And how would you do that?"

"Do you know Wade Panos?"

"By reputation, sure."

"And what's his reputation?"

"He does a good job. Maybe a little rough, but he keeps the scum factor down in his neighborhoods."

"And that's it?"

A shrug. "What else is there?"

Glitsky came forward again. "Do you know he's being sued?"

"Who isn't? People sue people all the time. What's that mean?"

"Maybe nothing, except when there's something like fourteen plaintiffs asking around thirty million dollars."

"Again, I ask you, what does that prove? Hell, you know. Somebody's *always* suing us. Brutality, invasion of privacy, stealing candy from schoolkids, you name it."

"True enough," Glitsky said. "You're probably right. Panos is a saint."

"I never said that." But Glitsky still had a look, and Gerson said, "But what?"

"Only that I'd think hard before I gave him point in any homicide investigation."

"He's not point. He had leads, that's all. The poker players."

Glitsky locked his fingers on the desk. Said nothing.

Gerson raised his voice. "And in fact the names he gave us took my boys someplace. You got a problem with that?"

"Not at all."

"So? What, then?"

"So, the usual suspects, huh? Two guys with sheets."

"Three, as it turns out. Randy Wills isn't any choirboy, either. So yeah, the usual suspects. Happens every day."

"No question about it." Glitsky turned a neutral face up at him. "Your boys find any evidence to go with their suspects?"

"They'll be getting warrants."

Glitsky clucked, then nodded, all understanding. "They looking at anybody else in the meanwhile?"

"Why do they want to do that when the guys Panos gave us look good for it?"

"You're right," Glitsky said mildly. "Waste of time. That'd be stupid."

Perhaps correctly, Gerson must have gotten the impression that Glitsky was including him among the less intellectually gifted. He'd burst in here ten minutes ago holding the high moral ground and for the past several minutes had been drifting into the lower regions, and losing territory even there. It didn't appreciably improve his attitude.

He stood up.

"Well, you know," he said, "stupid or not, I'm running the detail now. I'm calling the shots with my troops and what I came up here to tell you still goes. Silverman is my case. I'm controlling the investigation. Yesterday I'm a good guy and bend a little and you take advantage of it, hiding behind your old man. Well, I'm telling you now. You keep you and your father out of it, all the way out, or I'll haul your ass in before the deputy chief. Don't think I won't." His voice was rasping now, low-pitched with anger and the need for control in the cramped room. "In fact, you might want to remember that *every* homicide in the city is my case now and my guys work for me."

Glitsky knew he could a draw a punch with one sarcastic word and it hovered temptingly on the tip of his tongue. There'd be a great deal of pleasure in it. But he only leaned back, crossed his arms, and nodded. "I got it," he said.

David Freeman had to be at his office at 1:30 p.m. to hold the hand of another of his co-plaintiffs being deposed in the Panos lawsuit. Yesterday they'd started at 10:00 a.m. with a gentle, turbaned professor of Comparative Religion at City College. In his mid-fifties now, soon after the terrorist attacks Casif Yasouf had been walking back to his car, parked at the Downtown Center Garage, from a meeting at the St. Francis Hotel, when he had the bad luck to run into Roy Panos, in uniform. The assistant patrol special was abusing a homeless man in an alley, kicking him and his shopping cart down toward the western border of Thirty-two.

Mr. Yasouf's version of events was that he'd simply tried to intervene as a citizen, telling the policeman that he didn't have to use such tactics. Panos, he said, had then abandoned his pursuit of the bum and turned on him, lifted him easily by his shirt, slapped his face hard twice and told him to take his rag-head ass back to Arabia. Frightened and bleeding, Mr. Yasouf finally fled. He reported the incident to the regular police the next morning, complete with Panos's name from his tag. Two days later he abandoned the complaint. Again — his version — because someone had set fire to his car.

That deposition hadn't finished up until twelve-thirty the next morning and by the time Freeman had gotten back, walking as always, to his apartment at the foot of Nob Hill, it was after 1:00 a.m. and Gina Roake was asleep in his bed. It had been *their* bed now, since a few weeks after his physical confrontation with Nick Sephia.

About a year ago, things had started to change with Freeman and Roake. Before that, Freeman had maintained a discreet and rotating harem of up to a dozen women. He was, after all, a wealthy and successful old man with an established, urban, sophisticated lifestyle that did not include the sort of entanglements that he believed were the unvarying attendants of exclusive physical relationships. He had always kept an armoire of women's robes for his visitors. The medicine chest was well-stocked — toothbrushes, creams and so on.

Roake was, at forty-four, not exactly a babe in the woods herself. She, like Freeman, had had several long-standing but essentially casual relationships, and had never been married. They had seen each other in professional and social settings — courtrooms, fund-raisers, restaurants, even the occasional judge's chambers — for years, but had never shared more than pleasantries.

Freeman had a long-standing tradition that whenever he won a large case, he would celebrate alone — a fine meal at one of the city's restaurant treasures with an old and noble wine, then a final cognac or two at the Top of the Mark, or one of the other towers — the St. Francis, the Fairmont. That night, at the Crown Room in the Fairmont, he sat savoring his Paradis at a small table by the window overlooking the Bay side. He appreciated the walk of the shapely, grown-up woman as she got off the elevator, unavoidably registering that she appeared to be alone. It didn't matter, he told himself. This was not how he met women, ever.

He'd been playing the case over and over again in his mind throughout the night, all the high points up to and including the glorious moment of the "Not Guilty" verdict. People had no idea what a rare and lovely thing it was, even in San Francisco, to get a defense verdict. The best defense lawyers in the world won maybe five percent of their cases — Freeman himself hovered around fourteen percent, but he believed himself to be an almost unparalleled genius. And he was right.

Except now the case was over. There would be no need, even, of an appeal. His mind, consumed by its strategies for most of a year, was suddenly empty. He felt a mild euphoria and with the meal and wine, a deep physical contentment. The cognac was the essence of perfection. He stared out the window, over the sparkling lights.

He turned back to the room. The woman had materialized in front of him.

"David? I thought that was you."

Still half in reverie, he smiled. "Gina. Hello. What a pleasant surprise."

"I don't want to bother you if you're busy," she said.

"Not at all, at all. Please, join me if you'd like."

She'd sat and they had talked until last call, after which she took a cab home. In the next month, he asked her to lunch nine times — he preferred lunch dates because there was less expectation of automatic intimacy than with dinner. Either party, in the get-to-know stage, could back out without embarrassment or loss of face. In that way friendship, which in Freeman's opinion was always preferable to physical attraction, could be preserved.

In Roake's case, though, a strange thing happened. By the time it became obvious that they'd be sleeping together, he'd stopped seeing anyone else. Before he asked her to his apartment for the first time, and without any kind of agonizing analysis, he got rid of the contents of his armoire, the other feminine accoutrements. Then slowly, over time, she'd started leaving articles of clothing of her own at his place until she had her own drawer in his bureau and the entire armoire all to herself. She hadn't spent the night at her own apartment now for three months.

This morning, Freeman barely woke up in time to catch Roake as she was out the door on her way to work. He reminded her of the depositions that had now begun on

Panos, and wondered if she might make it back here for lunch, even a little early if possible, since they wouldn't get dinner together for who knew how long.

Now he checked his watch: 11:20. She should be home any minute. Billy Joel's CD of piano concertos — a Gina find — played almost inaudibly in the background. Rubbing his palms together, he was shocked to find them damp with nerves. He caught a glimpse of himself in a wall mirror and shook his head in amusement. David Freeman hadn't been nervous arguing before the Supreme Court. He couldn't remember his last attack of even minor jitters, but he had to admit he had them now. His eyes left his own image and went to the little eating nook in the cramped and narrow kitchen. Normally the table was a mess, piled high with yellow legal pads, lawbooks, half-empty coffee mugs, wineglasses and sometimes bottles, newspapers, binders and file folders.

Today, it looked perfect and elegant. He'd spent most of an hour removing the usual detritus and what remained were two simple place settings in silver, crystal champagne glasses, one yellow cymbidium in the center of the starched white cloth, echoing the sunlight that just kissed the edge of the table. There was a beaded silver champagne bucket to one side, a bottle of Veuve Cliquot's *La Grande Dame*, purposely chosen for the name of course, nestled in it in chilled splendor. He'd arranged for Rick, the chef downstairs at the Rue Charmaine, to deliver the light lunch — pike quenelles in a saffron broth and an artichoke-heart-and-pancetta salad — precisely at noon.

One last glance at himself, and he had to smile. Certainly, no one would mistake him for handsome. But he'd done all right, and today he looked as good as he could, which is to say he probably wouldn't scare most small children. He wore the one nice suit, a maroon-and-gold silk tie. He'd managed to shave without cutting his neck and his collar was free of his trademark brown specks of dried blood. It would have to do.

And here she was. On time, cheerful, kissing his cheek. God, he loved her.

"You're looking good today, mister. If I didn't have a meeting in two hours . . ." She kissed him again, then backed up a step. "I thought clients didn't trust nice clothes."

"This isn't for a client." He realized he had taken her hand when she'd come up to him and hadn't released it. "Come look at something."

She stopped in the doorway to the kitchen and turned to him. "Who are you and what have you done with my boyfriend?" Then, more seriously, "This is beautiful, David. Is it an occasion? Don't tell me we started seeing each other a year ago today and I didn't remember."

"It might be an occasion someday," he said, "in the future." He drew in a deep breath and came out with it. "I wanted to know if you'd be interested in marrying someone like me."

She looked quickly down to the ground, then back up, staring at him with a startled intensity. "Somebody like you? Do you mean hypothetically?"

"No. I said that wrong. I meant me. Will you marry me?"

For an eternal two seconds — they were still holding hands — she did not move, looking him full in the face. She brought her other hand up and held it over her mouth, obviously stunned. "Oh, David . . ." Her eyes filled. "I never thought . . ." She looked at him, hopelessly vulnerable, terrified. A tear spilled out onto her cheek.

But still the word didn't come. "I love you," he said. "Please say yes."

"Oh God, yes. Of course yes." Her arms were around his neck and she was crying openly now, kissing his face, eyes, lips again and again. "Yes yes yes yes yes."

"This Saturday?"

It was midafternoon and they were taking a break in the deposition of their old friend Aretha LaBonte while she used the ladies' room.

Panos's lawyer Dick Kroll was waiting, taking notes back in the conference room, a large sunlit enclosure resembling a greenhouse that they called the Solarium. Freeman and Hardy were ostensibly filling their coffee cups in the old man's office.

Freeman nodded. "If you're free."

"I'll get free. It's not that. I'm flattered that you'd ask me. I'm just a little surprised. No, I'm flabbergasted. I didn't know you were even thinking of it."

"Well, there you go. You don't see everything."

"And isn't Saturday a little soon if you just got engaged today?"

"Why would we want to wait once we decided?"

"I don't know. Most people do, that's all. Send out invitations, plan the party."

Freeman was shaking his head. "None of

that, Diz. We don't want a party. Just a best man — that's you — and a maid of honor and a judge. Oh, and Gina's mother."

"It's nice you remembered her. Can Frannie come?"

"And Frannie, naturally. Goes without saying."

Hardy drank some coffee. "You know, I've been a best man twice now in two years. I stood up for Glitsky."

"Good for you." Freeman's enthusiasm was restrained. "You'll be in practice."

"I didn't need it. It was pretty easy. Like Aretha here."

Again, Freeman shook his head. "Don't get complacent. Kroll's good, even if he's got no principles. In fact, it might be why he's good."

"I don't know," Hardy said. "I'm not seeing much yet."

Freeman opened the door out to the lobby. Aretha was back at her place in the Solarium, and smiling, Freeman waved at Kroll, who was staring angrily in their direction. He pointed at his watch in an impatient gesture. Freeman waved again, turned back to Hardy. "He'll come up with something."

"I'm just saying we've got him on the

ropes. I don't see him coming up with a *legal* something."

"You wait," Freeman said, "you'll see." Then, an afterthought, "What do you mean, legal something? What else is there?"

The law offices of Richard C. Kroll were located in one of the recently built and controversial loft spaces south of Market Street at Third and Folsom. For the past twenty minutes, Kroll had been turned around in his swivel chair, looking out of his second story, floor-to-ceiling window, for the familiar sight of Wade Panos to appear on the street below. It was the day after his latest deposition with Aretha LaBonte at David Freeman's office.

And now here Wade was, half a block down, on foot and in uniform as always, stopping to look into the shops as he passed them, even occasionally raising a hand to acquaintances on the street. An extraordinarily successful man in his element, Panos bestrode the pavement like a parade marshal, confident and unassailable.

Kroll's stomach rumbled, and he clutched at it. Taking a few antacids from a roll in his desk drawer, he stood up. In the mirror over the bar area, he got his face composed so that it wouldn't immediately telegraph the bad news he was about to deliver. By the time his secretary buzzed him with the word that Wade had arrived, he was back at his desk, apparently lost in other work. When Panos opened the door to the office, he looked up and motioned to the wing chair in front of his desk. He'd be done in just a moment.

Closing the folder, he finally found the nerve to look at his client. Wade, for his part, sat back comfortably, an ankle resting on a knee, his eyes half closed. He was always a patient man, and the small wait until his lawyer gave him his attention didn't seem to rankle in the least. Still, when Kroll closed the folder, he came out of his trance, suddenly all business. "So how bad is it?" he asked.

Kroll tried to smile. "How do you know it's bad?"

"You want to see me in person, Dick, it's bad. It's one reason I like you. Other guys, they get bad news, they give it to you over the phone, or leave a message. You? You got the balls to be here and try to break the fall. I appreciate that. So how bad is it?"

Kroll templed his hands on his desk. "Pretty bad."

Panos nodded. "Tell me."

"We got denied on the summary judgment."

"Which means what?"

"It means the judge decided that this thing's going forward."

Panos showed little reaction. If anything, he settled back a little more into his chair. "Okay," he said, "you said from the beginning that filing the thing was a slim chance. So it didn't work. No real surprise, right?"

"But there is a surprise."

Panos cocked his head, an inquisitive dog. "I'm listening."

Kroll noticed that his knuckles had gone white and he willed himself to loosen his grip. "You remember we decided that since you personally were not alleged to have harmed any of the plaintiffs, that you shouldn't be personally named as one of the defendants?"

"Right. It's just WGP and some of the assistants —" Noticing Kroll's look, he stopped midsentence. "What?"

"That's what Freeman and Hardy decided to hit. They were shooting to pierce the corporate veil, and it looks like they did it."

Still well back in his seat, still in a relaxed posture, Panos frowned. "You lost me, Dick. What's that mean?"

"It means. . . ." Panos stopped, shook his head, reached for another folder, and opened it. "I'll read the relevant part to you. How's that? 'Plaintiffs have introduced enough evidence to show that there exists a triable issue of fact as to whether WGP Enterprises Incorporated, a California corporation, and Wade Panos, an individual, are in fact alter egos of one another.' " He dared a glance up at Panos. "They're saying that the corporation is a sham and that therefore you should be personally bound in. Apparently the judge bought it."

"Dick, I've been incorporated for thirty years, and my dad before that."

"I know, I know." Kroll sighed. "But apparently they argued that the corporation is undercapitalized, among some other technical points. Also, since you're the only shareholder and you control the company's day-to-day workings on your own, they said the corporation is being maintained not as a legitimate entity but as an artificial dodge to avoid personal liability."

"Artificial my ass. I donate to all these charities through the corporation. I pay my guys and my bills with corporate checks.

The corporation's as real as a heart attack, Dick."

"I agree with you, Wade, and certainly that's what I'd argue in front of a jury, and I might even prevail. But the judge ruled that it would have to be decided by a jury, so that's what we're dealing with."

"And if we lose, then what?"

"Then you're exposed. Personally."

Panos seemed to go into another kind of trance.

"It gets worse, I'm afraid," Kroll said. "It also means you'll be deposed before the jury gets to hear anything. You and me go up to Freeman's office, there's a court reporter taking everything down, and you're under oath."

Panos opened his eyes again, but didn't respond. Folding his hands in his lap, he took a breath.

The lawyer continued. "It also means that Freeman and Hardy get to ask you where you get your money, all of it. And how you get it."

This brought a small rise. "So then you object, right?"

Kroll nodded. "Yes I do. Except in a depo the objection is noted for the record, but you've got to answer the question anyway. And later the judge rules whether the answer is admissible."

"Later?"

"Way later."

Panos's chest rose and fell, long and slow.

"The point is," Kroll continued, "once they've got you in a depo, they can ask anything. That's how they finally got Clinton, you know. Not because of anything he did with Paula Jones, but because he said under oath that he hadn't had sex with anybody else. Then when Monica came along . . ."

Panos held up a hand. "Spare me the history lesson, Dick. What's this mean to me in the here and now?"

Kroll picked his words carefully. "It means they're going to be able to look at any bank account you have anywhere. It could be — I'm not saying it *will* be, but knowing Freeman I'd say it's likely — that it's going to be open season on your books, and not just your corporate books. They want your net worth."

"Why? What's the big deal with my net worth?"

"That's largely what they base punitive damages on, Wade. The idea is that punitives are supposed to punish, to hurt. The more you're worth, the more they ask, the more —"

Panos raised his head, stopping Kroll. His face betrayed no deep concern. In fact, it had a controlled calm that, given the circumstances, Kroll found to be a little scary. A small laugh came from deep in Panos's throat. "You remember when this started? You called it a — what was it? — a nuisance lawsuit?"

"I remember."

Again, the frightening smile. "I'd say these two sons of bitches have taken it a little further than that, wouldn't you?" He came forward in the chair. "Okay, you're my lawyer, what's your advice now?"

Kroll appeared to be thinking, although he'd known all along that it would come to this. "We might want to offer to settle now."

Panos lived with that notion for a beat. Then, "How much?"

"A few million, at least. Say three, four."

Panos shook his head, uttered an obscenity. "You think they'll take it?"

Kroll shrugged. "I don't think I would, especially after this ruling, but it can't hurt to ask. There's no other option really."

Panos grunted. "There's always another option," he said. He cast his eyes about the room, then settled them on his lawyer. "But you go ahead. Make the offer."

9

Dan Cuneo lived in Alameda, across the Bay from San Francisco. He had a dentist appointment at eleven o'clock on Monday morning. Though it killed him to miss a day when they might be able to close in on a murder suspect, he also had a strong aversion to spending the day drooling with a numb lip next to his partner.

He'd read many, many magazine articles and listened to hundreds of hours of psychobabble nonsense about burnout, and the consensus was that if you wanted to avoid it, you had to keep some perspective on real life. Don't be a cop all the time. If you've got an appointment with a doctor, keep it. If you're really sick, stay home. The job isn't everything. So he had finally talked himself into believing that he wasn't abandoning the Silverman case by taking one day off.

He had accrued eleven extra sick days

from the past couple of years — times when the exigencies of the job had won out when he'd been sick. But today he had the damned appointment and as a conscious exercise he had decided, albeit before Silverman had been shot, that no matter what came up — and there would always be *something* that came up — he was going to keep the appointment. Mental health.

To quell the voice of his conscience before it could change his mind, he called his partner on Saturday morning and gave him the news that he was calling in sick Monday. Russell, who lived in Sunnyvale, forty-five miles south of San Francisco, took this as an opportunity to make plans to go fishing on the Bay. He had three unused sick days in his bank, and like every other city employee he knew except Cuneo, he believed that it was bad luck to let too many of them pile up. So on Monday he went fishing.

This morning, Tuesday, after three days out of the office, both inspectors had enormous amounts of busywork waiting for them when they checked in at a little after 7:45 — a couple of dozen phone calls for each to return, transcripts of the tapes of witness interviews to proofread for accuracy — and they stayed at their desks for three and a half hours before breaking for lunch, which took up most of an hour at the McDonald's next to the Hall.

At one, they had to be out at the Academy for a mandatory, previously scheduled four-hour sensitivity training class. Every cop in San Francisco made fun of these attempts to create social workers out of law enforcers. But if you didn't go, your pay got docked.

Today's topic had been transgender issues, timely and relevant because the city had recently decided to extend the insurance of city workers to cover sex-change operations. This change in policy also brought to light some sensitivity shortcomings among city service personnel. Especially the police, who needed guidelines on how to refer to those of questionable gender during the arrest and booking process. The critical element was the person's self-definition — if someone defined herself as a transsexual, officers should refer to her as a female; if she possessed a penis, however, she should be booked as a male.

But even with all the education, the concepts remained mostly elusive to some people. Drumming "Wipeout" on the steering wheel as he drove back downtown after the class, dusk descending, Cuneo turned to his partner. "So if I don't want 'em to cut off my dick, I can't be a girl."

Russell threw him a frown. "You've just failed the course. You realize that?" Then, seeing that Cuneo was apparently sincere, he continued, "It's not a matter of *wanting*, Dan. You can be all the way to a woman in your brain and still have a dick. You might not want to get rid of it anymore, or it might be too expensive . . ."

"Not here. It's covered by insurance."

"Okay, not here. But most places."

"If it were me," Cuneo said, "I'd just move here, get a job with the city, lop that sucker right off."

So it went, variations on the theme until they got back to the homicide detail where Cuneo hoped they could put in some time, finally, on Silverman. At least get caught up if there'd been any developments. But by now, the inspectors had each put in ten hours and he knew Russell was going to want to go home to his family. So more or less casually, Cuneo walked over and stood outside the open door to Gerson's office until the lieutenant happened to look up.

"Dan, there you are. You and Lincoln got a minute?"

The room had changed since Glitsky's

tenure. It wasn't a large space by any definition, but in the old days the big desk in the center of it had kept any meetings, by necessity, small. There had been one uncomfortable wooden chair across from the desk, affording any visitor maybe three feet of room. Anybody else would have to stand.

Gerson, by contrast, had installed a modular unit that hugged the back wall and turned the corner, where he had his computer, printer, fax machine and telephone. This arrangement left an open area in the middle of the room, made the office seem larger. The lieutenant was a bass fisherman and had brought in and hung on the walls a few of his mounted trophy fish and several framed promotional photos of boats and fishing equipment. On his last birthday, the unit had pitched in and bought him a mounted plastic bass that, when activated, sang "Don't Worry, Be Happy," and he'd hung it over his computer.

Now Cuneo, Russell and Gerson sat facing one another on their identical ergonomic rolling chairs. No one looked happy; all seemed angry, or at least worried. Gerson was telling them about Glitsky's input. "He thinks Wade Panos is screwing with your investigation."

Cuneo, paying attention, was whistling a tuneless melody. Russell, leaning forward, elbows on his knees, asked, "Did he say why?"

"No, not really, nothing substantive. Just that Panos doesn't have a great rep."

Cuneo stopped whistling. "The guy's a major philanthropist. What's he talking about?"

"I think he's talking about some of his guys, the beat patrolmen."

"What about them?" Russell asked.

A shrug. "Some of them, sometimes, get a little enthusiastic, it seems. Play a little rough with the residentially challenged, roust 'em out of their neighborhoods."

"Good for them," Russell said. "Somebody needs to."

"It's probably because they don't get the sensitivity training we real cops get."

"You're joking, Dan," Gerson said, "but you're not all wrong. Evidently it's a legitimate problem, at least enough so Panos is getting sued. He could probably run a tighter ship. But you ask me, the real problem is that Glitsky's old school and Panos isn't a righteous cop, simple as that. He doesn't like the patrols."

"So Glitsky's take is that Wade Panos

himself is personally screwing with our investigation?" Cuneo asked. "Why would he do that?"

"No idea," Gerson said. "But Glitsky's all over it. He went to Silverman's, you know. And yesterday morning he talked to Lanier."

"Lanier?" Cuneo straightened up. "What about? What's Lanier got to do with anything? You mean with Silverman?"

"I don't know." Gerson shrugged. "This Panos thing."

"What Panos thing?" Russell shot a look at his partner, came back to Gerson. "Are we missing something here, Barry?"

"I guess Glitsky's wondering why Panos got into it at all."

"Why?" Russell raised his voice. "I'll tell you why! He came down to Silverman's because one of his employees discovered the body, that's why. Then it turned out he happened to know about this poker game, which was the source of Silverman's stolen money. Next day he gives us names of the players in the game and one of them looks like he's with the guys who did it. What's the problem with that? Tell me that isn't good police work."

"I can't. It is. I don't have a problem, not with you. Not with the investigation either."

"I got another one for you, Barry," Cuneo said. "What's any of this to Glitsky anyway? Why would he give any kind of a shit?"

Gerson pressed his lips together, reluctant to diss a fellow lieutenant. Finally, though, he decided his inspectors needed to know. "My gut feeling is I believe he wants to get back into homicide, though God knows why. His dad knew Silverman. I guess he thought it gave him a wedge."

"And this helps him how?" Cuneo asked.

"I don't know, to tell you the truth. The kindest thing I can think is he's really trying to make himself useful somehow. I mean to us, to you. I've been trying to figure it out, but it baffles me." He shook his head. "Or maybe . . . no."

"What?" Cuneo asked.

"Nothing."

"You were going to say something," Russell said.

Gerson looked at each of them in turn, considered another moment. "Well, I don't really think this is too likely, but if Glitsky starts to make you guys doubt your sources, maybe you get tentative, don't make the arrests you need to. You look bad, which makes me look bad, and pretty soon they want a new lieutenant up here."

"And they pick Glitsky out of a hat?" Cuneo asked. "I don't think so."

"Are you really worried, sir?" Russell asked.

Gerson was matter of fact. "I can't say I'm losing sleep. But if you guys could bring in a quick collar here, it wouldn't break my heart. I . . ." He went silent again.

The inspectors waited. Finally Cuneo said, "What?"

He sighed with resignation. "When I mentioned this to Batiste, he said there might be something else in play. With Glitsky."

"What's that?" Russell asked.

Gerson paused again, lowered his voice. "I'd really like to keep this in this room, between us. All right?" Both inspectors nodded. "Well, it seems Lieutenant Glitsky has a couple of lawyer friends, we're talking *good* friends, *defense* lawyers, and they're the guys who are suing WGP. They can't very well have Panos get a lot of press for helping us solve a murder case right now — it'd make him look too good in front of the jury."

Russell came forward. "And you're saying Glitsky's working for these guys?"

Gerson backpedaled slightly. "I'm not

saying anything. I'm telling you what Batiste mentioned to me as a rumor, nothing more. To the extent it intersects with your investigation here, it's probably worth your knowing, although I don't know how much credence I'd give it. There's also talk that your suspect — Holiday, right? — he's been out working the streets, rounding up witnesses against Panos, too."

"Why? What would be in it for them?" Cuneo asked.

"They're asking thirty mil or so, which is ten to the lawyers if they win. Any small percentage of that is a nice payday for whoever was on the team helping them. How's that sound? Plus if we somehow screw up in homicide, maybe Glitsky gets the gig back here."

"We're not going to screw up, Barry," Russell said. "This one's falling in by the numbers. We brace Holiday in the morning, get him and his partners nervous about each other talking. Then somebody gives somebody up and we bring them all in."

"You're sure they're it?"

"The kid, Creed, he basically ID'd them." Russell spread his arms. "Show me anything else, Barry. No, this all fits."

It was full dark by the time Russell and

Cuneo checked out. They planned to arrive at the Ark tomorrow at 10:00. Holiday worked the early shift and they'd catch him there and have a long conversation.

Cuneo considered trying to talk Russell into going by and leaning on Clint Terry or Randy Wills more that night, but he knew that Lincoln would want to be home, a priority with him. Besides, Cuneo had his own date with Liz from Panos's office, and it made the second date difficult if you blew off the first one at the last minute. Finally, they'd already worked eleven hours today and there'd been nothing but stink about overtime lately. Cuneo knew that everything probably could wait until tomorrow and it wouldn't really make any difference. Certainly, nothing had happened since Friday. Cuneo was *always* frustrated by the pace of investigations; this case was proceeding as it should.

The two inspectors had not done any substantive investigative work on the Silverman murder since 8:30 the previous Friday night, when they'd gotten Creed's tentative identification of Terry, Wills and Holiday. It was now 6:30 on Tuesday, ninety-four hours later.

It was a small but welcome surprise. The

attorneys had all finished with Aretha LaBonte's deposition by early evening. Hardy would be home by dinnertime. Up in his office, he called Frannie with the news, then checked his messages — nothing crucial — and packed some file folders into his briefcase. Downstairs, he stopped in the doorway to the old man's office. Dick Kroll, who'd stayed for a little chat, had gone, and Freeman was alone at his desk, lighting the stub of a cigar he'd started early in the afternoon.

"Do you have any idea how great it is to be able to walk in here without Phyllis stopping me to ask what I want?" Hardy asked.

Freeman had the cigar in his mouth and spun it over a wooden match. When he had it going, he drew on it contentedly, then placed it in an ashtray. The firm's longtime receptionist, Phyllis, was a tyrant in the lobby, whose chief role was to block access to Freeman. Hardy's suggestions regarding her termination were a recurring theme that Freeman mostly ignored. "I believe Mr. Kroll is getting concerned," he said with satisfaction, "and not a minute too soon." He gestured ambiguously. "He just offered to settle."

"How much?"

"Four million. I must be losing my touch. I had him pegged at three and a half."

"I remember." Hardy stepped inside the office, sat on one of the chairs. "Still, it seems a long way from thirty."

Freeman blew smoke. "Yes, it does. Although, as Mr. Kroll points out, it's a mil and change for us right now. He seems to believe that our compensation — yours and mine, the firm's — is the critical factor. He doesn't even consider that it might be about our clients. Or his, really."

Hardy crossed a leg. "So the four mil, what's that break down to?"

"Call it almost three hundred grand per plaintiff, which after taxes is a hundred and fifty."

"Still," Hardy said. "That's real money."

Freeman waved that off. "Pah! It's gone in a year, maybe two. Besides, it's his first offer. I told him flat no, not even close. But I did learn something."

"What's that?"

"Panos has four mil of his own that he's willing to give us, forget the insurance. Where'd he get that kind of money?" He chewed his cigar for a moment. "Anyway, I told him flat out that my intention was to put his client out of business. The man's a common gangster and he knows it."

Hardy grinned. "You should have just been honest and told him what you really thought. So what'd he say to that?"

"He got a little put out. Said making this a personal vendetta wasn't doing either of us any good. I was being irresponsible to my clients." Freeman clucked. "He also said he was going to approach you directly."

"Me? What for?"

"Evidently he thinks you might be more amenable to reason. I told him to help himself. I hope you don't mind."

"Not at all. I'll just refer him back to you."

Freeman nodded, amused. "I told him that's probably what you'd do."

"And he said?"

"He said if it kept coming back to me, I was looking for trouble."

Hardy came forward. "He threatened you? Directly?"

But Freeman waved that off. "It wasn't even that. Cheap theatrics, that's all. That's what they do. They're cowards, basically. Wouldn't you agree?"

"Basically. But that doesn't mean they wouldn't try something."

"No chance. They're scared so they want to scare me. It's all just posturing, besides which, as you well know, I'm bullet proof."

Hardy grimaced. "I hate when you say that."

The old man grinned. "I know you do; that's half the fun. But you watch, this time next week, they come back with six, maybe eight mil. We get there, I might even start listening. But I might not." He smiled contentedly. "Have I mentioned that I love my job?"

"Couple of times," Hardy said. "And I my family, to whose bosom I now fly. Can I drop you home?"

"Naw." He indicated the clutter on his desk. "I've got some work here. Gina won't be home for an hour or two anyway."

"Is she picking you up here?"

"Are you kidding me? It's what, six blocks? I need the exercise. See you tomorrow. Drive carefully."

At the dinner table, Rebecca was making a face of disgust. "That is just so gross," she said.

"I think it's cool," Vincent retorted.

"It's not gross, Beck. They love each other."

"But he's so . . . I mean, you know what I mean."

"Old?" Frannie offered. "Ancient?"

253

"Not just that. I mean, yeah, he's old, but also, I mean, like . . ."

Hardy held up a warning finger. "Uh-uh, nice or nothing at all. This is David Freeman we're discussing. He is a great man and has every right to happiness and wedded bliss, just like I have with your mother." He gave Frannie a wink.

"And I with your father," she said.

"But, God." The Beck ignored them both, couldn't let the topic go. "I mean, think about Gina. She kisses him?" She shivered at the thought.

"More than that, I bet."

"Thank you, Vincent," Frannie said. "That's enough."

"And since it is," Hardy said. "I've got a fun new game. The Beck can go first." He turned to his daughter. "Here it is. You try to say a whole sentence without using the words 'like' or 'mean.' "

The Beck was a very intelligent child. She hesitated not at all before smiling cruelly at him. "Then I wouldn't be able to say that I like my daddy even though he's really mean."

This tickled Vincent, who held up both hands as though she just scored a touchdown. "Good one, Beck. Six points for the Beck."

Hardy grinned all around. "Six points, true, but unfortunately, grounded for life. It hardly seems worth it to me."

After dinner, the adults adjourned to the living room with the last of their wine while the kids cleared the table and started washing the dishes, a relatively new development in the Hardys' ongoing campaign to increase the quality of their life at home. Frannie sat on the couch with a leg curled under her, Hardy in his wing chair with his feet on the ottoman. Without benefit of the kids' comments, they had returned to the subject of Freeman's upcoming nuptuals. "Do you think he's all right?" Frannie asked. "I mean physically."

"David? He's a horse. Why do you ask?"

"Just that it seems so sudden. I wonder if he found out he's dying or something and maybe wanted to have his estate automatically go to Gina."

"He could just as easily put her in his will." He shook his head, smiling. "I think they love each other, strange as it may be."

"Why do you say that?"

Hardy sipped some wine, lowered his voice. "Well, the Beck wasn't all wrong at dinner. David's not exactly Brad Pitt, you know. He's not even Wallace Shawn."

"And this matters because . . . ?"

"It doesn't, I know. We should be above all that superficial stuff. Still . . ."

Frannie put on her schoolteacher look. "And we wonder why the Beck worries so much about how she looks."

Hardy was grinning broadly. "At her very worst, light-years better than David."

"I'd hope so, but just for your information, I would take a David Freeman any day over, say, a John Holiday."

"That's very noble of you, but I believe you'd be in the minority."

"And fortunately," she said, "I don't have to choose. I've already got a perfectly acceptable husband."

"Perfectly acceptable," Hardy said. "And people say the passion goes." He finished his wine, looked at the glass as though wondering where it had all gone. "But you just reminded me . . ." He was getting up.

"What?"

"I've been so swamped at work with these depos; I wanted to check in with John. The thing he called about Friday."

"Is he in more trouble?"

"Probably not. I hope I would have heard. I —" The telephone rang and got picked up in the kitchen on the first ring. He turned back to Frannie and made a face. "Well, if that's Darren, there goes an hour."

But his daughter yelled back. "Dad! For you."

Matt Creed tried the front door, then shone a light around the spacious lobby of the Luxury Box Travel Agency. Everything was as it should be, and this was not a surprise. This was the upscale portion of his route, close up to Union Square. In spite of the city's recent campaigns to discourage vagrancy in the high-tourist area, the vast majority of security problems this far north in Thirty-two still had to do with the homeless or mentally disabled population.

Unlike many of his colleagues, Creed didn't try to roust these unfortunates completely out of the beat. He didn't want them sleeping, parking their shopping carts, urinating or taking care of other personal needs in the doorways or elsewhere on the property of the client buildings, but beyond that, he was happy to leave them alone.

But tonight, late now, in the last hour of his shift, he had turned right onto Stockton and taken maybe ten steps when he saw an exaggerated movement, a shadow in the mouth of the alley across the street. Creed knew the spot pretty well. Since it ended at the delivery bay for a building on the next block over, it was more a driveway than a true alley. After the workday, in the lee of the prevailing winds and equipped with a dumpster that often doubled as a drop for leftover cooked food from some nearby restaurants, it had become a popular sleeping site for the area's homeless. Normally, Creed walked right by it on the last leg of his route.

But when some kind of bottle came skittering up the street toward him, slamming the curb and shattering at his feet, he stopped. He would never have done so normally, but perhaps because of leftover jitters from his recent shootout, tonight he pulled his weapon and crossed over. At the mouth of the alley, Creed could still hear the footfalls of the man running away. He stopped there, then stepped to the side against the adjacent building to catch his breath. After the excitement at Silverman's last week, he considered just guarding the opening and calling for some backup. Roy Panos was undoubtedly somewhere in the beat and could be here in ten, max.

But then he thought about the grief Roy would give him. A homeless guy throws a bottle in Creed's direction and he can't handle the situation himself. He needs *backup*. It might even cost him points with Wade, who made no secret of his disdain for cowardice, or timidity of any type for that matter. If you worked for Panos, you were macho or you were soon unemployed.

But Creed's jaw was tight, his teeth clamped down, all of his senses on alert. One part of him knew that it was all because of last week, of getting shot at. He thought of Nick Sephia's boast last night that getting shot at made him horny, and couldn't even find a shred of humor in it. Or truth. Even thinking about it now —

But what was he thinking of? This wasn't anything like a burglary in process. It was a homeless guy — Creed had *seen* him, or his shadow anyway. A homeless man who'd somehow scored a bottle of wine and got mad when it was empty. He probably hadn't even seen Creed, much less aimed at him. Shaking his head at his own demons, he realized with surprise that he still held his weapon, and he holstered it — whatever this was, he was sure it wouldn't call for a drawn gun — and turned on his flashlight.

Taking a last deep breath, he walked into the alley.

It wasn't much over ten feet wide, seventy or eighty feet deep. The beam on his light was strong, but at this distance still only dimly illuminated the dumpster at the end, on the left side. Normally, at this time of night, there would be a couple of guys sitting on the delivery dock, maybe three or four piles of debris that turned out to be men wrapped in their newspapers and layers of clothes at the small indentations of doorways along the alley. Tonight he saw nothing.

But the alley had no egress except the way he'd come in. The guy who'd thrown the bottle had to be hiding in or behind the dumpster. Creed walked another ten or twelve steps. "Hey!" he yelled, his voice echoing eerily off the walls on three sides. "Come on out here. We've got to talk."

Nothing.

Creed swore to himself, stood a long moment shining his light on the dumpster. "Come on," he said again. "Whatever it is, we'll get it worked out, all right?" He had half a mind to forget about it, to simply turn and walk out of the alley to Stockton and back to the precinct, where he could tell the lieutenant that there was this possible problem he might want to send some guys to look at. That wouldn't even involve either of the Panoses. And what was he going to do with this guy when he came out, anyway? March him down to the precinct? Knock him upside the head? Clean him up and buy him some coffee? Not.

Screw it, he thought. This is dumb.

He turned around and started back toward the street. He'd gone six or eight steps when another bottle exploded a few feet behind him, the broken glass spraying the ground around him with little diamonds. Creed nearly jumped out of his shoes.

But now, truly pissed off, he turned around. "Okay, asshole, you want to have some fun?" The beam from his flashlight preceding him, he raked the dumpster side to side and front to back. "Come on out! Don't be stupid." Ten feet back, he stopped again, gave the flashlight another pass.

Finally, movement at the back of the dumpster. He brought the beam over, took a step in that direction, then heard a noise — a second movement, to his left, at the front of the dumpster, maybe six feet from him.

He was turning in that direction . . .

And then he was dead.

Part Two

Sometime earlier today — time was routinely meaningless now — Gina Roake had been with them in Dismas Hardy's office, in David's building. These men, these unlikely avengers. She knew where they would be going when the meeting broke up, and why.

Now she was back where David had asked her to marry him. The most stunning, shocking and unexpected moment of all her life. She sat straight, unmoving, at the little rickety table, now reduced to its usual state, without the linen or china or crystal. Could that lovely service have been here? When was it now, that eternity ago?

She looked at her hands. The ring caught her short again and she held her left hand within her right and stared at it while more immeasurable time went by.

The kitchen was in a round turret that jutted from the corner of the apartment. The glass in the curved, original windows was probably sixty-five years old. Looking through them was a wavy vision through perfect water, and now she stared downhill at the impossible world going by as though nothing had changed. Cars passed at the intersection a block down; a couple embraced and kissed against a building; a woman pushed a baby stroller up toward her.

She hadn't dressed for work in several days, so she wore blue jeans and tennis shoes, a UOP sweatshirt, a blue band to hold her hair back. No makeup of any kind. She was rubbing her hands and looked at them again, surprised that now suddenly they struck her as the hands of an old woman. She'd been biting her nails, and the week-old red polish was chipped and pathetic. She made a fist of her right hand, let it go, made it again, and held it until it hurt. Old or not, she recognized that there was still strength in these hands.

Perhaps the biggest shock was what it had taken her this long to process — that her old friends in Hardy's office had truly scared her. She'd been playing with the big boys in her real life for a long time now, consoling or lecturing her clients, being a goddamned equal to her male friends and lovers, kicking ass in the courtroom, taking no shit and giving no quarter. That's why she was successful. That's why David loved her.

She thought it was who she was, but now even that wasn't clear. Nothing was clear. She didn't know who she was, who she wanted to be, what she wanted to do. But beyond everything else was raw rage. She'd never known anger like this before, nor even understood that such a thing could exist. The desire to hurt someone was almost a physical pain in her stomach. That scared her more than anything.

Her mind returned to the men in Hardy's office. She'd known them forever, it seemed. They'd been colleagues in her life with the law. She'd clerked for Dismas at the DA's when she'd been in law school and he'd just been starting out. Glitsky always a presence, even long before the homicide years, with his passion for justice, for fairness, a stickler for procedure.

But then this morning, these people of the law suddenly making common cause with a man like John Holiday? But Holiday, Dismas and Abe were in this all the way together now, there could be no doubt of that.

And good lawyer that she was, where did that leave her? With them? If she didn't believe in the rule of law under all circumstances, *then what kind of fraud had she been for all these years? If it seemed to these* men *that the law wasn't working as it should to protect them, did that give them the right to take*

267

it into their own hands? When the police didn't exactly move mountains to identify shooters in the various ghettos and barrios, did that condone or mitigate even slightly the violent retribution of a victim's relatives or friends?

She didn't think it did. No, she knew it didn't. She knew Glitsky and Hardy and they felt the same way. Or always had, until today.

Today everything was different.

And Gina now found herself with them. These men had become her true allies in this. The import of the collective decision as Abe had left Diz's office had been clear. He was going down to make the arrests himself if he couldn't move his own police department to do it for him. That was the pretext.

The subtext was that Panos and his gang would not go gently into the night. They'd proven themselves not only capable of violence, but committed to it as the way they dealt with obstruction. And the clock was running.

So Glitsky, left without an option, had come to his decision. He gave lip service to the arrest, but she knew without doubt that he'd get down to Pier 70 early, maybe a couple of hours early to avoid an ambush — in any event long before the four o'clock appointment he'd made with Gerson. And when they showed up, he'd be prepared to fight, quite possibly to kill. He had never asked Hardy or Holiday, and cer-

tainly not Gina, to back him up in any way. In actual fact, he'd been adamant on the point, expressly reminding them that he was a police officer acting in the line of duty. Diz, Holiday, anyone else who showed up to help him would, in the eyes of the law, be vigilantes. They must not be part of it.

To be part of it at all, if they lived, would ruin them.

But of course, he told them exactly where he was going, and when; what he planned to do, what he believed was going to happen.

A gust shook the ancient windows, then howled away down the street like the passage of the Angel of Death, the howl modulating down to a moan and finally fading to a dirge, then silence.

Gina had kept a Beretta .40 caliber automatic locked in her desk drawer ever since one of her early cop boyfriends had convinced her that one day she'd need it. She had often thought to get rid of it — lawyers needed to believe that they didn't have to carry guns — but could never quite make the decision. And because it really would have been the height of absurdity to keep a gun she couldn't load or shoot properly, she went to the range every few months and fired off a couple of hundred rounds of ammunition to keep herself sharp. Over the years, she'd not only become comfortable with her gun and, in the process, turned into a capable marksman, she'd come to enjoy the experience — the smell of powder, the deafening noise, the awesome kick and power so far removed from the cops-and-robbers fantasy she'd entertained when she'd started.

She knew now. To shoot a high-caliber handgun was to taste death, in some ways to embrace the idea of it. The thing ruined flesh, obliterated bone. It snuffed out life instantly. As fast, she thought, no — faster than God could take it. The feeling was intoxicating.

Still at David's kitchen table, she looked at her hands a last time. Her ring, again, caught her eye, and suddenly the reality of all she'd borne coursed through her body like a current.

She nearly ran to the front door and outside to the street. She had to get to her desk, then to her car. Enough reflection. She was who she was — equal in her heart and soul and body to any man, and to her allies in particular. She'd suffered along with them, and now belonged with them. They were all in this and they would need her.

She checked her watch and broke into a jog.

10

The smartest inspector in the San Francisco homicide detail if not on the planet worked solo. Paul Thieu, a six-year veteran, was on when the call came in at a little after one in the morning. A security guard named Matthew Creed had not reported back to his liaison at the Tenderloin Station at the end of his shift, and the ensuing search of his route by both city and private patrolmen had turned up his body. He'd been gunned down — two shots at very close range — and lay sprawled by a dumpster not two blocks from Union Square.

Although the pickin's were very slim, Thieu spent most of the rest of the night at the scene with the Crime Scene Investigation unit. He did notice a few potential anomalies that might possibly shed light on elements of the crime. There were two concentrations of broken glass, where bottles had obviously been broken — one out on Stockton across the street and up a few yards from the mouth of the driveway, and another at its mouth. It wasn't that broken glass rose anywhere to the significance of evidence — it was as common as the dew on many city streets — but Thieu believed in collecting all the data that came his way in the hopes that some of it would acquire relevance. He asked the CSI team to gather any shards that might be large enough to hold a fingerprint.

He also had a reasonably defined size twelve-and-a-half shoe print from a leather- or smooth-soled shoe. The dumpster had been dripping a stinky, gooey miasma and somebody had stepped in it and then onto relatively drier pavement. Thieu knew that the footprint might not belong to the shooter. The scene by the loading dock at the end of the long driveway was a known rendezvous for some of the city's homeless, so there was a strong likelihood that the footprint belonged to one of the bums.

On the other hand, Thieu was a stickler for precision and they'd done some preliminary blood spatter analysis, complete with photos — a difficult task in the middle of the night. The footprint location was at least consistent with where the shooter must have been standing, which was at the front, or Stockton Street corner, of the dumpster. This was hardly conclusive evidence, but it was something. He was going to take it. He asked the CSI team to gather some of the liquid and bag it as evidence.

He was aided in his work by the fact that the victim was in uniform. Even if he was only an assistant patrol special, Creed was in some ways one of them. Every man and woman on the CSI would take all the time Thieu wanted if it would help him apprehend a cop killer.

Although they found no casing, they also got lucky with one of the two .38 caliber bullets that had passed through the victim's body, leaving fairly clean small holes in the front and, even with two wounds, something less than a gaping maw of open flesh in the back. This had led Thieu to conclude first that the slugs were probably not hollow points and second that therefore they'd be able to find one or even both of the bullets. Not only was he proved right, but they discovered one of the bullet holes in a makeshift bumper someone had mounted against one of the buildings where the loading trucks would otherwise scrape. So the nearly perfect slug had passed through some rubber tire material that coated the bumper and lodged in the thick wooden beam beneath it.

Again, a slug by itself meant nothing. The odds of them finding the gun and matching it both to a person and to that particular bullet, and thus having it be any use in actually solving the crime, were all but infinitesimal. But Thieu was glad he had the piece of lead bagged and heading for the evidence locker. You just never knew.

Impressions, too, played a role, although in even a more nebulous manner than the other potential evidence. But impressions, unlike the other stuff, were ephemeral. Thieu was conscientiously typing his up so he wouldn't forget them, when Gerson came in at 8:30 sharp. Thieu had been technically off for two and a half hours, but he didn't care. He wasn't going to put in for overtime. He didn't need the money and he knew that eventually the bean counters who controlled promotion would discover that he solved cases and cost less. Besides, there was nothing he'd rather be doing. Nothing.

His colleagues had been drifting in for fifteen minutes and the homicide detail was filling with sound and the smell of coffee. Sarah Evans had discovered a female country singer with the same name as her, and she had her radio going low. Thieu tried to work through it all, concentrating mightily.

But it was not to be, at least not right then. Gerson made his way through the room and surprisingly — the two men tolerated each other at best — stopped in front of Thieu's desk, waiting until he looked up. "Got a minute, Paul? I'd appreciate it. In my office. Thanks." He turned and headed back.

This was a first, but Thieu took it for what it was, a simple summons, undoubtedly some bureaucratic folderol. Sighing, he pushed back in his chair and stood up. He couldn't help but compare the current lieutenant with his old boss Glitsky, who might have come over to his desk in the same way Gerson just had, but would have seen he was working intently — just possibly on a homicide he was expected to solve. Abe would have either had the sensitivity to let him alone until he was finished, or he would have wanted to know all about what he was working on, what if anything he'd discovered. They'd trade ideas and theories of the case.

But that wasn't Barry Gerson, who when Thieu got to his office was turned away from the door, studying columns of numbers on his computer screen. He knocked on the wall. "Sir?"

Gerson blackened the screen and spun round in his seat, motioned to the other chairs. "I don't want to keep you if you were going home," he began.

"No. I was finishing up, but I've got another half hour. What can I do for you?"

Gerson wasted no time. He pointed in the general direction of his desk. "I was reading the IR" — incident report — "on your call last night, what you're probably working on out there right now, the patrol special . . ."

"Matt Creed," Thieu said.

"That's him. I think there's a good chance he's part of another case, another homicide." At Thieu's unasked question, he went on. "I don't know if you've followed this Silverman case at all . . ."

"Sure." Gerson didn't know it, but Thieu followed *every* case. "Pawnshop on O'Farrell. Last what? Thursday night? Cuneo and Russell, right?"

"You know everything else and you don't know about Creed?"

Thieu ignored the facetious tone. "Not everything, sir. In fact, nothing but the bare facts." But he didn't want to get into one-upmanship with Gerson. He put on a receptive expression. "What was Creed's involvement?"

"He was the only witness to the robbery in progress at Silverman's. He chased the three suspects for a couple of blocks but lost them. Then he came back to the pawnshop and found the body."

"All right." For the life of him, Thieu couldn't figure out where this might be going. He'd let Gerson get to it without prompting him, though. Relaxed in his chair, an ankle resting on its opposite knee, he waited.

Gerson cleared his throat, finally went on. "The thing is, Cuneo and Russell interviewed Creed, and he pretty much identified the suspects."

This surprised Thieu, but he kept his expression neutral. "Pretty much?" he asked. He didn't know what that meant. "Positively? By name, sir? Or from a photo spread?"

"By name. The inspectors haven't had time to get photos together. But Creed narrowed it to a trio of losers in the 'Loin. Clint Terry, Randy Wills, John Holiday."

Thieu automatically filed the names away in the supercomputer he carried between his ears. He was stunned that ninety-six hours after a homicide, no one had shown the main witness a photo spread. Still, he waited, offering nothing but a civil expectancy.

"My point is that if these two homicides are related, maybe committed by the same hand, it might be more efficient to assign Creed to the same inspectors who are working Silverman since they've got the early jump. But I wanted to run it by you first."

Thieu was even more stunned. When two homicides seemed to be related, inspectors on both cases worked together. But he was being pulled off. "I've got no problem with that, sir," he said without inflection. "I'd be happy to brief them if you'd like, though there isn't much to talk about. But who works the case — that's your decision."

"No hard feelings?"

"Not at all." Then Thieu added, a brush at levity, "It's not like my caseload is about to dry up."

"No, I don't suppose it is."

But though Thieu in fact didn't really mind passing off the new case, he did have a question. He would always have a question. "So your assumption is that these suspects must have somehow found out that Creed had identified them and killed him to keep him from testifying?"

Gerson grimaced. "All I know is he was a witness in one case and the victim in another, and the other guys have got a head start. We might get two birds with one stone, is all I'm thinking." He spread his palms wide and stood up. "Efficiency. The brass loves it."

Thieu, standing himself, knew he'd been dismissed, but wanted to be sure that he and Gerson understood one another. "If you'd like," he repeated, "I could stay on awhile this morning to brief them."

But Gerson waved that off. "Thanks, but you're into OT now as it is. If you finish your write-up, that and the IR here ought to be enough to get them started. They have specific questions, they can always ask you later."

Cuneo wasn't sure that he liked the operating theory of the case, the very one Thieu had asked about. Cuneo had correctly identified the exact problem that had concerned Thieu. While there was an admittedly strong coincidence factor in Creed being involved in two homicides within Thirty-two in the past week, that very fact didn't compel Cuneo to believe that the cases were in fact related. It seemed to him that the *only* way the two *had to be* related was if the suspects had known that Creed had identified them.

"And how could they have known that?" He and Russell and Gerson were in the lieutenant's office an hour after Thieu had gone home and he was twitching his legs to some inner beat as he talked. "If the two are related, that's what *had* to happen, didn't it? I mean, they had to *know* Creed was a threat, right?"

"Right," Russell said. "So they knew."

"That's my point. How? I can't see him being so dumb. What did he do? Stop by the Ark and tell the three guys he'd picked 'em out?"

"Maybe not, but close." Gerson had no problem with it. "Come on, Dan. Look, the kid's involved in his first real homicide. He's the star witness, for Christ's sake. He's going to tell *somebody*. He's proud as hell of it. Right?" He looked to Russell.

And Russell agreed. "And that somebody told somebody else till it got back to Terry. Hell, it took four days as it was. That's plenty of time. More than enough."

Cuneo's legs stopped their jumping. "All right," he said. "If it sings so good for you both, I can run with it. But if that's the theory, we can settle it once and for all pretty quick."

Russell was right up to speed. "Ballistics," he said.

Cuneo gave him a nod. "We've got the bullet that did Silverman, too. Two bullets, same gun, and we've got connections. Connections, we get a warrant in a heartbeat and go on a treasure hunt."

After they'd left Gerson's office, Russell went over to the homicide computer and emailed the crime lab with the request, noted "Homicide — URGENT." The bullets from both scenes would by now have been filed away in the evidence lockup in the Hall's basement. Once the crime lab had physical possession of them — and a regular shuttle service ran between the Hall and the lab — they could do the actual comparison with an electron microscope. It shouldn't take more than fifteen minutes.

With any kind of luck, they could get it done today.

While Russell did the computer work, Cuneo checked their messages and found that Roy Panos had called early last night — he had some terrific 49ers tickets for this weekend that he couldn't use. If the guys were interested, why didn't they all meet at John's Grill down in the heart of Thirty-two, have an early lunch, pick up their tickets?

Of course, the call had been before Creed's death, so Cuneo called Roy back to make sure he felt he could handle a social lunch. Exhausted — he'd barely slept — Roy still wanted to meet with the inspectors. Maybe he could give them some thoughts on Creed while it was still early enough to do some good. If even by inadvertence he knew or had heard anything that might help them in finding out who'd killed Matt, he wanted them to pump him for it.

Finally, finally, finally, Cuneo and Russell got clear of the Hall. At five minutes to ten, they were parked across the street from the Ark, waiting for their chance to brace John Holiday at last. Find out where he'd been last night as well.

At a quarter after, Cuneo got out of the car and banged on the bar's door for fifteen or twenty seconds.

Quarter to eleven, and Russell couldn't endure another moment in the car with his hyperkinetic partner. He checked the door to the Ark again, then walked to the corner and around it to the alley that ran to the back entrance. It, too, was closed. There was no light within, no sign of any life.

They'd told Roy Panos they'd meet him at John's at 11:30, and ten minutes before that Cuneo turned on the ignition and put the car in gear. "How's the guy make a living, he never opens his shop?"

"Maybe he's not coming in at all," Russell said. "Maybe he's on the run."

Cuneo looked across, pointed a finger at him, pulled the imaginary trigger.

John Holiday's conquest stories to friends such as Dismas Hardy had lately been fabrications. The truth was that he had fallen in love and didn't want to appear to have been a fool if it didn't work out.

While Cuneo and Russell waited for him to show up at the Ark, he was in Michelle's wonderful apartment — a modest but extremely well-kept one-bedroom unit on the back, nontourist straight side of the "crookedest street in the world," Lombard. The place was only on the second floor of her building, but the street fell off in a cliff, so out the picture window she had a million dollar unimpeded view of the Bay and the Golden Gate Bridge. She'd started living in these three rooms while she was in college, eighteen years ago, and rent control had kept her there — in today's San Francisco, she couldn't have found an unfurnished lean-to for what she was paying. A freelance writer, Michelle occasionally published in national magazines and regularly in some of the local neighborhood papers and advertising supplements. She also had a couple of very nice steady jobs doing restaurant reviews, and these helped bridge the income gap by providing dinners out for her and, often, a guest.

The first communication between Michelle and Holiday had been faceless, via email. In fact, because Michelle signed her pieces "M. Maier," Holiday hadn't even known he was writing to a woman. In early summer, in an ad rag called the *Russian Hill Caller*, she reviewed a small new place called Tapa the Bottom — a Spanish *tapas* restaurant located at the foot of Russian Hill. Michelle's food pieces often had a kind of M.F.K. Fisher quality, where snatches of philosophy, cultural history, or personal experience would thicken the usual thin broth of menu and decor description, and this article had stirred up feelings in Holiday that he'd suppressed for a long time.

He'd spent his honeymoon with Emma on the Costa Brava in Spain, at a small fishing village called Tossa de Mar, about forty miles north of Barcelona. For Holiday, the very air there at that time had seemed imbued with promise, with a sense that everything in his life now was going to work out, that the emptiness of his early life was over forever. And that short season of hope had been steeped in saffron, garlic, oregano, onions.

As soon as Holiday finished the article, he'd beelined to Tapa the Bottom, where he felt himself transported by nearly every bite. Escargots in pepper sauce, baby octopus, the Spanish tortilla — really an omelette of onion, egg and potato — the crusty bread smeared with tomato and garlic. When he got back home, flushed with a full bottle of chilled rosé, he emailed M. Maier through the *Caller* to express his gratitude for the recommendation. He ended by adding, without much thought, "Happiness has been a bit elusive for a while, but while I was eating there, I was happy."

She'd written him back the next day, and they'd started corresponding regularly, breaking ground. Eventually, since they knew they must be neighbors, they agreed to meet. Michelle showed up in what turned out to be her usual outdoor attire, an army-navy coat over loose-fitting para-military camo garb, combat boots and a weird hat, one of her misshapen collection of thrift store headwear. In her heavy black-rimmed eyeglasses, with the hat pulled low and her tousled dark hair falling over her face, and wearing no makeup of any kind, she had attracted no undue attention.

Holiday had enjoyed the lunch, and though Michelle was nice enough, she wasn't the kind of woman he chose to pursue anymore. Clearly not a casual person, she brimmed with passion — thoughts and feelings, ideas, wit. Not his type, not since Emma. And certainly not the type he'd been taking lately to bed.

But he kept writing to her. She wrote back. They had another platonic lunch.

Gradually, as their relationship had slowly progressed, he began to appreciate her really magnificent beauty. Long-legged and deep-bosomed, with a sensuous wide mouth, an exotic cast to her eyes and strikingly perfect skin, she used the baggy clothes and funky headware and army camouflage as a form of deception that allowed her, mostly, to pass through the world unmolested.

In their early lunches, she'd always

looked barely thrown together. It came out that she'd been hurt a lot by men liking her only for her looks. She told him she'd always fantasized about marrying a blind man so that she could be sure he loved the person she was and not just because of, as she called it, the package.

The package fostered an odd mix of physical confidence and low self-esteem. As Holiday moved closer and closer to something resembling a commitment to Michelle, she had started to trust him less. If he let her know that he desired her body, too, it scared her. That's what the other men had wanted. So Holiday must in some way be like them.

The irony of this — that the first person with whom he'd tried to be faithful since Emma doubted him — did not escape him. They'd had their worst-ever fight about it on Thursday night. Holiday in his cups stormed out of the Imperial Palace before they'd gotten their pot stickers. They hadn't made up until Sunday, after a Friday night about which Holiday felt guilty. As well he should have.

It hadn't all been lies to Hardy.

This morning, in bed with Michelle, Holiday reclined propped on his elbow. Looking up from the newspaper, he was drawn back to that first meeting with her and had to smile that his initial reaction to this woman had been so neutral. At this moment, he was entirely smitten with the view of her. In stylish reading glasses, she wore orchid-print silk white pajamas. Barely buttoned on top, they gapped open as she leaned over to read.

He reached over and cupped her breast and she moved her hand over his, holding him there, never stopping her reading. He went back to the paper and turned the page. Some tension must have translated over to her.

"What is it, John? Are you all right?"

His hand had left her breast. He read on for another few seconds, making sure it confirmed what the headline seemed to promise. It did. He looked up at her, concern etching his features into something very much older. He hesitated, knowing that his ownership and management of the Ark was not her favorite thing about him. When he'd gotten home from work last night, he had started to tell her about Clint and Panos's people, to say nothing of the actual police. As usual, it hadn't sparked her interest, and he'd let it drop in favor of her query letters to *Gourmet*, *Sunset* and *Bon Appétit* to see if any of them would be interested in a story on the glories of grilled fruit.

He'd already told her the story about how he'd come to own the Ark. He'd known the owner, Joey Lamont, pretty well. Joey was pushing seventy and Holiday had had a pocketful of cash from the sale of the pharmacy, so they made a deal and the thing never even went on the open market. But now, like it or not, his bar was about to become the topic again.

"Somebody killed Matt Creed," he said.

"Do you know him?"

"Yeah, I did. He's the patrol guy. Kind of a cop. Private security."

"And somebody killed him?"

"Shot him." He was picking up details, scanning the small article. "Point blank, or close enough."

She pulled some covers up around her shoulders. "Tell me this has nothing to do with you or your bar."

He said nothing, eyes down on the printed page.

"John?"

Finally, a sigh. "He's the kid who found Silverman. It was in the paper Saturday. The thing they came and talked to Clint about."

"What do you mean, kid?"

"It says here he was twenty-two."

Michelle pulled her blanket more closely around her and got out of the bed. She walked over to the picture window and stood before it, looking out. "I don't want to have this in our life, if we're going to have a life," she said. "People you know getting killed. They're related, aren't they?"

He sat up, his voice defensive. "It doesn't say that here. There's no sign of it."

But he might as well not have spoken. "I guess I don't understand why you don't just sell the damn bar. Or if it's really important to you, at least fix it up?"

"It's not that important, really. It keeps my money working so I don't have to, that's all. I could sell it today for twice what I paid for it and then retire." Trying to inject some lightness, he added, "But then what would I do?"

"I've got a wild idea."

"What?"

"How about something worthwhile?"

A jolt of anger shot through him and he fought to control it. "I guess I don't remember," he said. "Were we having a fight?"

She lowered herself onto the ottoman by

her reading chair. Her head went down so that he couldn't see her face.

"Would you be happier if we broke up?" he asked. "The last thing I want to do is cause you pain."

When she looked up, she was close to tears. "You know two people who have been shot to death in the last week. Do you know how scary that is to someone who loves you? And then you say — you apparently believe — that they're not related, to you or each other." She shook her head back and forth with great sadness. "Of course they are, John. Of course they are."

Roy Panos was buying. He insisted.

He cut into his steak and met the eyes of both inspectors across the table. He put a bite of meat into his face, then put his utensils down and held up his right hand. "I swear to God. Terry was off. I stopped in around eight . . ."

"I thought they'd quit paying you guys," Russell said.

Roy nodded. "Yeah, but since Silverman, I figured it can't hurt to keep up on 'em, am I right?"

"You're right." Cuneo was having petrale with capers and lemon sauce, humming as he chewed. "So Holiday worked the night shift last night?"

"Yep."

"You talk to him?" Russell asked. He was having the special — lamb chops with asparagus and garlic mashed potatoes.

"Said hi when I looked in. I bought a coffee. He asked me where Mattie was."

"Creed?" Cuneo put down his fork. "Why'd he ask that?"

Roy shrugged. " 'Cause normally Mattie walked the north beat first. But last night I took it."

"Why?" Russell asked.

"No reason, really. Change of pace."

"He say anything else? Holiday?"

Panos had had a rye on the rocks before lunch. Now he finished his second glass of wine and started pouring the next. He drank some more, put the wineglass down, twisted the stem of it pensively. When he spoke, it was almost apologetically. "I didn't want to spook him. I wanted to let you guys get him fresh."

"So you didn't mention anything about Creed?" Cuneo asked.

"Anything like what?"

"Like he pointed the finger in their direction."

Roy gave this some more thought. "I didn't go anywhere near there, but now

292

you mention it, Holiday did say if I talked to Mattie, would I ask him to stop in? He wanted to ask him something."

The two inspectors exchanged a look.

Suddenly, Roy's heavy eyes lit up with the significance of what he'd revealed. "He wanted to make sure Mattie was on, didn't he? Son of a bitch. And I told him. Shit." For a moment, it looked as though Roy would cry.

Russell reached out and patted the table between them. "It would have been another night, that's all. It's nothing you did."

"The sons of bitches," Panos repeated. "And now, without Mattie's ID . . ."

"Don't worry about that," Cuneo said. "They made some mistakes last night. We're close."

"How close?"

He was one of them, another cop, so the inspectors told him.

11

The night before, Hardy drove twice around the downtown neighborhood and could not find a place to park even quasilegally. Nearly out of his mind with frustration and worry, he had finally given up and driven the extra few blocks to his own office, where he had his own spot under the building. Back up on the street, he'd run back to the emergency room entrance of St. Francis Memorial Hospital, where Gina Roake had stood waiting by the admitting station.

"How is he?"

Her face was blotched, but she held it now under tight control. "Not good. He's been in there for two hours. He's still unconscious. They won't let me in."

"What happened?"

"Somebody beat him up, Dismas. I'd been home an hour and some policemen knocked at the door. He had his wallet on him, which had his driver's license with the address, and . . ."

"He had his wallet? Was there still money in it?"

"I don't know. I didn't even . . ."

She caught Hardy's shift of focus and turned. A young woman in green scrubs had come out into the waiting room. Roake touched his arm and went to her. He followed, noting with a sinking heart the grave look on her face.

"We've done all we can for the moment," she was saying. "We'll be bringing him to the ICU, where we can keep a close eye on him."

"But how is he?" Gina asked.

The young doctor's eyes quickly went to Hardy, came back to Gina. "He's taken quite a beating. He's got severe head trauma and internal bleeding and he hasn't regained consciousness." She took in a deep breath and let it out. "I'd have to call his condition critical."

Roake closed her eyes. Her shoulders seemed to collapse. After a short moment, she opened her eyes and nodded. "Is there anything at all I can do?"

There wasn't. The doctor said she had to go and supervise the transfer to the ICU, and she went back behind the door to the ER.

Without a word, Roake and Hardy sat down next to one another on the waiting room chairs. To his surprise, Hardy realized that they weren't alone in the room — a young black woman rocked a baby across the room and stared into empty space in front of her. An elderly Asian man was reading a newspaper.

A young person let out an agonizing moan somewhere behind them, and sirens cried somewhere close in the night.

After a minute, an orderly came out holding a large plastic sack. He looked around and came over to them. "Are you with Mr. Freeman? I've got some of his personal effects that you might want to take."

Roake reached out for the bag, and for the first time Hardy noticed the ring — twice the size of Frannie's diamond, newly mounted and bright. She opened the bag and looked inside, then closed it back up. "His good suit," she said as though to herself. "I bought it for him." Turning to Hardy, her lip quivered for an instant. She bit down on it. "How could this happen?" she asked. "Who could have done this to him?"

After a sleepless night, Hardy's first stop

at a little after 6:00 a.m. this morning had been the hospital again. It was still long before visiting hours and though he believed he had no chance to get in and see Freeman, he knew he'd get more information talking to a human being than to a voice on the telephone.

Sure enough, at the nurse's station, he had learned that Freeman's condition was unchanged from the night before, but that at least there had been no deterioration. He was no more critical than he'd been. Armed with that news, he walked down the hallway and looked in on the ICU waiting room, where the nurse had told him another of Freeman's visitors had spent the night.

Roake clearly hadn't spent it sleeping either. Alone in the room at this time of the morning, she'd aged five years in the past six hours. Her eyes were heavy, red-rimmed, her hair all over the place. As Hardy got to the door, she was running her hands through it as though trying to still the ravages of a severe headache.

Seeing him, she stood and walked over, put her arms around his neck and sagged for an instant. He saw the plastic bag that held Freeman's suit on the floor next to the couch where Roake had been sitting —

she really hadn't gone home.

After they'd sat, Hardy delivered the latest prognosis in the best possible light, then asked if he could do something for her, drive her home, anything.

Her first reaction was to shake her head as though she didn't understand the question. A random syllable escaped, stopped again. She ran a hand through her hair again, squeezed at her temples. "I suppose I've got to get to my clients. I know there's something this morning, but . . . but that's not you, is it? I'd better leave a message for Betsy." She looked out beyond Hardy. "It's morning already, isn't it?"

"Getting there," Hardy said. "You ought to go home and get some sleep, Gina." It was hard advice but she had to hear it. "Nothing's happening here. The nurse told me this could go on for a while."

"I know." Then, again, "I know. I just wanted to stay. I thought . . ."

He waited, but no further words came. "I can drive you to David's now," he said. "You get a little sleep, call your office when they open. If they need you here, you can be back in five minutes. How's that sound?"

She was perfectly immobile for half a minute or more, then finally let out a heavy breath, reached for the plastic bag, stood up. "You're right. You talked me into it."

Fifteen minutes later, he couldn't believe the amount of legal curb that was available just around the corner from the Hall of Justice. Then he remembered, of course, the time. But he'd wanted to get down here if he could while someone from the night shift might still be in the building.

Miraculously, he was talking to Inspector Hector Blanca within ten minutes. Blanca was a dark-skinned Hispanic sergeant with the General Work Detail and he'd pulled the call on the Freeman beating. It was not only fresh in his mind, he was reviewing the incident report, written by the patrolman who found Freeman, as Hardy got to his desk. After the introductions, and Hardy's reassurance that he was a friend of Abe Glitsky and used to be a cop himself, that he wasn't some ambulance-chasing dick of an attorney looking to make trouble, Blanca must have decided it was okay to talk. "So, this man Freeman. He was your partner?"

Technically David wasn't, but Hardy didn't think it mattered. "I hope he still is."

The sergeant grimaced. "Sorry. I didn't

mean that. What's the word at the hospital?"

Hardy told him, but he'd come to Blanca to get information, not give it. "His fiancée, Gina Roake, told me he still had his wallet. That's how you guys knew to come to his house."

"That's right. Beat him near to death, but didn't take his wallet, his watch, nothing."

"Was there money in it?"

Blanca tried to keep his face neutral, but it wanted to react. "Six hundred fourteen dollars, right there in the regular section."

Hardy sat with that a minute. "So it wasn't any kind of robbery. You saw him. What was it about?"

"I've got no idea. It was about as brutal as I've seen. He fucking somebody's wife, anything like that?"

"No," Hardy said.

"What I mean is, maybe if it was personal . . ."

"Yeah, I know. I can't think of anything —" He stopped.

"What?" Blanca asked.

"I just thought about this pretty ugly lawsuit we're working on. But I've never seen anything like that before and I've been practicing twenty years."

Blanca gave him another chance. "You sure? I'll grab at anything."

But after another minute with it, Hardy shook his head. "No. Couldn't be."

"All right. But whatever it was, let me tell you, this was deliberate damage. Boots and blunt objects. Not just fists."

Hardy didn't want to think about Freeman lying helpless, curled on himself, as a group of vicious assailants worked him over. "So there was more than one guy?"

A shrug. "I can't say for sure, but I'd bet on it." He drummed his fingers on his typewriter keys, then met Hardy's eye. "I guess there's no nice way to put it, sir. Whoever it was, these guys left him for dead."

"But took nothing?"

He shook his head. "Nothing obvious, at least."

"So what's that leave?"

Blanca frowned in concentration. "It leaves the whole universe, to tell you the truth. People nowadays, you wouldn't believe how many are just nuts."

"I bet I would. You think it was just some kind of rage?"

"It looked like that, but who knows? It might have been just for the thrill." Something seemed to nag at him. "An old guy like this, though? It doesn't make any sense, not that it has to. Tell you what I'll do. I'll pull some other reports from the general vicinity. Maybe come up with something similar. MO. Something."

"Thanks," Hardy said. "I'd appreciate it."

Okay, Hardy told himself. He'd done his little bit with detective work, and without any conclusive results, but the real reason the hospital and the Hall had had to come first and early this Wednesday morning was because he had to get to his office.

Freeman & Associates kept formal hours, from 8:30 to 5:30. Like most law firms, F&A expected its associates to bill two thousand hours every year. With a two-week vacation, that computed to forty billable hours every single week, even weeks where there was a holiday or two. Working at perfect efficiency, the best attorneys could perhaps get all their administrative and other unbillable work, such as lunch for example, done in two hours every day. This meant that, if they did not double-bill — if discovered, a firing offense at Freeman's — associates averaged about ten hours at their desks every single day, often working weekends to make up for holidays or the rare day off when they needed to bill but the office was closed.

The awesome burden of billing two thousand hours was perhaps the main reason Hardy had never joined Freeman's, or any other, firm. Not that he didn't work round the clock and then some when he needed to, but at least in theory — though meeting his monthly nut kept it from being his common practice — he could make his own decision to put in fewer hours and therefore make less money. This wasn't an option for Freeman's full-time associates. But since it was the norm everywhere else, what were they going to do?

So although it was still a few minutes short of 8:00 a.m. when Hardy walked up the stairway and entered the lobby, the place wasn't deserted, but the somber tone was decidedly unusual. Word must have gotten out.

At the receptionist's desk, although Phyllis wasn't in yet, they had the radio tuned to the all-news station. A group of maybe ten associates stood around, listening, murmuring. Hardy knew three of them quite well — Amy Wu, Jon Ingalls and Graham Russo — and Russo broke from the knot when he saw Hardy. All the other eyes followed him. "Do you know anything about David?" he asked. "Amy heard the end of something in her car, but . . ."

Russo and everyone else could tell from Hardy's expression that what Wu had heard was both true and bad. The knot coalesced around him and Hardy gave them the very short version and answered as many questions as he could. While he was in the middle of one of them, Phyllis came up the stairs behind him — her usual grim-lipped, uptight self. She stood behind Hardy for a moment, clearly perplexed at the gathering.

Hardy stopped midsentence and, cued by his audience, turned. "What's the matter?" she asked. "What is this about?"

"David's in the hospital," Hardy said simply. "Somebody beat him."

"What do you mean, beat him? He's not in trial."

"Not that kind of beat. Somebody mugged him, beat him up."

For a long moment, she still appeared not to comprehend. Finally, she backed up a step and put a hand over her heart. "Why? I mean, is he all right?"

"I was just telling the folks here. It's bad. He's unconscious."

Phyllis looked down to Freeman's office

door as though she expected him to appear from behind it. One of the associates yelled from back at reception. "Here it is, here it is!" And as a body, the mass of people turned and fell silent.

". . . flamboyant and famous attorneys in the city was found beaten last night a few blocks from his home. Police have no known motive yet in the brutal attack, which has left Mr. Freeman in critical condition at St. Francis Memorial Hospital. Robbery doesn't seem to have been a factor, although police are refusing . . ."

Hardy and the rest of the associates all missed the rest of the report. At the word "critical," Phyllis had uttered a small cry and crumpled to the ground.

In his office, Hardy had three voice mails from Jeff Elliot, his friend and the writer of the "CityTalk" daily column for the *Chronicle*. They shared the basic information that each had independently gathered; then Elliot asked, "So where does this leave you?"

"You mean me personally or the firm here?"

"Both."

"Well, he's the rainmaker here, so people are freaked. If he's even out for a couple of weeks, the work dries up. Phyllis fainted. You know he'd just asked Gina to marry him?"

A short silence. Elliot, Hardy knew, trying to digest it. "What'd she say?"

"She said yes. He gave her a ring."

Another pause. "Was she seeing anybody else?"

"Who'd want to kill David and thereby eliminate the competition? I don't think so. She was at the hospital all night."

"Still . . ."

"I think it's a dry well, Jeff, but you can ask her if you want."

Elliot seemed to accept that. "So how are you doing?"

"I'm worried. Unconscious isn't good. They're saying critical, and the nurse this morning wasn't what you'd call optimistic. Blanca — you know Blanca — he seemed to think that whoever did it meant to hurt him bad at least."

"What for?"

"No theories. Not robbery, unless he was carrying something unusual with him, which he never did. But not his wallet, not his watch — a Rolex by the way."

"So what do you think?"

"I'm totally stumped. At the moment, I'm tempted to think it might even have been random. Easy target. Cheap thrills. It's been known to happen. Hey, I'm getting another call. You want to wait?"

"No thanks. I'm crankin' here. I hear anything, I'll let you know."

"Dismas Hardy," he said, punching into his call waiting.

"Diz. Dick Kroll. I just heard about David. My God . . ."

"Yeah. I don't know what's happening yet. Did we have a depo today? We do, don't we?" Hardy brought his hand to his forehead, squeezed his temples.

Kroll was sympathetic. "We can put that off as long as you need. The important thing now is David. How's it look?"

For the hundredth time, Hardy ran down what he knew. Answered the same questions. No robbery. No motive. No clues. A senseless beating of an old and defenseless gentleman. When he finished, the line hummed open for a long beat.

"I don't know what to say, Diz. I'm in shock, really. Is there anything I can do?"

Hardy gave it an instant's thought. "Maybe see if any of your client's men noticed or heard something. Or will. It wasn't one of Wade's beats, though, was it?"

"I don't know. Where did it happen exactly?"

"Two blocks north of here. Right around the corner, actually."

"No, then. Thirty-two ends down at Post."

Hardy kept on. "It was his usual route home, which he always walked because he was bullet proof. Jesus . . ."

"What?"

Hardy blew out. "Nothing. I just remembered I offered to drive him." He swore.

"Don't blame yourself. It wasn't anything you did." Kroll cleared his throat. "So listen, I don't want to add to your troubles today. Why don't you dig out, call me when you want to start up on these depos again. I'm assuming if David's out, you'll be taking the lead."

"It's too early, Dick, okay? I don't want to go there yet."

"Fine, fine. I'll wait till you call me. Meanwhile, is there anything else I can do? Anything at all?"

"I can't think of anything, but thanks."

"I'll pray for him. How about that?"

Hardy hadn't ever considered Kroll much of a religious man — certainly he was an unscrupulous attorney and dirty fighter, but you never knew. "Couldn't hurt," he said. "Thanks." Yet another call was coming in on the heels of the last. He looked at his watch — regular workday still wouldn't begin for seven minutes and he'd already been going for two hours. He punched the button on his phone, stifled a weary sigh. "Dismas Hardy," he said.

It was the first time Hardy had been to Glitsky's new domain on the fifth floor. The lieutenant was leaning over a computer terminal in a claustrophobic room occupied by two women, one of them with an enormous girth. Glitsky was saying something to her about the new software they should be getting sometime in the next decade that would do it all faster and better. Hardy, in low enough spirits already, found the moment nearly unbearably sad.

Perhaps sensing a shadow behind him, Glitsky stopped in midsentence, straightened up and turned around quickly. Everything from his stance to his fierce glare announced his readiness to fight whoever it might be. When he saw it was Hardy, something went out of him. For an instant, he seemed almost disappointed, but immediately the expression shifted to concern. "You all right?" he asked. "Is everybody all right?"

By this he meant, of course, their families. Hardy showing up unannounced in the middle of a Wednesday afternoon, looking shell-shocked and drawn, set off every alarm in Glitsky's head.

Hardy's reply didn't ease his mind. "Got a minute?"

Excusing himself to his staff, he led his friend to the next office and closed the door behind them. "What?"

"You haven't heard about David?"

Glitsky read his friend's face and his gaze went flat. "Don't tell me he's dead."

"Not yet, but it doesn't look good." The telling took less than a minute, during which Glitsky took a seat behind his desk. Hardy remained standing, drained, hands in his pockets. "I've just come from the hospital. Again. Gina's back down there, too."

Glitsky slouched in his chair, fingers templed at his lips. Hardy was rambling on. "I don't even know why I'm here, to tell you the truth. I answered calls all morning at the office, but the thought of work . . ." He shrugged. "Sorry to just barge in."

"If memory serves," Glitsky said, "I've done it to you a few times."

But the usual banter couldn't find a toehold, and the two men filled the space managing their silent emotions. Finally, Hardy pulled a chair around and sat heavily. "I really don't know why I'm here," he repeated.

Glitsky let another minute pass. "He was walking home? That's it?"

Hardy nodded. He was wrestling with something, and finally came out with it. "I almost told Blanca I thought it was Panos."

At this, Glitsky's eyes sharpened. He stirred in his chair. "Do you?"

He shook his head. "I can't see it. Kroll called me up this morning as soon as he heard. He seemed genuinely upset."

"And that rules out Panos? That he didn't inform his lawyer? I wouldn't tell my lawyer if I was planning to beat up or kill somebody. Not before, not after. But what was David to Panos? I know you've got that lawsuit, but . . ."

"Just keep repeating thirty million dollars, Abe, and everything will become clear. If we win all the way large, say, it's not impossible Panos is on the street." Talking about specifics somehow took Hardy's mind off the big picture, and he too became more animated. "Kroll offered David four the other day to settle."

"Four million? What'd the old man say?"

"He laughed at him. Kroll then got huffy and said he was going to go around David and talk to me directly, I guess on the theory that I'm a wuss and I'd cave. David said he was welcome to try, but I'd probably just send it back to him, which was true. Anyway, Kroll got a little mad and told him he'd better watch out."

"For what?"

"Maybe for what happened."

Glitsky cocked his head. "You really think that?"

"I'm not really thinking anything, yet, Abe. We're talking boots and clubs, maybe nightsticks. Your average street banger doesn't have a sap."

"But you said 'maybe' nightsticks."

"True. But we're also talking downtown. Unless you're walking around with lumber, you're not going to find a club lying on the street, are you?"

"Maybe a tire iron. Or the butt of a gun."

Hardy shook his head, disagreeing. "A couple of whacks on the head with a tire iron and you're dead directly, wouldn't you think? Maybe a gun, though."

"So what are you saying?"

"It's coming to me as we're talking, so I'm not sure. Whoever did it didn't come to rob him. They showed up carrying heavy tools and ambushed him."

The phone rang twice. The answering machine picked up with its warm and sunny greeting. "Glitsky, payroll. Leave a message." Some sergeant left his number and asked if he could get a call back about his accumulated comp time.

Neither Glitsky nor Hardy acknowledged the interruption. As soon as the sergeant had rung off, Hardy continued. "You might as well know the other thing that happened yesterday. Both Blanca and Jeff Elliot thought it might have something to do with it, but I just came from talking to Gina, and it doesn't."

"Okay. What?"

He told Glitsky about the engagement, the ring, the remote question about Gina's possible involvement with another man. "Anyway, I asked. I don't know whether it set our friendship back two years or if she was flattered that I could think she was somehow keeping a stable of men on the side, but either way, she wasn't lying. Enough for me, anyway."

"I'd take that."

"So. There we are." Suddenly he found he had talked it all out. And again, it left him exhausted. "And so what, huh? Nobody's even looking."

Glitsky almost said that if Freeman came to, he would be able to tell them what happened; if he died, the case would go to homicide and maybe Paul Thieu would get it and discover something, but he realized this wouldn't be a consoling thought. And if anybody else besides Thieu picked up a case like this, an old man who lingered, no clues, it would remain a mystery forever. So he shrugged. "Blanca's okay," he said. "Maybe he'll get something."

"Yeah." Hardy dragged his old bones up and stood. "Well . . ."

The phone rang again. Glitsky glared at it, then got up himself, making no move to answer it. He was coming around to let Hardy out when he heard the voice of Marcel Lanier. He stopped and picked up the receiver.

"Talk to me," he said.

Hardy was at the door and raised a hand in silent farewell. Glitsky, listening with one ear, snapped his fingers, got his attention, waved him back in. "Yeah, I'm here," he said into the mouthpiece. He listened intently for almost a full minute, then said, "I appreciate it, Marcel. Thanks."

Hardy stood right at the door. "What was that about?"

Glitsky raised a hand and settled a haunch on the corner of his desk, his face hardened in concentration.

Hardy couldn't take it. "What, for Christ's sake?"

Glitsky expelled a lot of air. "One of Panos's guys got shot last night. The kid who found Silverman. Creed. Matt Creed."

"You knew him?"

"I only met him once, Monday night, a couple of hours after I left you, in fact. But he made an impression. Remember I told my dad it was a bad idea to go to Silverman's when nobody in homicide called him back?"

Hardy nodded. "Sure."

"Well, he went that night anyway and I had to pull him out. Creed was there."

"Doing what?"

"Just walking the beat. He saw the light and stopped. Then I showed up. We had a little party together. But a nice kid."

"And somebody shot him?"

Glitsky's head dropped, came back up. "Last night. On the beat." He paused to let Hardy digest it. "Marcel was just talking to Paul Thieu and heard about the connection to Panos. He thought I'd want to know."

"Why's that?"

"We had a talk about Wade recently, Marcel and I. I thought maybe he could pass a message along to Gerson. Save him some trouble." A shrug. "Turns out he couldn't."

"What was the message?"

"That maybe Panos wasn't the guy to help out homicide on Silverman. Or anything else, for that matter."

"And he'd been doing that?"

"Trying. He'd given them some names, among them your friend Holiday, who Creed originally ID'd as one of the guys who broke into Silverman's, by the way."

"Well, that's wrong. John had . . ."

Glitsky held up a hand. "Relax. Creed changed his mind. No ID. He was calling the case inspectors and letting them know."

"Did he?"

"I don't know. I'd assume so. Besides, what does it matter? You said Holiday has an alibi, and you'd never lie for a client."

Hardy declined to comment, found his chair, and was sitting again. Finally, he said, "Suddenly I'm willing to believe that Panos had something to do with David."

Glitsky nodded slowly, the professional cop in him less than completely willing to commit. "It does invite inquiry."

"So how do we do it?"

"Do what?"

"Inquire."

Glitsky scratched his cheek. "You might profitably mention something to Blanca. Maybe something got left at the scene. David's. But this could be nothing. Just a coincidence."

"Theoretically, I agree with you. I'll keep it in mind."

"Just so we're on the same page. And also, so you're clear, I'm not going anywhere near it. The latest poll results are in, and the consensus is it's not my job."

12

San Francisco's crime lab, one of several buildings in a facility that had originally been built by the Navy, had recently been refurbished and was now pretty much state of the art. The facility also housed the TTF unit, or Tac Squad, and served as the PD's armored car lot. Although its location in Hunters Point was as far from desirable as possible, the ancient hamburger stand called Dago Mary's just outside the compound made it something of a destination for the law enforcement community.

Russell and Cuneo had finished their lunch with Roy at John's Grill. Then they'd gone back to the Ark, pounded on the doors again, sat outside for most of another useless hour. Apparently the place wasn't opening today, at least not before nighttime. Finally Cuneo gave up on the stakeout and they'd driven to the Marina District, to Holiday's address, where several newspapers in the doorway argued that he'd been away for a while.

Russell couldn't pass Dago Mary's without a pit stop. Hell, they were right here anyway, Russell argued. It wouldn't take fifteen minutes. They would have plenty of time to pick up their ballistics results from the lab and roll back uptown on the undoubtedly related Creed/Silverman murders. Get some warrants. Kick ass.

By the time they got past the guard tower, parked, and arrived at the lab's reception, they'd burned fifteen more minutes. A small room with a desk, phone and computer, enclosed on their side with glass, blocked any view of the lab itself within. When the inspectors entered the lobby area, there was no one at the desk. They waited awhile in the hopes that a body would appear.

Cuneo craned his neck trying to be seen. He sang out a strong, "Hello!"

"Here we go," Russell said. There was a button next to the door that led inside and he pressed it. Silence. "Maybe it rings inside." He pressed and held it this time.

"Hey! Hey! Enough with the bell! We're coming."

The door finally opened to reveal a small, pale, middle-aged man in Dockers and a button-down plaid shirt. A wash of wispy dark hair fell sideways across his forehead — if he'd had the right mustache, he would have been a ringer for Hitler. The plastic name tag over his left pocket read "M. Lester," and Mr. Lester was frowning. "Keep your shirts on, boys, what's the problem?"

Cuneo pointed at the reception desk. "Nobody seems to be minding the fort, is all."

"Yeah, well, Sherry's out today. Sorry."

"Well," Cuneo said, "we're here for some ballistics results. Homicide. My partner here, Russell, he marked it urgent."

The frown grew more pronounced as Lester turned to Russell. "I emailed you about that."

"I never got it."

The man persisted. "I sent it off as soon as I got yours. Couldn't have been five minutes later."

"I still didn't get it," Russell said. "What was it about?"

"Your evidence. I asked if you could pick it up while you were still at the Hall and bring it down here. We're getting killed by the flu. Half the staff is out sick. We got nobody to drive the shuttle even."

Cuneo drew a breath, kept an exaggerated calm in his voice. "And so, because my partner had marked his email 'Homicide — Urgent,' and you didn't hear back from him, you called a patrol car or got a messenger to bring this critical evidence down to your lab so that we'd have our ballistics results in time, perhaps, to save a life or two, or at least get some scumbags off the streets. That's what you did, right? Tell me that's what you did."

In spite of the strikeout on ballistics, Cuneo reminded Russell that for all their efforts, they still needed to talk to John Holiday. He might have come in to the Ark since they'd last been there, and Cuneo voted that they go back for the third time that day and try again.

"There's no way, Dan. He's gone."

"I don't think so."

"Why not? He doesn't come to work. His apartment's deserted. He knows we've put him with Terry and Wills on Silverman. If it were me, I'd be long gone."

"Except that, if you recall, Roy Panos said he talked to him last night. Stopped by the Ark and there he was working behind the bar. Nothing's changed between last night and today."

"Except Creed got shot. Not exactly nothing."

Cuneo glanced across the seat. "Agreed. But if Holiday was bartending, and Roy says he was, then he didn't do Creed, did he? He knows we're not after him for that. So no way does it get him to run if Silverman didn't."

This shut Russell up for a half block or so. "Don't get me wrong," he finally said. "I'm itching to drive back uptown and talk to him, but if we don't have ballistics, what are we talking to him about? Especially if he wasn't any part of Creed?"

"I never said he wasn't any part of it. He just didn't pull the trigger. But that still leaves Terry and Wills. In which case Terry's the shooter both times. We might mention some chance of immunity for Holiday if he'll give them up, see if he bites."

"If he's there."

"Even if he's not, we'll learn something. Maybe get another chance to talk to Terry."

"And if he is, we're his friends."

"That's the ticket," Cuneo said. "Give him a chance."

Randy Wills checked his lipstick in the bathroom of his apartment. He'd bathed and shaved all over less than an hour ago.

Looking down, he smoothed the front of his skirt, then came back to the mirror. Luckily, he'd never had a heavy beard, and now a close shave and makeup base gave him the smooth cheeks of a very pretty woman with luminous eyes, a delicate nose and jawline. He wore a luxuriant, natural-looking chestnut wig. A black turtleneck covered his Adam's apple — the only give-away that he wasn't what he seemed.

Outside, it was coming to dusk. The back window in the bedroom let in a thin late-afternoon light, and he looked around the room and then into the front rooms — the kitchen and living room — with something approaching real contentment.

He and Clint lived in a street-level apartment on Jones, less than a quarter mile from the Ark. It didn't look like much from the outside, but they'd turned it into a nice home — the best place Randy had lived in since he'd left New Mexico at sixteen.

When Randy got to the Ark, he struck a momentary pose in the doorway — hip cocked, breasts thrust out. Clint was behind the bar, of course, talking to a couple of customers, and he looked up without any sign of recognition at all. Only a friendly nod, as if Randy were just another customer. Could it be he didn't recognize him at all? Was he that beautiful tonight?

Taking a stool next to one of the customers, he crossed his legs and arranged himself at the bar. "Hello, Clint," Randy said, "I'd like a vodka gimlet, please."

Clint's customer, a puffy-faced man, was staring at him. The other man, black, leaned over the bar. "Who's your friend, Clint?"

Randy smiled all around and made some eye contact. He offered his hand to the closer man. "I'm Randy Wills," he said, in his most feminine voice. "Randy with an 'i.'" Then, to the other man, "Hello." He'd get a rise out of Clint yet, he thought.

But Clint simply looked down, shaking his head. Surprisingly, the puffy-faced man didn't take his extended hand. Instead, he proferred a badge, introduced himself and his partner.

Clint reached across the bar and put his big hand over Randy's. "I'm sorry," he said. "They just got here. They're looking for John."

"Why?" Randy turned to the inspectors. "What did he do?"

"We want to talk to him," Russell said. "We understand he was working here last night."

"That's right," Terry said.

"But you're here tonight?"

"For another hour or two. Then John comes on."

"Tonight?" Cuneo asked. "I understood he worked mostly days, though."

"Mostly, I guess, you're right. But it varies. We're pretty flexible here, really."

"Good for you," Russell said. "So you weren't here last night then?"

"No, I already told you, we . . ."

Cuneo butted in. "That's right, you did." He turned to Randy. "We were just talking to Clint here about what he did last night. I'd like to ask you the same thing. What you did."

Clint started to say something to him, but Russell leaned in, one finger extended in warning. "Uh-uh-uh. No hints."

"What I did?" Randy checked with Clint, who nodded almost imperceptibly. "When? Last night?"

"That's right, last night," Cuneo said.

Eyes over the bar. "I was with Clint. Why?"

"We'll get to why," Russell said. "Just now we'd like to know how you spent your night last night. Unless there's some reason you'd rather not tell us."

"No. Nothing like that. Why would there

be?" Another look at Clint. "Well, early we had dinner at home; then we went to Finocchio's for the show," he said. "We were there together. I used to work there." Into their stony silence, he added, "I'm a dancer. Well, used to be."

Cuneo said, "That was pretty good." He turned to his partner. "They've got some code."

Russell jumped right in. "You talk to anybody at Finocchio's while you were there? What time was that, by the way?"

"I don't know. What time, Clint? Eleven, twelve? Somewhere in there."

"No hints," Cuneo repeated. "My partner asked if you talked to anybody."

"I suppose the waiter. He might remember."

"Uh-huh. And what time did you get there?"

"I really don't know exactly. I don't remember."

"Later than ten?"

"Maybe. It seems like it. Why? What happened last night?"

"What happened last night, he asks," Cuneo said to Russell. Back to Randy. "As if it's news to you, a patrol special named Matt Creed got shot dead about three blocks from here."

Shocked and appalled, Terry put his hand to his heart. "Not Matt," he said.

Cuneo pointed a finger at him. "Spare me that shit." He threw an ugly look at his partner, tapped twice on the bar, obviously reining himself in. After a minute more, still fighting himself, he picked up a glass from the gutter and spun it. Finally he whirled on Randy. "So I'm asking you again, tell me what you did last night?"

"I told you. We ate and then went to a show."

"And you were there until what time?" Cuneo pressed.

"Where?"

Suddenly Cuneo grabbed a glass from the bar's gutter and flung it at the bottles behind the bar, where everything exploded in a spray of glass and noise. *"You want to fuck around, you fucking queen? You want to fuck around with me? I'll show you fuck around!"*

But Russell was up, next to Cuneo, ready to restrain him if he took it any further.

Terry had ducked, then backed away, and now he'd come back forward, his hands shaking on the bar. "Really, inspectors, really. We didn't do anything. We didn't do *anything*."

For a long dead moment, there was nothing but the sound of labored breathing in the bar. Then Russell leaned over and punched a finger into Clint Terry's chest. "This isn't close to over," he said. "Don't leave town. Stay where we can find you." He turned to Cuneo. "Let's get out of here before somebody gets hurt."

The inspectors killed an hour at the building housing the Tenderloin Task Force, talking to the Patrol Special liaison to see if any information had surfaced on the beat or with any of the regular patrol cops during the day. Nothing.

Then, calmed slightly and primed to finally get a word with John Holiday, they came back, yet again, to the Ark. It was full dark outside and the place had six paying customers. Terry and Wills were gone and a man fitting the description of Holiday was behind the bar. Before they'd even sat, he had napkins down in front of them.

"Good evening, inspectors," he said. They hadn't even started and he was ahead of them. "What're you drinking?"

"We're not," Cuneo said. He put his badge on the bar and sat on his stool. "We'd like you to answer a couple of questions."

"Sure," he said, then smiled. "Give me just a minute, though, would you?" He walked down the bar, had a word with a customer and pulled a bottle of beer out of the refrigerator. After he'd opened and poured it, he was back in front of the inspectors. "It's bad luck in the bar business to let your customers get thirsty." Another smile. "You sure you don't want anything? It's on me."

Cuneo had gotten himself seated. The fingers of both hands were already tattooing the bar. "Enjoying yourself, aren't you?"

A nod. "Every minute, inspector. Life's short enough and this isn't dress rehearsal. Now what did you say I could do for you fellows?"

"You can answer some questions," Russell said. "Like where were you last Thursday night?"

Holiday clucked as though he were sorely disappointed. "Oh, *that* kind of question. This is about a crime, isn't it?"

"You know what it's about," Cuneo snapped.

"Actually, I'm not sure," Holiday said. "I was working here last night when Matt Creed got shot, so it's not for that. But if it's about any crime at all, I'm sorry, but

I can't help you."

"Last Thursday night," Russell said again.

"Darn," Holiday said. "It's sad, too, because I know the answer to that one and I think you'd like it. But my lawyer told me he'd kill me if I answered questions from you guys about any crimes without calling him first."

"So you talked to your lawyer?" Russell said. "Why'd you do that?"

Holiday had his smile stuck in place. "We're close friends," he said. "We talk all the time. He's a great guy, really. Dismas Hardy. You know him?"

"And he told you not to talk to us?" Cuneo asked. "Why was that?"

"I had some legal troubles a while ago. He just found it a better policy. Your lawyer's not there, some policemen take advantage. You wouldn't believe."

"So call him," Cuneo said. "Tell him to come down."

"I would, but it's Date Night. He and his wife, they go out every Wednesday. He says it's the secret to his happy marriage. It wouldn't do any good, anyway — if he came down — he wouldn't let me talk to you. He's really strict about it."

"How much money did you lose at

Silverman's?" Cuneo asked.

Holiday sighed. "Can't say. Question. Oops, look at that. Another customer with an empty glass. Back in a New York minute. Don't go away."

Holiday went down the bar again, took two drink orders. As he was pouring the second, the inspectors filed past him on their way out.

"Nice talking to you!" he called after them. "Have a nice night!"

13

Date Night might have been the key to the Hardys' marriage, but they weren't having a happy one.

It had started, naturally, with another stop at the hospital. Hardy hadn't wanted to go again — it would be his third visit there today — but Frannie insisted that she wanted to see David. Before she'd seen the damage, she had some sense that in some way she could help. Make him more comfortable, maybe bring him cookies tomorrow. Something.

She'd heard the word "unconscious," of course, but the concept and reality of deep coma hadn't yet struck home. She confessed this forty minutes later to her husband, before she'd even gotten her glass of wine, while she was silently crying in their back corner booth at Fior d'Italia. "I couldn't even see him, really. I've never seen anybody so bandaged. His whole face

. . ." Her eyes pleaded with him, as though somehow hoping he could make any part of it better.

Hardy knew that she was trying to find a place to order her impressions, but they'd assaulted her too violently for that. He put his hand over hers on the table. She just needed to talk. "It didn't even happen to me and I feel so violated," she said. "I don't know how this kind of thing can even happen."

"That's almost exactly what Gina said."

"And poor Gina. And after the whole wedding . . ." She stopped while the sensitive waiter, delivering their drinks, averted his own eyes from her. Hardy had ordered Pellegrino. The waiter took their meager orders — they were splitting the antipasto and then a plate of carbonara. Sensing that it wasn't the night either for a sales pitch on the special, or for glib, he retreated.

"No appetite," Hardy said. "Except for maybe killing whoever did that to David."

"You think that would help?"

"I don't see how it could hurt." Hardy wasn't speaking ironically. He had no humor left in him. With his jaw set, staring fixedly ahead, he slowly turned his glass of water in the circle of its condensation. "Sons of bitches," he said. "If they think this is going to soften me up, they're making the biggest mistake of their lives."

"Who is? I thought nobody knew anything about who did this."

"Nobody does."

"So who's trying to soften you up?" Clearly, he'd let slip something he'd have preferred to hold close. His mouth twisted in a slight grimace. Frannie knew his looks, and in his rage he was very close to losing control. "Dismas?"

He picked up his glass and drank it all off. "I don't even know how to find out."

"Find out what?"

"How to prove it." He hung his head in disgust. "I should just go shake their tree."

"That is definitely not a good idea. If they did this to David . . ."

"And of course that's what they're counting on. Everybody's scared and nobody does anything."

She leaned in toward him. "Do you really think you know who did this?"

"I've got some idea. I might be wrong, but I bet I'm not."

"Well, then. Tell the police. I know they'll look. They know you."

"Uh-uh. You and I may remember me as the cop I once was, or the hard-hitting prosecutor I became, but that's all ancient history. Now I'm a defense attorney. I'm not on their side anymore. . . ."

"There's no side. Whoever beat up David . . ."

But he was shaking his head. "According to the cops' best guess, whoever beat up David is probably either a bunch of kids or a well-coordinated band of random muggers, neither of whom stole anything. Do either of those theories make even the tiniest bit of sense to you?"

"No."

"Which leaves what?"

"Somebody with a reason."

"Exactly. Somebody who stands to lose thirty million dollars if David takes him to court, for example."

"The man in your lawsuit, what's his name?"

"Wade Panos. Good guy. Private cop. Pillar of the community."

"He's not beating people up, Dismas. That doesn't make any sense, either."

"He doesn't have to do it himself, Frannie. He's got people."

"So we're back to where we were. Tell the police."

Hardy calmed himself with a deep breath. "No, now we're back to where we were, I'm a defense attorney."

"What does that mean?"

"It means you, Susie Citizen, can have something bad happen and you go to the cops and give them some reasons why your suspects might have done it and they'll listen to you with something like an open mind. Whereas, I, defense cretin that I am, I say something and first it's got to make it through the prism of doubt. And especially when I'm accusing somebody who's facing me in court. You, knowing me as the caring human being that I am, possibly can't see that in reality every word out of my mouth is a self-serving lie and every act of kindness is a cynical manipulation."

"I think you're exaggerating."

"Not by much."

"Abe doesn't see you that way."

"Maybe not all the time, but you'll recall we've had our bad days. And even with Abe, it's always been over this same issue, this inherent lack of credibility. When I walk in the door, first it's what's my agenda? What am I *really* doing? The idea that I've got something to give them for free that might help in some way just never occurs to them, and they wouldn't believe it if it did. And besides, Abe's not really a cop anymore."

She frowned at that characterization. "I

bet he'd help you with this if you asked."

"It's funny you should say that, because just this afternoon I did, and he didn't."

The frown grew deeper. "What did you say, exactly? Maybe he didn't realize it was personal."

Hardy raised his shoulders an inch. "He knew it was David. That's close enough. He knows the lawsuit is my case now. He's even the one who got me really considering Panos."

"Well, that's helping you."

"Okay, as far as that goes. But he's not intervening with any other cops, I'll tell you that. It was loud and clear. Not his job."

Frannie was swirling her own glass. "So who's investigating what happened to David? Have you talked to him?"

Surprised, Hardy sat back in his chair for a moment. Sometimes the obvious solutions could be the most elusive. Everything he'd told Frannie about the police prejudice against defense attorneys was absolutely true, but just that morning he'd actually encountered a great deal of cooperation from Hector Blanca. Maybe the General Work inspector would be the exception that proved the rule.

In their conversation back then, Hardy

hadn't even mentioned Panos in the Freeman context because it had been the barest wild notion on his part, with nothing to support it. But since then he'd learned about Matt Creed and his undeniable connection to the Patrol Special. It wasn't much, but if Blanca in fact wanted to find David's assailants — not a sure bet by any means — Hardy thought that with suitable up-front disclaimers, he might get him to listen.

"What?" Frannie asked. "What are you thinking?"

"Just that sometimes you're a genius. You're right. Freeman's guy — his name's Blanca — he might look."

"Why wouldn't he, Dismas? It's his job, isn't it?"

"Yep," Hardy said. "Sure is. And guess what? It's still his job, whether he does it or not."

"What does that mean?"

"Well, it means he's got a guy beating his neighbor up, let's say, or there's a fight in a bar. Both cases, and most of his other cases, he's got a victim and a suspect who's got a motive. With an apparently random mugging case like Freeman, and leaving me and my ideas out of it, the odds are good to great that they'll never, no matter

338

what, get to base one about who actually did it, so every minute Blanca spends looking is potentially a pure waste of his time."

Frannie stared disconsolately at the tablecloth between them. "And even if they find him, it doesn't help David, does it?"

At the truth of that, the futility of the entire discussion, Hardy blew out heavily.

The waiter returned with their plates to a silent table. Picking up the mood, he said nothing as he checked the basket of bread and placed the antipasto platter between them — olives, red and yellow roasted peppers, anchovies, salami, caponata. The restaurant was one of their favorite places and the antipasto a long-standing traditional beginning to their meals here, but neither Hardy nor Frannie reached for a bite. After a minute or so, Frannie sighed and took a tiny sip of her wine. "It seems a shame to come to a great place like this and not want to eat. Should we just pack it up and go home?"

But they didn't get to go straight home.

They'd found a parking place three blocks straight up the hill, in a dark stretch of Union Street above Grant. The wind was cutting into them, even huddled together, and they leaned into it as they walked. Neither really looked up or paid much attention until they came up near their space.

Hardy drove a five-year-old Honda on which he had long ago disconnected the alarm, since alarms only went off by mistake, anyway, never to alert you of anything.

But this time it might have been worth having.

The front windshield had been completely and thoroughly smashed. There were four or five obvious impact points — two of them had pierced the safety glass. The rest of the window was a network of weblike fissures — white lines in the distant dim light from Washington Square down the street.

"Oh, God!" Frannie said, her hand over her mouth.

Hardy didn't hear her. He was caught up in his own reaction, a veritable flash flood of unleashed obscenity. Spinning all the way round in frustration and anger, he whirled again and threw a vicious backhand fist up against the windshield, spraying more glass inside the car and onto the street. Another spasm of swearing overtook him as he was cupping his bleeding hand against himself, and again he lashed out at the windshield. The immediate anger spent now, he leaned heavily with his one good hand on the car's hood, ragged and desperate gasps punctuated by staccato exhalations.

Frannie had found that she'd backed herself against a building. Shivering in her heavy coat, she couldn't have said whether it was the biting wind or the chill of fear. Her husband's reaction struck her as more upsetting and in some ways almost worse than the vandalism itself, the violence and obscenity so unlike him. Under normal circumstances, something like this — a car window smashed — would make Dismas mad, of course; he'd be scathing in his wrath for a while, and probably funny about it. But that was nothing like this, nothing close to how she'd just seen him. Whatever this was, it had rocked Dismas to his core.

Coming forward tentatively, she reached out and touched the windshield briefly — it crinkled almost like cellophane as some glass chipped off onto the dashboard inside. Involuntarily, she backed away a step, another one. "Dismas, what is this?"

His face was as grim as his words. "This," he said, "is a warning."

"Against what?"

"Me. The lawsuit."

She didn't know what to say to that. He was obviously reeling from David. Of course that would occur to him, but she didn't think there was any way he could be certain. But this was no time to argue, or even discuss. He was too wrought up and, obviously, in pain. Moving close next to him, she put a hand on his back. "Is your hand all right?"

It was Frannie who took control, getting ̶ ̶p̶a̶s̶s̶e̶n̶g̶e̶r̶ ̶door for her husband, helping him inside. Eventually, they were both inside the car against the wind. They turned on the engine for the eventual heat to kick in. Now her husband sat beside her, unspeaking, cradling his injured left hand. She finally ventured a suggestion. "We ought to call the police."

It didn't call for a reply, and none came. Frannie got out the cell and reported their problem and location, then called her brother at home to ask if he'd like to come and get them. All the while, Hardy sat ramrod straight, well back in the passenger's seat. He stared straight ahead through the kaleidoscope of broken glass.

Since they were patrolling in North Beach anyway, the squad car got there in under ten minutes. By the time Hardy saw the red-and-blue lights turn up at the corner, he felt he could face another human, talk with some semblance of reason. He and Frannie opened their doors and were standing out in the street as the two uniformed officers — Reyas and Simms from their name tags — approached them.

It was obvious enough what had happened, and the officers took their statements with professionalism and even sympathy. While Simms went back to his car to call the towing service, Reyas began walking around the car with his flashlight. He hadn't gotten very far when he stopped and leaned over for a closer look at the hood. "This looks like blood here," he said.

"It is," Hardy said. "It's mine. I lost my temper and popped the windshield." He held up his hand. "Not my finest hour," he added, "or my smartest."

Reyas nodded, shifted his attention to Frannie. "Mrs. Hardy," he asked, "you two haven't been fighting, have you?"

The question surprised her and instinctively she threw a look at Hardy before coming back to Reyas. "No, sir. We were just coming back from dinner, as we said. At Fior d'Italia."

He appeared to be considering something. Coming back around the front of the car again, he sprayed his beam over them both. "Mrs. Hardy," he said. "Would you mind accompanying me for a minute over to the squad car?"

Again, she looked at Hardy, and though not happy about this development, he nodded once. "It's okay."

He turned and watched them walk away. Hardy knew what was happening here. Officer Reyas wanted to get Frannie alone so she could answer a question or two without interference or coercion from her husband. He also wanted some better light — the squad car was parked directly under a streetlamp — where he could observe her more closely to see if she had any visible bruises. If it seemed that the broken windshield was really part of a violent domestic disturbance, Hardy knew they'd handcuff him and take him downtown. As well they should, he thought.

But they wouldn't find anything to indicate that.

His hand was throbbing now. Looking down, trying to make it into a fist, he realized that he might have broken a bone in his little finger. The blood had mostly dried by now, but even with the cold, the swelling was substantial. The pain and this inconvenience to him and to Frannie struck him as being a two-pronged and just sentence for having been such an idiot.

A fierce and quite deadly calm settled upon him. He *knew* without any doubt what this had been here tonight. It was part of David and perhaps part of Creed. His earlier explosion was the wrong use for his really unprecedented anger. The calm would serve better.

He looked again across the street. Reyas and Simms were both talking to Frannie and fortunately, Hardy thought, his fiery, redheaded wife was keeping her own famous temper in check. After perhaps three minutes, both policemen escorted her back to where he waited. Frannie had evidently explained to them that Moses was on his way to pick them up.

But they weren't done yet. Simms had a notepad out. "Mr. Hardy. Your wife tells us you've got some suspicion of who might have done this?"

Hardy struggled for a genial tone. "Some," he said. "I'm suing somebody. If I win, and I will, they're out of business."

"You want to give us a name?"

"I could, but it wouldn't do you any good. He wouldn't have done this himself.

345

He'd have sent one of his men." He drew a breath to maintain his control. "And there won't be any evidence here. They wouldn't have touched anything. The windshield looks like your traditional blunt object." He indicated the car. "You can see where they hit it."

"Yes, sir," Simms said. "But if you want us to include anything specific in our report, now is the time. As you say, there's a chance we won't get anywhere with an actual investigation on this incident, but it would be good to have a name if something else happens later. You call us and say, 'This is the second time,' and somebody's going to wonder why you didn't report the first one."

"What do you mean, if something else happens?" Frannie asked.

The two cops looked at each other. Surely this was clear enough. But Hardy saved them from having to answer. "Nothing's going to happen," he told his wife. "They see they're not scaring me off and they'll stop trying."

"Like they did with David?" she asked with some asperity.

"Who's David?" Reyas asked.

Hardy sighed. "My partner in this lawsuit. David Freeman. He got beaten up last night. He's still hospitalized."

"In a coma," Frannie added. "In critical condition."

Again, Reyas and Simms consulted silently. Finally, Simms tapped his notepad. "Maybe you better give us a name," he said.

Moses McGuire arrived a little after the tow truck and after the Hardys' car was on its way, he packed the two of them into the cab of his pickup. It hadn't been a cheerful ride back from North Beach, but Moses had talked them into stopping by his bar to eat their dinner and calm down. Now he'd plied his sister with wine and Hardy with some first aid for his hand and then a double martini. Most of the immediate tension had passed. They were eating their Fior d'Italia antipasto at one of the coffee tables at the back of the Little Shamrock.

McGuire tipped up the last of his scotch. "I've got an idea," he said.

"Ideas are good," Hardy said. "I'd take an idea."

"Paul!" McGuire called to the bartender and held up his empty glass, pointing at it. Then, back to Hardy, "Where does Panos live?"

"Uh-uh." Frannie shook her head. "Bad idea."

"No, really," Moses said.

"No really yourself. You don't escalate things."

"You don't? Why not? I think it's a fine idea. Drop by his place, pop a window or two, have a little fun."

Hardy thoughtfully chewed an olive. "It does have a quaint sort of in-your-face appeal."

McGuire was getting into it. "Especially if I just do it and don't even tell you." He smiled at his sister.

She put down her wineglass. Her face had gone hard. "Don't even think about it. I mean it, Moses."

She turned to her husband for support, but he just shrugged. "I can't control him, Fran. He's a big boy."

"Boy is the key word." Then, to her brother, "You just don't do this."

McGuire got his new drink. Service tended to be good for him at the Shamrock. But he hadn't lost the thread. "So what do *you* recommend?"

The question seemed to fluster her. "I don't recommend anything. The police said they were going to look into it."

McGuire barked a deep and scathing

laugh. "And then, when they find nothing, what?"

"Maybe they'll find something," Frannie said.

"She's right," Hardy said. He'd had enough discord for one night. Moses and Frannie were threatening to really go at it, and he thought he'd try to slow them down. "Maybe they will, Mose. It could happen."

A couple of scotches now into the wind, McGuire fastened a cold eye on Hardy. "Traitor. And how, pray, is it going to happen? One of Panos's guys leave a card in the gutter?" He took in both of them. "Get real, guys. You've already told me that they don't have anything on who beat up your Mr. Freeman, and he's a moderately important person. You think they're even going to look with your stupid car? This, my naive friends, is not going to happen."

"My car's not stupid," Hardy replied. "In fact, now that I think of it, it's smarter than some of my clients."

"Go ahead, Diz. Make a joke of it. I don't think it's funny." McGuire put a spoonful of caponata on some focaccia and stuffed it into his mouth. "These guys really piss me off."

"I intuited that." Hardy was working on his newfound calm. He put his injured hand on Frannie's knee, shot her his craggy grin. "We're a little angry ourselves, tell the truth."

"But you don't go breaking *his* windows," she said. "Then you're just like he is."

"Sorry, li'l sis, but no you're not." Before Vietnam had killed the scholar he'd been as a young man, McGuire had earned a doctorate in philosophy at Berkeley. "There's one tiny little difference."

"No. There's no difference. And don't 'li'l sis' me!"

"All right, strike the 'li'l sis,' but don't give me that 'no difference' bullshit."

Hardy's efforts to defuse the sibling fireworks weren't working. The area at the back of the Shamrock was small enough to begin with — maybe ten feet across and twelve deep — and McGuire's voice reverberated off the close walls, drowning even the jukebox.

"There's a fucking *huge* difference. And you know what it is? *They started it!* How 'bout that for a concept?" He pointed at his sister, his brow knit, his eyes dark. "They did it to you first. You don't think that makes a fundamental difference, you're dead fucking wrong."

"Easy, Mose," Hardy said. "We're just talking, okay?"

McGuire whirled on him. "What do you think that was? You see anybody throwing a punch here? I don't think so. But don't tell me we're just like them, 'cause that's just plain *bullshit*. We're nothing like them."

But Frannie was evidently much more accustomed to McGuire's outbursts than even Hardy was, and he'd seen a lot of them. She got up and sat down next to her brother, put an arm around him. "And people wonder where I got so feisty," she said. She kissed him on the cheek. "Okay, you're nothing like them. Just promise me you won't go shoot out anybody's windows."

Not completely mollified, McGuire came forward heavily. He grabbed for his scotch, picked it up, then put it back down and sat back. After another moment, he leaned over and kissed his sister. "I wasn't going to shoot them," he said. Smiled. The fight was over. "I was thinking maybe a slingshot," he said.

14

The call came into homicide at 4:38 a.m. As soon as he heard the tentative identifications, Paul Thieu thought he knew what he had, but for his own reasons, not the least of which was pride in his work, he proceeded in his own ordered, methodical fashion. He had to get to the scene and make his own determination first.

Gerson wouldn't thank him for a call at this time of the morning anyway. If the crime scene was anything like what it promised to be from the dispatch — double homicide or possibly homicide with suicide — the CSI team wouldn't even have gotten a good jump by the time it was reasonable to call the lieutenant.

In the cold, dark morning, Thieu left the Hall of Justice through the front doors. A couple of black-and-whites were parked on Bryant just down the steps — the dim light of cigarettes visible in the front one. Thieu didn't want to waste even the few minutes it would take to walk to the back lot and get his assigned Ford Taurus. He walked up to the driver's window and pressed his badge up against it. The window came down in a fog of smoke and coffee. "Sorry to interrupt your coffee break, officers, but I've got a very hot homicide eight blocks away and I'd like to be there ten minutes ago." He slapped the roof of the car. "How fast can you make this thing go?"

Sirens screaming all the way — Thieu saw no reason why commandeering a squad car couldn't include an element of fun — they dropped him at his address in under five minutes. Two other squad cars were already parked in the street, but there was no sign yet of the coroner's van or any of the CSI people.

The building had no aspirations to stand out among the other worn and tawdry four-story structures on the block. With its common entrance, yellowing paint and graffiti in a hundred hands and colors, the apartment house squatted all but anonymously amid its identical neighbors, each more depressing than the next. Inside, Thieu knew, the apartments would also be more similar than not, every one squalid. Stained ancient mattresses with no coverings, broken furniture without upholstery, bare walls and sagging wallpaper hanging in sheets no one ever thought or cared to remove. In every kitchen, dirty dishes would lie piled in the sinks and on every flat surface, the stoves would be buried in grease and carbon, the refrigerators nearly living with mold. The stench of the rooms — of tobacco, urine, alcohol, vomit, decay and musk — would, Thieu supposed, never come out.

When homicides are reported, the sergeant from the local precinct is supposed to come out and maintain security at the sight until an inspector from the homicide detail arrives. In this case, things were working as they should and Sergeant R. Penrose, from his name tag, out of the Tenderloin Task Force was standing, talking to another uniformed patrolman at the building's entrance. Out of the wind, inside the open doorway.

Thieu introduced himself and noted the look of relief on Penrose's face — the scene wasn't his direct responsibility anymore. Thieu pegged him at about his own age, mid-thirties, but a kind of rigid nervousness made him seem younger. "This is Officer Lundgren," he said. Although Thieu was anxious to get inside, he knew it was smarter to get everything from the beginning. "He and his partner out in the car there, they got the original complaint."

In this part of town, complaints to the police were decidedly unusual, so this in itself piqued Thieu's interest. "Who complained about what?" he asked.

"The landlady." Lundgren pointed into the half-shadow behind him where a small Asian woman, dressed now in a heavy overcoat, hovered by the stairway. "Mrs. Chu. Her English isn't so good, but evidently she was trying to sleep and —"

"Excuse me, Officer," Thieu said, stopping him. He turned to Sergeant Penrose. "Maybe I will see if I can just talk to her for a minute, please."

Penrose nodded. If he was surprised, he didn't show it. He motioned to Mrs. Chu to come forward. Thieu was not a tall man, but Mrs. Chu didn't reach his shoulders. She looked to be about sixty years old, and as she emerged from the shadows, Thieu took in her threadbare coat, the thin, short gray hair, a pair of red Converse tennis shoes. She, too, like Penrose, exuded wariness.

That was it, Thieu was thinking. Everybody here looks spooked.

He addressed her in Mandarin, in which

he was fluent, and at the familiar sounds, she relaxed slightly. She told him that she'd been watching television (not in fact trying to sleep as Officer Lundgren had volunteered), trying to drown out the loud radio from directly below her. Usually the tenants down there were quiet and polite, but tonight it seemed they were partying. They came in a little after midnight — yes, she thought, several people, at least three but maybe more — and first thing had turned on the radio, very loud. She couldn't hear her television over the blaring radio. But noise was a fact of life in the building, and people tended not to get involved. (Thieu knew that interrupting "parties," that is, drug use or sex or both, was a typical cause of violence in the Tenderloin.) Besides, one of the men downstairs was very big and she did not want him to become mad at her, so she put it off a long time. But eventually, about an hour ago, she needed to sleep and so came down and knocked.

But no one answered, although the radio kept on and on. Finally, she called the police and they . . .

Thieu thanked Mrs. Chu and turned back to Sergeant Penrose. "I'd better go in. I expect the coroner and crime scene investigation unit any time. I'm afraid you're not going to be getting much sleep, Sergeant. Sorry."

"I think it's going to be a while anyway," Penrose said. "Every time I close my eyes, I . . ." He stopped, motioned toward the closed door. Again, that spooked quality. He reached out and touched Thieu on the arm, a dramatic gesture under any circumstances, and not at all coplike. "Prepare yourself," he said. "It's bad."

Dawn ambushed him.

One minute Thieu was opening the door to the apartment, flipping on the light against the blackness outside, thinking not only that it wasn't bad, it was incredibly well-kept — the flowers, the polished surfaces, a sense of order and cleanliness, to say nothing of the matching furniture, high-end magazines, framed prints on the faux-painted terra-cotta walls. A minute later, he stood squinting up at blue sky through the back window that opened on an alley. In three plus hours, he hadn't grown appreciably inured to the sight of the carnage behind him in the bedroom.

He'd been wrong about the CSI team hardly getting a jump before it was time to call Gerson. They were getting close to finished. Already they wanted to remove the bodies, but much as it sickened him to refuse, that's exactly what he did. After a long while working here, someone had opened both the back windows and the front door and the temperature in the apartment now barely made it into the forties, although it felt like one hundred degrees to Thieu.

He knew it was time to call Gerson, but he checked his watch anyway and made sure. Turning around, he resolved to go outside for a moment — he wanted to get out of this room — and patch into the detail from one of the squad cars, or maybe the coroner's van. He stepped carefully to avoid the blood, tried again without much success to avert his eyes from the horrific tableau.

But before he'd made it out of the room, Lennard Faro stopped him. Faro was the crime scene specialist. Thin and intense, he had recently begun sporting a soul patch under his lip which he called his bug. Both of his ears were pierced, the right one twice. He wasn't yet thirty years old, yet in his profession believed that he had seen everything. Even the almost unfathomably grisly scene here today failed to elicit any response, and Thieu found himself wondering if it was all simply a defense. He knew that he, himself, came across as very professional, and knew the reality behind that guise. Maybe Faro was simply better at it than he was — but even if it was your job, Thieu didn't think most humans could handle the butchery they had here without reacting viscerally.

But Faro seemed to be holding up. Certainly better than Thieu was. He and Thieu had both spent the previous night crawling around the driveway where Matt Creed had been shot, so when the specialist had first arrived, he greeted Thieu with the old, "We've got to stop meeting like this." But that was before he'd seen the bodies.

Now, having seen them, his voice held a suitable gravity, but no real sign of personal revulsion. Suddenly Thieu realized what it was — Lennard Faro wasn't spooked. And it was hard not to be. "So we got a refrigerator here, Paul. You still wanna leave 'em where they be?"

"I do," Thieu said. "I'm going out to call Gerson on it right now. Couple more hours isn't going to hurt them, I don't suppose."

Faro cast an unfeeling eye back at the room. "No. They'll keep. But the team's

going to want to wrap it up, and —"
Seeing Thieu's expression — anger and resolve — he stopped. "I'm just saying it's two nights in a row now. People get tired they don't do as good. We got the place sealed off. We come back early, say. Or bring out the day team to tag and bag. What do you say?"

Thieu knew that he could appear peremptory. He forced a smile, pointed to the front door. "Let's go out a minute, get some air, okay?" By the time they had reached the front door, finally out of sight of the bedroom, Thieu found he could control himself much more easily.

Turning back to Faro, he spoke with an easy assurance, even sympathy. "I hear what you're saying, Len, but I think in this case, it'd be helpful if your team stayed around just awhile longer, at least till the lieutenant's here to let you go."

"You think Gerson's gonna be coming down here?" Faro, clearly, didn't envision that possibility. "That would be a first, wouldn't it?"

Thieu didn't comment on that. "What I think is that whether or not he comes down himself, it's very likely he's going to assign this case to Cuneo and Russell, which is what he did with Creed last night." Faro's hand went to his bug as he processed this. "I'd bet you anything that this one's part of that, which is part of Silverman. So if you don't mind, I think it'd be helpful if you guys were around to answer questions when the new guys get here. Probably in fifteen minutes or less. Plus," he added, "they need to see it."

Faro's face suddenly went slack. "Nobody needs to see that," he said.

Thieu felt a wash of something like relief. He decided to speak. "You know, Len, I'm glad to hear you say that. I thought it rolled right off you."

Faro pulled at his bug, shook his head slowly side to side. "Nope," he said.

When Thieu reached Gerson on the phone, the lieutenant as expected wasn't enthusiastic about coming down and checking out the murder scene himself, but he wasted no time at all with his administrative duties. Upon learning that the victims were Clint Terry and Randy Wills, the two chief suspects in both the Creed and Silverman homicides, he told Thieu — again, if he didn't mind and with other suitable disclaimers — that it sounded like efficiency would be better served if Cuneo and Russell were assigned to this homicide as well as the other two. He told Thieu that the two inspectors were running a little late getting into the office this morning since they were stopping at the lab for some ballistics results before reporting in. But Gerson would call dispatch and send them directly to the crime scene just as soon as he got off the phone with Thieu.

Which he did shortly, leaving Thieu and Faro standing out in the street by the coroner's van. But when Thieu started explaining Gerson's decision about Cuneo and Russell to Faro, the crime scene specialist stopped him before he'd gotten very far. "Wait a minute. Wait a minute. You want to run that by me again? You're telling me those guys in there, they were *suspects* in the Creed thing?"

Thieu nodded. "Yeah, and them plus a third guy named Holiday for Silverman."

Faro pulled at his bug. "So the theory is what?"

"What do you mean?"

"I mean, you just told Gerson this homicide was related to Creed and Silverman, so he's sending over Russell and Cuneo, right?"

"Right."

"So what's the relation?"

"The relation is that they're suspects in

both those murders."

But Faro was shaking his head. "They killed Silverman. Then they killed Creed. Now they're both dead. And this guy Holiday, he's the only one left?"

"Yeah, looks like. Which makes him . . .'" Thieu cocked his head. "What's the problem, Len?"

Faro took a long beat deciding what he'd say. Finally, he said, "This might be a hell of a coincidence, okay, and we're trained to hate and mistrust them, but they happen. My take is that this isn't any of that — Silverman and Creed, I mean. It's completely unrelated."

"It can't be. These are the same guys."

"Be that as it may, I've seen a half a dozen of these."

"Like this? Not like this." Thieu motioned toward the apartment. "Like that?"

Faro's head bobbed down, then up. "Spittin' image, or close enough. This is a pickup gone bad. I'd bet my badge on it. Which might close Silverman and even Creed, okay, except maybe for this other guy, Holiday, but these stiffs here, this case — they ought to stay with you."

"With me? In what way with me?"

"Your case. They've got nothing to do with Cuneo and Russell's other work."

Thieu rubbed his hands together against the cold. "They do if . . ."

"Nope. Not unless you think Holiday did this, which I'm betting he didn't. You're thinking he did?"

"I didn't know. I just assumed he must be in it somehow. He fits."

"A falling out among thieves, something like that?"

"Something like."

Suddenly Faro shivered. "Jesus, it's cold. I'm going to go tell the team we're hanging fire another hour or so. Send 'em out for coffee." He fished in his pockets, brought out his keys, pointed. "That's my car over there, the brown one." He flipped the keys to Thieu. "Get the heat going, would you? Have a seat. I'll be right back."

Thieu was still pondering the pickup gone bad theory when Faro opened the door and slid into the passenger seat. "So where were we?"

"This should stay my case."

"That's it. And hey, no offense to Dan and Lincoln, nothing personal. It's just that their theory don't hold."

Thieu crossed his arms, hugging himself. It hadn't warmed up much. "So what's yours?"

"What happened? Easy. The two vics in

there went out to party last night and found some guy who wanted to play, so they brought him back here. You see some of that powder on the bureau? Ten to one it's coke, maybe heroin or crank, one of those. So they're getting a lot high and a little kinky, maybe one of 'em's already naked — I'm thinkin' the big guy . . ."

"That's Terry. Why him first?"

"We'll get to that. But see if this don't play. So Terry's tied up in the chair just like he is now, maybe they're playin' a little with him and the two other guys — well, the guy they picked up and the one he thinks is the girl . . ."

"Wills."

"Yeah, whatever, so those two start to get it on. Then the pickup guy reaches down and — whoops! — gets a handful of surprise."

"Wills isn't a woman."

"He sure isn't. Not even a little. So the perp goes ballistic — the coroner will tell us exactly what he did next, but my guess is he strangled Wills, maybe knocked him around a little first. But he's still flying on whatever drug they're doing and completely out of his mind now with being fooled. His masculinity, if you want to call it that, is all fucked up. Except he really knew all along. Plus he's just killed Wills with Terry tied up sitting there watching him. What's he gonna do? He's in a rage and completely freaked. He's got to get out of there, but first there's business. So maybe he's gone to the bathroom since he's been there, seen the straight razor Wills shaved his whole body with. He goes back in there . . ."

"I think I get it from there," Thieu said. He might have been a hard-boiled six-year veteran inspector of homicide, but he was shaking now not with the cold, but with the recitation. He didn't think he could bear to listen to Faro's certain-to-be-vivid clinical description of how the throats of both of them had been slit, or the individual steps as Randy Wills was undressed, trussed, and finally castrated.

Faro needed a moment to extract himself from his imagination. At last, he turned to Thieu. "Anyway, my point is that whatever happened here, this was separate. Nothing to do with Creed or Silverman or anything else. This was its own thing and the case ought to belong to you if you want it."

John Holiday loved Clint Terry — he really did — but he was going to have to fire the irresponsible son of a bitch. He was thinking this as he pulled the chairs off the tables that he'd put them on when he'd closed the place last night at two o'clock. Why did he bother? He set the last chair in its place and checked his watch. Noon. He'd closed the place up a mere ten hours ago, and thank God he'd come by just on a random check to find the door closed and nobody behind the bar. This was his only source of income and it had to be open for him to actually make some money, stay solvent and not be forced to sell cheap.

He still believed he could get a lucky streak going, maybe at poker. Lucky streaks weren't out of the question. Look at him and Michelle. With just a few solid months and a bit of luck, he could make the Ark presentable, and then maybe sell at a profit, go back into something more legitimate.

What was the matter with people? he wondered. A gay ex-convict like Clint with a questionable reputation and no real skills, where was he going to get another job as good as this one? With a laid-back boss, flexible hours, decent pay. What, if anything, was he thinking as he undoubtedly slept in this morning, making it two days in a row, knowing he was blowing the job off? All Holiday asked, essentially, was that the big galoot show up, and especially — *especially!* — when Holiday had pulled the night shift the day before. But first yesterday, then today. Enough was enough.

He was going to have to do it. That was all there was to it.

Fortunately, when he'd closed last night, he'd prepped the back bar and cleaned up every bit of the glass and mess — good guy and great employer that he was — so that Clint could have it easy when he opened. Now, at least, he was close to ready, albeit two hours late, as he unlocked the front door and flicked on the OPEN sign.

As sometimes happened, a man was waiting just outside and pushed open the door while Holiday went around the bar. The man, a wiry Asian of some kind, was seated by the time the two men were face to face, a cocktail napkin down on the bar between them. "Morning," Holiday said. "What can I get you?"

"How about a beer?"

"Bottled? Draft? We got Sam Adams and Anchor Steam."

"Which one's colder?"

"Anchor," Holiday said, naming the city's own brew. "It's lived here longer so it's had more time to chill. But you sure you want cold today? There's plenty of that outside."

But the play had run out. "Anchor's good," the customer said.

Holiday turned and grabbed a glass from the refrigerator, tipped it up against the Anchor spigot and drew off the pint. Coming back to the bar, he noticed a twenty dollar bill in the gutter, the man's wallet out on the pitted wood. The badge.

He put the beer down carefully. "I told the guys who came by yesterday that I wasn't talking to you without my lawyer here. I'm still not. You want me to call him?"

"I'm off duty and I've got the world's simplest question, I promise. Whatever answer you give me, I drink my beer and go home and get some sleep."

For some reason — Clint's absence, or this man's easy manner, or even his own fatigue at having his guard up all the time — Holiday called him on it. "Okay. What the hell? One," he said.

"Where were you last night at midnight?"

Holiday actually laughed out loud. "That's it? That's the one question? We could play this all day. I was here, and by here I mean *right here*" — he tapped the bar twice — "tending this twenty-two feet of antiquated glulam with dedication and some might even say panache."

"So you had customers? People you knew?"

"Six or eight at least. But I just gave you another question."

"Two actually," Thieu said. He lifted his glass and, closing his eyes, drained half of it. "Great beer," he said. Then, "Thank you."

He picked up his wallet, got off his stool, and walked to the door, where he stopped and turned again. "Keep the change."

The evidence bonanza that was the Terry/Wills apartment was almost enough to overcome the revulsion felt by both Cuneo and Russell when they had first arrived and taken in the appalling scene. Thieu had still been there with them, of course. They didn't know it, but Gerson had overruled his request, based on Faro's theory of the case, that on reflection he should remain the inspector of record. Thieu didn't argue with the lieutenant, but simply hung around until all three inspectors signed off on the release of the bodies to the medical examiner's with a great sense of relief.

Once the overwhelming presence of the corpses was removed, and Thieu had gone, Faro and the other members of the CSI unit began walking the two new inspectors through the masses of evidence they'd acquired and bagged in plastic. Cuneo and Russell were both tightly focused and slightly flushed with the successful results of the ballistics test they had finally shepherded through the crime lab. That test, performed on two remarkably undamaged slugs, had conclusively shown that Sam Silverman and Matt Creed had been shot with the same .38 caliber weapon.

And now, among other items, they were looking at just such a gun, a Smith & Wesson revolver with its serial number filed off, found under a pile of socks in the bureau drawer in the bedroom. Two empty bullet casings remained in the cylinder with four live rounds. Additionally, the same drawer yielded a box of .38 ammunition minus eight shells, a stack of bills of various denominations — $2440 in all — each one marked with a small red dot in the upper right-hand corner. Wade Panos and Sadie Silverman, both and separately in their respective interviews, had mentioned this habit of Silverman's, red-dotting the bills he'd be depositing.

When they had nearly finished — Faro had already gone home for the day without burdening the new inspectors with his theory of the case — Cuneo had an idea and went to the bedroom closet. The CSI team had already looked inside it and found nothing, then had reclosed the door. Of course, the clothes the two victims had been wearing were already bagged and tagged, but Cuneo had read Thieu's report on the Creed crime scene and had something specific in mind. He wasn't a minute looking before he stopped humming "Bolero" and turned back to the room. "Lincoln, get me another bag, would you? Good-sized."

He came out holding a pair of large shoes. They were nicely made, expensive-looking loafers of light brown braided leather with a tassle. The soles were worn smooth, but there was some gunk — still tacky — stuck where the heel started, a little more around the edge, on the right one. "If this is what I think it is," Cuneo said, "we got this thing wrapped up."

As it turned out, they didn't need the analysis of the garbage effluent. This time the two inspectors of record didn't email the lab and request that someone drive up to the Hall and pick up their new evidence. They had the gun — the probable murder weapon — and, since they hadn't been back to the Hall to return the earlier slugs to the evidence locker, they had possession of them, too. So they had another hamburger lunch at Dago Mary's while the lab fired the gun and compared this new bullet to the earlier rounds.

By one o'clock, they were back uptown talking to Gerson in his office. Ten minutes after that, they appeared in the chambers of Judge Oscar Thomasino, a venerable presence on the bench, who was on his lunch break from the trial over which he was presiding. This was his week as duty judge, which meant he was the person responsible for approving search warrants, and he was already well disposed to both Cuneo and Russell. The DNA evidence that had led to the arrest of the alleged rapist and murderer Shawon Ellerson last week had come from a search conducted by these two inspectors at the suspect's apartment, and Thomasino had signed off on the warrant for that search.

He got up from his desk and the paperwork on it and ushered the two men over to a small seating area by the room's one window. "You boys are having yourselves quite a week," he said.

Russell nodded soberly. It never did to gloat. "We're getting a few breaks, your honor. That's true."

"It's funny how breaks come to the good cops. I've noticed a definite correlation."

"Thank you, your honor."

"This one looks pretty solid," Cuneo added. He handed the warrant across to the judge.

Thomasino looked it over carefully. These may have been good cops, but the decision to violate a citizen's residence by allowing a legal search was never a casual one, and Thomasino took it very seriously indeed. When he'd finished reading, he looked up. "So this man, Holiday, how does he fit exactly? I'm not sure I see it."

Cuneo took point. "We believe he was with the other two men — the victims this morning in the apartment where we found the gun — during the Silverman robbery and murder. Plus, we've confirmed that the same gun was used to kill a security guard two days ago, Matt Creed."

"But these men were not shot? This morning?"

"No, sir. Somebody had cut their throats," Russell said.

"And you think it was this Holiday?"

"Yes, your honor." Cuneo, exuding urgency, came forward in a kind of a crouch. "We didn't get a positive match on the slugs for Silverman and Creed until this morning and based on them, we were planning to arrest Terry and Wills, except they went dead on us."

"But not Holiday? Why not?"

Russell shifted in his seat. "He's a bartender. He was working when Creed got shot, so we think that Creed was just the two of them, Terry and Wills."

"Maybe Holiday didn't even know they were planning on killing him," Cuneo added. "He might have felt they were getting too trigger-happy and were a risk. Which is why Holiday decided he had to kill them."

"But," Russell said, "it's probable he did know about Creed. That they all decided."

"And why would they do that?" Thomasino asked.

Cuneo straightened up, the tag team continuing. "Because Creed had identified all of them as the guys who'd killed Silverman. So they figure he can't testify if he's dead."

Russell jumped back in. "And me and Dan repeating what Creed told us would be hearsay and inadmissible anyway, isn't that right?"

A faint trace of smile tugged at the judge's mouth. "The rules about hearsay have fooled better men than me. But you're saying you had an ID on Holiday? Then why isn't he in jail already?"

"The ID was in the dark at fifty feet, your honor," Russell said. "The DA wouldn't have charged it if that's all it was."

"We needed physical evidence tying him to Silverman," Cuneo added. "And we didn't get any until this morning, when we got plenty."

Thomasino stroked his chin, pulled at his ear, rubbed his neck. Something about all this still bothered him. "I see you've got a lot for these two dead men, although it's a little late now. I'm still not sure I see the connection to Holiday so clearly."

Cuneo had started tapping his thighs in agitation. "Your honor, he killed them both last night. The other dead man, Creed, put Holiday with them both during the Silverman robbery and murder. I'm a hundred percent certain we'll find evidence we can use at his place tying him to four murders. This man needs to be off the street."

"But you need probable cause for a

search warrant. You gentlemen know this. And I'm not sure you've got anything yet that rises to that standard."

"Your honor." Russell reached over and touched his partner's arm, stopping the agitation. Playing counterpoint to Cuneo's intensity, he leaned back in his chair, crossed a leg over his knee. "I personally heard Matt Creed positively identify the three men who robbed and killed Mr. Silverman as Clint Terry, Randy Wills and John Holiday." He pointed to the form in Thomasino's hand. "As the affidavit indicates, we found bills with Mr. Silverman's distinctive mark at Wills's and Terry's apartment. We will be searching for similar bills at Mr. Holiday's. We *know* they were together."

Chewing the inside of his cheek, the judge sat with it for another moment. Finally, he narrowed his eyes and leaned forward. "Inspector Russell, you heard this Mr. Creed's identification with your own ears?"

"Yes, sir."

"Inspector Cuneo? Same question."

"Yes, your honor."

Thomasino nodded. "All right. Perhaps the warrant application just isn't as clear as it needs to be. I want you to handwrite that right here, initial and date it, each of you. I'm calling that good enough for me." He came all the way forward and placed the warrant on the small table between them. The pen's scratch was the only sound in the room.

Holiday called Michelle at her apartment from the Ark. She had a restaurant review for a place on Chestnut Street and they'd been planning to go there together for lunch, but now that wasn't going to happen. He told her that Clint still hadn't shown up and he was going to have to pull a double shift. He'd see her tonight, late, after he got off. He wondered, since the restaurant was near his own duplex, if she'd mind swinging by his place for a clean shirt or two and some underwear. He might be pulling back-to-backs at the bar and he could be with her sooner tonight if she could save him the long walk or bus ride home. He'd lost the last car he'd owned at a poker game, then found he didn't need a car for his normal life, anyway, since he lived all of it within such a relatively small radius. Most days he walked to work — Chestnut to Taylor or Mason, then all the way down to O'Farrell wasn't even two miles and the hills gave

378

him some badly needed exercise.

So after lunch, sometime between 2:00 and 3:00, Michelle found herself climbing the stairs to his flat. He'd lived in the same upper duplex on Casa Street in the Marina for over fifteen years, had bought it with Emma, lived there with her for their three years together. In a fit of fiscal probity during Emma's pregnancy, the young couple had actually bought mortgage insurance and because of that, after her death, the place was now paid off. It still had ghosts for him, evidently, and he spent as little time there as possible, although he had told her that he recognized the necessity of holding on to it. He could never afford to rent a similar, or even a far less desirable, place. It was just something he possessed, like his bar. Part of his life.

There had been three newspapers in the little area at the foot of the stairs, and Michelle was carrying them as she got to the upper landing and noticed that his door was open. She pushed at it gingerly and it gave another few inches. Inside, she heard unmistakable sounds of movement and male voices.

"Hello!" she sang out. "Is anybody home?"

The voices ceased. Footsteps approached. The door opened all the way. A well-dressed, clean-cut black man stood in front of her, scowling. "Can I help you?"

"Is John home?" she asked. "Who are you?"

The man pulled out his wallet and showed her his identification. Another man, this one white, appeared in the hall behind him. "Inspector Lincoln Russell. My partner, Dan Cuneo. We're with homicide."

"Homicide?" She backed away a step. "Is John okay?"

"That would be John Holiday? Yes, ma'am, as far as we know."

"All right, but then what are you doing here?"

"We're searching his apartment." Inspector Russell reached into his coat pocket and produced a piece of paper. "We have a warrant."

The other man came forward. "While we're getting to know each other, can I please see some identification?"

"From me?"

"Yes, ma'am. If you don't mind."

It didn't seem to her that it was a request she could refuse. Flustered, going for her purse, she dropped the newspapers around the welcome mat. Finally, she fished around and brought out her driver's license, which she handed to Russell, since he was nearest to her. He glanced at it, showed it to his partner, then gave it back to her and said, "All right, Ms. Maier, you mind telling us why you're here?"

Michelle was thinking as fast as she could, showing them nothing. "I've been trying to get in touch with John and he's not answering his phone, so I thought I'd come by and leave a message on his door. I'm going away for a couple of days and he always watches my cats." She knew she was blurting and realized at the same time that this might not be a bad thing. "He's really good with cats. He never forgets. Anyway, so when I got here I thought I'd pick up his papers when I saw them all down there, and then the door was open a little, so I . . . well, you know." She stammered to a halt. "I'm sorry to have interrupted you," she said.

The black inspector turned to his partner, came back to her. "You don't know where Mr. Holiday is?"

"No. That's why I came by, to see if . . ." She gave them both her most plaintive look. "Is he in trouble?"

Cuneo came forward a step. "You might want to find somebody else for your cats. If he comes by, we'll see he gets the papers."

It was a dismissal. She couldn't believe it, but as long as she stayed cool, they were letting her just go away. "Okay, then." She forced herself to wait another moment, then raised her hand tentatively, as though wondering if it would be appropriate to wave. "Sorry to have bothered you. 'Bye."

"So . . . what?" Gerson said. The three of them were in his office, sitting around in something like a circle. The door was closed. "You left his copy of the warrant taped to the front door? Inside?"

"Yes, sir."

"I don't want any technical error to screw this up."

"No, sir," Cuneo said. "Neither do we. It was a righteous search, by the book."

"And where was all this? Just lying out?"

He was referring to the three baggies the inspectors had brought in with them — their winning streak growing to truly absurd proportions. In Holiday's bathroom, one of the drawers under the sink didn't appear to be as deep as the counter over it. Upon pulling it out, Russell discovered a battered, old dull red leather pouch stuffed to near bursting with over $3,700 in mixed bills, each one marked with a red dot in the upper right-hand corner. As if that weren't enough, at almost the same instant, Cuneo — in the bedroom — let out a yelp when he opened a cigar box on a shelf in the back corner of the closet. It rattled when he picked it up, and he found that it contained seven rings, five of them women's engagement rings with large diamonds, two of them for men. One of the men's rings was truly distinctive, inset with what looked to the inspectors to be a huge and brilliant star sapphire. Two of the rings, including the sapphire, still had the tiny price tag attached with a small length of thin white string. The price tags also had red dots on them — Silverman's.

Cuneo nodded. "We talked about it on the way in," he said. "If I were more cynical, I wouldn't believe this could have fallen together so perfectly all by itself."

"You are more cynical, Dan," his partner said. He turned to Gerson. "It wasn't just lying out, sir. Holiday had it hidden. Just not well enough."

"Don't get me wrong," Cuneo said. "I'm not complaining. I'll take it. Makes up for all the times nothing works. It's just so weird. I'm tempted to go buy a lottery ticket."

Gerson nodded. "And Thomasino

signed off on the search?"

"Yes, sir," Russell said.

"Okay, so what I suggest you do is go back to him right away . . ."

"He's at trial," Cuneo said.

"Interrupt his honor," Gerson replied. "He won't mind, I promise. Print yourselves out an arrest warrant and show him what his wisdom allowed you to discover. You'll make his day. You have any idea where Mr. Holiday is at the present time?"

"Dan called the Ark, sir, from the phone at his place as soon as we found this stuff. When a male voice answered, we hung up. We figure he can't have a clue we've made this kind of progress. Enough to arrest him. And it's got to be him working there now. His other bartender's dead."

"Good point. All right. So after the judge signs your warrant, you're going down to pick him up? You want some backup?"

Cuneo answered. "We can handle it, sir. He won't give us any trouble."

Gerson considered for a beat. "Okay, but by the book."

"Every time, sir," Russell said, nodding in agreement. "Every time."

"Glitsky. Payroll."

It rankled every time.

"Lieutenant? Barry Gerson again."

"Yes, sir." No emphasis. "What can I do for you?"

"Well, first I wanted to apologize for going so territorial on you the other day. I can't blame you for being interested in Silverman. Your father knew him. Of course you're interested. I was out of line."

"Thank you. What's second?"

The brusqueness of the reply slowed Gerson for a second, but then he recovered. "Second is I thought you'd want to know that Cuneo and Russell have been doing some incredible work these last couple of days. I believe they've gotten to the bottom of this thing with Silverman. At least they've got plenty that you can pass on to your father."

Suddenly the flat tone left Glitsky's voice. "I'm listening."

Gerson gave him the rundown on the evidence that so unambiguously pointed to Terry, Wills and Holiday — the gun in Terry's drawer, so clearly and demonstrably both the Silverman and Creed murder weapon. But also the red-dotted bills from both the Jones Street apartment and from Holiday's duplex in the marina. Although the lab hadn't finished its analysis of the gunk yet, Gerson threw in for good measure the shoes found in Terry's apartment and their probable relation to the Creed killing. The pawnshop jewelry articles in Holiday's closet. The case was solved, soup to nuts.

When Gerson finished, Glitsky exhaled heavily. "So that's it?"

"That's it."

"And Holiday killed the other two. Last night, was it?"

"Looks like. There's really no other option. Thomasino gave Cuneo and Russell a warrant in about five seconds. They've gone on down now to pick him up."

Glitsky spent a second or two adjusting to this new reality. The fundamental rule of his thirty years of life as a cop was that evidence talked, and in this case it positively screamed. He had been completely wrong, and his meddling had possibly even inconvenienced the good inspectors working the case. Maybe, he thought bitterly, payroll was where he belonged after all. He'd obviously lost his edge. He drew in a deep breath, let it out slowly. "Then I'm the one who should be apologizing, Lieutenant. If Wade Panos put your guys on the trail that led here, I must have pegged him wrong."

"That's not an issue for me, Abe." Glitsky noted the first name, a far cry from the "lieutenant" he'd started with. "You thought you were doing me a favor."

"I really did."

"I believe you. Some of these rent-a-cops . . . well, you know. They're not all righteous, we can go that far. But Panos had something real this time. We're lucky he felt cooperative. Anyway, if you've got something I need to hear in the future, my door's open. You put in a lot of years at this desk. I'd be an idiot if I didn't take advantage of that."

"Thanks, Barry. I appreciate it. But it's your gig now. I'm out of it."

"Maybe. But I'm reserving the right to come to you if something stumps me. Deal?"

"Deal."

When they hung up, Glitsky sat unmoving, turned away from his desk, staring out the window into the bright afternoon. He heard the wind whistling around his corner of the building. A deep sigh escaped. In spite of the kissy-face words, the hard truth settled over him like a shroud — in the real world, Glitsky would probably never set foot in homicide again. No one was even going to have to try to keep him out. The thing was done, a fait accompli.

It was the termination of all those years.

After a minute, he swiveled his chair, stood up and went over to the printing room to see how the paychecks were coming along. They were due out tomorrow morning. That was the priority now, the sum total of his professional importance — making sure those checks got out on time.

15

Holiday got Michelle's frantic call to the Ark during the afternoon lull. He had one customer, a fifty-something dot-com bankrupt named Wayne, and he shooed him out pleading illness. He was going to have to close up. After he'd locked the door behind Wayne, he took all the money from the cash register, walked to the back room, and unlocked the bottom left drawer of his desk. The drawer contained a Walther PPK .380 automatic wrapped in a greasy old T-shirt and a quarter box of ammunition that was at least six years old, and possibly more than that. Holiday had bought the gun when he'd first opened his pharmacy fifteen years ago — he had no memory of when he'd last taken it to the range, or bought any ammunition. In all his years in business, he'd never had occasion to take it out, even to brandish.

But he believed with all his heart that he had a reason now. He cranked a round into the chamber and snapped the safety off. He tucked the gun into his belt and the bullets into the pocket of his three-quarter-length leather coat. Letting himself out the back door of the Ark, he double-locked it up and started walking. He arrived at Michelle's an hour later.

Now they had been holed up inside for about another hour. It turned out, when Michelle accidentally saw the gun, that she wasn't much a fan of firearms. There had never been a gun in her parents' house when she was growing up. She wasn't going to tolerate one now. She had wanted to warn John about the police, but had never considered what it might really mean, who this man she'd been seeing really was.

When he showed up with a loaded gun, it more than worried her. It made her feel as though he'd duped her somehow.

So she'd told him no gun, he didn't need it here, she wouldn't have it in her apartment. If he was intent on keeping the gun, he had to leave. In the end, she reluctantly agreed to a wimpy compromise — he would unload it and put the gun and the ammunition out of sight in one of the bedroom drawers. She agreed not because she wanted to, she realized, but because suddenly some part of her was afraid of him.

She'd been attracted to him at the beginning — and consistently since — because she'd chosen to ignore all the outward signs that he might finally, at heart, not be the man he pretended to be. Now she was forced to consider that he might, in fact, be a true criminal. The seedy bar, the nomadic lifestyle, ex-convict associates, heavy drinking, even his own drug arrest. He had explained away all of those dark and telling realities with a lighthearted and eloquent insouciance, and she'd wanted to believe him in large part because of the powerful chemistry between them.

Clearly he had a sensitive side. He'd apparently endured great pain and loneliness after the loss of his wife and child. He was smart as a whip. He could be very funny. He was a great lover. She had convinced herself that most of the time he simply chose to hide his essential goodness from the world because people would take advantage of it. The same way she handled her physical beauty. This was something she could relate to, a defensive coloration.

But now, here he was in her private and special place with a loaded gun. The homicide police had been searching his duplex. *How blind was she?*

And now she'd not only helped him escape, she was harboring him.

When he had stowed the gun, he came over to where she stood looking, holding a crack in the blinds open with her finger, out the window over the city. When he put his arms around her from behind, he felt her stiffen. "What's the matter?"

She let go of the blinds, shrugged out of his embrace, took a step away, turned to face him. "Oh, nothing, John. Whatever could be the matter?"

He smoothed the side of his mustache. "I just put the gun away, Michelle. That's what you asked me to do."

She crossed her arms. "Where did you go Friday night?"

He cocked his head. "What was Friday night?"

"The night after Thursday, a week ago today, when you walked out on me. I know you remember. Chinatown. Where were you?"

"I don't know. Home, I guess." He strove to sound casual. "I can't believe how many people are interested in where I was every night this past week. Maybe I should make up a calendar and pass it around."

"Or maybe you could answer me."

"I just did, didn't I? I was home."

"On Friday night?"

He gave every indication of counting back the days, making sure. "Yep. I worked the day, handed it off to Clint, ate at Little Joe's, went home, watched TV, went to sleep."

"That's funny," she said.

"What is?"

"When I went by there today, when the police were there, I picked up your papers down at the bottom of the stairs, and there were three of them — Friday, Saturday, and Sunday."

"Michelle . . ."

She held up a hand. "Never mind. Don't even start. I'm going out for a walk. You and your gun don't have to be here when I get back."

Roake had been a defense attorney for twenty-one of her forty-eight years. After graduating from King Law School at UC Davis, she passed the bar and, at twenty-five, took her first job with the San Francisco District Attorney's office. Two years later, genetically predisposed to favoring the underdog and the dispossessed, the unfortunate and the unlucky, she switched to the defense trade. There she was often unsuccessful, although typically defense attorneys would under the normal definition be considered to fail most of the time. (A ripping success is often an accepted plea to a slightly lesser offense, or eight years in the slammer for the client instead of twelve.) After thirteen years working mostly with and for other lawyers, she finally hung out her own shingle and had done exceedingly well exclusively handling criminal cases.

Unlike Lennard Faro, who believed he had seen it all, Gina Roake *had* seen it all. She had defended clients — and come to know them as people, as far as this was possible — from the netherworld of the gene pool all the way up to educated professionals and wealthy business people: suburban housewives turned murderers, children who'd killed their parents, addicts of every drug known to mankind, sexual criminals from simple misfits to the truly perverted, thieves, rapists, con men, pickpockets, shoplifters (lots of shoplifters!), lowlifes, gangbangers and muggers. A million drunk drivers. Nothing surprised her. Humans were flawed, but worth defending.

And so, she felt, was the system. Her job, her lifework — keeping some balance between the two — meant providing the best defense the law allowed to those who had fallen. Everyone had a demon; most people had several, from grinding poverty to sexual abuse, from unseen psychic trauma to pampered irresponsibility, and these demons *would* be served, forcing their victims to commit crimes against themselves and against the society that had maimed and scarred them. She'd always believed that the crimes should be justly punished, but that the criminals themselves — the human beings who did these things — ought to be viewed with an eye to mercy, with an understanding of what had led them to their acts.

This was why now she felt so adrift, so foreign to herself. Along with the grief to which she had not even begun yet to grow accustomed, her desire for vengeance against the people who had done this to David — *to David!* — was making her feel, quite literally, insane. "If I knew who they were, Dismas. I swear to God, if they were here in front of me, I would personally beat them to death. Gladly."

Unable to concentrate, Hardy had left work early again. He had a Band-Aid of a splint around the pinkie and ring fingers on his left hand, but the others were intertwined on the table between them in the hospital's tiny coffee shop. Cups sat untouched in front of them. "I'd say that's natural, Gina."

"It's not for me; that's my point. It's the polar opposite of everything I've ever believed. I would literally kill the sons of bitches."

"I doubt that."

"Try me." She brought her hands up to her face and wiped a palm down each side of it. "Oh, God, what am I saying? I'm losing it here, Dismas; I really am. What am I going to do with this?"

"Have you slept yet? At all?"

A brittle laugh collapsed into a pitiable cough. "I'm sorry," she said when she'd caught her breath. "No. Sleep has not happened. Not to you either, I'd say."

He didn't want to burden her with his own problems, his own fury and fears. He forced a smile. "I had a little bit of a tough night last night, that's all. Car problems. Have you seen him?"

She nodded. "They let me in whenever they can now. An hour or two. I try to tell myself he's squeezing my hand back or something, but . . ." She shook her head in misery, bit her lip. Then, as though if she said it aloud it would be more true, she whispered, "His kidney function seems to be slowing down."

"Is that bad?"

"It's one of the things they measure. Of course if it stops entirely, it would be bad." Closing her eyes, she sighed deeply. "I'm trying to prepare myself. I just feel so . . . so helpless and then so goddamned furious. I'm in there pleading with him, talking out loud like he can hear me, like I'm . . ." The words stopped. She looked across at Hardy. "You don't need to hear this. You know."

He reached across the table and put his hand over hers. "You're a big girl so I don't have to tell you, but if you could sleep, it would help. Especially if you can't do anything here."

"I keep thinking maybe he'll wake up and if he does I won't be there."

"He'd get over it. He might not even notice. No, never mind. It's David. He'd notice." He shrugged. "Still . . ."

"Still, you're probably right. Oh, and Sergeant Blanca came by here for a few minutes. He said he'd talked to you. He didn't have much."

"He still doesn't, not as of about a half hour ago."

A silence. Then Gina said, "They're not going to find anything, are they? I wonder if it's somebody I got off. If some scumbag was back on the street because I was such a goddamned whiz of a lawyer. Wouldn't that be special?"

Hardy squeezed her hand. "Don't go there."

"I don't know where I'm going."

Hardy hesitated for an instant, then decided that he'd known her for a long time. He could push a little. "Gina. Sorry to be a broken record, but how about going home, then to bed? Give the nurses your number. They'll call you if there's any change. This isn't doing anybody any good."

"I'll still want to kill them," she said. Somehow the comment didn't seem off the subject. It was as though they'd been talking about it all along.

"I hear you," Hardy said gently. "If it's any help, so do I."

When she saw Holiday wasn't gone, Michelle stood just inside her doorway, uncertain about whether she should simply turn and give him more time, or walk out and call the police herself. But she hesitated long enough for him to start explaining.

The television droned near him. He stood in front of it, his coat back on. She assumed he had rearmed himself.

"I'm sorry. I didn't expect you back so soon." He took a tentative step toward her, then stopped. "Look, I'm sorry about everything. I didn't mean to lie to you. I've got a bad habit of . . . never mind, it doesn't matter anymore. I'm going now in a minute. I just wanted to catch the news. Maybe see if they'll show what I'm up against."

Still in her camo gear, including hat and boots, she came up next to him as the program began, then backed up and sat on the corner of the bed.

Since it was both local and lurid, they didn't have to wait long. The handsome and serious anchor hadn't gotten twenty words into the lead story when Holiday nearly jumped forward to turn up the volume. " . . . these grisly Tenderloin murders. The victims have been identified as Clint Terry and Randy Wills. Terry, a bartender at a downtown watering hole, was a former football star with the . . ."

"Oh my God." Holiday folded himself down to the floor, cross-legged. As the anchor continued with the details, his head fell forward. After a minute, he reached up to support it with his hands, rocking his whole body from side to side.

On the television, the story continued, running through a cursory review of the related killings and a tantalizing film clip of Crime Scene Investigators removing allegedly "highly significant evidence" from the scene, and closing with the not entirely surprising news, though no less unwelcome for that, that the chief suspect for that crime and also the murders last week of Sam Silverman and Matthew Creed, was John Holiday.

He finally glanced up again at the mention of his name. His four-year-old mug shot filled the screen as the anchor finished up with the words that a warrant had been issued for his arrest and that he should be considered armed and dangerous. As they cut to the next story, Michelle walked to the set, picked the remote off the top of it, killed the power.

Head in his hands, Holiday still rocked his whole body on the floor — back and forth, side to side.

"John?" She reached over and touched his shoulder. "John, are you okay?"

When he looked up, she wasn't sure he even saw her. His eyes shone with panic. His voice, when it came, was a suddenly ravaged and hoarse whisper. "I don't believe Clint and Randy are *dead*. They can't be just dead."

She lowered herself down to the floor, facing him. He kept shaking his head from side to side. She reached out and put a hand on his knee, and she left it there.

The sun descended enough so that a few bars of sunlight through the blinds inched up the wall over her bed. A dog barked somewhere in the neighborhood, the call was taken up by another; then both died away.

Eventually, Holiday cleared his throat one time, again, didn't meet her eyes, then began quietly, matter-of-factly. "What I do, see, is find somebody like you and then try to fuck it all up, cheat on you or do something else you can't forgive . . ."

"Shut up," she said. "Just shut up. I get it. You don't think I get it? I know what you do, what you always do. You know why? 'Cause I do it, too. It keeps things manageable, doesn't it, making people you might love hate you when they start to get close? So my question to you is, 'What are you going to do now?' I'm talking with you and me."

"You told me to get out."

"Right. And you didn't leave. You had most of an hour. What does that mean about us? Anything? Or were you just afraid to go out because of . . . because of all this? And don't tell me you needed to find out what they were saying on the television."

"No."

"What then? If your plan is to hang around and have a few more fights and go out on me to make me hate you, I can save you some trouble. Just walk out now, no hard feelings. Because do it again and I *will* hate you. I promise." She stood up and went back over to the window, checked the blinds again. She turned back to him. "You didn't kill any of those people, did you?"

"No. I've never killed anybody."

"Do you know who did?"

He nodded soberly. "The same people who planted whatever they found in my apartment." He looked up at her. "I don't understand this at all, Michelle. The last I heard, the police were talking to Clint about Mr. Silverman, and now they're both dead."

She'd been pacing and now stopped over by the bed. "That lawyer who defended you last time . . ." Suddenly, her hands came up. "Christ, I don't believe I'm talking about this. Lawyers and killers and planted evidence. I don't want this stuff in my life, John. I really don't."

402

He got up and came over to her. "It's not my first choice either, Michelle. I'm not making this happen. I don't want to be around it, either. I don't even know what it is. If this thing ever ends, maybe I'll make some changes."

"Maybe. Some. Wow."

"All right, not maybe. Definitely, and maybe a lot. But first there's this, wouldn't you agree? What were you asking me about my lawyer?"

"Just that aren't you still friends?"

"So where are you now, John?"

"At a friend's. I locked up the Ark and I'm not going home."

"Ah, intelligent behavior at last. And so what do you want me to do?"

"I don't know. Talk to somebody. Whatever you do. I didn't do this, Diz, none of it. I loved Clint. I liked Sam and Matt. I don't know how anything got into my apartment. This whole thing is too weird."

"I haven't had much luck with the too-weird-to-be-real defense, John." Hardy sighed. "All right. You said there was a warrant? For your arrest?"

"That's what was on the news. You can check it out for yourself."

"I will. But in the meanwhile, I want you

to think about something. If in fact there's a warrant out on you, my only option as your lawyer is to advise you to turn yourself in. If you don't, I can't have anything more to do with you."

"Turn myself in for what?"

"See if you can guess, John."

"But I didn't do it."

"All right."

"You don't believe me?"

"That's beside the point. If there's already a warrant for your arrest, about the best I can do is arrange your surrender."

"That's you the lawyer, Diz. What about you my friend?"

"I'm afraid we're the same person, John. Look, if you won't take my advice, why don't we both think about it overnight? You think about it, I'll think about it. One of us might come up with something."

"What about now?"

"What about it?"

"I come over now to your place. We get something figured out."

"Then if I don't call the police, I'm harboring a fugitive and lose my license. And though I love you like a brother, I couldn't do you any good if I'm disbarred." He paused. "Look, why don't you call me at my office tomorrow morning? Something might have changed by then. I'll talk to the DA, see what they're going with. Meanwhile, you say nobody knows where you are? I'm guessing you're not that uncomfortable. Just lie low."

"Diz . . . this isn't exactly what I was hoping to hear."

"What can I tell you, John? It's the best I can do."

Watching his television at home, Nat Glitsky had heard the news of the awful Tenderloin murders and then of the arrest warrant that had been issued in Sam Silverman's death. Now he was in his son's kitchen, sitting at the table having tea with his dessert, Abe's day-old macaroons. For the first time since Rachel's birth, the Hardys hadn't shown up yesterday at the conclusion of their Date Night, so there was a full plate of them.

Nat dipped his cookie into his tea, blew on it, put the softened morsel to his granddaughter's lips. "Your daughter, she loves these," he said.

"Everybody loves them." Treya was standing behind her husband's chair, her hands on Abe's shoulders. "Dismas Hardy thinks Abe should go into business making them. Abe's Manna Macaroons."

"Such a name," Nat said. "A name is an important thing. That Dismas, he's not so dumb."

Abe liked that. "I'll tell him you said so. He's a glutton for praise. 'Not so dumb' ought to make his week."

Nat teased Rachel's lips with the remainder of his macaroon, then brought it to his own mouth and popped it in. The baby's little hand reached out. Her face fell in shocked surprise. A second later, her smile returned as a fresh cookie appeared in Nat's grasp. He let her grab it and they played tug of war for a second or two before he let it go. She laughed in pure joy, stuffing the spoils of victory into her mouth. "Such a good girl," Nat said. "I see great things. Someday she becomes the owner of Abraham's Manna Macaroons."

"Abe's," Treya said. "Not Abraham's."

"Shorter," Glitsky said. "Punchier. Maybe I will go into baking after all." Treya had come around behind Rachel and gave him a look.

He gave her the same look back. "Baking's a noble profession. Baker's have been baking probably longer than cops have been . . ."

"Copping?" Treya offered a tight smile. "It won't be too much longer. A couple of months, he said."

"Two months can be a long time if you're in thumbscrews."

Nat nearly sprang forward out of his chair leaning over the table. "He says thumbscrews, plural. I don't even see one." He sat back down as though he'd proven something. "And for all the moaning and groaning, who did they call as soon as they knew about Sam?"

"I believe that was Lieutenant Glitsky," Treya said. "The pariah of Bryant Street."

"Courtesy only."

"Courtesy, he says." Nat wasn't buying.

"I heard him." Neither was Treya. She finally sat down at the table. "And since the only thing of interest and importance in the world, and hence the only thing worth talking about — never mind the precious lives of infants — is a homicide investigation, it just occurred to me that I'll bet this is why Dismas and Frannie didn't come by last night. He's still John Holiday's attorney, isn't he?"

Abe nodded. "I would think so."

But Nat exploded. "Wait a minute. What am I hearing here? This man who killed Sam? He's with Dismas?"

"He was," Abe said. "I'd bet he still is."

"He's trying to get him off?"

"I haven't heard Holiday's even been arrested yet, Dad. But when he is, yeah. That's what Diz does."

Nat sat unhappily with this intelligence for a second. "He'd do this, this defense work, for a man who's killed four people. Did you see what this animal did to those men last night?"

He shook his head. "No. I'd only heard they'd been killed."

"Only killed would have been mercy," Nat said.

He went on to tell his son some of the details he'd picked up. When he finished, Treya made a face of disgust, then asked, "And Holiday is wanted for all of these murders?"

Abe picked up something in her tone. He wasn't going to pursue it aloud right here. But in the past year, he and Treya had met John Holiday a few times at the Hardys'. He had seemed okay to Abe; Treya had positively liked him. And Glitsky very much trusted his wife's instincts. He had seen enough of killings and murderers that he considered almost anyone, under the right conditions, capable of the act. But he'd never seen a sign nor heard from Hardy that Holiday used drugs, the great instigator of horrible, irrational violence. If Holiday had been robbing Silverman's store and got interrupted, if Creed had chased him into a blind alley, maybe . . .

But the scenario with Terry and Wills, as his father had just explained it?

"What?" Nat asked, seeing the look between them.

Abe hesitated. Then, "Nothing," he said.

16

Rebecca sat down to the plate of scrambled eggs her father had cooked for her. This morning, he'd cooked them for Frannie and Vincent as well, but neither of them typically appeared at the breakfast table until ten minutes after the Beck. By this time, whatever hot meal Hardy had prepared would have cooled — to him, cold scrambled eggs were an affront to nature — although his wife and son didn't seem to notice, much less mind.

His daughter took a first bite, said, "Yum!" then looked around. She didn't miss much and wasn't easy to fool. "Where's the paper?" she asked her father.

He casually sipped his coffee. "I don't know."

She put down her fork. "What's in it?"

"What do you mean? What's in what?"

"The paper."

"I just said I didn't know where it was."

She gave a theatrical sigh. "As if."

"As if," he repeated, striving to match the teenage inflection.

She ignored that. "As if you didn't go out to the porch and get it like you do every single morning. Is it one of your clients?"

It was his turn to sigh. He and Frannie had discussed it, along with the spin they would put on the smashed car window, and had decided it would be better for the kids if Hardy could get a few facts about the crimes for which John Holiday was likely to be arrested before he tried to explain it to them. Holiday wasn't exactly Uncle John yet, as Uncle Abe was, but he'd been by the house a few times in the past year, almost immediately endearing himself to both children, although for different reasons. He treated Rebecca in a sincere and courtly manner that flattered her vanity; Vincent he treated like a grown man, no kid stuff. He played catch with him, arm-wrestled, had taken both Hardy men to 49er and Giants games.

As the kids had gotten older, they had both become, as Hardy was, addicts of the morning *Chronicle*. Rebecca, particularly, loved the back page of the Scene section — the columnists and the In Crowd. Vincent, emulating his dad, would peruse Jeff Elliot's "CityTalk" column every day, but his favorite was Thursdays, when McHugh and Stienstra did their respective great stuff on the Outdoors page. Hardy and Frannie had promoted this interest from its first flowering over the comics — it was important to keep up on the news, on what people thought, what was happening in the world. Life wasn't lived in a vacuum.

But there could also be the occasional drawback, as for example when your client and friend happened to be the main suspect in four murders, two of them incredibly grotesque.

"Who is it?" Rebecca asked.

Hardy threw a glance at the ceiling, then looked straight at her. "John Holiday."

"No way!"

"I'm afraid so."

"Not John. There's no way, Dad. What are they saying he did?"

She was going to find out anyway. Still, he hesitated, then decided it would be impossible to soften it. "They're saying he killed some people."

"That's the stupidest thing I ever heard. John wouldn't ever kill anybody. He *couldn't!*"

"I don't think so either."

"And what you do mean, *some?*"

"Four."

"*Four?* Dad, come on."

"It's not me, Beck. I don't think he killed anybody, either. But they found some evidence in his house . . ." He stopped, reached out, and put a hand over hers. "Look. Beck. I'm going to talk to him today; then I'll have a better idea where we stand. But I didn't want you guys to see the paper this morning, okay? Two of the —"

But her temper was up, and she cut him off. "What are they saying he did?"

"Well, that's just it. You don't want to know. Not right now."

"*Yes I do!*" Suddenly, she pushed back from the table. Her chair fell over and she was on her feet. "He's my friend, too. You can't censor us like that."

Hardy knew he sounded like a pathetic adult. Still, he couldn't stop himself. "It's not censoring, it's . . ."

"It is, too. Where is it? I want to see."

"Beck . . ." He was up, too. "Please don't . . ."

But she ran by him, through the kitchen and out to the little anteroom in the back where they stored their recyclables. By the time he got to her, she'd already dug it out

413

from where he'd buried it. She was emitting little whimpering noises, as an injured puppy might. Finally, she turned to him with her hand over her mouth, her eyes overflowing. "Oh God!" she said. "Oh God!"

Then Vincent was standing behind them. "What? What's going on?"

Most of an hour got killed while Hardy dropped his rental and picked up his own car with its new windshield. Again he stopped at the hospital. Again David had not improved.

When he finally arrived at Sutter Street, it was close to nine o'clock, normally a bustling hour, but the office had an extremely subdued feel. The reception desk, Phyllis's domain, sat empty. As he stood there, one of the phones started ringing. He just let it go.

The lights in the lobby had yet to be turned on. The door to the office at the far end of the lobby that housed Norma, the office manager, was closed and through the blinds he could see Phyllis in there. She seemed to be wiping at her eyes. The Solarium was empty. No secretaries were gossiping by the coffeemachine/Xerox area. Hardy took a few steps so he could

414

see down the hallway, and was relieved to see people — secretaries and paralegals — at their desks, but most of the doors to the associates' cubicles seemed to be closed. People were hunkering down, lying low.

One of the doors was open in the long hallway on the main floor, and he walked down to it and looked inside. Amy Wu was at her desk, scribbling furiously on a yellow legal pad. Hardy knocked on the door and she looked up, smiling feebly out of politeness. "Hi. How's David?"

"The same, I'm sorry to report. It's pretty quiet out here."

"Is it? I haven't noticed. Jon — my paralegal? — he called in sick so I've been running pages to word processing all morning. I've got this memo that needs to be filed today, so —" Suddenly she stopped, put her pencil all the way down. "I'm sorry. Who cares, right? How are you doing? What happened to your hand?"

He held it up. "Stupid accident. Me, I'm trying to get motivated to go upstairs and face some work."

"Join the club. I think I'm the only one down here who's been able to get going on anything, and that's only because I'd fire myself if I was late on this filing after all the work I've already done." She motioned

415

with her head. "Everybody else . . . well, you noticed."

He nodded. "I can't blame anybody. I feel the same way." He paused, took a breath, came out with it. "But I wonder if I could ask you a favor."

"Then you'll owe me one, but sure. What is it?"

"Could you keep an eye out down here, give me a call when people start coming out their door, getting back to work?" At her questioning look, he added, "I was hoping I could tap some of the talent down here. I need some people in a hurry if we want to keep up with depositions on Panos. We're talking megahours."

Something was going on in Wu's brain. Her eyes narrowed; then she nodded. "Sure. First sign of life, I'll buzz you."

"Thanks. In fact, after you're done with your memo, maybe . . ."

But she was shaking her head no. "I can't, Diz. I'm overwhelmed, especially if David's out for a while. I've got to call Jon at home though. It just occurred to me, if he's not really sick, if he just decided this was a sinking ship . . ." She stopped and sighed heavily. "If he dies, then what? Is all this keeping up with his work just me being stupid?"

"He's still got clients, Amy. They're still going to need good lawyers. That's what David's been training you for, isn't it? It's why I need a few bodies around here. David or no David, Panos is going to be huge."

"So you're really going ahead on that?"

"I really am." He narrowed his eyes. "Of course I am. Why would you even ask that?"

"No reason, really." But after wrestling with herself for a minute, she came out with it. "I've just heard some rumors around here that that's why David got beat up, that it had to do with Panos, with scaring him off. Evidently, David himself mentioned something about it to Graham, talking about his bullet-proof self of course. Now, with this — everybody's heard it by now — so even if you're assigning billable hours, people might be a little reluctant, especially with you not really in the firm."

This was the first time Hardy had run up against this question. He'd always considered his irregular status vis-à-vis Freeman & Associates an unalloyed good thing. He was merely the upstairs tenant and friend of the firm's owner, and as such was neither fish nor fowl — not associate, not partner, not even Of Counsel, and a bit of a loose cannon at that. He loved the freedom of it, the independence. When David threw him work, he was often happy to take it.

But now he wondered if he could successfully assign it back to the formal associates, who in David's long-term absence (to say nothing of his death) might be out pounding the pavement for work before too long.

Among the associates, Hardy thought he could count on Graham Russo, who had once been his client and with whom he still had a good personal relationship. And maybe, in a week or more — after she worked down her current load — he might be able to use Amy. But other help from among David's legions was problematic at best. And if David died, the ancillary support — Norma and Phyllis and the secretaries and paralegals who worked with the other associates — would all dry up overnight. With his limited resources, Hardy wouldn't stand a chance.

He could promise all the billable hours in the world, but none of the associates would be laboring under any illusion. Since it was a contingency lawsuit, if they didn't win, those hours would be written off. And what could he pay them in the meanwhile? Hardy couldn't float an island of suits, betting on the come, the way Freeman could.

The Panos lawsuit would be over before it began.

It was a morning of first revelations. Aside from his realization about the tenuousness of his position among the associates, for the first time it struck him how effective the violence against Freeman had been. Was. Especially if he didn't survive. Far from being the blunt instrument it had first appeared to be, the mugging was effectively a scalpel that separated him both from the lawsuit and the other associates.

For the sad truth was that Hardy alone had no power in the Panos matter. The plaintiffs were all the clients of David Freeman, not Dismas Hardy. Some he hadn't even met. Hardy wasn't any kind of real player, any kind of significant danger or threat to Panos, but merely a fly to be flicked away without a second thought. The realization washed over him like an acid bath. He must have shown it.

"Diz? Are you all right?"

He flashed a false grin. "Fine," he said. "I'm fine. I'm just thinking about how to do all I've got today. If Norma comes out of her office, would you ask her to please give me a call?"

Hardy's office was one flight up from the lobby, the only occupied room on the third floor. He took the stairs two at a time. His office door was closed, but a light shone under it from within. He stopped short of the opening, heard a quiet and dull but unmistakable thud, then after a moment, another one — someone was pounding something against his wall while he waited for Hardy to arrive. Putting down his briefcase, he stealthily tried the knob, which didn't give at all. He'd had enough experience with muggings and surprise mischief over the past couple of days that he wasn't anxious to get any more, and he turned back to the stairway.

The police could be here in ten minutes and whoever had broken into his office could explain it all to them.

Halfway down the stairs, a voice stopped him. "Diz?" Holiday stood at the top of the stairs, grinning down at him, holding three darts up. "I thought I heard somebody pounding on up the stairs, but I wanted to finish my round. Where are you going?"

Hardy climbed back up the seven steps he'd just descended. "I was just going to call the police, John. That would have been a good time." He reached the landing again and led the way inside, then closed the door behind Holiday. "How did you get in here? Wasn't the door locked? It was. And what were you doing?"

"Just shooting some darts. There was a bunch of keys down at the reception desk, and nobody was there. I thought you'd be up here in your office, to tell you the truth. Then when you weren't, I figured I'd just let myself in. I put the keys back."

"Good for you."

"This place is a ghost town today. Where is everybody?"

"It's a legal holiday." Hardy said it without a trace of irony.

"Hm. Well. But you're here, I notice, although you are a little late, aren't you?"

Hardy wasn't even slightly in the mood to explain his various delays of the morning, especially since the beginning of it all had been the breakdown of his children over the very client he now faced. "We had an appointment," Hardy said by way of explanation, "except if you remember, you were supposed to call me. Do you remember that? Wasn't that what we decided?"

Holiday shrugged and walked back over

to the dart line. "Either way, we're talking."

Hardy got around his desk and put his briefcase on the top of it. "That's true, John, but I'm your attorney and I happen to know that there's a warrant out for your arrest, so all I can do now, as I thought I explained rather clearly last night, is help you turn yourself in." Hardy's voice took on an edge. "How about putting those things down a minute and talking to me?"

Immediately, Holiday whirled, all contrition. He placed his two remaining darts on Hardy's desk and spread his hands apologetically. "I thought we were talking. What happened to your hand?"

Hardy glanced down at his Band-Aid splint. He was going to have to invent a witty response pretty soon, but he didn't have the energy for it right now. "I whacked it against something." He sat down behind his desk. "Look, I'm sorry, John, but I'm a little stressed. But I suppose you are, too."

"Naw. It's just another arrest warrant." Holiday went over to the couch, plopped himself down on it. "So what do you think? What's the plan?"

"I wish I had one. I'm assuming you're not inclined to give yourself up."

"Good guess."

"Well, as your attorney, that's all I'm allowed to suggest."

"How about not as my attorney? I haven't paid you anything, have I? Can't we just be friends?"

Hardy's mouth turned up an inch. "Can't we all just get along?"

"Exactly, and apparently not too well. But you and me, we could."

"But even as just your friend, I'm still harboring you, and you're a fugitive."

Holiday shrugged. "Tell them I held you hostage or something."

"Though it might not be a bad idea, you know. Turning yourself in."

Holiday's eyes went wide. "You're out of your mind, Diz. I wouldn't last fifteen minutes in jail."

"Why not? You've been there before. It wouldn't be any worse than last time."

"Yeah, except this time someone would kill me."

"Why would they do that?"

"Because that's what these guys are doing, Diz. Think about it. I'm the only one left and the case is closed. As soon as I'm dead, it's a tight little package. Nobody goes looking for who really did it."

"And who are these people?" A grin

flickered around Hardy's mouth. "You're saying they're cops? They can get you in jail?"

"They planted stuff in my apartment."

"The cops did? Why?"

"I don't know why, but it's not as far-fetched as you think. It happens."

"I'm sure it does, John, I'm sure it does." Hardy scratched at the top of his desk blotter. "Look, humor me a minute. If you've got solid alibis for all the murders, we could press for a quick prelim and have you out of there and cleared of all this in a week or two at the most."

"Not if I'm dead first."

"That's not going to happen. Not in jail. Do you know where you were when any of these last three men got killed?"

"Sure. Two of them, Randy and Clint, I'm positive. I was at work. In fact, you know, a cop came by the Ark the other day, before I even knew about Randy and Clint, and asked me if I'd been tending bar there the night before."

"What do you mean, a cop? A real cop? SFPD?"

"I thought so. The badge looked right. Some Chinese guy. He wasn't with Panos, I'll tell you that."

"And he asked you what?"

"Just if I'd been working at midnight the night before and could I prove it? I told him yeah and it seemed to satisfy him. That's why I'm blown away they got a warrant for me. I mean, they *know* I didn't kill Clint and Randy. I don't get it."

"So what about Creed?"

"Same thing. It was a work night, though there weren't as many customers, but somebody would remember. So maybe they think I wasn't the actual shooter with Creed anyway. I was just in cahoots with Clint and Randy." Holiday had gone into a full recline on the sofa, his hands crossed behind his head.

Hardy sat for a long moment, picking at the Band-Aid. "You mind telling me again where you were the night Silverman got it? Last time we talked about it, not to put too fine a point on it, your alibi sucked."

Holiday got himself up to sitting again. He ran a hand through his hair, tugged at the side of his mustache. When he spoke, he wore a sheepish expression. "If you want to know the truth, my girlfriend and I had a fight and I went out and picked up somebody else, who I couldn't find again to save my life."

"That's what it might be, John. To save your life."

He shook his head.

"Did you go to her house?" Hardy asked.

"Yeah. Well, apartment, I think."

"So where was it?"

"She drove," Holiday said. "I dozed. I don't know."

"What about in the morning?"

Holiday made a face. "There wasn't any morning. I left right after . . . anyway, I think I wandered around a bit."

"Drunk?"

"Possibly. Likely."

Hardy frowned. "Which means you really have no alibi at all for Silverman, is that right?" He didn't wait for an answer. "So where did you call from yesterday?"

"My girlfriend's."

A beat. "Another one?"

"The real one."

"The one you broke up with on Thursday?"

"Yeah. Her name's Michelle. I'm staying at her place."

"I'm happy for you. That's so special. So the story about the important man's wife . . ."

"I made it up."

"Great!" Hardy said. "Swell. Let me ask you this. The paper said you lost a lot of money at Silverman's game the night before he died. Is that true?"

"Okay, but I didn't go to steal it back. I didn't, Diz. I swear to you."

"You swear to me. That helps. You swore to me about your alibi." Hardy shook his head angrily. "It might have been nice to know some of this a week ago." Collecting himself, he drew in a long, slow breath and let it out heavily. "Okay, John, suddenly my idea that you turn yourself in because you couldn't have committed any of the murders isn't so doable. Any one of them is good enough." He looked straight at him. "How am I supposed to believe you didn't do this after all? You got any suggestions?"

"I'm telling you. You know me, Diz."

"Right. But these lies, John. I can't think of a reason you'd lie to a *friend* if you weren't trying to hide something."

"I felt bad about the way things had gone with Michelle. I didn't want to bring her into it. That's the truth. I swear to God."

Hardy was still working on his response to that when on his desk, the telephone rang, his direct line. He reached for it. "Dismas Hardy." Listening for a moment, he sat up straighter, uttered a syllable or two, listened some more. He put a finger

427

to his lips and pointed at Holiday. He talked into the receiver. "Sure, I read all about it this morning. I wondered whether —"

As he spoke, he reached out and pushed down on the button, breaking the connection in his midsentence. "That was a homicide inspector named Russell," he said, "asking if I'd seen you recently. Somebody must have told him that I represented you last time and he thought you might have looked me up again."

"That was probably me. He and his partner came by the bar."

"And you gave them my name?"

"Yeah."

"Terrific, John. Just great. You're batting about a thousand here with bad moves."

"I know, Diz. I know. I'm sorry. Did he say where he was?"

"He didn't get a chance. We can hope it was the Hall. But I think you'd be smart to get out of here right now. I don't want to know where you are when they ask me, which they will. I'd be surprised if they think you're here now, but to be safe go down through the garage and out the back. Now go! Call me in an hour. We'll think of something. I'll be here. Go! Go!"

When the phone rang a minute later,

Hardy picked it up again. "Inspector Russell? Sorry about that. We're having the devil of a time with the phones lately here. I don't know what it is, except aggravating. You, too, huh? I think it's everybody. But you were asking about John Holiday? I'm afraid I don't know where he is. He's no longer my client."

Russell said he'd talked to Holiday just two days before and he'd mentioned Hardy by name as his attorney. Said they were close friends. Saw each other all the time.

"I hate to say this, Inspector," Hardy said. "But the man's been known to lie. Sure. Anytime. Good luck."

The lab tests from the Terry/Wills crime scene indicated that the stuff on the shoe in Terry's closet closely matched the gunk Thieu had collected at the Creed scene the day before — brake fluid, animal fats, peanuts and pepper flakes, no doubt from Kung Pao chicken.

Thieu was at his desk comparing the written transcription of a taped recording of one of his witness's interviews to the tape itself. While Russell was on the phone with Holiday's lawyer, trying to track the suspect down, Cuneo read over the lab report on the shoe and decided to thank the veteran inspector and to share the good news with him. "Pretty cool, huh?"

Thieu put the report down. "That's enough matches for me. It's the same stuff, all right. Nice work. And I see you found more evidence at Holiday's place."

"It's been a lucky couple of days," Cuneo said.

"If you believe in luck."

"What do you mean by that?"

"Nothing, really. It's just so rare when things fall together so well."

"I said the same thing to Gerson, but what am I supposed to do, look a gift horse in the mouth? This is about as solid as it gets."

Thieu made no comment to that. He had put down the transcript and his pencil. Now he took off his earphones and hooked them around his neck. He looked piercingly at Cuneo. "After I left the Terry/Wills scene yesterday, did you find anything that put Holiday there?"

"Not directly, no. But later in the day we did find money and jewelry from Silverman's at his place."

Thieu acknowledged that with a nod. "I heard about that. But no bloody clothes or shoes? Anything tying him directly to

Terry and Wills? There was an awful lot of blood."

"He hadn't been back there, where he lived. There were three or four days' worth of newspapers down on his stoop."

"Ah, that would explain it then."

"Maybe he slept in his bar, I don't know. Or he's shacked up with somebody." Cuneo had pulled a chair around and was straddling it backward. He started tapping a beat with his fingers. "But that's a good call. We'll check the dumpsters and alleys between the Ark and Terry's."

"You can't ever have too much, I don't believe." Thieu leaned back in his chair and folded his hands over his middle. Then he smiled politely and, wishing Cuneo luck again, said he had to get back to his editing.

17

Holiday's phone call did not come one hour later as Hardy had suggested, so he had filled his increasingly wide-open morning with visits downstairs to less-than-enthusiastic associates and calls to his deposition witnesses in the Panos suit. He needed to bring them up to date on Freeman's condition and rearrange his calendar so that they could get back on some kind of schedule by, say, the middle of next week. If David still wasn't up to appearing, then Hardy would try to go it alone, or with minimal help, for a while.

It galled him, but he knew he might have to revisit the question of Kroll's settlement offer — four million was starting to look pretty good to him about now. But whether that or any offer was still on the table was uncertain. Hardy himself had already billed something in the order of three hundred hours to the matter in the past four months and now stood to lose all of that time and money if he couldn't make some magic in the relatively short term. So he talked to clients and filled time.

Three full hours after Holiday had ducked out of his office, his call-waiting signal went off. In his mind, by now he had just about come to the conclusion that Inspector Russell had staked out his office after all and that John had been arrested leaving it. And that after he was processed, Hardy would get the phone call.

He asked the client to hold a second, connected to the other line.

No hello, no identification of any kind. Just the words, "Big Dick," repeated twice. Then a dead line.

After he finished talking to the client, Hardy hung up and stared into the empty space between his desk and his dartboard.

The voice had been Holiday's, and he had obviously formed the impression that Hardy's phone might be tapped. Hardy reflected that he also thought someone might kill him in jail. He might have found this paranoia amusing if he had any patience left.

Hardy thought about it for another thirty or forty seconds, then stood, threw the last two of Holiday's morning darts into his board — two elevens — and walked out, making sure the door was locked behind him. In the lobby, some semblance of normalcy had returned. Phyllis had returned to reception and her presence was somehow reassuring. One of the associates sat with a client, visible through the glass walls of the Solarium. Norma's door was open and he saw her at her desk, talking on the telephone. Above all, a slight but audible hum permeated the open space. People were here, trying to carry on.

Okay, he thought. Okay.

When Hardy pulled his car out of the garage, he saw that the day had become overcast again. Gray, with hovering wisps and banks of fog that he drove into and out of as he fought the noon traffic. He decided that the first thing he would do when he got to Holiday was have the billing conversation. Friends or no friends, he was going to get a retainer up front before doing any work for John Holiday. He couldn't afford to work for free anymore. He was going to charge his top defense fee and three times that for every minute he spent in the courtroom. Holiday could sell his bar or his duplex to cover his costs for all Hardy cared. He was done with charity.

Fortunately, the phrase "Big Dick" meant something to Hardy besides the standard reading — it was Holiday's name for Coit Tower, the phallic landmark and vista point at the apex of Telegraph Hill. Hardy had worked himself up to a fine fettle by the time he serpentined up the winding streets and reached the parking lot. This spot with its mounted binoculars all along its retaining wall, was premier sightseeing turf — Alcatraz, the Golden Gate Bridge, Sausalito and the Marin headlands, seemingly a stone's throw across the Bay.

At this time of day, normally the lot was cluttered with vacationers and tourist buses. But as Hardy pulled into one of the parking spaces and opened his car door — he'd had his windshield wipers going from halfway up the hill — he marveled at the sense of desertion. The place was wrapped in a thick, bone-chilling gauze of cloud and drizzle. He could barely make out the tower itself, looming there right behind him. He was completely alone up here today, his car the only one in the lot.

Leave it to Holiday, he thought. Why couldn't they meet at some restaurant, or even his new girlfriend's house? Hell, any-place else would be more convenient and comfortable than here. But of course, Holiday hadn't given Hardy any chance to argue, or suggest an alternative.

And now there was no sight of him here, either. Hardy looked again back toward the tower, out over the low retaining wall into the empty fog. "John!" he yelled into the nothingness. He walked halfway through the lot, into the very middle of it, toward the tower. He called out again. Turned. Waited. Cupped his hands around his mouth. "Hey, John! Ollie, ollie oxen free!"

"I haven't heard that in forever."

"Jesus Christ!" When Hardy landed, he whirled around and found himself facing Holiday, who stood a foot in front of him, grinning. "Where did you just come from?"

"Right here. Did I scare you? I did, didn't I?"

"No. I always levitate when the fog's in." Hardy put his hand over his heart. "God!"

"A little jolt like that's good for you. Clears the arteries."

"Well, they're clear then. Now all I've got to do is start breathing again." He looked all around. "Great place you picked here. Especially today. Why don't we get in my car before we freeze to death? You make any decision?"

They started moving. "About what?"

"Oh, I don't know. How about . . . ?"

Hardy paused as out of the corner of his eye he noticed a gray sedan pulling slowly into the lot maybe fifty or sixty feet off to his right. The driver-side window, all the way down, possibly gave him some subliminal sense that something was not right, and he instinctively grabbed Holiday's arm just above the elbow. "What?"

Before he could answer, the car suddenly accelerated and turned hard to its left, exposing them to the passenger-side window, from which an arm protruded . . .

Hardy could be wrong and look like a fool, or they could both be dead in two seconds. It wasn't a hard choice. "Down! Get down!" he yelled.

Hardy crouched and pushed Holiday away, then hit the pavement rolling himself as two quick shots, then two more, exploded behind him.

He rolled again and came up, running and stumbling — his dress shoes slipping on the wet surface under him — toward the protection of the retaining wall. Behind him, tires screeched. Two more shots, deafening, in rapid succession.

The low wall directly in front of him pinged with a ricochet. He saw the gray mist of a shatter of concrete, felt a scratch across his cheek. Had the bullet hit him?

But he was still moving; he had to keep moving forward.

And then he was over the wall, rolling and sliding steeply downhill under the canopy of low evergreen and bramble.

The thick trunk of an ancient cypress stopped his free fall and knocked the breath out of him, a murderous blow high on his ribs under his arm. But he didn't stop.

Were they still up there? Had he heard another peal of rubber? Did it mean the car was gone?

Whatever, he was still exposed.

Forcing himself to roll, he half collapsed into the fall line of the slope and didn't come to rest again until he was within a first down of Lombard Street, still within the treeline, sheltered from below and hidden from above.

He couldn't move, never wanted to move again. His ribs. Was he shot? In shock?

The silence all around him was complete, the fog enveloping but now not cold. He was sweating heavily. His breath came in gasps. The pain from his broken left finger kicked in again. Agony.

He squeezed at the skin around his mouth, took his hand away, and saw blood. He rubbed at his cheek — a faint sting, a smear of red.

Suddenly aware of movement behind him and to his right up the slope, he turned and saw Holiday traversing, half sliding toward him. But he was moving smoothly, quickly, unhurt. He was with Hardy in seconds.

"Diz? You all right?"

Hardy tried a deep breath. His ribs hurt, but he could breathe. He definitely wasn't shot. The scratch on his cheek — he'd done worse damage shaving.

Then they were both on their feet, dusting themselves off, checking back up the hill. A car passed below them on Lombard and they both froze until they saw it was a large white SUV, nothing like the gray sedan. For a moment, neither man could find anything to say.

The right arm of Hardy's suit coat hung by a thread and he shrugged himself out of it and rolled it into a ball. Under it, his shirt, too, was badly ripped at the sleeve.

Holiday reached over and flicked at the tear. "I've got to get myself a real lawyer. Clothes make the man, Diz," he said. "You look like absolute shit."

★ ★ ★

From a certain point, there was only one way up or down Telegraph Hill, and deciding they didn't like the odds of taking the only street up, where their assailants might still be lurking, they made it back to the retaining wall uphill through the trees and brush. Hardy's car was still the only one parked in the lot, right there ten feet away. Crouching, he got to the door and opened it, got his cell phone, made it back behind the retaining wall. He and Holiday moved a few yards back down the slope where they could still see any activity within the lot. But there was none.

"Okay, you've got your phone. Now what?"

"Now I call the police."

"I don't think so. Not while I'm here."

"So you go. But I'm reporting this."

"Why? What are you going to say?"

"I'm going to tell them what happened."

"And then what? They're going to investigate? They're going to find something you don't already know? And thank you for it?"

"I don't know, John. What do I already know?"

"You know somebody followed you here and tried to kill us. Your pal Freeman's in the hospital. Put it together. It's Panos."

"I'm not arguing with you, John. I'm telling you the cops need to know it, too."

"And then they'll move right on it?"

"That's the theory."

Holiday shook his head. "Man. You're hopeless."

Twenty-five long minutes passed before the patrol car showed up.

In that time, two tour buses had pulled up into the center of the lot, the exact spot where Holiday had surprised Hardy. Additionally, several cars had arrived and parked willy-nilly all around. It had turned, Hardy was thinking, into a goddamned tourist extravaganza. A fitful breeze had blown off the worst of the fog, revealing the usual stunning panorama. A knot of Japanese tourists in overcoats had gathered at the retaining wall where the bullet had chipped it near the front of Hardy's car. They were enthusiastically sharing the mounted pay binoculars and exclaiming over the view.

Hardy didn't even see it. His ribs throbbed. He'd turned the car's heater on so he was no longer cold, but he was still shaking.

As he opened his door and raised his

hand to call the black-and-white car over, he was struck with a sense of the surreal nature of the whole afternoon, of what he'd gone through, of what he was doing now.

When he'd first returned from Vietnam, before he'd gone to law school, Hardy had been a cop, walking a beat with Abe Glitsky. He liked cops, empathized with them, generally understood their concerns, prejudices, methods. And now here were two more, twin tight ends named Jakes and Warren, and at a glance very much like the men from the other night with his windshield in North Beach — hardworking, sincere, dedicated — and most importantly, living every day in the line of fire, which tended to breed a certain defensiveness, even cynicism.

They pulled over and parked in the space next to him, got out of their car together, expressed their concern over Hardy's appearance, asked him if he needed medical attention, which he declined. Finally, Officer Warren took out a pad of paper, and the interview began.

"So what happened here? Dispatch said there was a report of a shooting? You mean right here?" Checking out the tour buses around them, Warren couldn't quite picture it.

Hardy really couldn't blame him. "This was about an hour ago, and the place was pea soup with fog. You couldn't see twenty feet. There was nobody else up here."

"Nobody?"

"Not a soul." The two cops looked at each other, but Warren's expression remained neutral. "Just myself and a client I'd come here to meet."

Hardy knew this would be tricky, but once he'd decided to call the police, he had to tell them the truth. It was the only way the system worked. So he told them about Holiday.

But the truth wasn't scoring points. Jakes broke in to ask, "You mean to say that this client of yours, he's wanted for murder? There's a warrant out?"

"That's right."

"So where is he now?"

"I don't know."

"You don't know," Jakes repeated.

Hardy started to shrug. His ribs stopped him. "When I called you, he thought it would be smart to leave. I couldn't really argue with him."

"You didn't try to make him stay?" Warren asked.

"Of course," Hardy kept it low-key, "I told him he should turn himself in. He might be safer in jail after all. But he didn't see it that way." Hardy met their eyes in turn. "But the point is that he was here earlier with me. If you don't mind, I'd like to get back to what happened."

Finally Jakes said, "Okay, shoot."

Hardy gave it to them succinctly in less than five minutes. "We waited for a while down there at the bottom," he concluded, "then climbed back up here through the brush . . ."

"Wait a minute," Jakes said. He walked over to the retaining wall and looked down. "You came back up through that? Why didn't you use the road?"

Hardy explained, but by now no longer felt they believed him. He walked them over to where the tour buses were parked, describing the gray sedan and its course through the then-empty parking lot. Hardy had distinctly heard the tires squeal, but the pavement had been wet, and now there was no sign of skid marks. Six shots had been fired, but no one had been hit and there were no bullet casings. The chipped cement at the retaining wall could have happened an hour or a week or six years ago.

Back where he'd parked, he said, "I know how weird this sounds. But it happened." He indicated his own ruined clothes, his face. "I didn't do this to myself, really. And my partner David Freeman is in the ICU right now, mugged a few days ago. That's real and verifiable. So is the fact that somebody smashed my windshield a couple of days ago in North Beach. There ought to be a report of that on file."

"So you're saying you think you know who did this? All this stuff?" Warren asked.

"Yes, sir. His name is Wade Panos. He's a Patrol Special. You may know him."

"And you're saying you think he's trying to kill you? And your partner?"

"I do."

"And what about your client? Holiday? How does he fit in with all this?"

"That," Hardy said uneasily, "gets a little complicated."

18

Clarence Jackman did not normally hold open office hours for defense attorneys, nor for anyone else. After a long and successful career in the private sector, Jackman, a darkly hued African-American sixty-five-year-old, physically imposing and impeccably dressed, had been appointed to his position of District Attorney of San Francisco by the mayor about three years ago. Since then, he'd come to appreciate the power and influence that came with the job, to the extent that he was committed to running for election to his second term. He was now, even more so than when he'd been in the lofty reaches of the private sector, a true august personage.

But Abe as well as Treya Glitsky, who was his personal secretary, considered him something of a friend. So did Dismas Hardy and, for that matter, so did David Freeman. All of these people, along with

Gina Roake and a few others, had been regularly meeting at Lou the Greek's for a couple of years with the DA and serving as his informal kitchen cabinet.

So when Hardy had called requesting a meeting with the DA, saying he *needed a word* with Jackman *right away,* Treya cleared it with her boss and set to work rescheduling the afternoon. When he actually arrived battered, worn and dirty, and gimped his way into the outer office, sans coat, his hands and face scratched and bloody, she ushered him directly in, closing the door behind them.

After expressing his genuine concern and making sure Hardy was comfortable in one of the office's easy chairs, Jackman listened with his trademark intensity. He sat slumped at the near end of the couch, leaning heavily on an elbow, the thumb of his right hand under his chin, the fingers regularly caressing the side of his mouth.

When Hardy finished, Jackman sat still for a very long while. Hardy knew better than to interrupt his thoughts, or try to prompt him. At length, the DA straightened up slightly and looked Hardy in the face. "Panos?"

A nod. "Yes, sir." Hardy knew that Jackman couldn't take this as anything like good news. It was no secret that Panos contributed to every major political campaign in the city so that, no matter who won, he never lost influence.

"You seriously believe he's behind these attacks?"

"Not personally, probably not. But some of his people, yes."

"You'll pardon me for saying so — you're obviously upset right now, Diz, and I can't say I blame you — but that seems like just one hell of a reach. Wade's not a gangster."

"With respect, Clarence, maybe you'd like to take a look at some of my deposition testimony. He's not exactly Mr. Clean."

Jackman shook his head. "Maybe not. He's in a tough field, where admittedly some of his tactics, especially with, let us say, not the cream of society, might have come close to crossing the line. But here you're talking attempted murder of regular citizens. There's a huge difference and frankly, I can't see Wade going there. Why would he even risk it?"

"Maybe because David and I, we're threatening to put him out of business."

"And how would you do that? Do you think he doesn't have insurance?"

"No, he has insurance."

"Well, then." A pause. "You know and I know how it works, Diz. Panos sees this as just another nuisance lawsuit. In all probability, he won't personally pay a dime, even if it goes to trial, which it probably won't. All parties will settle. It's not personal."

Hardy sat back. "Take a look at me, Clarence. I'd say it's gotten personal. I'm going to try like hell to shut him down. I want the son of a bitch in jail."

Jackman sighed. "Well . . . but all right. So then, assuming you're successful, he'd be out of business. He's close to retirement age anyway. He might even welcome the break." He came forward to the edge of the couch and spoke with a quiet intensity. "Look, Diz, there's no denying that something bad is going on. David and then you today. I'm willing to concede that they're related. Hell, they'd all but have to be. But related doesn't mean it has to be Wade."

"Except that it is."

Jackman frowned. "If it is, there are two very good and experienced inspectors investigating David's mugging and they should come up with something."

"Two?"

"Two." Jackman played it as a trump. "It may not be clear to you, Diz, but I myself am *really, really* pissed off about David. I don't think you or anybody else has any idea how angry I am. So I asked Dan Rigby" — the chief of police — "to assign another inspector to assist Hector Blanca. They had the CSI team out all morning combing the site, and you know how often that happens for a simple mugging? Never. But it happened now, and it happened because I wanted it to. And they get anything else they need, too. I've even given the investigation an event number." This was a huge commitment from Jackman. The assignment of an event number meant that all expenses related to the event were paid out of the city's general fund, and not out of any department's budget. It essentially meant unlimited resources.

Jackman continued. "So if they find anything that points to Wade Panos — hell, I don't care if it points to the Pope — I'll charge him or whoever it is so fast it'll make your head spin." In his agitation, Jackman had stood up. He leaned back against his desk, arms crossed. "So if you've got even a small show of proof that Wade's any part of this, of you or David, I'd like to hear about it right now."

Hardy sat silent, wrestling with how far he should push this thing. "It's not just me and David," he said. "And it's not attempted murder. It's murder. And in fact it's more than one."

His patience clearly frayed, Jackman nevertheless nodded cautiously. "I'm listening."

Hardy launched into his conspiracy theory that led through Silverman and Creed, Terry and Wills, and on up to the arrest warrant that had been issued for his client. Jackman's scowl had grown darker as the recitation progressed. By the time Hardy finished with the suggestion that the DA convene a grand jury to investigate Panos's company — he was sure they'd find something tying at least his employees to these murders — Jackman finally lost his temper, albeit in his quiet fashion.

"In other words, your client didn't kill these people. Panos did. Now he's a murderer."

"Yes, sir."

"And what about the police, about the evidence they've collected, the witnesses they've talked to?" The DA kept talking. "If I'm not mistaken, Diz, when you defend people, it's often not because they didn't do *something*, but because no one can prove what they did do, isn't that right?"

"Yes, but . . ."

". . . but without proof of any kind, you're telling me you *know* your client is innocent and that in his place Wade Panos is guilty. Am I stating your position accurately?"

Hardy spread his hands. "I'm saying it's worth looking into, that's all."

"No, that's not all, as a matter of fact. You want me to use the power of this office to investigate a private citizen who happens to be your opponent in a lawsuit . . ."

"Clarence, that's neither here —"

But Jackman raised a finger. "Please, let me finish. And at the same time you accuse this same private citizen of the very crimes your own client stands accused of. And all in the name of what? Of David's mugging, is what it comes down to, and the rage I feel about that. If I didn't believe I knew you so well, I might be tempted to think you were a cynical lawyer trying to manipulate the DA to harm his adversaries."

"That's not any —"

But again, Jackman stopped him. "Let me tell you something, Diz. If one of your clients suggested you try something like this to me, you'd laugh at him. If you were Wade's lawyer and I called you in to talk about any of these charges, you'd laugh at me. Where's the proof? Where's any *sign* of proof?"

"I'm betting it's out there."

"Well, if it is, apparently neither you nor the police have found it. And what they have found seems to implicate your client. Rather strongly, from what I hear." He crossed back and took the chair next to Hardy, where he leaned forward with some intimacy. The vitriol seemed to have passed. "Diz, look what's happened to you today. It's got you shook up. What you're telling me is that sometimes the process doesn't work — you and I both know that."

"No one's looking in the right direction, Clarence."

"I'm sure the police are looking where the evidence leads. That's what they do."

"And they're never wrong, are they?"

And this, finally, was the wrong note.

Jackman's shoulders fell and, sighing heavily, he stood up and went over behind his desk. "I encourage you to make sure the report on what happened to you and your client today is complete. I will talk to Chief Rigby and try to make sure that Inspector Blanca gets a team out to Coit Tower before every trace of what happened to you is gone."

"Thank you." He was standing up. The meeting was over.

But Jackman stopped him a last time before he got to the door. "Diz."

Hardy turned back. Jackman was pointing a finger for emphasis. "I want to be crystal clear here. If we ever do get to the point where we can charge Panos with something, and there's any suggestion that the criminal charges were brought because you're my friend rather than because there's evidence sufficient to convict, this case won't just go down the tubes, it'll embarrass us both. *Capisce?*"

"*Capisce.*"

"So we won't ever have to talk about this again, right?"

More than anything else, Hardy wanted to go home. He knew he looked a mess; his ribs ached; his whole left hand throbbed anew. But it was already early Friday afternoon, and though he might get lucky with Blanca deciding to pull weekend work, his luck wasn't something he wanted to count on. Not today.

Again, the inspector for General Work was in. When Hardy gave his name and they called Blanca, he said to bring Hardy back to his area. But when Hardy got there, Blanca looked right through him until Hardy spoke. "Sergeant Blanca."

Blanca's eyes settled on him. Recognition dawned. "Mr. Hardy? Sorry. I thought I was waiting for a man in a business suit. What the hell happened to you?"

"That's why I'm here."

"Well." Blanca got halfway out of his chair. "Come on back where we can talk."

He got Hardy settled, brought him some water, picking up some of the details as he did so. The smashed windshield. The report he'd be getting from the responding officers on the Coit Tower shooting today. Blanca wrote the names down, made a note to look them up. Finally the sergeant got seated in his chair. "So you're thinking it was the same person who shot at you . . ."

"Two people, at least," Hardy said.

"Okay, two, maybe three. And you say these might be the same people who beat up Mr. Freeman?"

Hardy nodded. "I've got no proof, none at all, as Mr. Jackman just reminded me. But yes, I'm let's say morally certain it's the same guys."

"Last time you didn't want to give me a name."

"But I did tell you about a lawsuit we were preparing . . ."

"Sure." Suddenly, his eyes alight with possibility, Blanca pulled the yellow legal pad he'd written the officers' names on up in front of him. "You also said that in twenty years or so of practice, you hadn't ever seen anybody take it out on the lawyers."

"True. But I'm seeing it now."

Blanca quickly took in his dishevelled appearance again. "So you got a name now?"

"Wade Panos."

Blanca reacted almost as if he'd been struck. "The Patrol Special? Actually, the king of the Patrol Specials?" He put his pencil down.

"His people. Especially a thug — I think he's Wade's nephew — named Nick Sephia."

Blanca didn't need to consult any notes. "I've heard of him."

"I'm not surprised. When he worked for his uncle, his specialty was planting dope on working girls, but he's been known to hit people, too. Now he's muscle for the Diamond Center. A real sweetheart." Finding a receptive official audience a nice change of pace, Hardy leaned back in his chair. "Jackman tells me you got a partner to help with the Freeman investigation."

"Yeah," Blanca said, "but what investigation? We don't got witness one to interview and Freeman still isn't telling us anything." He looked up with some real sadness. "Anyway, even with CSI going over the place a second time, we got nothing, and I mean nothing. So unless somebody walks in off the street and confesses, the investigation as you call it is closed."

"I was thinking maybe what just happened to me might reopen it. If there were two of you, maybe you could shake a tree or two. At least see if Sephia's got an alibi."

Blanca shook his head skeptically. "That's an awful cold trail, and if he had partners, they'd cover each other anyway."

"Okay, but I'm not a cold trail. Somebody shot at me in the last two hours. Sephia's someplace to start. Maybe you can find out what he was doing."

"No maybe about it. But you didn't see him?"

Hardy shook his head. "I saw the car. Gray sedan, late model. Then the gun, which I'm afraid took all of my attention."

Blanca chuckled. "Yeah, they tend to do that."

"I guess I just wanted to put what's happened to me on your radar as part of Freeman. Which, of course, I can't prove. But if you could find anything, either up at Coit Tower or talking to Sephia . . ."

"Hey, I'm hearing you. I'm on it."

It wasn't the kind of story he was dying to tell his wife. In a fair, just, and kind world, she wouldn't have been home in the middle of this Friday afternoon, and he could run upstairs, shower, change into a new suit or even some hangout clothes — "Oh, with David out of the office, there wasn't much to do, so I thought I'd spend some extra time with you and the darlings." He could bury his ruined clothes under something in the garbage can, explain away his scrapes with a humorous anecdote about one of his client's vicious cats.

Except that Frannie was sitting on some cushions in the bay window in the living room, studying, and saw him when he got up on the porch. She made it to the door and opened it before he did. "What happened?"

"It's not as bad as it looks," he said.

Twenty minutes later, he was soaking in a hot bath upstairs. Aside from the scratches on his hands and his face, the upper right quarter of his back was badly scraped and already swollen. Frannie sat on the edge of the tub, twisting a towel anxiously as they talked. "I must be missing something, then," she said. "So who shot Silverman?"

"That I don't know. Not specifically. Maybe Sephia."

"Which gets you to Panos?"

"Right, maybe, if he even knew about it." He let out a breath. "But there were three of them. And another problem. I've got the same people killing Silverman and Creed, right?"

"Okay."

"So why did Creed have to get killed?"

"So he wouldn't get to tell the homicide cops he wasn't sure about identifying John and his friends."

"Right. And who does that benefit?"

"The real killers, whoever they might be."

"Exactly. So then they decide — actually, they probably decided at the same time as Creed — if they do away with Terry and Wills, it's going to look like John. It's got to. The cops still were working with the three names and there's nobody else left. So they plant the Silverman/Creed gun and some of the Silverman loot in both places and bingo."

"But they really don't want John arrested."

"No. They want him dead. Then all the questions stop because there's nobody around to ask them. It's just lowlifes purging each other from the gene pool. It's a tightly wrapped, self-contained case, and everybody involved is dead."

"Not exactly. There's still you."

He looked up at her, shaking his head. "They had us both there for a minute . . ."

"But how could they have known about that? That you'd be together?"

"I don't know for sure, but I'd bet they figured John would eventually come to my office, or I'd go to him, so they just decided they'd tail me for a while. And everything worked like a dream. Except I saw them in time."

"So if it isn't about David's case after all, why did they attack him?"

"Or us, for that matter, with the windshield. Maybe it's both."

"That seems like such a reach, Dismas. I'm sorry, but it really does."

Hardy nodded ruefully. "Those were Jackman's exact words, I believe."

"And planting evidence in two apartments? Does that really happen? Are you *sure* John wasn't at Silverman's?"

He hesitated, then shook his head. "No."

"Or that this Nick Sephia was?"

No answer.

Frannie tsked, twisted the towel some more, stood up and walked over to the door. "I mean, I can't imagine John killing anybody either, but . . ."

"He sure didn't kill his bartender and his boyfriend, Frannie. Not that way. I don't believe that."

"Okay. I can't see that either." She turned back to face him. "Maybe you could talk to the man who's got Abe's old job."

"No. That's not going to happen."

"Why not?"

"Because he's got a suspect and I'm the guy's lawyer. My only function is to deliver John so they can arrest him. As I mentioned to you the other night, as a defense attorney, I have no interest in justice, only in getting my client off."

"But Abe used to talk to you about cases."

"And it's one of the things I always loved about him. But it got him in trouble more than once and he's already told me he won't talk about this one."

"He might, though, when he finds out

461

they shot at you. That might make it different."

He shifted in the tub and an involuntary groan escaped. Finally, he got through the pain. "It's worth a try, I guess," he said. "I've got to do something."

She was over by him again. She sat on the edge of the tub, put a hand gently on his shoulder. "You're not going to want to hear this, but maybe you should consider dropping this lawsuit. See what happens to David, then take it from there."

He gave it a minute of real consideration. "It might get to that anyway. I can't afford to keep it going by myself, although I might be able to talk one of the big firms into taking it on. It would be a big payday."

"If you win."

"There is always that. But what I'd really like is to try to bluff them into making another settlement offer at least, pay for expenses and the time I've already worked. Although I can't believe this thing this morning was about that. With Freeman out of the way, the thing's going to pretty much dry up on its own anyway. So I'm thinking it had to be mostly about John."

She rubbed her hand over the skin of his shoulder. "You want to hear another hard one?"

"From you? Anything."

Unhappy, she came out with it. "You could always drop him, too, Dismas."

He sighed, hung his head. "No," he said finally. "It's tempting as hell, and maybe he deserves it, but that I can't do."

"And meanwhile, someone's trying to kill you."

"Maybe. Maybe me or maybe John. Probably not me."

"Notice the clever rationalization. Even though they broke your windshield and shot at you, they're not really after you."

He smiled at her. "I'm not saying it's impossible, just unlikely. Besides, I've finally got this Sergeant Blanca looking at Sephia. If he finds anything, and I bet he will, then suddenly it all falls into place. I'm talking Silverman and the rest, the murders."

"It all falls into place? How does it do that?"

"Inevitably?" Hardy going for the light touch, but he couldn't quite pull it off. "What do you mean? How does it do what?"

"How does it go from you and David getting attacked to the murders? I mean, what's the point of contact that connects them? Because from where I sit, I must tell you I only see one."

"And what is that?"

"John Holiday."

Blanca had what he considered a legitimately hot lead and wasted no time after Hardy left. He picked up the phone, got information, and found the number of Georgia AAA. He endured the usual runaround for a few minutes until he was finally connected to the Diamond Center's Chief of Security, who told him that Nick Sephia was off today. He was taking a three-day weekend.

A good sign, Blanca thought. If he was off, it left him free to drive around in a gray sedan and cause mischief. So, all right. He knew where Sephia wasn't. The trick now was to find where he was.

The obvious answer was WGP — Panos's company — and sometimes obvious worked. The efficient-sounding woman in the Panos office said she had no idea where Nick Sephia was — he no longer worked for the company — but she took his number and said she'd try to reach Wade and have him call back. Three minutes later, his phone rang, and it was the man himself. His tone was relaxed. "Do you mind, Sergeant, if I ask what this is about?"

"Not at all. I wanted to have a few words with Nick Sephia. I tried where he works, but he's taking a day off."

"And you think I know where he might be?"

"I understand he's your nephew."

"That's right." Panos paused. "And you think I might know where he is? How many nephews do you have, Sergeant? Do you know where any of them are? If he's not at work, he's probably at home, and I don't know his address offhand, somewhere near Gough, I think. Maybe we've got it or his phone number in some files back at the office, though. He worked for me for a while, but you probably already knew that."

"Yes, sir."

"But you know, my little brother Roy hangs out with him sometimes. I could page him and see. He's on the beat today."

"I'd appreciate that."

"Good. But you still haven't told me what this is about."

"I thought I did. I wanted to have a few words with him."

Panos chuckled. "Excuse me, Sergeant, but as one cop to another, you can cut the bullshit, okay. The question is what do you want to have a few words with him about?"

Blanca thought for a minute. "His possible involvement in a crime. A violent crime."

After a rather long hesitation, Panos spoke in a heavy tone of sadness. "I hate to hear that. I was hoping he was doing better. I heard he was, what with the new job and everything. He's got a temper, sergeant, but he's a good boy."

"This wasn't temper," Blanca said, "and whoever did it wasn't a good boy."

Panos sighed. "God. Poor Rosie, his mother. What that woman's been through." He sighed again. "Why don't I page Roy, see if he can help you? Oh, but one thing . . ."

"Yes, sir."

"I'm curious how you knew that Nick used to work for me, or that he was my nephew for that matter."

"Somebody I talked to knew him," Blanca said.

"Oh yeah? Was the guy's name Hardy, by any chance?"

"It was just a witness. I can't give out the name."

"No, of course you can't. But you might like to know, not saying it was him, that this guy Hardy and I are involved in some big litigation — he's a lawyer; in fact, he's a sleazy lawyer if you want to know the truth — and he's not going according to Hoyle." Panos spent a minute or so outlining some of the salient points of the lawsuit — the plaintiffs and some of the issues and money involved.

He concluded earnestly, "Look, the truth is the guy makes things up if he needs to, if things aren't going his way. I'm not saying he has anything to do with your questions about Nick — Nick's a hothead all right. But this Hardy is well known for being unethical. Seriously unethical. Do yourself a favor and ask around. Only if it was him you heard about Nick from, of course. Anyway, there's my warning for what it's worth. And you can probably expect a call from Roy any minute."

It came as advertised, and Roy told Blanca that Nick and a friend of his had gone up to Nevada last night to spend the weekend gambling — he was a serious poker player — before the crowded and crazy snow season began next month. Roy was planning on going up and joining them tonight when he got off work. He expected they'd probably be just hanging around the cabin they rented during the day — they hit the clubs at night. But Roy had the cabin's number if the sergeant would like it.

The area code was 775. Nevada.

"No, this is Julio Rez, but Nick's here. Hold on."

"This is Nick. Who's this?"

Blanca had never spoken to Sephia before and so had no idea if this was truly him on the telephone. But it seemed an impossibly elaborate ruse for someone to cook up in the fifteen minutes or less since he'd first called Panos's office. It would never be proof in a court of law, but Blanca personally had no doubt that he was talking to Nick Sephia, and that if he'd driven where he was in no traffic, he was four hours east of where Blanca sat now.

Which meant, conclusively, that he hadn't shot at Dismas Hardy three hours ago.

What it meant about Hardy, Blanca couldn't quite say. He wanted to trust and even like the guy because of David Freeman and what had happened to him, but now suddenly he didn't have a good feeling even about that.

Blanca looked at the receiver in his hand. He had everything he needed from Nick Sephia. He hung up.

Strikeout.

At the end of the day, at the end of the

week, things were getting a little hot in Barry Gerson's office in the homicide detail. The small and airless place was packed with mostly large men, and all of them were standing. The two squad car officers who had responded to the Coit Tower call, Jakes and Warren, had come directly up at the end of their shift. That had started the whole thing. They knew that whatever had happened that noon at Coit Tower — and they were very skeptical — the fugitive and murder suspect John Holiday had been part of it. If they did nothing else, they felt they had to take their information to homicide. As soon as he determined what the officers' visit was about, Gerson had naturally called in both Cuneo and Russell, who were finishing up some paperwork, getting ready to go home.

After he'd hung up on Nick Sephia, Hector Blanca had had a full and interesting afternoon looking up and noting the name Panos on the report on Dismas Hardy's broken windshield. Deciding to take Panos's advice and ask around about Hardy, he went directly to the best source he could think of — he called the District Attorney to whom he'd had increased access since Freeman had been mugged.

Jackman had stopped far short of a glowing character reference. "He's a good lawyer." Then, "*Defense* lawyer, I should say." In fact, when Blanca first mentioned the name Dismas Hardy, Jackman's tone had unmistakably cooled, then changed by degrees until Blanca concluded he was furious about something, about Hardy.

After that conversation, he was trying to locate Jakes and Warren to get the story on the events at Coit Tower and was suitably stunned when their sergeant at Central Station told him that, even as they spoke, the two officers were possibly reporting to the Homicide Detail on the fourth floor of the Hall of Justice, just upstairs from him. Maybe he could catch them there, get their report in person.

So Blanca was with them as well, the last one to arrive. For some not exactly rational reason, when he'd first heard the word homicide, he'd imagined that David Freeman must have died — although of course Freeman had nothing to do with Jakes and Warren. But it was the only even remotely related homicide that came to his mind, and so for the first few minutes after Gerson — somewhat grudgingly — admitted him to his office, he stood against the door, trying to pick up the gist of things as they went along. Finally, he had to interrupt.

"Excuse me, I keep hearing the name Holiday," he said. "I thought we were here about Hardy and maybe Freeman."

"Who's Freeman?" Gerson asked.

"Hardy's partner," Blanca said. "He's in the ICU over at St. Francis right now. Somebody beat him up. Bad. But who's Holiday?"

"Hardy's client," Gerson said. "Arrest warrant out on him for murder. For four murders, to be more precise."

"Wait a minute, excuse me," Blanca said. "This guy Holiday, he was with Hardy today? When?"

"When they got shot at," Warren said. "About noon."

"Maybe," said Jakes.

Russell decided to get into the discussion. "Maybe what? Maybe Holiday was there, you mean?" he asked.

"No. Maybe they got shot at," Jakes answered. "Or, alternatively, maybe it was just Hardy."

"No, that's wrong!" Obviously Warren and Jakes had discussed it between themselves and didn't agree. "Jakes watches too many movies."

"Hey!" Jakes said. It wasn't playful. "You

show me anything proves it happened."

"I saw the guy, Hardy, is what proves it happened. He was beat to shit."

"Doesn't prove squat. He could have done it to himself."

"Yeah, but why?" Warren shook his head. "People just don't do this shit."

"Hold it, hold it, hold it!" Gerson had the rank, and he pulled it. "Officer Jakes, what are you trying to say?"

The young man gathered himself. "Only, sir, that we examined the area pretty carefully, and several aspects of Mr. Hardy's story seemed, well, a little questionable."

"Like what?"

"Like first, his story is nobody else was there. We're talking Coit Tower. Noon . . ."

"It was foggy, Doug, get it?"

Gerson snapped at Warren. "Button it! Go on, Jakes."

"All right, it was foggy. Like it's never foggy? Hello? This is San Francisco, people have heard of fog. They still go to Coit Tower. So anyway, the first thing is he and Holiday are all alone up there, except when we arrive twenty minutes later, it's a car lot, plus buses. Okay, so then he talked about screeching tires. Except no tire marks. Then some chipped concrete where a slug hit it, or maybe not. Oh, and finally six shots fired, just about point blank . . ."

"Moving car," Warren blurted, held up a hand to Gerson. "Sorry, sir."

"Okay, moving car, but nobody even scratched. We then interviewed down on Lombard, right below. Seven people home. Nobody heard a shot."

The only sound was a low musical note — Cuneo. No one seemed to notice.

"All right," Gerson said. "And all this means what?"

"He doesn't think it happened," Cuneo said. "He thinks Hardy faked it."

"That's right, sir. I do."

Warren raised his hand. Gerson pointed at him and nodded. "Go ahead."

"I saw the man, sir. Hardy. He was ripped head to toe. Brand new nice suit. Cuts and scratches all over."

This didn't bother Jakes. "That hill's a monster. You roll down it in a suit, you'll ruin it, too. You'll get scratched up."

"Okay, maybe, but why would anybody — *anybody*, much less a successful lawyer — want to do that?"

Blanca had gradually found himself growing astounded that Hardy had spent so much time with him earlier in the day, discussing the Coit Tower incident in some detail and never once seeing fit to mention his representation of the murderer John Holiday, or the fact of Holiday's presence at that scene. Deciding he had to speak up, he cleared his throat, raised his hand, addressed himself to Gerson. "If I may, Lieutenant. I might have something to say to that."

"All right." Gerson looked around. "We're all listening."

Blanca, still by the door, held up some paper. "This is a report about another incident that happened Wednesday night in North Beach, also involving Hardy. While he and his wife were at a dinner at Fior d'Italia that they didn't eat, supposedly somebody smashed the windshield of his car. He first told the officers he suspected who it might have been, but didn't think they needed to investigate. The vandals, he said, wouldn't have left any sign. He admitted that he'd hurt his hand and that his own blood was on the hood of the car — he'd lost his temper when he saw the damage and slammed the windshield, he said."

"All right," Gerson said, "what's the point?"

"There are two points, Lieutenant. First, maybe it happened the way it looked, but maybe he hurt his hand trying to break the window himself before he went to a tire iron or whatever got used. Again, just like this incident today, there seems to be no evidence that anything happened the way he said it did."

Every man in the room was locked into Blanca's narrative. He went on, "The second point goes back to Officer Warren's question of why anyone would do this kind of thing, and the answer is that in both these incidents, Hardy accused a man named Wade Panos as . . ."

"Wade Panos!" Cuneo exploded out of his trance. "Wade Panos isn't going around breaking car windows. That's the stupidest thing I ever heard."

Russell was just as outraged. "You mean to say that Hardy actually told you Wade was the person shooting at him?" He was looking for corroboration from Warren and Jakes, and they were both nodding.

But Blanca answered, "Not exactly. He said it probably wasn't Panos himself. He has a nephew named Sephia . . ."

"Sure," Cuneo said, "Nick."

"Except Nick was up at Incline Village today," Blanca said. "Since last night. Roy Panos gave me his number and I checked. So he didn't shoot at anybody."

"Roy's a good guy," Cuneo said.

"You know him?" Blanca asked. "Either of them?"

"Both," Russell said. "They gave us the list of names that led straight to Holiday."

The room, this time, went completely silent. Jakes said, "Shit."

After a long beat, Blanca picked up the thread again. "So here's the missing piece of this puzzle. Hardy's suing Panos right now, damages in the millions for abuses in his Patrol Special beats. And guess who else?" Nobody offered. "The San Francisco Police Department. For negligent supervision."

The room grew blue with the obscenity of comrades. When it had run its course, Warren was the first to get back to the issue. "So he faked all this to . . . what?"

"I'm hearing two reasons," Gerson said. "First, to ruin Panos and give himself more ammo in court. But even more, and this really sucks, to maybe try to get a jury to think this Nick Sephia's got something to do with the people Holiday offed. The old Soddit defense."

"What's that?" Jakes asked.

"Some other dude did it," Gerson said. "Hey, maybe the other dude was this guy Sephia. All Hardy needs to get to is reasonable doubt. If he can make the jury believe Sephia shot at him and his client . . ."

"Scumbag," Cuneo said. He was one man, but he spoke for the whole group.

Unanimously.

Part Three

Holiday had borrowed Michelle's car and was riding south through the city on surface streets. Hardy had ordered him that no way was he even to consider going outside until this thing had gotten settled. The arrest warrant on him was still in force. Glitsky evidently was going down to make the arrests on the others that would somehow clear Holiday; then he'd present the DA and even the homicide detail with a fait accompli. Glitsky said he had the evidence he needed. It was going to happen. Holiday just had to wait.

Except that this was Holiday's fight, far more than it was even Glitsky's or Hardy's. Fuck if he'd let someone else fight it for him. They'd already killed two of his friends, tried to kill him, set the police on his ass. Hardy could say what he wanted, but after everything that had happened so far, nobody doubted that if Holiday got into custody, they would find a way to get to him. Panos was connected inside the system. Enormous sums of money were at stake — they had killed to protect it and they would kill again. As often as they needed to, wherever it needed to be done. Even in jail.

Holiday looked down at the gun on the seat next to him, what was left of the box of old cartridges. Reaching over, he picked it up, felt the heft of it, put it back down. He wiped his hand across his forehead. He was sweating. He rolled the window down an inch. Outside, it was cold, overcast and windy. He lowered the window further. Kept sweating.

He knew he could just keep driving south. Michelle wouldn't be home until late so nobody would even be looking for the car. He could zip over to the freeway and be out of the Bay Area within a couple of hours, out of the state easily by nightfall. Maybe even out of the country. It wasn't yet 1:30. If he pushed it, he could cross into Tijuana well before midnight. And, after Glitsky and Hardy had fixed things up for him, after the authorities had come to believe that it was Sephia and his friends after all, he could simply come back, re-open the Ark, continue as before. It was his fight, sure, but did that mean he had to be in it? Wasn't that the sucker play?

And what about Michelle?

Holiday for years had been playing himself as the tragic figure who didn't commit. He was too bruised by life, too battered by love and loss. The women had always understood, as Michelle would come to understand. He felt his pain too deeply, he was too sensitive. The idea that his broken heart would ever heal just wasn't really on the table.

Was he really ready to abandon that charade for good?

He was. All the running around, the scoring, the drinking, the moving on from woman to woman hadn't given him one minute of true happiness. But Michelle had. By the same token, Dismas Hardy had taken him into his life, endured his jokes and visits and hangovers, made him part of the family — God knew why. So Diz and Michelle, were they just to be more sacrifices that he'd burn on the altar of his pathetic self-pity?

He'd come to his last turn if he wasn't going to get on the freeway. He didn't take it. Suddenly putrid with fear, he realized that he wasn't going to Mexico or anywhere else except Pier 70, where Glitsky was going to need all the help he could get. Hardy had never said anything definite about going himself — in fact, he'd outright denied he would be there. It was police business, he'd said. Civilians didn't belong, would be out of place.

But Holiday knew Hardy. He would be there.

When they got this cleared up, Holiday would start taking care of the Ark, of Michelle, of the rest of his business. His life.

19

On Saturday afternoon, Vincent Hardy opened the front door of his house and stood in the entrance to his living room where his father and Abe Glitsky were speaking in measured tones, having a serious discussion. He wore a long-sleeved Jerry Rice 49er T-shirt, tennis shoes and calf-length baggy shorts; mostly, though, what he wore was mud. Hardy looked at him with a wary expectancy, but mostly with a poorly concealed lack of patience.

"Dad," he said without preamble, "I need a chainsaw."

Glitsky, not really in the mood for it, nevertheless broke a rare smile. "As who does not, Vin? As who does not?"

"A chainsaw?" Hardy's back was still sore and he was reclining, feet up, in his reading chair. "A *chainsaw?*"

"Everybody needs one sometime," Glitsky said.

Vincent didn't get the joke. "Maybe, but I need one now. We really do, Dad."

"What for?" his father asked.

"To cut stuff."

"There," Glitsky said, the question settled for all time. "What did you think he wanted it for, Diz? To cut stuff. You can't do much else with a chainsaw, can you?"

"I saw some guys juggle one down at Venice Beach one time," Hardy said. "A chainsaw, a bowling ball and an egg. It was awesome." He whipped on his son. "What do you want to cut, Vin?"

"Some trees, over in the park." He pointed vaguely outside. "They're hanging over the sidelines at the football field."

"What football field?"

"Just at the end of the block. Where we practiced for Little League."

Hardy grimaced as he came forward slightly. "There's no football field down there."

"Yeah, there is. We're making one."

"That's why they need the chainsaw," Glitsky said. "Obviously."

Hardy knew the Little League practice area well. It was a small plot just to the left of the entrance to the elegant and majestic Palace of the Legion of Honor, one of San Francisco's premier tourist destinations.

Hardy had been one of a contingent of local dads who a few years before had gone down to the Parks Commission and requested that they be allowed to bring in a backstop for baseball so that the kids could have a flat, grassy place to practice. The commission finally agreed, but only under the condition that it would be a revocable permit, good for a few months in the spring, and that the lot should otherwise remain pristine. And now, judging from his son's appearance, the place was at best a mudhole, and they needed a chainsaw to clear more land.

After Hardy had finally, with much gnashing of teeth, made the sad truth clear to Vincent, and he'd gone down to break the news to his friends and teammates, he lay back in his chair, covered his face with his hands briefly, let out a deep breath. "So where were we?"

"Do you realize that none of my three sons ever said those words to me?"

"What words?"

"Dad, I need a chainsaw. It kind of choked me up."

"It is a beautiful phrase."

"Every dad should hear it at least once. Well." Glitsky let out a theatrical sigh. "At least I got to hear *your* kid say it. That's some consolation. When the guys in Venice juggled it, was the chainsaw going?"

"Yeah."

"With a bowling bowl and an egg? Was the egg hard-boiled?"

"I don't know. I'd assume so."

"But if it wasn't, imagine? I would have loved —"

"Abe." Hardy held up a hand. "Please."

Glitsky's mouth turned down. "Okay, but I think I've got a chainsaw in my garage, if you change your mind and want to borrow one."

"I won't. Can we drop the chainsaw?" Then, reading Glitsky's mind, Hardy said, "Don't."

Glitsky's frown grew more pronounced.

Hardy took his opening. "But on this other thing . . . I'm still trying to imagine who might have shot at us if it wasn't Sephia."

"And you're sure it wasn't him?"

"Blanca was sure enough when I talked to him last. Said he checked around and called Nick up in Nevada, where he'd been since last night. So it wasn't him. But who does that leave?"

"Maybe Wade's got some other shooters on the payroll?"

Hardy had thought of almost nothing else in the twenty-six hours that had elapsed since he'd arrived at Coit Tower. It showed in his drawn and worried face. "But there's no reason to come after me. I'm no threat anyway if Freeman . . ." His voice wound down.

"Maybe they don't know that."

Hardy's voice grew hard. "Meaning maybe you think I should tell them I'm out of it? Just roll over?"

Glitsky spread his hands. "Meaning nothing. My favorite theory is they weren't after you anyway. Whoever it was, they wanted Holiday."

"How'd they know he was there?"

"How'd they know you were? Somebody followed somebody, that's all. Happens all the time. The tail figures out your destination is Coit Tower, calls for the cavalry in the gray sedan, you're there when they arrive twenty minutes later. Then it's sorry, no hard feelings, but it's bad luck to leave witnesses breathing."

"Maybe," Hardy said. "But what's the deal with Blanca? I mean, early afternoon yesterday he's the perfect cop. Wanted to know everything I had. Impressions, suspicions, you name it. We talked about David, getting a lead on these cretins . . . anyway, three hours later he's a different guy."

"Maybe he ate lunch at Lou's in the meanwhile, got a stomachache."

Hardy kept talking. "He knows it wasn't Sephia. Plus he wasn't going after Panos until he got some physical evidence. Then he asks me how come I hadn't told him I was with Holiday up at Coit? Didn't I think that mattered? It's like, suddenly, I'm the bad guy. What, I'm making this stuff up to ruin his day? I wanted to go, 'Hey, remember me? I'm the guy who got shot at. I am the *victim* here.' Anyway, he tells me he'll call if something comes up, but I'm not holding my breath."

"Probably smart." Glitsky stood up, walked over to the fireplace, moved some of the glass elephants on the mantel. "So what's your next move?"

"That's why I called you. Though it pains me to admit it, I think I need some advice."

"Strategic?"

"Emotional, philosophical, strategic, I don't care." He came forward with some difficulty, rolling his shoulder against the pain. "They whack my car Wednesday, they shoot at me on Friday. Tell you the truth, I'm a little concerned."

Glitsky stared out through the blinds of

Hardy's front window. A muscle worked by his temple. When he spoke, it was with an exaggerated calm. "For what it's worth, it's probably not you. It's Holiday."

"It was my car, Abe, on Wednesday. Holiday wasn't anywhere near it."

"That, in fact, might really have been random. Vandals."

"Right. Just like David was." Hardy took a beat. "Come on, Abe. Two attacks in three days. You know it wasn't random. I'd like a little hint about what to do here. I don't like people coming after me. To say nothing about my family. It makes me a little uptight. We had two crying kids last night. Frannie's talking about taking them out of school, all of us going away for a week or two."

Glitsky just nodded.

"What?" Hardy asked.

"You already said it. If you're absolutely sure it's Panos . . ."

"Of course it's Panos! Whether the target is me or Holiday, either way it's Panos."

"Okay, so what you do is you call Dick Kroll and tell him you're out. At least until Freeman's up and around again. Explain the situation without threatening him or accusing him or his client, if that's in your arsenal of legal moves. That takes you out of it, am I right?"

"So far. Maybe."

"All right. Meanwhile, make friends with Blanca again. Find out what happened. It's probably just some misunderstanding — you know how cops can be if they feel you haven't been completely straight with them. Apologize. Then, of course, turn over Holiday."

"No way."

Glitsky's mouth went tight. "There's that flexibility you're so famous for."

"He's not going to jail again, Abe. He's been there once and didn't like it. He thinks Panos will have him killed."

"In jail?" Glitsky barked a laugh. "That's just stupid and you know it, Diz. Wade may be the big bad wolf on the streets, but essentially he's a *rent-a-cop*, okay? He doesn't have secret operatives working in the jail to enforce his wishes. Trust me on this. The truth is that if somebody is out to get your client, he's safer in jail than he is out of it."

"And then what?"

"And then what, what?"

"I mean, after I drop my lawsuit and John's in jail, then what? They just win?"

"What's the hurry? You let things cool

492

off awhile, see how things stand with Freeman, get some new partners to work on the lawsuit later. Then, with Holiday, you press for a speedy trial and get him off on the evidence. You said he's got alibis for all the murders. If that's true, he's out after the prelim."

"And back on the street, where they can try again."

Glitsky broke his second smile of the day, a personal record. "You can't have it both ways, Diz. He's either safer on the street, or safer in jail."

"How about neither? Whoever really did these killings wants to pin them on him. If he dies, with the evidence they found at his place, the case is closed."

Glitsky walked back to his chair, stood looking down at his friend. "Because you've been through recent psychological trauma and I don't want to embarrass you, I've kind of been avoiding that pesky little evidence problem."

Hardy's eyes narrowed. "Abe, I swear to God, somebody shot at us yesterday. Really. I'm not kidding you."

Glitsky registered surprise. "I don't doubt it. But what's that got to do . . . ?"

"Somebody planted that evidence. Get used to it. That's the truth. And that happens to be Nick Sephia's specialty."

"Which makes it especially unfortunate he wasn't here in the city."

"I'm working on that."

"Well." Glitsky stood again. He checked his watch. "You get something, let me know. Meanwhile, call Kroll at his home, talk to your client. Be convincing. It could all be settled by tonight."

Glitsky met his wife and daughter where he'd dropped them at a bookstore on California Street. They presented a Saturday Children's Hour that Rachel enjoyed — it also got everybody outside of the duplex, which was to the good. In the car, Treya drove while Abe turned himself around and sang some nonsense songs to his daughter, then tickled and laughed with her, enjoying himself. Treya put a hand on his thigh. "What are you so happy about? Not that I'm complaining."

"I've successfully resisted temptation, so I'm taking a few minutes to bask in my virtue."

She threw him a look across the car seat. "That's nice. Was the temptation female?"

He put his hand down on hers. "Never in the world. He was subtle enough about it, but Diz wanted me to check up on the efficiency of the current homicide team. I politely declined."

"What is it," Treya asked, "some kind of virus? First your dad, now Diz."

"I know. But I can't be mad at him. He's legitimately worried."

"I'd be worried, too. But what did he expect you to do about it?"

"He thinks John Holiday's getting framed. He wanted me to pass it on."

"To Lieutenant Gerson?"

"Who else?" He grunted. "My close friend Barry, who is hanging on my every word. I told Diz that wasn't the way to go. You would have been proud of me."

"Always," she said, "but somebody's trying to find who shot at him, aren't they?"

"Absolutely. He reported it, so that's what they've got to do." He glanced across at her. "What's the problem?"

"People shooting at our friends. That's a pretty serious problem, don't you think?"

He shook his head. "They weren't after Diz."

"No? What would have happened if, say, they'd killed Holiday after all?"

"What do you mean, what would have happened? He'd be dead and . . ."

"And that would be the end of it? What about these other killings he supposedly did? Those cases would be closed, too, wouldn't they?"

Glitsky didn't answer right away.

"You see what I'm asking? Doesn't it make sense?"

He nodded. "It's more or less what Diz was getting at. But it doesn't have to be Panos, or anybody connected to Panos."

"But whoever it was had to be at Silverman's, right? I mean, the money, the jewels. And didn't the young man you talked to . . ."

"Matt Creed."

"Right. He told you it *wasn't* Holiday and his friends, didn't he?"

"No. He only said he couldn't say for sure that it was."

"But did he ever get to tell that to the inspectors in homicide? Did he have time before he got shot?"

"I don't know."

"Now *that* might be worth finding out."

They were going shopping next and pulled into a space at the Safeway. Treya turned off the engine, but Abe didn't move to get out of the seat. Instead, he sat there, rubbing his scar with his index finger. "I thought you didn't want me getting in-

496

volved in any of this. It's not my job. Remember?"

"I know. I do remember." After a long moment, she said, "You're right. I just hope somebody really is looking for whoever shot at Diz."

"I might be able to ask around about that. It's not homicide."

"That might not be bad."

They got out of the car and Rachel, who'd fallen asleep in the baby seat, was making some discontented noises as Glitsky leaned in, pulled her out, and brought her in close to him, bouncing her gently. While Treya walked a few steps ahead, he kept up a singsong patter all across the lot. By the time they got her fastened into the seat in the shopping cart, she was gurgling happily again, mimicking her father's words. "Ay-so, ay-so."

"What do you have her saying?" Treya asked, smiling.

Glitsky, his smile quotient for the day all used up, fixed his wife with a serious look. "Key childhood words," he said. "One in particular."

"What's that?"

"Chainsaw," he said.

Nat had his own key and had let himself

in. Abe and Treya heard the stertorous rumbling that marked Nat's sleep from down on the sidewalk.

He was on the living room couch. The rule was not to wake him up on purpose, although occasional, accidental noise in the background was considered kosher and often did the trick. So Abe put on a CD of the opera *Turandot*, which featured his middle son Jacob in his first commercial recording, albeit among the chorus, where Abe swore he could pick him out. With the music at conversational level, they parked Rachel in the playpen with some toys and began unpacking their groceries in and around the kitchen.

They hadn't quite finished the first bag when Nat was in the doorway, scratching his white hair around his yarmulke, pulling his sweater down over his belt. "For a minute with that music," he said, "I thought I must have died and gone to heaven."

"He sounds great, doesn't he?"

"Outstanding."

"You guys talking about Jacob?" Treya asked. "I don't think he's on this track."

Father and son exchanged a look. "You don't hear him?" Nat asked. He paused, listening, pointed. "There!"

"Ah." Treya smiled at her father-in-law, turned back to her groceries. "Oh, there."

"She doesn't hear him," Abe said.

"I do," she insisted. "Right in the middle of those other voices. He really stands out." She pushed it for her husband's benefit. "It's like he's in the next room." But then something struck her and she turned, suddenly all business. "But wait a minute. It's Saturday, Nat. What are you doing here? Is everything all right?"

Nat was an observant Jew and spent a great deal of time inside his synagogue. He took the Sabbath seriously, and normally he would not move from his apartment except to walk to temple, where he'd remain until sundown. But at Treya's question, his expression went blank for a beat. Then he remembered. "Ach, this Silverman thing again."

Abe stopped pulling groceries from his bag. "What about it?"

He shrugged. "I'm talking to Sadie today outside temple."

"How's she holding up?" Treya asked.

"You know. A good few minutes, a bad day or two. It's still so soon. We only just laid him down, when . . . ?" Nat lost his thread to sadness for a second. "Anyway, she asks would I please thank you for telling her about this man they arrested, this friend of your friend Hardy."

"They haven't arrested him yet, Dad. He's still at large."

Nat took on a querulous tone. "I swore you said they arrested him."

"No. Not yet."

After a moment, Nat shrugged again. "Well, maybe that's just as well."

"Just as well? Why do you say that?"

"Because this morning she's watching the television and the news has the story of all the evidence they found at this man's house — the money and the rings and so on. Especially this one sapphire ring."

"What about it?"

"What about it is that Sam only had one ring like they described — this one — and it definitely wasn't missing when Sadie and I went to take the inventory there. Remember? When you came that night? We never got too far, but we looked in the jewel case. The ring was in there that night. She was sure of it."

"Maybe the one they found was another ring like it, Dad. This one had Sam's tag on it."

He shook his head. "That's what I'm saying, Abraham. Listen to me. It was Sam's, all right, but it was still in his case

500

when we went there. So whoever killed him didn't take it during the robbery. Something's got to be wrong with this, don't you think?"

Treya, too, had stopped unpacking groceries. She stood with her arms crossed, leaning back against the counter. "Does Sadie think she's sure about this, Nat?"

He looked at the two of them. "Not just Sadie. I saw it, too. We even talked about it, how it was good Sam never had to sell that one, his favorite piece in the shop. He thought it was lucky, for the cards, you know. So no. No question. It was there."

"Anybody shoot at you recently?"
"No."
"You call Kroll yet?"
"I'm still deciding."
"How about Holiday?"
"How about him? Why, what's up?"
"You know how I wasn't going to get involved?"
"It filled me with admiration."
"Me, too. But alas, short-lived. There's been a development."
"Talk to me."

The way Glitsky decided he had to play it was to have Sadie call the police and appear to take care of the matter herself. His own involvement under any guise wasn't going to be appreciated, no matter what spin he put on it. He felt pretty much out of spin in any case.

Sadie lived in a stand-alone bungalow on Palm Avenue, not far from the synagogue. Inside, the place was a pin-neat kitsch warehouse. Every conceivable surface — the top of the television set, the bread-basket in the kitchen — every inch of flat space was covered with a doily and then a knickknack or doll, a porcelain piece or souvenir. Coney Island! Disneyland! Niagara Falls! The Grand Canyon! Tiny dogs and cute little cats. Pincushions.

Sadie cleared a spot big enough to hold a teapot and cups on the small table in front of the sofa in the living room. It had grown dark outside by now. With two small sconced wall lights by the door providing the only illumination, Glitsky thought it probably wasn't light enough to read, but neither his father, who sat next to her on the couch, nor Sadie herself seemed to mind, or even notice.

She poured his tea and sat expectantly while he tried to explain. "I know that because I'm with the police, it seems like I would be the natural choice to take your information, especially since I know you. You know Nat. We're all a little like family. But that's not really how it works."

"I know how offices work," she said, laying a frail hand on his. "Somebody's afraid you're going to get the credit."

"Maybe there's some of that. But basically there are two inspectors in the homicide detail who are handling the case — in this instance probably all of these cases — and whatever information comes to the police ought to be funneled through them."

Sadie was smiling at him as though he were somehow feeble. She had left her hand, cool and crepe-skinned, over his, and now she exerted some slight pressure for emphasis. "I'll do whatever you tell me and talk to anybody you want. All I know is what I saw."

"I saw it, too," Nat repeated, and Sadie rewarded him with a grateful look.

"And that's the ring, this sapphire ring?"

"Well, yes, that one stands out. But really, there wasn't any jewelry taken at all, although that would of course be harder to prove."

"And why is that?"

"Because they may have taken something I'd never seen. Maybe Sam had taken in some stones or something that day. I wouldn't have known they were there, then, would I?"

"No. Of course you're right." Glitsky decided he'd fallen into the error of assuming that Sadie wasn't as sharp as a younger person might have been. Enough of that. "So you could swear that the sapphire ring was in the case when you went there with Nat?"

"Yes. No doubt of it. We — Nat and I — we even wrote it on the inventory before you stopped us. I've got it saved."

Given the condition of the house, this didn't surprise Glitsky, but he was still glad of it. "That's good. You might want to bring that with you when you talk to the inspectors."

"Well, shall we call them now?" she asked. "I'd like to get this out of the way. It just doesn't seem right that this other man . . ."

"John Holiday?"

"Yes, that was it. That this Mr. Holiday — well, I don't see that he killed Sam, let's put it that way. I think somebody must have been trying to be too clever by half. Maybe they didn't know — they must not have known — that Nat and I had been in the shop that other night. If it had only been the money, that would have been stronger."

Glitsky felt a small shiver at the back of his neck. "Let me ask you something else, if I may. Didn't I hear that Sam had stopped using the Patrol Specials last summer?"

She nodded. "It just didn't seem to be worth it. Mr. Panos was asking more and more. We hadn't had any kind of trouble for years and years. We talked about it, but just finally thought . . ."

Nat reached over and patted her hand. "It's all right," he said. "They were there that night and it didn't save him anyway, did it?"

"No," she said with great sadness. "You're right. You're right. It wasn't that."

"But my point," Abe said, "is whether they still had a key to the shop."

20

The 49ers had a good day and beat Green Bay 21–3. The tickets Roy Panos had given Dan Cuneo were at the forty-five yard line, fifteen rows off the field. Perfect seats. The sun was out and there was no wind, though it was chilly enough here at Candlestick Point that now, walking back to his car, Liz snugged up close up against him, her arm around his waist.

She felt the vibration, too. "What's that?"

"Pager," he said. He pulled the little unit off his belt. "My partner, from home."

As he held it, it vibrated again, and he sighed, smiling at her. "And here's another one."

"Mister Popularity," she said.

"That's me." But when he saw the number, his smile faded. "My boss, from *his* home."

He had a cell phone in his car, and he

called Gerson first. The lieutenant told him that the Silverman widow had called earlier in the day, saying she had discovered some new and important information about her husband's murder. Gerson wanted Cuneo to go and talk to her. He gave him the address.

"I'm on it," Cuneo said. He hung up, turned to Liz. "Work."

Liz wore a half-mocking pout. "You don't really seem too sad about it."

"It's a big case," he said. "This Silverman thing again."

"I thought you had a suspect for that."

"We do. Maybe somebody's found where he is. That could be what this is."

"And then what?"

"And then maybe I get to make the arrest."

"All by yourself?"

Modest, he shrugged. "If I have to."

She smiled at him now. "You love what you do, don't you?"

"Yes, ma'am, I sure do."

"But how do I know for sure those two calls really weren't other girlfriends?"

He turned to her in the car seat. "First, because I'm a policeman, and cops don't lie. Second, I don't have other girlfriends. I'm not even sure I have one girlfriend, to tell you the truth, although I was kind of hoping to find out about that before too long."

Smiling, she took the cue and leaned across the seat, brought her lips up to his. The kiss went on for close to a minute, and there was nothing platonic about it. When they separated, she said, "On that girlfriend question, you can say you have one if you decide you want to."

For the first time in quite a while, Cuneo was tempted to let something else come before his work. He struggled to get a breath, leaned over and kissed her again. His hand found her breast. One of her hands went to his leg. His pager went off again. The kiss ended and he groaned, pulled the pager from his belt. "Lincoln again," he said. "Would you like to call this time, make sure it's really him and not a girl?"

"That's all right," she said. "I think I believe you. Will whatever it is you're doing this afternoon take a long time?"

"It's hard to say. I don't even know what it's all about yet. But if I'm done early, I could stop by again and maybe we could . . ."

Her finger traced his lower lip, shutting him up. "No maybe about it," she said.

On its way back to San Francisco from the Truckee Airport, the Kamov Ka-32 helicopter *thwacked* its boisterous way down the Little Grand Canyon, the little-sung but majestically beautiful passage cut into the Sierra Nevada by the American River. Its two passengers, Nick Sephia and Julio Rez, were sitting strapped in behind Mikhail, their pilot. Perhaps they should have been relaxed from two nights of gambling and four women between them, but this morning Sephia's Uncle Roy had called, waking them at ten o'clock, not even five hours after Nick had paid off Trixie and finally fallen into a comalike sleep. Roy told Nick he needed them both back in the city — he was sending the Kamov back up for them. It seems they had made some mistakes and still had work to do.

Even with the windows closed, they could barely hear inside the chopper. But that didn't stop the sleep-deprived Sephia from bitching about things. "It's not like we didn't do enough these last couple of weeks. Roy's crazy to want us back in town. We ought to be lying low."

Rez shrugged.

"He told us to make it look good, didn't

he? Didn't we both figure the ring would lock it up? So now he's all, 'What if somebody noticed?' Who the fuck's gonna notice? And what are we going to do about it now anyway? It's done."

Rez put a fish eye on his partner. "You shouldn't have shot Sam."

"I had to shoot him. He had us made. *Me,* anyway. And fuckin' Roy, stopping to admire the jewelry. He's the only reason . . . it's his fault as much as mine."

"Yeah, but he's getting us out of it. So we just let him work it."

"Hey, Julio. Here's a tip — he's not working it. *We're* working it. Maybe you didn't notice who was there with Creed, who didn't even show up for the faggots."

"Whatever. It's working. It's his plan. We just stay cool; it'll be over."

"I am cool."

Rez looked over at him, snorted. "Oh yeah, you're cool."

"Hey, who missed Holiday? And Hardy? Both of 'em. Six shots. Didn't touch either one."

Rez threw it back at him. "Who drove like shit?"

They lapsed into a sullen and angry silence. Sephia closed his eyes and crossed his arms, trying to get some more sleep.

After two or three minutes of looking down into the wilderness, Rez leaned forward and put on his pair of headphones. "Hey, Mikhail!"

The pilot tilted his head. "Yah!"

"How much time we got?"

The pilot shrugged. "All we need. Shipment till tomorrow."

"You mean *not* till tomorrow, you dumb Polack. Why don't you swing us around?"

Mikhail didn't completely understand the complicated and unexpected request, so he turned in his seat. Rez pantomimed that he should turn the craft around and fly lower.

"Got to piss?" Mikhail asked.

Rez laughed and shook his head no. He repeated the order.

Sephia felt the lurch, the change in altitude and direction, and sat up, eyes open. "What's happening?" he yelled across to Rez, who didn't appear to hear. Sephia hit him on the arm and asked again.

"You'll see. A little fun." He pointed at his earphones. "Put them on. You're going to need 'em." Then, into his microphone, "Mikhail! Good! Down! Down! Okay, now. Slow."

The pilot put the helicopter into a steep dive, leveling off over the river, at perhaps sixty feet. The sides of the canyon rose up on both sides, towering over them. Then, suddenly, on the right, one of the canyon walls disappeared to reveal a grassy plain upon which grazed a herd of deer. Rez unstrapped his seat belt and suddenly pulled open the door. Rez tapped Mikhail on the shoulder and pointed down. "There!" he said. "There!"

He pulled a .45 automatic from his shoulder holster and turned to smile over at Sephia. The herd of perhaps twenty head didn't seem to know what to make of the noise from above them. As a body, it made a false start, then stopped again, and huddled together. Mikhail, getting the idea, hovered over them, circling.

The .45 fired three times in quick succession, deafening even over the noise of the prop. Rez whooped with a mad laughter as the chopper dipped and turned and he squeezed off two more rounds.

The remainder of the herd was moving now, out under the helicopter. Rez slammed his own door, crossed to Sephia's and yanked it open, slapping the gun with a yelp into his partner's hand, pointing down. The deer were right under him, forty feet below, milling in confusion.

Sephia nodded, took the gun and aimed

with both hands, then fired three times in three seconds. He pulled the trigger again, then noticed the slide all the way back, the chamber exposed. No more ammo.

But Rez pulled a fresh clip from his jacket pocket and handed it over. Sephia ejected the old one, dropped it onto the floor, and jammed the new one up in place. The slide slapped forward, the first round in the chamber. He took aim again. The standing deer had at last begun to run and Mikhail was chasing them toward a grove of trees.

Sephia took his shot. Squeezed again, but this second time, there was another empty click. Misfire. The first cartridge had jammed, bent now, halfway outside the chamber. Sephia swore again, but the sullen look had left his face. The two partners were ecstatic with the noise and the mayhem.

The rest of the deer reached the grove and Mikhail pulled up steeply, then whirled back around. Rez leaned out the open door and looked down, smiling.

In the pasture, six deer lay still in the brown grass.

Cuneo rang Mrs. Silverman's doorbell.
Out here in the western half of the city,

the wind had come up. Intermittent high clouds scudded overhead, permitting only a milky sunshine through them. Suddenly, Cuneo realized, from a sunny morning of great promise at his home in Alameda, it had become a depressing late-autumn afternoon.

Mrs. Silverman looked worn out, as though she hadn't slept well. Still in mourning, she wore a black skirt and matching sweater, a demure string of pearls. After he'd gotten seated at the dining room table and declined her offer of something to drink, he placed his tape recorder between them, delivered the standard test and preamble with his name and badge number, the date, and the identification of the witness. Then he asked Mrs. Silverman to tell him why she had contacted the police. She got to the crux of it immediately, with no prompting by Cuneo.

When she'd finished, for a long moment he couldn't think of a question. He sat back in the dining room chair and crossed one leg over the other. Finally, "But the ring was at Holiday's place, ma'am. I found it myself."

"I'm not denying it was there. I'm saying it wasn't taken the same night my husband was shot. It couldn't have been."

"And what does that mean to you?"

She settled back in her chair, a blackened figure in a dim room. "I don't know exactly. I was thinking it meant that Mr. Holiday couldn't have taken it, after all."

"Why not?"

"Well . . ."

"Maybe he saw the rings while he was there the first time and went back another day."

"But I locked the place up after I left, the night I started to do the inventory. I don't know how he could have gotten in."

"Maybe he had a key. Wasn't he a regular at these poker games?"

"Yes, but Sam didn't give those men keys to our shop. Sam wasn't stupid, Inspector."

"No, ma'am. No one's implying anything like that. But maybe he found an extra key somewhere in the shop when he was there the first time. Or even in the red pouch itself?"

Cuneo's suggestions seemed to upset her. "I didn't think of that. But I'm not sure Sam had many extras. Certainly he wouldn't have left any of them lying around."

"It would only have taken one." Cuneo came forward, put his arms on the table.

"Mrs. Silverman, we appreciate your coming forward with this. This is a very difficult time, I'm sure, and you want to do all you can to help. If nothing else, you've given us something else to look for at Holiday's place. If there's a key to your shop we've missed there, we'll go back and find it, I promise."

The little speech didn't seem to help much, but Cuneo got the feeling that nothing would. Mrs. Silverman sighed deeply. "I just wanted to make sure that the wrong man didn't suffer for what Sam's killer had done."

"I wouldn't worry about that. We've got the right man. The money proves that without any question, wouldn't you say?"

"I suppose."

Unambiguous as it was to Cuneo, somehow Mrs. Silverman seemed doubtful. "You don't seem too convinced."

"No, I . . . it's just that I had a thought that it might have been — what's the word? — planted there."

"Planted? By who?"

"Someone who could have gotten into the shop."

"Which brings us back to the key, doesn't it?" he asked gently.

"Yes, I suppose it does. But then I think

Wade Panos and his people might still have one, really are more likely to have one than this man Holiday, don't you think? From when they patrolled for us?"

Cuneo, suddenly, was all attention and focus. On the drive out, he had tried to dredge up from his memory all he could recall of Mrs. Silverman. Her name had stuck with him, and not just because she was a victim's spouse. He finally had remembered the name from Gerson's story about Abe Glitsky. Now when he heard the name Panos again, the connection came back to him. Glitsky's earlier use of Mrs. Silverman as a wedge to get back into homicide. Glitsky helping out some lawyers in their lawsuit against Panos. Beyond that, *John Holiday* out beating the streets for witnesses and plaintiffs in that same lawsuit.

Holiday and Glitsky. And by extension the lawyer, too. Hardy, the guy Blanca had told them about yesterday. All of them, co-conspirators.

And now Glitsky hitting a new low, using this grieving old woman to float the idea that the ring had been "planted," a word she hardly knew. Cuneo smiled and kept his tone as pleasant as he could. "Mrs. Silverman," he said, "I wouldn't torture myself with all these dark imaginings, if I were you. Are you still talking to Lieutenant Glitsky about this case?"

"Just last night," she said. "His father, Nat, was Sam's best friend. I called him when I remembered about the ring. He told me to get in touch with you."

I'll bet he did, Cuneo thought. After he'd coached you about your testimony. But to her, he simply nodded. "Well, that was smart of him. But if you ask him, he'll tell you the same thing. We're so used to TV and movies nowadays, we sometimes feel there's always got to be some unlikely twist, like somebody planting evidence. In the real world, most things are just what they look like." He came forward in his chair, lowered his voice to a near whisper. "If it eases your mind at all, whenever and however he got the ring, John Holiday probably wasn't the one who shot your husband. But he was there, doing the robbery, getting his poker money back, when Clint Terry lost his head and panicked and shot Sam. All the evidence supports that, ma'am. That's what we've got."

Pumped up with adrenaline, Cuneo walked up the dark driveway to the refurbished garage that Liz rented just off Silver

Avenue. Around at the side door, he saw candlelight flickering on the walls through the window. He knocked once, lightly, and a bulb came on over the door. "Who is it?"

"Liz. It's Dan Cuneo."

"Dan who?"

But then another light came on in the window and the door opened. She stood there smiling at him. Barefoot, she wore a green terry cloth bathrobe. Her hair wasn't yet completely dry and framed her pretty face in a black halo of curls. She had a glass of wine in her hand. He became aware of the thump of a jazzy bass line, caught a heady whiff of a musky perfume and, unmistakably, marijuana. "Did you get to arrest him?" she asked.

An hour later, Cuneo was as relaxed as he could ever remember feeling.

The bed was a mattress on the floor and he lay naked flat on his back upon it, one arm thrown back over his head, the other around the shoulders of his new lover. The music she'd had on when he got there had ended and now the apartment was silent. More incredibly to him, his own head was silent. Liz had pulled up the blanket and now lay pressed up against him, her left hand resting flat against his belly, her leg thrown over both of his. The candle cast the room in an amber glow.

"So somebody ought to tell Wade and Roy to watch out," he said. "These guys are serious. I mean, Glitsky's up there in the department. He's also tight with Clarence Jackman, the District Attorney. His wife, get this, is even Jackman's personal secretary."

"And they're all in this together?"

"My boss didn't know how high up it went. He didn't want to think it went to Jackman, but it might. But there's no doubt a conspiracy here."

"Trying to frame Wade?"

"That's what it looks like. Glitsky had this poor old lady prepped like you couldn't believe. Didn't Wade still have a key to Sam's place? I doubt she even knew what she was saying, but Glitsky sure as hell knew what he was feeding her."

Liz came up on an elbow and the blanket slipped down to reveal the arc of her breast. "I haven't heard Glitsky's name before around this. Although I know Dismas Hardy, of course, and David Freeman. They've been out to get us for most of the past year now. I don't know why. Wade's the nicest man. Secretary's Day last year he took me to Masa's. It must have cost him three hundred dollars. And flowers every day that week."

"You don't have to sell me. He basically did my job for me on this one."

"You're being modest."

"I don't know about that. But I do know Wade had better be careful. This Glitsky is a very serious man. Wade's got to be clear on that."

"I'll sit him down and make him listen. Except what can he do, really? That's the problem with being a good guy. You can't stop anybody until they do something to you first."

"So maybe somebody will do something."

"To Wade? I don't want that, either."

"No. I mean stop Glitsky. The DA or somebody might step in."

"I can't believe he's with the police and he's so bad."

"I know," Cuneo said. "It's a problem."

21

Motor running and heat on, Paul Thieu's car was parked across the street from Glitsky's duplex on Monday morning. When he and Treya came down their steps at a little after 7:30, Thieu turned off the engine, opened the door, and got out. Glitsky stopped, said something to his wife, and left her on the sidewalk while he crossed over.

"You could have come up and knocked, Paul," he said. "We would have let you in."

Thieu said, "I thought it would be better if we didn't talk at the Hall."

Thieu wasn't yet thirty-five years old, and Glitsky suddenly realized that except for Marcel Lanier, he was now the oldest inspector in homicide. He recalled when he'd pulled Thieu out of Missing Persons six years ago to translate as he'd interviewed the Vietnamese mother of another murder victim. Then, as now, the face had been grave — if the man had a flaw, he was too serious. This morning, he exuded gravity.

"I was going to be driving in with Treya," Glitsky said.

"I could take you, drop you off a block down."

It wasn't really a request. Glitsky had years and rank on Thieu, but neither played much of a role in their connection. Thieu's brains commanded respect, and Glitsky simply nodded, then walked over to Treya to give her the news.

She didn't exactly embrace it. "Unless I'm mistaken," she said, "Paul's still in homicide." Then, "You didn't sneak out and call him, did you?"

He tried a feeble joke. "Maybe it's about his overtime."

"Maybe it's about Sam Silverman."

Last night, Nat had called with a recap of the interview Sadie had had with Cuneo. Not that the inspector's theory was any less defensible than Glitsky's. Certainly it was possible that Holiday had reentered the store with a key and then stolen the ring on another day. But at the very least, Glitsky thought Cuneo should have been open to the possibility that someone — not necessarily Panos but necessarily Silverman's killers — had planted the ring at Holiday's. It made him wonder. Somehow homicide and Panos kept seeing facts — even ambiguous or incriminating facts — in the same light.

When he'd been in homicide, he'd never had that experience with the Patrol Special.

It still wasn't his job, but with the attack on Hardy, it was at least his business. Treya, even, had come to agree with that.

She kissed him good-bye and said she'd be around if he wanted to have lunch. He watched her walking away for a few steps, then put his hands in his flight jacket pockets and crossed the street.

"I've been wrestling with guilt," Thieu began after they were rolling.

"Who's winning?"

"I guess the guilt. I'm here." He threw a quick look across the seat at his old boss. "You know anything about this double in the 'Loin?" Wills and Terry.

Glitsky chuckled. "Treya just called it."

"What?"

"Silverman."

Thieu took that in, nodding as though it confirmed something he'd been thinking. "I didn't draw Silverman. It wasn't ever my case. You know Cuneo and Russell?"

"Not personally."

Thieu shrugged. "Well, they got Silverman. Few nights later, I pull this kid Creed, who was the main witness for Silverman."

"I heard," Glitsky said.

"You know about this?"

"Some." He looked over, qualified it. "What I read in the papers."

Stopped at a red light, Thieu tried to find a clue in Glitsky's expression. Apparently, there wasn't one. "All right, I'll cut to the chase. Creed and these two poor schmucks in the 'Loin, suddenly they're connected because Creed had ID'd them for Silverman. Then a gun's at their place, ballistics confirms it killed both Silverman and Creed, everybody's happy, right?"

"I know I am," Glitsky said.

"Except there's a third guy Creed named."

"John Holiday."

The trace of a smile lifted Thieu's mouth. "But you're not following the case."

Glitsky shook his head, straight-faced. "Hardly at all."

"Then maybe you wouldn't know they pulled a warrant for him."

"I did hear something about that."

"Okay, here's where the guilt comes in.

None of these are my cases. Gerson yanked two of them out from under me after I'd already worked the scenes."

"Let me guess," Glitsky said. "You're conflicted about telling them they screwed up."

Another red light had stopped them. Thieu turned to his mentor. "Worse. I *want* them to screw up."

Glitsky sat with it a minute. "What'd they miss?" he asked.

It wasn't a long laundry list, but it was compelling enough. Thieu told Glitsky that when it had become obvious that Holiday, by default, was going to become the prime suspect in all the murders, Thieu had gone by the place he worked and, to his own satisfaction, verified that he had a reasonably good and, more importantly, verifiable alibi for the time of his bartender's — Terry's — death. Thieu had questioned dozens of killers and witnesses in his six years in homicide, and was all but positive that if the arrest warrant hadn't been hustled through so quickly, Holiday would have supplied the names of his customers who would have eliminated him as a suspect at least in the deaths of Wills and Terry.

Beyond that, Thieu said, it flew in the

face of reason that this grotesque and sexually tinged double murder had been a result of thieves falling out among themselves. There was also too much of Silverman's money lying around — if it was about the robbery, Holiday would have known it was there somewhere and at least searched for it. Then taken it.

In Thieu's opinion, and he'd given it a lot of thought, only two scenarios worked here. One was Faro's: this was a pickup gone bad. The other was his own: that whoever killed these guys was some kind of psycho who enjoyed it all right, but whose true motive was to implicate the only suspect left alive, Holiday. Who, unfortunately for the actual bad guys, had an alibi. The whole thing screamed overkill. It was far too neat a package. The dope, the money, the gun, the shoes.

"Oh, and while we're on the shoes." Thieu had been talking for five minutes and now suddenly paused for a breath. "You read about the gunk? All well and good. Nice Italian shoes, size thirteen. But guess what? Terry wore a thirteen, all right, but the Italian thirteen is at least a half size smaller than our thirteen. No way he wears those shoes. They weren't his. Especially when every other pair in the closet was crappy. Six pairs of sneakers, some Birken-stocks, flip-flops, one lace-up wingtip. Anybody who looked would see which pair didn't belong there."

"But they didn't look. And you didn't tell them."

"Another source of my guilt. I figured if they're going to be on the case, they can work it. So the closet's got all these junk shoes, and then this Italian braided beauty with the gunk on it, and half a size too small." Thieu shook his head. "It doesn't make any sense. You want my opinion, somebody knew what we'd be looking for and planted this stuff."

Glitsky kept his face impassive. "Funny you should use that word," he said, and gave Thieu the gist of Sadie Silverman's testimony, Cuneo's interpretation.

After Thieu heard it out, he sat drumming his fingers on the steering wheel. "I've got to tell the lieutenant about these clowns, Abe. I've got to. Except then . . ." He didn't have to say it. Cops didn't fink on other cops. Gerson might appreciate the news, but Thieu would forever be tainted in some way, out of the club more than he already was by virtue of his race, brains, physical size. "It'd be sweeter if Gerson found it out by himself."

It wouldn't only be sweeter, Glitsky knew, but it would save the good Inspector Thieu from the sure-to-be-thorny explanation of why he hadn't told Cuneo and Russell everything that he'd discovered and theorized instead of leaving them to find out for themselves. Thieu felt guilty about it, and Glitsky empathized with where he was coming from. But the fact was that he should have felt guilty. He hadn't done the right thing.

They pulled up to the curb a couple of blocks before they reached the Hall. Glitsky had his hand on the door handle, but paused a last second. "Look, Paul. I happen to know Holiday's lawyer. He'd be motivated to verify some of those alibi names. Maybe he could talk one of them into volunteering to come in. Tell his story."

"You know," Thieu said, "it's not that I care about this John Holiday. I sure as hell don't want to help his defense if it needs it. But I don't believe he did Wills and Terry." He wiped his eyes as though banishing the image. "I screwed up, too, didn't I?"

"It's a big club, Paul. Welcome to it. At least you feel bad about it."

"Maybe not bad enough to tell Gerson."

"Well, the plain fact is that he done you

wrong, too." He opened the door, got out, and leaned back in. "Give it a day or two. I'll call Holiday's lawyer. Make something happen."

Holiday's lawyer felt a hundred years old. The bruise on his back had blossomed into a dinnerplate-size black-and-blue mark that woke him up whenever he shifted in bed over the entire weekend. The whole left hand continued to throb.

Glitsky called. On and on about Sadie, Cuneo, Holiday, the planted or not-planted ring. And of course, the client never got in touch.

Sunday night he'd taken a Vicodin left over from somewhere, then drunk two scotches with his brother-in-law before dinner. Two bottles of red wine with Moses after. Up too late, near midnight, Moses at his most passionate and most drunk, pressing for retaliation against Panos and his people *now!* Before they could strike at Hardy again. Hardy halfway — more than halfway — into it. Really, really pissed off. Embarrassingly so, he supposed. Foolishly. Frannie supervising the kids' homework far in the back of the house where maybe it wouldn't sound so awful. Susan finally packing Moses up and driving him home.

Both women angry with their men. Frustrated, exhausted, afraid.

Out of bed, badly hungover — dying — at 5:30, and no chance of going back to sleep, not with the back, the head, the hand. For the first time in months, he couldn't even be bothered with the newspaper. Out of the house before anyone else was up, he stopped at St. Francis to check on David, who perhaps on his deathbed looked just like Hardy felt. An hour in the office produced a cup of coffee and fourteen minutes of disjointed dictation. He was never going to drink alcohol again.

Getting nothing done, he went back down to his car, which was parked under the building. Paranoid, he knelt and looked under the chassis, not really knowing what he was looking for. Moses's warnings kept replaying in his brain — the brother-in-law had not been mellow at all about Hardy getting shot at. He got into the driver's seat, stopped himself, then pulled the lever to open the hood, got all the way out and around the front again, and lifted it. "Motor," he said aloud. Disgusted with himself.

At the Hall of Justice, Hector Blanca was busy; he'd be a while. Hardy waited in the outer office while time passed. A half hour. Forty-five minutes. He asked at the desk again, was told that it might still be a few minutes.

An hour.

The secretary finally suggested he come back another time. Sergeant Blanca really wasn't going to be able to spare any time this morning. "Well, I wonder if you'll be able to help me, then." He heard himself, the clipped and impatient tone guaranteed in any bureaucracy to produce glassy-eyed, unfeeling incomprehension, if not outright hostility. He reined himself in, fooling no one, however. "Listen. Someone shot at me last Friday — shot at me! — and I was hoping to find out if Sergeant Blanca or anybody else had made any progress finding out who it might have been."

The secretary shook his head. "Did you make out a report? Well then, as soon as we have something, the sergeant will let you know."

He walked back down a long hallway to the main lobby, where the day had now progressed enough to where the familiar vulgar din reigned, maybe even louder than usual. The traffic court line stretched from the ticket window, out past the elevator banks, over to the coffee kiosk, where he waited in another line to place his order. A baby was crying up front while, closer to him, a couple of five-year-olds chased each other, screaming. In the entrance to the courtroom hallway, a man in a frock and collar was lecturing a group of fifteen or twenty people in Spanish. A shaggy young man, barefoot, fell into line behind him and hit him up for some spare change. Reaching into his pockets, he found some coins and dropped them into the man's dirty, outstretched hand.

The coffee line wasn't moving, or maybe he had mistakenly wandered into the traffic line after all. Either way, he walked to the elevators and stepped into an open one, pressing 4, Glitsky's old floor, out of habit. Six people shared the car with him — he didn't hear a word of English. When it stopped at his floor, he got out and stood lost in the suddenly empty, almost eerily quiet, space.

The elevator area on all the floors looked almost identical, so he'd gotten well into the hallway that should have led to Glitsky's new digs when it struck him that something was wrong. Familiar, but wrong.

He stopped again, looked around.

Out of a doorway further along on the

right, two men emerged and turned toward him. One — gray-haired, heavy and be-spectacled — wore a well-tailored tan business suit. The other was a policeman in uniform. They were coming toward him, talking easily to one another, and at about twenty feet, recognition kicked in. Hardy moved into their path. "Richard," he said to Kroll.

"Diz! How you doin'? I think you know Roy Panos. Roy, Dismas Hardy."

"Sure." Roy's smile evaporated. He nodded cautiously, but neither man offered to shake hands.

Kroll put on the proper face. "So how's David coming along?"

"Not well, I'm afraid."

"No change at all?"

Hardy shook his head. "It doesn't look too good, Dick."

He put a hand on Hardy's arm. "I am so sorry to hear that. Is there anything I can do? Or anybody can do? Anything at all?"

"I think they're doing all they can." Hardy motioned with his head. "So you been down at homicide?"

"What? Oh, yeah." Kroll laughed out of all context. "Following up on poor Matt Creed. Did you know Matt?"

"No. Afraid not."

"Good kid. A real tragedy."

"Yeah," Hardy said. "I'm aware of the case."

"Oh, that's right. Sorry."

"No need to be. It wasn't my client. He didn't do it."

"No. Of course not. You going down now to explain about that to Gerson?"

Hardy forced a cold grin. "Something like that."

"Well, good luck."

"Thanks."

Hardy started for homicide as Kroll and Panos walked toward the elevators. He heard their talking resume in modulated tones. Suddenly, Kroll's voice pierced the silence again. "Oh, Diz!"

Hardy turned.

"On the other matter." He walked a little back the way he'd come, lowered his voice. "I don't know if you've heard. Your witness LaBonte?"

"Aretha? What about her?"

He moved two or three steps closer, started to talk, stopped, started again. "I just heard about it from Gerson. You know they hauled her in for hooking again yesterday." He hung his head for an instant. When he looked up, he met Hardy's gaze. "I know you're getting a lot of bad news this week, Diz, and I hate to add to it, but I guess she couldn't take the life anymore. Sometime last night she hanged herself in her cell."

Hardy never intended to go to homicide anyway, so deciding to climb to Glitsky's floor by the inside stairs wasn't much of a change of plans. But he didn't go up them right away.

When the hallway door closed behind him, he turned around and sat heavily on the second step. He leaned over, feeling sick, elbows on his knees, his pounding head resting on the heel of his one good hand.

Hardy hadn't been Aretha's criminal defense attorney because, frankly, she couldn't afford him. She was a professional girl who got busted two or three times a year. Nevertheless, in the past six months, he'd come to know Aretha fairly well. She was twenty-four years old, black, functionally illiterate. The fact that she did not have a pimp contributed to the continuing difficulties in her life because she had no street protection, but she did have a steady boyfriend, Damoan. Quiet and polite, although unkempt and gang-dressed, Damoan often accompanied her to depositions and court appearances. It seemed to Hardy that the couple was happy with each other, unlikely as that might seem.

With Freeman, Hardy had spent several hours with her, coaching her, taking her statements. But also having coffee, joking, driving someplace or another. He'd come to know her as an honest, uncomplicated person with a surprisingly sunny disposition and outlook. Things — sometimes terrible things — seemed to roll right off her. She'd probably spent two hundred nights of her life in jail. She'd told Hardy, and he believed her, that she viewed the experience as a neutral one. On the one hand, it gave her some time off; on the other, it was a hassle and an inconvenience.

Kroll's statement that she must have "grown tired of the life" didn't wash with anything Hardy knew about the woman. She hadn't begun to lose her looks yet. Sephia's plant on her notwithstanding, she didn't use hard drugs. Unless she and Damoan had broken up, and he'd seen them apparently happy together within the past week, she was as unlikely a candidate for suicide as Hardy could imagine.

He opened his eyes and raised his head, slowly got to his feet. He turned around, looked at the stairs, wondered if he could muster the strength to climb them.

When Hardy first came in, Glitsky brought him a glass of water and four aspirin. Now the door to the office was closed. Glitsky sat behind his desk, scowling, tugging absently at a rubber band. "She must have, though."

"I can't accept it. Somebody got to her."

"In her cell? Not as easy as it sounds, Diz." He snapped the band a few times. "But don't get me wrong. I'm not ruling it out entirely." After a minute, he added, "Maybe you were right keeping Holiday outside."

"It wasn't my decision," Hardy said, "but I'd advise against it now. Not that I've had a chance."

"You haven't talked to him?"

"Not since Friday. I don't even know where he is."

Glitsky pulled the rubber band apart and sighted through it.

"You can give me that look all you want," Hardy said, "but it's a true story. He's gone to ground."

"All right, let's say I believe you. I'm still having trouble with Panos somehow connected to the jail."

"Maybe he passes the word through homicide."

Glitsky snorted. "Now you are dreaming."

Hardy lifted his shoulders and immediately regretted it. He didn't care if Glitsky couldn't see *how* it might happen. Something *had* happened. Aretha LaBonte was dead in jail and he didn't believe she killed herself. And that left only one other option. "You can laugh," Hardy said, "but I just saw them down there."

The laughing, if that's what the snort had been, stopped. "Who? Down where?"

"Roy Panos. Downstairs. One floor down."

"In homicide?"

"With my close friend Dick Kroll. Evidently checking up on the Creed investigation."

Glitsky sat up straight. "What were they checking on, the shoes?"

"What about the shoes?"

It didn't take Glitsky long to tell it.

"So you're saying Terry didn't shoot Creed after all."

"He still might have. Half a shoe size is close."

"Going up, okay, but not going down. If the shoe don't fit, you gotta acquit."

Glitsky frowned at the reference. "Please," he said, "spare me. But my question is: Does Panos even know about that? Thieu hasn't even told Gerson yet."

Hardy reached for his paper cup and sipped some water. He realized that the aspirin had begun to kick in. Only slightly, but he'd take it. "If it's any help, I got the impression that they weren't there about Creed anyway. Kroll just said the first plausible thing that came to mind."

"Okay. And this means what?"

"I don't know. Maybe nothing. But maybe they're all pals, sharing information."

Glitsky was back with his rubber band, his face set. "So Panos would know what evidence they still needed? Which would tell him what to plant and where to put it?"

"You said it, not me."

"It's just what I warned Gerson about."

"When was that?"

"When this whole thing started, back with Silverman. Right after Wade gave the inspectors his list of suspects."

A short silence settled; then Hardy said, "Somebody's got to tell him. Gerson."

"He doesn't want to know. At least not from me."

"How about Clarence?"

"How about him?"

"He's not going to want to try this thing if the evidence is bogus. You'd be doing him a favor. Plus, he'd listen to you, as opposed to someone else in this room."

"Why wouldn't he listen to you?"

Hardy didn't think he needed to give the complete explanation. "It's my client, Abe," he said. "Think about it. You're an objective third party."

Glitsky knocked, got Jackman's "Yes" and opened the door. The DA, reading something at his desk and perhaps thinking it was Treya, looked up in mild, pleasant expectancy. But as soon as he saw Glitsky, his expression hardened by a degree. His eyes went down, then came back up. Flat, controlled. He smiled in a perfunctory way.

Feeling something in the gaze, Glitsky stopped halfway to the desk. "Sorry to bother you, Clarence, but Treya said you might be free, and this is important."

The smile stayed in place. Jackman gestured at the papers spread around his desk. "Freedom's relative, Abe, and everything is important. The job is important. What can I do for you?"

"How do you get along with Barry Gerson?"

Jackman took a beat. "You mean professionally? About the same as I did with you when you had his job. Why?"

"Because he's being used. He's going to be badly embarrassed. Somebody's got to get the message to him, and it can't be me."

"Why not?"

"He thinks I want his job."

Jackman pushed himself back a bit, folded his hands on the desk. "You haven't made that much of a secret, Abe. You've told me the same thing ten times in the past year and a half."

Glitsky took one of the chairs in front of Jackman's desk. "True. But for some reason he's thinking I'm interfering with one of his investigations, trying to make him look bad, get him fired or transferred so I can get back in."

"Why do you think that would be?"

"That's a long story, but essentially because I've asked him for some information on the Silverman homicide, which has turned out to be connected to a few other cases."

"You're right." Jackman delivered it as a surprise. "Gerson is thinking that."

Glitsky crossed a leg, scratched at his scar. "You've talked to him?"

A nod. "Yesterday." All trace of warmth had left Jackman's face. "On Sunday. At home. Actually, it was both Lieutenant Gerson and Dan Rigby, conferenced in."

Glitsky sucked in a breath. Dan Rigby was the chief of police.

Jackman continued. "The chief said that since you and Treya were in my inner circle, as he called it, as is Dismas, maybe I should have a word with some or all of you and see if between us we can bring some reason to bear here. So your dropping in today is fortuitous after all. And, as you say, important."

His formal smile appeared briefly, then vanished. "The chief mentioned the possibility of filing charges against both you and Diz for conspiracy to obstruct justice in this rash of homicides for which his client — Holiday is it? — has been accused. But the chief thought that in view of your record, your past heroism and so forth, I might be able to exert some influence and get you to stop what he called this misguided campaign to smear Wade Panos."

Glitsky shook his head in anger and disbelief. "This is not misguided, Clarence. This is real. They shot at Diz. You know what they've done to Freeman — you've seen him."

"And that was Panos?"

"Yes."

"You're sure?"

"Yes, sir. Absolutely.

"And your certainty is based upon what? Incriminating physical evidence?"

At this, Glitsky sat back, planted his elbows on the arms of his chair. A muscle worked at the side of his jaw. "I've got a witness," he said, "who gave them something that strongly indicates that *their* evidence is bogus. I'm assuming that's what they called about. Sadie Silverman."

"That's accurate." Jackman inclined his head an inch. "Let me ask you this, Abe. Why did you get this witness? What's your role here? Why are you even involved at all?"

"She came to me, Clarence. Through my father. I didn't seek her out."

"All right, grant that. Did you then speak with her about her testimony?"

"I didn't coach her, if that's what you're implying. I heard what she had to say, then told her to call homicide."

"You didn't indicate to her that perhaps one of Mr. Panos's men planted some bogus evidence?"

Glitsky squirmed in the chair, chewed at the inside of his lip.

"I'll take your silence for a yes." The DA sighed. "You know, Abe, I hate to say this, but some people seem to think you're involved in this for your own personal gain."

"I won't dignify that with —"

Jackman held up a hand. "If you're any part of Diz's team in this lawsuit and he wins, some people think you'd stand to make a bundle. And at the expense of the city and the police department."

"But I'm not on his team."

"You haven't supplied him with information about this lawsuit against Mr. Panos?"

"Yes, but . . ."

"Then you'll admit there's an appearance."

"Nobody's paying me anything, Clarence. Even if they win."

"I don't know if I'd brag about that if I were you," Jackman said. "It doesn't make you look very astute." He paused. "But I'm not getting into the truth or falsehood, or even the wisdom, of any of this. I'm simply telling you as a friend that the money motive is plausible to the point of certainty to several men of good will *within the police department*. You are on very, very thin ice here, Abe."

"Clarence —"

The hand again. "Let me just add a personal note, if I may." The voice was modulated, controlled, no sign of anger, but Glitsky wasn't much fooled. This was the sound of Jackman's purest fury — he'd heard him press for the death penalty with the same inflections. "It's absolutely true that you and Treya, even Dismas and Gina Roake — and certainly David Freeman — are all in my 'inner circle.' We're professional colleagues, but more than that, I think, we've developed a real bond in the years since we've been meeting at Lou's. We're friends."

"Yes, sir. I feel the same way."

"Good. So you'll understand." He came forward. "Can you possibly imagine that I wouldn't do all I can to use the power of this office to help any one of you if there were facts, evidence, proof, *anything at all*, that could justify an investigation of Mr. Panos and his activities? Or anybody else. Of course I would. It hurts me that you could doubt that."

"I don't doubt it, Clarence. It's why I've come to you today."

"But you don't have anything I can use, Abe. And by contrast, Lieutenant Gerson has two experienced inspectors, eyewitness testimony and lots of physical evidence. I cannot in good conscience ignore all of that. Frankly, I'm not even inclined to. And closer to home, I will not let it appear that I'm willing to manipulate the system to help my friends. My problem is not Mr. Panos. It's you and Diz, putting me in an untenable position. Surely you can see that?"

"That's not our intention."

"No. I'm sure it's not. But it is the result." Jackman straightened up, drew a deep breath. "Now I told Diz the same thing that I'm going to tell you now. Unless and until new evidence comes to light through the proper channels, and that means the homicide department, I don't want to have to discuss this with you again. I *won't* discuss it with you again. Is that clear, Abe?"

"Yes, sir."

"All right, then."

22

Michelle was out shopping for food, picking up something they could eat at home since dining in a restaurant together was not in the cards. Holiday stared out through the blinds at the overcast day, then brought his eyes back to the sheet of paper in front of him on Michelle's kitchen table. It was a little past noon and, out of habit, he'd poured himself the last couple of ounces, neat, from the bottle of bourbon he'd bought maybe a week ago and nipped at nearly every day since.

But today the taste for it wasn't there. He hadn't touched the glass. Looking at it now, his hand started to reach for it, then stopped.

He came back to the paper, on which he'd written four names — Tom, Evan, Bryan (or Ryan?), Leslie. He knew there had been at least four others, maybe five, at the bar with him the night that Clint and Randy had been killed, but he couldn't dredge them up from the sludge of his unconscious. Hardy, when he finally got over berating him for not calling sooner, said it could be extremely important, the verification of his alibi. His friend Glitsky, the cop, had evidently suggested he try to come up with his customers' names. Holiday had been his usual confident self, telling his lawyer no problem, he'd have some kind of a list for him within an hour at the most. And then Hardy could run around checking up on them.

Well, he had made up some weak kind of list, true, but it wasn't likely to do him or anybody else much good. These were the first names of his customers, who were not even acquaintances of his, and no sooner had he begun in earnest than he realized he had no more notion of their last names than he did of their occupations, addresses, the kinds of cars they drove. They were, in essence, complete strangers. Cash customers.

He found it ironic that any one of them, if they could be found, might be able to save him from a murder conviction. But what was the likelihood of that? They were talking about last Wednesday night, already five days into the past. It was the last night Holiday had worked the bar, and now even he, highly motivated, could only remember four possible names.

And in another day or two, he knew it wouldn't be worth the effort at all. The typical customer at the Ark probably drank in some dive every night, so his possible saviors were in all probability unsure about which night exactly they had been at the Ark. Wednesday? Or was that Lefty O'Doul's, or John's Grill? Or was that Tuesday? John had been on, bartending both nights. He put the pen down and closed his eyes, trying to remember anything distinctive that would set Wednesday apart, to him or to any of his customers.

Nothing came to mind.

He opened his eyes and there was his neat bourbon. He picked up the glass and took of sniff of it — great stuff, Knob Creek — but suddenly there seemed something distasteful about it. Not the bourbon itself, but the hold it had over him. The blurred memory that was right now hampering his efforts to save his own future had come a shot at a time from a bottle much like this one.

The blurred memory . . .

He stood up and walked over to the window, separating the blinds slightly. The city wasn't pretty today. The Bay churned gray-green, dotted with whitecaps. He closed his eyes again and tried to reimagine the bar as it had been that all-important Wednesday night, the people who'd been sitting there right in front of him. No doubt he'd had conversations with some of them, told jokes, listened to their stories. He hadn't gotten anywhere near to blacking out that night, and still, now, five days later, none of it was there.

Nor, he was sure, would it be there for any of the others.

It was as though he hadn't lived those hours. They were simply gone. As today would be, he knew, if he picked up that glass and drank it off.

And after all, what difference did it make?

All he knew was that suddenly, for some reason, it did. He shouldn't be so willing to fight for his life, to try to clear his name, if the days were just going to continue on, a succession of empty and forgettable moments. He did not want empty anymore. If it took someone trying to take his life away to enable him to see it, then at least he'd seen it in time.

The feeling came as unheralded as it was undeniable. He wanted Michelle to come back through that door. He wanted to be alive for it. For her.

For him.

He picked up the glass and poured its contents into the sink. He rinsed every trace of alcohol out of the glass, went to the refrigerator, filled it with orange juice and drank.

She did come back. They had tomato and mozzarella slices on sourdough bread with olive oil, vinegar, sea salt. The grocery store sold fresh basil in little handfuls, and they ate it leaf by leaf with the sandwiches, with Pellegrino water. They were just finishing when Michelle's cell phone went off. She answered and gave it to him. His lawyer.

"Any luck with your list?"

"Three and half first names. I don't know if one guy was Bryan or Ryan."

"Any last names?" Hardy wasn't in a good mood today, hadn't been for a while. "First names don't do us any good."

"I know. I'll keep trying. Meanwhile, what?"

"Meanwhile, not much. If you're okay where you are, stay put."

"That's my plan, Diz. But is anybody having any luck finding who shot at us?"

"Not much. In fact, there's a healthy skepticism about whether it happened at all."

"Of course it happened."

"Except there's no sign of it. Apparently, I'm capable of faking these scratches and bruises to make Panos look bad."

"You tell 'em it was Sephia?"

"He was in Nevada."

"When?"

"When we got shot at. Well, a couple of hours later."

"So?"

"So it's four hours away."

"Not by helicopter. The Diamond Center's got a helicopter, remember. Sephia works for them." The line hummed with silence. "Diz?"

"I'm here. I've got another question for you."

"Battle of Hastings. Ten sixty-six."

"No. Good answer, though. The question is what made Sephia go to Silverman's? I mean in the first place."

"That's too easy."

"Humor me."

"Okay. How about fifteen thousand dollars or so?"

"That might do it. But what was that?"

"That's what he lost the night before."

Hardy spoke hesitantly, as though afraid

he'd unhear what he'd just heard. "I thought *you* were the one who lost so big."

"I did. We both did, although Nick lost more. Sam had a great night."

"John, why didn't you tell me this before?"

"You never asked, Diz. Nobody asked. It never came up."

He heard a sigh over the line. "Okay. So who else would have known about it?"

"Anybody else who was at the game. I heard the cops knew. That's how they got to me."

"I hate to bore you with another list, but I doubt I can get my hands on the police version."

Thirty seconds later, Hardy had the names of the poker players and another question. This, to Holiday, was as easy as the first one. "Sure. Julio Rez and Roy Panos. The three of them are always together. You notice they were at the game, too?"

"So who's Rez?"

"There's a woman in the room with me. It's hard to be frank."

"But trouble?"

"That would be a fair assessment. I bet it was him."

"Who?"

"Rez. Who shot at us. Nick driving. Or vice versa. It doesn't really matter."

"But with Roy Panos, it gives us three, doesn't it? And that does matter. That's the magic number."

"Well, whatever it is, it sure looks like you've kicked up a lot of shit."

After a short pause, Hardy's voice came back, the tone harsh. "What's that supposed to mean, John? I'm doing all I can here for you."

"I'm not denying it. You have my undying gratitude. But the sad fact of the matter is, all you're doing is exactly what you should be doing for yourself, anyway."

"I *should?* There's no *should* here, John. I'm doing you a favor, plain and simple. You'd be advised to count your blessings."

"Kiss my ass, Diz. You're doing this because I wouldn't be here in this mess if it wasn't for you."

"Me? Jesus Christ . . ."

"Jesus Christ yourself. Who do you think started this whole thing? Here's a hint. It wasn't Panos, who was minding his own business until some lawyers decided to take him down and make a pile of cash in the process."

"You know what kind of business it was, John?"

"So? They broke some rules. What are you and Freeman all of the sudden? The guardian angels of the Tenderloin? You're telling me you guys went after him because of your concern for justice and goodness? My ass."

"Talk to some of my clients."

"I have, Diz. Remember. I know a lot of them. Hell, I *found* half of 'em for you. Hookers, thieves, robbers, con artists every one. And yeah, okay, so some of them had dope planted on them, big fucking deal. None of them are strangers to dope, anyway. Better than getting beat to shit, which Panos could have done to them just as easily as planting dope."

"And just as illegally."

"Please, please. Sanctimonious crap. You got in it for the money. The fact is Panos was providing a service the cops don't . . ."

"So you're defending him now?"

"No. I'm saying you were in it, too. From the beginning. It's never been a moral issue between you guys, just a conflict of interest."

"Great. I appreciate your input. So nobody's right? What was Silverman? Or Freeman?"

"Collateral damage. Both of 'em. The inevitable next step, that's what. What was

556

Panos going to do, let his nephew go and take this rap? Be sued to death? I don't think so. Hell, he offered you *four million dollars* to just go away and you said no, remember? What'd you expect him to do, send you a Hallmark card?"

"I think we ought to just go," Michelle said.

"Where?"

"Anywhere. Away from here."

"And then what?"

"I don't know. We just live."

"We wouldn't be living. We'd be hiding."

He was on the ottoman in front of her. She was sitting in the chair by the window. She reached over, flipped the blinds open, then closed them again. "Isn't that what we're doing now?"

He smiled at that. "It won't be too much longer. My lawyer's got some ideas."

"Oh yeah, it sounded like you were great pals."

Holiday glossed over that. "Besides, if I run it looks like I'm guilty of something."

"I hate to mention it, John, but so does not turning yourself in."

"I was hoping maybe you wouldn't notice that part." He took her hands in his. "This is going to work, Michelle. All of it.

Our life. I don't want to start it out on the run. I didn't do any of this."

"I believe you," she said, "but it seems like they have so much."

"It's all easily explained. A little turn of the prism. It was three other guys, and now Hardy knows who they are. He'll get their names in front of the right people. You'll see. Another two or three days, they'll cancel the warrant and it'll be all over."

Hardy was going to write a book someday and call it *Nothing Is Ever Easy*, his companion volume to *Nothing Easy About It — A Parent's Guide to Raising Happy and Well-Adjusted Children*. The inspiration for today's chapter, after his fury at his client had ebbed slightly, came from trying to get interviews with the two names — Fred Waring and Mel Fischer — that Holiday had given him from Silverman's poker game.

Both were listed in the telephone book. In hindsight Hardy realized that he should have recognized this right off as one of nature's head-fakes, making it look as though something about these interviews might, in fact, be easy. He could have used some easy.

The morning had already wiped him

out. Waking up with the world's worst hangover hadn't helped. Then there had been David at the hospital, then the long and fruitless wait for Blanca, running into Kroll and Roy Panos, their news about Aretha. Finally, the argument with Holiday about whether he was to blame for some of this. He really didn't need that shit from his client, not today, not ever.

Even if, being honest now that his blinding anger had somewhat subsided, he admitted that it might be partly true.

For most of the past two hours, he'd been holed up in his office, lying on the couch, damp paper towels over his eyes. Finally, still hurting, he'd looked up the numbers of his two witnesses, found them, then punched up the one for Fred Waring. Hardy found himself on the Bernard Rulker & Co. broker hotline, press one if you'd like to continue in English, now press one if you'd like to open a new account, two if you're an existing Rulker client and so on. Eventually, Hardy negotiated the maze and reached the point where he foolishly thought he'd soon be speaking to an actual person, but the "Please hold until one of our brokers can assist you" was in itself merely a prelude ("We appreciate your patience, please continue to hold") to an actual timed four minute Musak version of "Satisfaction."

When a pleasant-sounding woman finally came on, Hardy got off his speakerphone, asked for Fred Waring, and learned that he was on vacation in Hawaii this week. No, they didn't have a number where he could be reached. Could someone else help him?

Mel Fischer had an answering machine and Hardy left three phone numbers — office, home and cell — and a message: who he was, what this was about. The matter was urgent. He considered adding that it was a matter of life and death, but didn't wish to appear too dramatic.

Twenty minutes later, he raised his head off the couch again. This was ridiculous. He was doing nothing worthwhile, and much needed to be done. The telephone book once again held the promise of good luck — Fischer's address was on Taylor, apparently only a few blocks from his office. Filled with self-loathing as he was anyway, Hardy thought that the steep climb over Nob Hill would be just the kind of torture he deserved. He fought his nausea enough to get him up and down the stairs.

At the reception area, really an ovoid island in the center of the rotunda that was Freeman's lobby, Norma the office manager, her elbows on the counter, was in deep conversation with Phyllis. Both women had been with the firm forever, certainly since before Hardy had arrived as a tenant, and neither could be said to be big fans of his. After all, he didn't work for David or the firm, and yet he took great swaths of the great man's time and used the firm's Xerox, fax and other machines, and even associates' time, according to his own idiosyncratic whims. Hardy couldn't say he was overly fond of either of the two women, either. Still, the sight of them — they turned to look at him when he emerged from the stairway — forced him to square his shoulders, put forth a positive image.

Unexpectedly, Norma straightened up and motioned him over. She was a big-boned, solid woman in her mid-fifties who exemplified the competence that Freeman demanded. Fashionable without attempting to be glamorous, completely lacking the gene responsible for humor, she might have been the prototype for all of the legal office managers Hardy had ever encountered.

"Hello, ladies," he said, his voice a completely sincere and solemn monotone. "How is everybody holding up down here?"

"Not too well," Norma said. "Really not well at all." Hardy had picked up the pervading malaise downstairs ever since the day after the mugging, but he couldn't really imagine what Norma would have to say to him about it. But she continued, "With all of Mr. Freeman's many talents, it appears he never really considered the possibility of anything like this happening. As long as he came in every day, things just seemed to run smoothly."

"He's always had a good manager," Hardy said.

Norma smiled, grateful for the praise. "Well, thank you, but I was just saying I'm very much out of my depth just now. I can't even sign paychecks and some of the associates need to be paid soon." She hesitated, looked to Phyllis. "And frankly, so do we, the staff."

Phyllis, unbidden, chimed in. "Clients have been calling every day. Where's David? When's David coming back? What am I supposed to tell them?"

The panic in the voice of Freeman's dogmatic, capable and strong gatekeeper came as something of a shock, and brought

Hardy up short. "I'd just tell them that their work is in good hands, that we're hoping David will be back before too long. . . ."

"But they want to know when and I can't tell them that."

Norma handed a Kleenex down to her, came back to Hardy. "I just don't know what to tell everyone. And we thought — Phyllis and I — that even though you're not really a member of the firm, you've got more . . . Well, you're more mature than any of the associates and . . . we thought maybe you could say something." Her own composure broke suddenly. "Mr. Hardy, it's all coming apart. I don't know what to do."

Hardy hung his head briefly. His head throbbed. His eyes didn't want to focus. "I'll do whatever I can, Norma, but I can't say anybody will listen to me. I just rent upstairs and everybody knows it. But if you think it might help . . ." He looked around the expanse of the floor, into the open Solarium, the empty Xerox room. A truly ominous silence reigned. "How long do you think you'll be able to hold it together? Assuming David doesn't . . ." He found he couldn't finish.

"David always kept a lot in petty cash.

We used to argue about that, but now maybe I could use some of that . . ." She bit at her lip, closed her eyes in thought for a second. "The associates are still billing and we're getting payments. Maybe I could access some of those assets . . ." Again, she stopped. "Best case, Mr. Hardy, let's say a month, if he doesn't recover."

"But he's going to, right?"

She nodded, shaky. "Of course. I didn't mean . . . but it's just that no one else can do what he does."

"No. I know." He put a hand on her shoulder. "You just tell me when, I'll be there."

Much to his surprise, she stepped forward and put her arms around him, squeezing and sending fresh spasms of pain across his back. "Thank you," she said, "thank you."

After a few more words of encouragement, he crossed the lobby, then descended by way of the semicircular staircase that opened into an ornate street-level foyer. It was the middle of the workday, just after lunch hour. Normally, the place hummed with activity and even enthusiasm — Freeman might be a slave-driver, but he was also a great lawyer with an immense talent for motivating his associates.

Hardy stopped and listened again to the silence above.

In some very real way, the world seemed to be ending.

Hardy carried his cell phone with him. It didn't ring as he labored up the steep slope of Taylor Street, over Nob Hill, three blocks back down the other side. It still hadn't rung when he got to Fischer's address. Reasoning that anyone getting home and finding an urgent message would of course call right away, Hardy didn't really expect anyone when he rang the bell. But then the voice came through the intercom.

"Who is that?"

"Mr. Fischer. My name is Dismas Hardy. I called about John Holiday?"

It was turning into a cold November. The overcast had thickened again, and the breeze had freshened to a true wind that had chilled him thoroughly and now gusted around him as he waited on the stoop. A full ten seconds passed. He was about to ring the bell again — nothing was easy — when he heard the buzzer and pushed against the door.

It was a two-story building without an elevator, and when Hardy got to the second floor, Fischer was standing in his open doorway as though guarding the sanctum within. He looked like he was pushing seventy. Thick-shouldered, with a tonsure of gray hair, he wore khakis, tennis shoes and a black Oakland Raiders sweatshirt. Though he barely reached Hardy's shoulders, the old man projected a pugnaciousness and even resentment out of all proportion to the apparent situation. "All right," he said before Hardy got to the last step. "What's so urgent about John Holiday, the son of a bitch? May he rot in hell."

Still a dozen feet away, Hardy paused. He held up his hands for a second, advanced another foot or two. "I have a couple of questions, that's all."

"You're his lawyer?"

"That's right."

"Then I got a question for you. How do you live with yourself?"

"John didn't kill anybody."

"Hah! How'd Sam's stuff get in his house, then? Aliens?"

"Maybe something like that," Hardy said. "I hear you were at that last poker game."

"Yep. What about it?"

Suddenly, Hardy found himself asking a

question he hadn't even thought about. "Have the police talked to you yet?"

And gratifyingly, it slowed Fischer down. "What do you mean, talked to me?"

"You know. Taken a statement about the game, who was there, who won what?"

Fischer eyed him suspiciously. "No. Nobody's talked to me. Not the cops, I mean."

"So somebody has?"

"I didn't say that." His look was pure defiance. "Nobody talked to me."

"Doesn't that seem strange to you? That you were at this game the night before Sam got killed, and nobody from the police wanted to question you?"

"I wasn't there when he got killed. They knew who they were looking for. They didn't need me."

"So you believe that John went back and tried to get back the money he lost?"

"That's what they're saying. Yeah."

"Did anybody else lose money that night? A lot of money?"

Fischer did an overdone impression of thinking about it. "Nope," he said with finality. Shaking his head, he repeated it. "No."

"You had to think that hard to remember?"

This riled the old man even further. "No. I remember perfectly. Holiday was the big loser that night."

"Nobody else?"

"Hey, Jesus, what do you want? I answered your question, all right? That's enough." He backed into the doorway, put his hand on the door behind him.

"You seem a little nervous, Mr. Fischer. Are you nervous? You think maybe I'm going to hurt you. Did somebody else tell you they'd hurt you if you didn't change your story?"

Now the nerves were unmistakable. "I never changed any story! They found all that stuff in John's place. There's no doubt he did it."

Hardy stepped up closer, anger in his voice. "So there's no point, then, in bringing up who else might have lost money that night, is there? They didn't kill Sam. They just don't want people asking questions that might be embarrassing, that might make the police think it looked like they had a reason, too. Isn't that it, Mr. Fischer? Isn't that it?"

For a lengthy moment, Fischer stared with wide-eyed fear at Hardy. Then, suddenly, he brought himself up straight. "I don't have to talk to you," he said, and ducked behind the door, slamming it in Hardy's face.

Hardy yelled at the door, his voice reverberating in the hallway, "You'll have to talk to me at the trial!" Breathing hard, in a fury, he waited.

Eventually he turned and walked back downstairs, out into the bitter and windswept afternoon.

Hardy called Glitsky on his cell phone walking back to his office. Maybe Abe's meeting with Jackman had gone well.

"No," Glitsky said.

"He wouldn't even listen to you?"

"Oh, he listened all right. But he didn't hear."

"Abe, this is just plain weird. Clarence knows us."

"Apparently not well enough. Apparently, you and I are conspiring to obstruct justice. I'm screwing with Gerson, going behind his back, undermining his inspectors so I can expose his incompetence and get my old job back. I'm also working with you on this Panos lawsuit so that if you win, I get to retire in style."

"You want to run by me how that's going to work exactly? How are *you* making anything off of my lawsuit?"

"I'm sure there's some way."

"When you find out, let me know, would you?" A pause. "And Clarence believes this?"

"I can't say that for sure, not personally. But we're smeared enough that he can't be perceived to be involved."

"Abe," Hardy said, "these people shot at me."

"I mentioned that."

"And what did he say to that? Hell, he saw me afterward. He knows I'm not making it up."

"Not the issue. Not for Clarence."

"But he *knows* us. We're the good guys." Although, after his debate with Holiday on this issue, the statement nagged at him. "Relatively," he added.

"Not even that. Not today. Today the system's working as it should. As people are so fond of saying, evidence talks. And *all* the evidence says John Holiday's a stone killer and you're on *his* side. Which makes you one of the bad guys, no relativity about it. And, of course, because you and I are friends, so am I."

"Except that the evidence is no good."

"Yeah," Glitsky said, "there is that."

23

Back in his office for the third separate time that day, Hardy was killing more time before the five o'clock meeting Norma had scheduled for him to address Freeman's staff in the Solarium. His shoes and jacket were off. He lay on his couch again, eyes covered, and realized that he had no other quasilegitimate legal venue where he might be able to make his case. He hadn't swayed Jackman, had no chance with the homicide inspectors.

But he might be able to get to them through public pressure. He and Freeman had done this many times and he was a little surprised that he hadn't thought of it before now.

Jeff Elliott, his friend and the writer of the "CityTalk" column for the *Chronicle*, had finished his column for the day. He told Hardy that if he could save him the handicapped space under his building — Elliot had multiple sclerosis — he would be happy to drop by for an hour of gay repartee, as long as there was a story involved. Hardy went down and stood in the spot until Elliot pulled into it. In a trice, the columnist had done his magic with his wheelchair. The two men rode the back elevator up to the third floor.

While Hardy had brought over some coffee and eased himself down in one of his client chairs, Elliot watched him move. "So who beat you up?" he asked.

Hardy tried to smile. "I thought I was hiding it pretty well."

"You thought wrong. You're walking like the living dead." He put his cup down. "So what happened?"

"Leaving out the hangover, which is another story, that's what I wanted to talk to you about." He gingerly rearranged his body in the wing chair, went on to outline the high points of the situation as it had developed. "So now the whole world thinks that Abe and I are illegally conspiring to get Panos and take him."

"And why are you doing this exactly?"

"So we can win this lawsuit that David and I had been working on."

"Past tense?"

"It's starting to look like it. Although let's keep that off the record for now."

With some difficulty, he changed position in his chair. "It was one of David's brilliant ideas that had some chance of success as long as he was around to pursue it, but I can't keep it going on my own. I can't even pay me, much less the associates we've been using. And that was before my witnesses started dying. In jail, no less." He filled Elliot in on Aretha LaBonte. "Although the official line is she killed herself."

"But you think, somehow, it was Panos?"

"I don't know how, but yes."

"He's got people on payroll in the jail?"

Hardy lifted a hand. "I know. It stretches credibility."

"That's a fair assessment."

"But the only thing more incredible is that all of this stuff is coincidence. David, okay. Maybe even the windshield thing with me. But the shots at me, Aretha dying. Somebody's behind all that. It's not just happening."

Elliot had a pad out and was taking notes. "Okay, we've got Freeman's lawsuit. Panos wants to drive you out of it."

"He's already done it, Jeff. He did it when he took out David."

"But you've got no proof?"

"Zero."

573

Elliot was clicking his pen.

"What?" Hardy asked.

Elliott shook his head. "I'm trying to understand the connection between your lawsuit and all these murders, beginning with Silverman. They don't seem related."

"They're both Panos, Jeff."

"I'm not saying they're not. I'm perfectly willing to believe that they are. Just tell me how, that's all."

Hardy slumped back in the chair, drew a heavy breath and started at the beginning. Ten minutes later, he'd laid it all out. He brought his right hand up to his forehead and squeezed at his temples, sighed a last time, looked across at Elliott. "Don't think I don't realize how bad this sounds, Jeff. But it's not John. He didn't break my windshield. He didn't hire some stooges to take shots at both of us. This is Panos and his gang." He lifted himself from his slump, came forward urgently. "And I can't get a soul to believe me. How am I going to stop them before they try it again?"

Elliot held his coffee still on the arm of his wheelchair. He'd given up all pretense of note-taking. Now, to buy himself another few seconds, he sipped at the cup. "Here's the thing, Diz. I believe you. Just so that's out of the way between you and me. Okay? Okay. Absolute belief. You say it, I buy it. Good enough?"

Hardy nodded.

"Good. But that said, the question now becomes what can I do to help you? Which I would love to do if for no other reason than it's a terrific story."

"So write it up. Crime boss bamboozles city hall. You'll win the Pulitzer Prize."

"That'll be fun," Jeff said. "But first I need one little thing that an objective party, such as my editor, might take as evidence that there is something real here, and not just the wild conjecture of a defense attorney who wants to get his client off. No offense."

"No. Of course not. None taken."

"But we're talking murder here, Diz. Multiple and very ugly murder. And Wade Panos isn't some small-time gangster. If I print any part of this without some show of proof . . . well, you know this."

"What do you need?"

"Not much," Elliot said. "But you've got an enormous big edifice going here. It's going to need at least a little tiny foundation in unassailable fact."

Hardy took another run at it, pointing out the various holes in the police case —

the planted rings at Holiday's, along with Sadie's testimony and Cuneo's interpretation of it; the slightly off-size, fashionable Italian shoe; Thieu's checkup on and belief in Holiday's alibi.

At the end of it, Elliot was frowning. "None of which, I'm sad to say, rises to the level of proof."

Hardy had gotten out of his chair, was creaking around the office. Elliott's words stopped him over by the dartboard. "They can't have done this so well. If somebody searched their places . . ."

But Elliot was shaking his head. "Who? And why? You need something to start with." He closed his notepad. "Maybe next time they'll make a mistake."

"Maybe next time will be me, Jeff. Or Abe. And maybe next time they won't miss. I don't want any next time."

"I hear you." Elliot looked toward the window. Dusk had settled. He looked at his watch. "I don't mean to run, but I've got to go. Dorothy batters me horribly if dinner's done and I'm not home."

Out at the elevator, Hardy pushed the button for the basement, then stepped out in the hall. As the door started to close, Jeff wheeled forward a couple of inches and stopped it. He looked up at Hardy. "The first thing you do, the first bit of real evidence you find, you call me, hear?"

Thirty people, more or less, had gathered in the Solarium. Some, like Graham Russo and Amy Wu, were Hardy's friends. Some of the others — Phyllis and Norma, for example — had been at best politely adversarial. The rest comprised a pretty decent microcosm of the adult world. The ages ranged from perhaps twenty to Phyllis's sixty-something. A quick glance around revealed every major ethnic configuration, about half men and half women. Hardy thought it ironic that Freeman, who found San Francisco's endemic, runaway political correctness as offensive as affirmative action of any kind, had staffed his own firm with such an incredibly diverse talent pool.

As Hardy came into the conference area, stooped and drained, he gathered some sense of the room's expectation. He might be an outcast in the other professional aspect of his life, but here he felt a strong and unexpected acceptance, mixed with a real pride that he was affiliated with this quality group of individuals. He wasn't really part of them, yet clearly he had their respect — everyone had gathered to hear him. Someone closed the door behind them all and after a minute, the room was silent. Hardy stood at the head of the oblong table, made eye contact with Norma, Graham, Amy, some others, and in his natural voice, began.

"We've all been attacked," he said. "We feel violated, angry and victimized. We're all of us afraid of what's going to happen next, whether it's tomorrow or next week, or even beyond that. We've all been working hard on projects and cases that may now have to be abandoned, and we're wondering what will have been the point of all those hours and all that work. All I can say is that the value of the things we do lies in doing them as well as we can, and that what we continue to do does matter.

"I know that we are all hoping and praying that things here will return to normal. But we must face the possibility that they may not.

"So the real question is how we, all of us, deal with this uncertainty and this changing order. My only suggestion is that we take solace and comfort in our families and friends, our faiths if we have them, and our work. If it all ends here tomorrow — and it might — then we'll at least have had the satisfaction of knowing that we've done everything we can to preserve a great legacy with integrity and class. If things do change, we'll be no less ready to deal with that change for having kept up our spirits. If on the other hand life here returns to normal, how proud we'll all be of the fact that when everything looked the darkest, we held our course."

24

Treya and Abe Glitsky sat in their car where she'd parked it near their place. Her last few comments sounded like she was defending Clarence Jackman and Abe wasn't much in the mood to hear it. "So he accuses me and Diz instead?"

"He's not under the impression that he did that."

"Then he wasn't paying attention."

"Well," she said, "he's politically bound. Don't look at me like that; I'm completely with you on this. I'm just explaining his position. And for the record, I think it stinks. I'm well into serious anger myself. What else does he expect you to do?"

"That's easy. Stay completely out of it."

"Can you do that? Do you *want* to?"

"I don't know," he said. "I keep telling myself it isn't my case. It has nothing to do with me."

"Except that they shot at Diz."

"And beat up Freeman. And maybe had something to do with this prostitute who hanged herself. And nobody seems to be trying to stop them."

"Which still doesn't make it your job, does it?" She reached over and touched his leg. "That's not a criticism. It's a real question."

He put his hand over hers. "Okay, here's where we are then, it seems to me: Diz tells me the lawsuit is pretty much over. The attacks on Freeman and Aretha and maybe Diz worked. Let's say it is Nick Sephia and his pals. They're done on that score, right? Nobody caught them, but the threat's over. They don't need to do anything else. So I can let that go, clear conscience, not my job. You with me?"

"All right."

"But the other side, where's Holiday in the picture? That part's not over, not even close. Even leaving out whoever killed everybody in the line leading from Silverman, meaning Creed and Wills and Terry, they've still got to take out Holiday if they want to be able to rest easy. And maybe knock off Diz."

"And maybe you, too."

Glitsky pulled at an ear. "Okay, maybe that. But it doesn't change the fact.

They're going to have to try to get to Holiday. And maybe Diz after him. So, given that, if there's some way I can help stop them, I don't see how I can keep out of it."

"No." She sighed. "I don't see how you can, either."

"Which leaves what? Play by the rules? Whose rules?"

"I know," she said. "I know."

"Jesus Christ, Roy, this was originally going to be one of the famous quick and dirties, you remember that? Bang bang bang bang and it's all over. Now, shit." They were in Wade's enclosed patio, where he was finishing another jigsaw puzzle. He'd summoned his brother to his home after Liz had told him about this new wrinkle she'd found out from her boyfriend — that some lieutenant named Glitsky who used to run homicide and now was somehow tight with Silverman's widow had put it together that the ring hadn't been taken during the Silverman robbery. "What kind of stupidity made 'em think up taking some rings? Nobody needed the rings. And without 'em it's foolproof. What were they thinkin'?"

Roy, straight in from his shift, was still in uniform. A jumpy wariness clung about him as it often did when he had to confront his intelligent and powerful older brother. "I told 'em that, Wade, the same thing. The money and the pouch, that's all. But Julio thought the ring locked it up tighter."

Wade grimaced. "Julio's an idiot. A psychopathic idiot."

"He's not so bad. He was trying to help."

"Don't give me that," Wade said. "You see what the little fuck did to Freeman? I say go out and put the old man off his feed a few days, maybe get him thinking about his workload, and what's he do? Fucking kills him."

"I didn't hear that. Freeman's dead?"

"Not literally. Not yet anyway. But not because Rez didn't try." He shook his head with disgust. "I tell you, that guy scares the shit out of me. I don't know why Nicky's got to hang with such an animal. What he did to those two faggots, Jesus, when a couple of quick shots would have done it as well. Better. Then the two of them get their chance to finish it up, and they miss Holiday, for Christ's sake. And again, once he's dead, it's all over." He saw something on the table in front of him and placed a large piece he'd already connected into a corner of the puzzle. "So now it's the loaves and fucking fishes. We get rid of everybody we need to and we've still got three more, and one of 'em's a lieutenant. Christ! When's it gonna end, Roy? *How's* it gonna end?"

Roy wiped his palms on the arms of his chair. "Same as always, Wade. Same plan. It's going to end with Holiday. He'll turn up, maybe at his house, maybe with his lawyer again, maybe jail, but someplace. Then he goes, and after that nobody's going to worry about whether he's guilty or not anymore."

"What about the lawyer?"

"With Holiday gone, who's going to pay him? Why would he care?"

"But if he does? If this guy Glitsky does?"

"They won't. Stop worrying."

"Worrying's what I do."

Roy forced a grin. "Come on, Wade, you know how it is. Holiday's a *job* to these guys, something they do to get paid. Hardy and Glitsky, they both have families, for Christ's sake. On the off chance one of 'em might get a wild hair around this, we give 'em a nudge and they drop the thing like a hot potato. Maybe we even do that soon, get them out of the way now."

"What kind of nudge? You hurt them,

you're asking for more trouble. And if Rez is part of that, you'll be covering up for what he does the rest of your life."

"I'm not thinking about hurting anybody. Just make 'em think."

Wade held up a hand. "Don't tell me. I don't want to know how. Just make it happen."

Hardy was on his way out of his evening hospital visit when Roake was coming in. She was professionally dressed and told him she'd had to be in court all afternoon. Life was going on since it had to. How were things here? Any change?

There wasn't any news and the two found themselves again in the gift shop, sitting at the one table. Roake in the nicest, most concerned way imaginable commented on how terrible Hardy looked, how lousy he sounded. Was he eating? Getting any sleep? He should try to take better care of himself.

"I'm working on it," he told her. "But in the meanwhile, I've got a problem maybe you can help me with."

She nodded. "If I can."

He took a deep breath and came out with it. "I know who beat up David. Does the name Nick Sephia ring a bell?"

It did. Roake remembered the earlier "mistaken" battery when Sephia had turned and knocked Freeman to the floor outside the courtroom during the summer. "You're sure it's him?"

Hardy considered for a second. "Beyond a reasonable doubt, and you would be, too."

"Okay. So what's your problem?"

He gave her a truncated version of his own interaction with Blanca, backfilled through Jackman and Glitsky, then brought it around to Silverman and Holiday. "In any event," he concluded, "Blanca started out fine, but recently hasn't been too inclined to bust any hump for me. Somebody convinced him I'm just scamming to get Holiday off."

"But somebody shot at you."

"If you happen to believe that." He shrugged. "I can't explain all this, Gina. I don't think, though, that you have the stink that Abe and I have somehow developed. You're Freeman's fiancée. You've seen Blanca here. He'll talk to you."

"And what do you want me to say? Or do?"

At this, Hardy tried to smile. "First, just deliver a message. When I originally told Blanca I thought I knew who'd shot at me

— this was like two hours after it happened — he checked on Sephia and found out he was in Nevada, at least four hours away."

Roake's brow furrowed in thought. "Which leaves him out."

"That's what Blanca thought, too. And that seemed right, even to me, until John Holiday pointed out that Nick's got the use of the Diamond Center's helicopter. Forty-five minutes to state line."

Roake seemed to be waiting for more. At last she said, "Excuse me for thinking like a defense attorney, but since that's what I've been my whole life, Nick having access to a helicopter doesn't mean he shot at you."

"No, of course not. But at least it means that my accusation wasn't whole cloth. I wasn't just getting in a random dig at Panos and his people, which is apparently what Blanca has been thinking. The thing is, I believe that both Jackman and Blanca really do want to find who did this thing to David. I'm telling you it was Sephia. If *you* mention this incident between David and Sephia last summer, or maybe Kroll's threat to David the night before . . . before this happened, maybe they'll listen at least enough to call Sephia in to talk. If there's a god, it's not even impossible Blanca could be convinced to pull a search warrant."

Roake's eyes had taken on a faraway cast.

"What are you thinking?" he asked.

"What? Oh." She lifted her left hand, displaying the diamond ring. "Just imagining what I thought I'd be feeling like today. Married to him, I mean." Her smile didn't come any more easily than Hardy's had. "Not like this." Then, abruptly, "But the answer is yes, of course I'll go see Blanca, or anybody else you suggest. He's on in the morning?"

"Yes."

"All right." Again, her focus shifted. "Can I ask you another question? How do you know?"

"Know what?"

"That it was this Sephia person. Do you have any proof?" The question obviously struck a nerve — Hardy visibly reigned in a rising tide of temper. She put out a hand and touched his. "Don't get mad at me, Diz. I'm on your side, but it's a legitimate question."

"I'm sure it is. Jeff Elliot had the same one."

"Well?"

"Well, I'm getting damn tired of it, to tell you the truth. I *know* it was Nick. What am I supposed to do, let him kill more people while I try to find proof that he's killed others?"

She drew a deep breath. "The short answer to that, I'm afraid, is yes. If he did kill somebody else, or even beat up David, and God knows I want pure, sweet revenge for that. But still, you need . . ."

Hardy cut her off. "So he shoots at you, you don't fire back?"

"No. Somebody shoots at you, you fire back at where the shot came from. That, as you know better than anyone, is self-defense. If you happen to kill the shooter, two things, you've proven he was behind the gun, and you get your revenge. But you don't get shot at, decide who it must have been, then go to his house and shoot him back two days later. Because what if it could have been, even *should* have been your guy, but it wasn't?"

"That didn't happen here."

"No? What's different?" Again she touched his hand. "My only point is you'll hurt yourself, Diz." After a minute of silence, she added, "You've got to find something, that's all. At least for yourself, if not for the law. You've got to *know*. Really know."

Hardy shook his head and swore under

his breath. Another silence built. Broken finally again by Gina. "Here's a terrible thought," she said.

"Terrible is my favorite. What is it?"

"Just that I've got the key to David's apartment." She started running with the fantasy. "If something David owned found its way into Sephia's, say, pocket, and Blanca happened to see it, that might get to probable cause for a search. I can't believe I'm saying this."

"They do a search of his place, they got him," Hardy said, rising to the idea. "The plant would only get them inside. It would take some real evidence after that — say blood splatter on his clothes, and my guess is that there would be plenty — to arrest him."

"Right. We'd just be facilitating a legal search."

They looked at each other with a thrill almost of illicit love, both of them wondering how it would be to play outside the rules. To beat these criminals at their own game.

Finally Hardy pulled out of it. "It's a beautiful idea, Gina, but maybe we won't need it."

"I couldn't do it anyway," she said.

"I don't know if I could either."

"Probably that's a good thing," she said. "It's why they're them and we're us."

"Right," Hardy said. "If we don't do it by the book we're as bad as they are. Does something seem wrong with this picture somehow?"

Hardy and Frannie hadn't had the best night of their lives so far, and now with Glitsky's urgent and atypical call inviting himself and Treya over to talk about their options, it didn't look as though it was going to improve. They were in the kitchen, an hour after a dinner that had featured a meltdown of sorts from the kids, who had finally processed the reality that their father had been shot at and badly hurt in the bargain.

They might not know exactly what it was, but they understood that something truly bad was happening. Uncle Moses and Aunt Susan had been here until late last night, Rebecca and Vincent banished with their younger cousins to the back of the house while the adults drank and argued. This morning, their father and mother had barely spoken — were they getting divorced? Why was someone trying to hurt Dad? Were they actually trying to *kill* him? What were they going to do about that?

What was Dad going to do? He was trying to find who it was, wasn't he? Get them arrested? What were the police doing? Were *they* in danger?

Hardy found it difficult to finesse these questions, particularly since Frannie wasn't helping much. She was still mad at the situation, mostly at her brother, true, but beyond that she'd been dealing with the kids' blossoming reaction to all this since six o'clock this morning, by which time her hungover husband was already long gone for work. Tears and fears. What was going to happen to them? What if Dad died? What was this all about?

"I don't want to live like this," Frannie said. "I don't know how these people have done this to us." They were keeping their voices abnormally low so that Vincent and Rebecca, doing their homework in the rooms directly behind the kitchen, would not have more cause to worry. To Hardy, the tension in the house twanged with every sound.

He crossed the kitchen and put his arms around his wife. She leaned up against him. "I don't know what to do," she said. "I just feel so helpless."

"That's what Abe and Treya are coming over for," he said. "We'll come up with some plan, the four of us."

"But I don't understand why the police, or Clarence Jackman for that matter, why they don't believe you in the first place. That's the part that's making me crazy. You didn't do anything wrong."

"That's funny. John Holiday seems to think I started the whole thing. Me and David." At Frannie's look of disbelief, he explained. "Going after Panos."

"Hel-lo?" Frannie didn't want to hear this nonsense. "You've got over a dozen clients he's harmed one way or another. That's not you starting it."

"I tried to make that same point myself. Evidently Mr. Panos can do whatever he wants, and if somebody like me calls him on it, I'm at fault."

"John really said that?"

"More or less."

"That really makes me mad."

"You must be a bad person, too. Anyway, I tried to explain that maybe I'm not a moral paragon, but what I'm doing is within the law, whereas everything Panos has done and is doing is against it. Call me delusional, but that's a big difference."

"Did he get it? John?"

"Not really. He's not much into right and wrong. He simply pointed out that I should have been prepared to handle this stuff before I started in on Panos to begin with."

She moved back into his embrace. "It's like this bad dream where you're drowning and calling out the names of everybody who could save you on the shore right around you, but nobody hears."

"I know," Hardy said. "I know." What else could he say? That's exactly what it was like. He and Frannie were having the same nightmare.

Or maybe not exactly the same. She boosted herself up onto the kitchen counter, and she sat with her ankles crossed, her hands clasped between her legs, her head held low. "This has always been my biggest fear, you know that? That somebody was going to take all this law stuff personally and come after you. Or us. Me and the kids. And you always told me that that never happened. Except now it has."

"I know." He rested his own weight against the opposite counter. "What do you want me to say? I never thought it would."

"But now that it has . . . maybe we should reconsider . . ."

"What?"

She raised her eyes. "Maybe everything, I guess."

Hardy didn't like the sound of that at all. "Everything takes in a lot, Fran. You're not saying you and me, I hope."

"Not specifically, no. . . . But the life we have. If it's not safe . . ."

"This is one moment, Fran. It's not our life. Our life has been good. It still is good."

"But not living like this. If we lost the kids . . ."

Hardy stepped toward her. "That's not going to happen —"

"Don't!" She snapped it out, stopping him. "Don't say it's not going to happen. You don't know what's going to happen. You've always told me that *this* wouldn't happen."

Hardy backed off, took a breath. "So what are you saying? What do you want to do?"

"I don't know!" Anger flashed in her eyes. Then, after a beat, with some measure of calm, "I don't know. Maybe we should just leave here. Start over someplace else, with you doing something else?"

"And how do we do that exactly? What do we live on, for example?"

"We'd find something."

"Something that's going to support four of us, with two kids in college in a couple of years? I don't know how we're going to do that. And then what? Sell the house?"

"We could."

"Frannie. We can't." He approached again, but more cautiously. "Listen to me. I don't want something else. This is what I do. I'm trained in it and I'm good at it. I may even be doing some good from time to time."

"But your life is threatening all of us, Dismas. Can't you see that?"

He gathered what he felt to be the last of his reserve. He'd come to where she sat and he set his hands on either side of her hips. He felt that it would take all his strength to keep his voice modulated, and when he spoke, it was almost in a whisper. "Can't you see that what's at stake here is exactly that? The way we live, the way we want to live. Some crop of assholes comes in and threatens us, threatens *that*, what do you want me to do? What do you want us to do? Pack up and move? I don't believe it. Because then what?"

"You're alive at least."

"We're alive now. And we're where we belong. We're just scared."

"And so we live with this fear?"

"Sometimes, yes. Sometimes we have to. Hopefully not for too long." He brought a hand up and touched her cheek. "Look, Fran, I don't like it any more than you do, but you just can't let the bastards win. Sometimes they push you far enough and you've got to fight or else they'll take it all. They'll just take it because they can, because nobody will stop them. And that's wherever we move, whatever we do."

25

At a little before midnight, in her camouflage outfit and with her heart pounding against the wall of her chest, Michelle walked all the way up one side of Casa Street, crossed where it abutted on Marina Boulevard, then all the way back on the other. There were several mature trees sprouting from squares cut in the sidewalk, and these blocked some of the illumination from the streetlights. Still, she thought she could tell if a person, or even two, was sitting in any of the cars parked solidly against the curbs on both sides. She saw none.

This time, she left the newspapers where they were and took the steps to the landing quietly, but two at a time. At the top, a sudden light-headedness came over her so strongly that she thought for a second that she would faint. Straining to hear any sound that would mean discovery, she could hear nothing except the beat of her heart throbbing in her ears. Unable to stop herself, she walked back down the stairs and peeked out for another look at the street.

Back upstairs, she opened the screen door, wincing at the squeak, waiting another minute, listening. Then suddenly in a great hurry, she inserted the key, opened the door and closed it behind her.

She stood in blackness, letting her eyes adjust. After a time, some faint illumination of the streetlights through the front windows seemed to create spectral shadows, and eventually these resolved into shapes and spaces, and she felt she could walk safely. The errand was simple enough — she was picking up some of his clothes, whatever bills might have accumulated, a checkbook and ATM card if she could find them in his rolltop.

Michelle hadn't worried until she'd gotten to the front stoop, when suddenly the entire idea struck her as foolish beyond imagining. Except now she was already here, inside.

It was an older building and the hardwood floor creaked as she moved back down the hallway toward John's bedroom. She'd made the walk several times and had never noticed the sound before, but now the boards seemed to be screaming in agony at her light and cautious tread. What if the people downstairs woke up and called the police? She stopped, pinned to the wall, sweating now even in the chilled hall. She was not cut out for this kind of work. But there seemed nothing to do but continue, and the back half of the hallway was blessedly more quiet. If she walked faster . . .

She had brought a small but powerful Maglite flashlight and a string shopping bag that could stretch to accommodate everything she needed, and she went right to his dresser — socks and underwear in the top drawer, a couple of shirts in the next one down, an extra pair of jeans, tightly rolled. Her bag was nearly full, but then she was almost done — just the checkbook and the mail.

The rolltop did not budge at first. Nor at her second try. Straightening up, she took several deep breaths, took hold of the two handles. When she jerked at it sharply, the old wood released and the top flew up with a rattle and a crash. For a full minute, she didn't move, barely trusted herself to breathe. But there was no sound from below, from anywhere. Far in the distance, a siren wailed, but then stopped almost immediately. It wasn't about her.

The checkbook with his ATM card was in the top middle drawer, where he'd told her she'd find it. Farther back, a picture frame, face down, stopped her completely. Carefully, she lay the flashlight on the desk and reached in, lifting it with both hands, setting it upright in front of her.

It was, of course, Emma and Jolie. She should have known. Unable to tear her eyes from the image, by the flashlight's beam she studied the faces of John's lost loves. It was the furthest thing from a posed shot with say-cheese smiles and orchestrated effervescence. Perhaps because of that, she knew why this was the one he'd kept, the one he'd framed. It was a feeding moment, the baby in a high chair anticipating the bite, which judging from her clean face might be the first of that meal. The mom bringing a spoon toward her. Although she immediately recognized John in the infant's face, the mouth especially, the baby took after her mother even more. Particularly in this picture, where they wore the same expression, a kind of rapturous expectation. Both so vividly alive. Both so young.

A noise, close by, shattered her revery. In her nerves and haste she reached both for the flashlight and the picture. The frame escaped her grasp in the now-sudden dark and it came down, the glass breaking with its unmistakable, sickening sound. In the aftermath, the silence was complete again.

But, she thought, not quite as it had been before. Now, glued to the chair, shaking but immobile, she imagined someone else within hearing distance, listening as she was for another sound. She put her hand over her mouth to stop her own breathing, tried in vain to summon some saliva, to swallow.

Someone was at the screen door, which creaked again. A second later, she heard a key turn, and the hallway light came on. A man's voice called out, "This is the police. I have a weapon drawn. Come out where I can see you."

Michelle went to stand up, then thought better of it. "I'm in the bedroom, down to your left," she said. "My hands are over my head. I won't move until you say so."

Like last time, there were two of them, but not the same two. The Asian man, the one who'd been holding the gun when he walked in, put the thing in its holster, then approached her with his wallet out and badge showing. After asking her to stand up, he introduced himself as Sergeant Inspector Paul Thieu of San Francisco homicide. He didn't waste any time at all. He patted her down quickly and thoroughly, then asked what she was doing here.

She thought she'd go with the same basic story that had worked before. "I watch John's apartment when he's away."

"You do, do you? Can I see some identification, please?"

She fumbled in the breast pocket of her camo shirt and brought forth a wallet insert with her driver's license, which he took, examined carefully, and showed to his partner. The partner carried a briefcase. He was short, dark, well-dressed, with a soul patch under his lip. Returning the wallet insert to her, Thieu looked her up and down, seemed satisfied with something. "All right, let me ask you again. What are you doing here?"

"I just told you, I . . ."

He was shaking his head no, patiently but with a determined look. He pointed to the string bag at her feet. "That bag is full of men's clothes and what looks from here like a checkbook. Which makes me believe that we've come upon you here in the act of burglary."

"No! That's not it. Really." She implored each of the men in turn. "Look." She reached into her front pocket. "I have a key. The key John gave me. I didn't break in here. He's a friend of mine. I watch his stuff."

"Clothes," Thieu said, pointing again.

Thinking fast, she offered a hopeful face. "I wash them. He leaves them in the hamper. I was bringing them back."

"In the dark? At one o'clock in the morning? You're one heck of a friend. Do you expect us to believe any of this?"

"Well, he pays me, of course. Not much, but . . ."

"Do you know there's a warrant out for Mr. Holiday's arrest? For murder?"

"I . . . I know. I heard that. But that must be a mistake. John wouldn't hurt anybody."

"Do you know where he is?"

"No. You mean now?"

Thieu turned to the other man. "Do you think I meant now, Len? Did you get that impression?"

The other man nodded, shot her the straight line. "He means now."

"No. I don't have any idea where he is. I mean, that's why I came here. I haven't heard from John in a few days, almost a week now." Suddenly, her eyes lit up. "Look, I came by here on Friday, too," she blurted. "When the other officers were here."

"What other officers?"

"The men with the search warrant. They had identification. A black guy and a white guy."

"Cuneo and Russell," the other man said.

"All right, and these inspectors talked to you?"

"Same as you. Checked my ID. Everything."

"And you were here, again, why?"

"That day, the same as now, then picking up John's newspapers."

"They're still down there, I notice."

She shook her head. "Just the last three days. I was going to get them on the way out and throw them away."

"And you told all this to Inspectors Cuneo and Russell?"

"If those were their names."

"And they just let you go back home?"

Thieu was in a pickle.

Earlier tonight, at the house of Glitsky's lawyer friend Hardy, Thieu had told the lieutenant that he'd come here with Faro. It seemed a reasonable risk. But it was turning out to be true what everybody said

— that no good deed ever went unpunished.

And that's what, in theory, this trip to Holiday's was intended to be, a good deed, albeit with elements of self-interest. Glitsky, Hardy and their wives had been truly distraught over this problem with Panos. Thieu hadn't seen Abe so angry in years and Treya — in Thieu's opinion a rock of sanity, patience and good humor — was if possible even madder.

Thieu had come to Glitsky this morning with his problem. And this was, he supposed, why Abe was such a valuable friend and mentor. Coming here could be the solution for both of them, and for Hardy as well. Thieu got the feeling that Glitsky and Hardy had come to their decision after quite a lot of internal debate between them, and that neither was thrilled with deciding that their only viable option was to find evidence linking Sephia, Roy Panos and Rez to these murders. Clearly, they would both have preferred some kind of confrontation with these men, but in the end they were lawmen, and they'd do it according to the law.

Finally, Hardy suggested that Thieu come here with Len Faro and dust the place for fingerprints. The CSI team had already done the places where they'd discovered the incriminating evidence from Silverman's. Photographed the stuff in place, dusted the actual articles for prints where possible. But they hadn't done a general sweep of the entire duplex unit — dishes in the sink, doorknobs, bathroom fixtures.

The other three suspects had never been at Holiday's house and Glitsky thought that Thieu ought to be able to get some kind of statement to that effect. Even a verbal admission might do the trick, though written or taped would be better. Once they had that, if they found fingerprints of any of the suspects at Holiday's home, the question of where the planted evidence had come from was going to drive the investigation either to one of the true conspirators' doors, or to Wade Panos.

The only wrinkle from Thieu's perspective was the imperative to keep himself out of it. The problem as well as the source of his pique was that he wasn't assigned to any of the murders that came in the wake of Sam Silverman. So what excuse could Thieu plausibly invent for why he had to go to Holiday's duplex in the dead of night and dust for fingerprints?

He had to give it to these defense lawyers. They were a devious group and Hardy clearly belonged among them. Thieu simply wouldn't mention it until he had the results. As far as Lennard Faro was concerned, Thieu was doing a routine favor for his two homicide colleagues Cuneo and Russell, just being thorough with housekeeping at the home of a murder suspect. The print lifts would go to the lab — Faro would neither know nor care what they were about, and would never ask. After the results came in, if the fingerprints of Sephia and/or Panos and/or Rez came in, then having at least established the Panos connection to the case, Thieu could come to Gerson and, man to man, admit to his earlier reservations about the evidence and the interpretations of Cuneo and Russell.

Perfect.

Until this woman.

He believed no part of her story. In his heart, he was even insulted that she could *think* any part of it was plausible. He ached to put handcuffs on her, take her downtown and do a serious interrogation. But that would leave him with the really insoluble problem of explaining to Gerson why he'd been here in the first place. The entire house of cards would come down if he didn't have a positive match on some Panos-connected prints to fall back on. He could certainly find himself out of homicide, possibly cut in rank.

And then there was the even bigger problem. Thieu was morally certain not only that this Michelle Maier knew where the fugitive John Holiday was at this moment, but that he was at her own home. She had come over here to get him some changes of clothes, obviously. Access to his money. He and Len could drive her back to her place, put the cuffs on Holiday and be heroes tomorrow.

Except Glitsky didn't think Holiday did it. From Thieu's perspective, the evidence didn't say he did, either. It was simply good police work to verify whether an alternative set of suspects had a substantial evidentiary problem. And the woman, Ms. Maier, had given him a rationalization — she'd actually been here with Cuneo and Russell just three days ago, and they hadn't seen fit to follow up. It blew Thieu's mind. It wasn't what they were looking for, and so they hadn't seen what it so obviously was. No doubt her explanations had been as lame then as now.

By her own admission, they'd checked her identification. So in theory, Cuneo and

Russell knew as much about her as Thieu did, though he'd be surprised if either one of them had thought to write down her last name or address. Or remembered them, as he did.

John Holiday was *their* suspect. It was *their* case, not his.

Let them work it.

All this passed through Thieu's agile mind during his brief questioning of Michelle Maier. She had just begun blowing more smoke about the newspapers, how she was planning on picking them up on her way out tonight.

"And they just let you go back home?"

"Yes, sir."

He turned to Faro, shrugged extravagantly. "Well, Ms. Maier, it appears to be your lucky night. Inspector Faro and I have a lot of technical ground to cover here and if you gave your name and address to the other inspectors, I'm going to assume they followed up as they should. That okay with you, Len?"

Faro tugged at his bug. He held the rank of inspector but wasn't an investigator. He did forensics and crime scene analysis. As far as he was concerned, the woman's presence was only significant to the extent that it sullied the scene. The sooner she was gone, the better. "As long as she doesn't touch anything else going out. Leave the mail," he told her.

Michelle knew what she was hearing, but wasn't sure she believed it. Thieu lifted his hand and waved as he would to a child. "Drive safely," he said.

"Really? I can go?"

Thieu nodded impatiently.

"Thank you. I mean, I'm sorry. I just . . ." She noticed the string bag at her feet and leaned over to pick it up. Then she walked past the two policemen, and out the front door.

26

Ever since he'd finally gotten his doctor's permission to go back to work after his year and a half of recovery, Glitsky hadn't missed a day. Over a very early breakfast, though — the baby wasn't even up yet — he was telling Treya that he thought he could spend his time more profitably outside today. "But do you want to hear something funny?"

"More than anything."

"I feel guilty about it."

"About what? Taking the day off?"

"Calling in sick when I'm not. I've never done that before."

"You're kidding?" Treya put her bagel down. "Never, not once?"

"I told you it was funny."

"Hysterical. Except I don't think I have, either. No wonder we're a good couple. We're probably the only two people in America."

"Which leaves me with a problem. I was

hoping you'd be able to tell me the proper etiquette for when I call in, but now it turns out you wouldn't know."

"I don't think there's really much of an etiquette. You call, leave a message . . ."

"Yeah, but I'm supposed to be sick. So, for example, do I try to sound miserable?"

"How would they tell the difference?"

Glitsky faked a pout. "That was cruel."

"I'm in a cruel mood." This was and had been true since yesterday, since soon after Glitsky's meeting with Jackman. Glitsky thought she was proving herself to be one of the premier grudge holders. "I haven't decided if I'm going in, either," she said. "And I'm talking about ever. How *dare* that man treat you that way?"

"It wasn't personal."

"That's kind of my point, Abe. It should have been personal. You and Dismas are about half the reason he got that job in the first place."

"Maybe true. But we're not going to be why he gets to keep it." Glitsky picked up a slice of lox, rolled it up, and popped it into his mouth. "When I was a kid, I thought the ultimate food was lox, you know that? If you ate lox, you were a megasuccess like a movie star. If somebody had ever told me that one day I, a mere cop, would commonly eat lox at home, I wouldn't have believed them. And yet look at us. Sometimes I still can't believe it."

"That was subtle," she said, "but I caught it. You're changing the subject away from Clarence and I want to vent some more."

"You can if you want, but he wasn't all wrong. Diz and I really have nothing, and Clarence's reaction was probably a good portion of why we decided we had to look rather than just accuse. Besides, if he's getting calls from Washington and Rigby" — the mayor and police chief, respectively — "on the weekends, it's helpful for us to know how high Panos's influence extends. In a way, his coming down on me was a pretty good heads up. He might have even meant it that way."

"I'm sure."

He shrugged. "As you so astutely observed, he's playing the political game. Right now he's got his hands on the power and he's the best DA we've had in years. So he wants to keep it. I can't blame him. It's high stakes."

"And the ends justify the means?"

"Sometimes. Not always. I think Clarence is trying to figure out that balance himself. If Diz and I actually get something that does break this case, he'll jump on it with both feet."

"Do you really think that? After what he's already done to you both?"

"Absolutely."

Treya chewed silently, sipped at her tea. "All right, I'll go to work. But he can get his own darn coffee."

At a quarter to eight, Glitsky flashed his badge at the manager of the Diamond Center lot. At 9:45, he and Hardy were still in Hardy's car, in a VIP parking space just to the side of the entrance, and directly across the street from the Georgia AAA Diamond Center. Hardy still hurt. He dozed fitfully behind the wheel until Glitsky backhanded his shoulder. "Panos," he said.

It was Roy, on foot and in uniform. Stopping at the huge double doors, he checked his watch, paced to the corner, looked both ways, then came back to the doors and looked at his watch again. He wasn't sixty feet from where they were parked. Both men slumped in their seats, awaiting developments. They weren't long in coming. Two men coming up out of the lot passed within five feet of Glitsky's window. Again, he ticked Hardy's shoulder, and pointed. Sephia in a black leather calf-length coat and Rez in tight black chinos and a tan, torso-hugging sweater that he tucked into his pants.

They crossed to where Roy waited at the doors. He wasted no time but immediately grew animated, gesticulating, all bulldog. "Next time we bring one of those distance microphones, tape everything they say," Glitsky said. When Hardy didn't reply, he said, "That was a joke, Diz."

But Hardy still didn't answer. He just sat, watching the trio across the street. After a few minutes of back and forth, Roy seemed to have shot his wad in terms of aggression, and then the meeting, abruptly as it had begun, was over. Roy resumed the walk on his beat. Sephia and Rez went to the double doors of the Diamond Center and disappeared inside.

"Well," Hardy said, "they're all involved in something together, but we already knew that. I'd love to go inside and have a few words with Nick."

"What good would that do?"

"I don't know. Maybe none. But it would be fun to bait him a little. Cast aspersions about his mother's heritage or something. See if I could get him to take a poke at me with witnesses around."

"It's nice to see you thinking about having fun again. I wasn't going to mention it, but your company's been less than scintillating this morning."

"Yeah, but I had all the ideas last night. Speaking of which, no word from Thieu?"

Glitsky shook his head. "Too soon." His eyes had never left the double doors, and now he bobbed his head that way. "See? You wouldn't have had any time anyway. Keep low."

But they needn't have worried. Sephia carried a plain paper bag and he and Rez passed them again close enough to touch, but they were deeply into their own conversation now and never slowed.

"Now what?" Hardy said.

"Gentlemen, start your engines."

So they were ready. Glitsky, looking back over his shoulder, said "Okay." Hardy let them pass, said, "That's the car!" and fell in behind them.

"What car?"

"The gray sedan. The one they were driving when they shot at me and John. The bastards are so smug they didn't even use a rental or a throwaway. Can you believe that?"

Glitsky had his pad out and got the license number. They were heading west on

Geary now, back a couple of carlengths, but no one in between. "Speaking of fun, if we can ever get somebody to start issuing search warrants, it might be fun to dig around in that thing."

"There it is," Hardy said, "fun again." But as he said it, he was rolling the muscles of his back. He didn't look like he was having fun.

They followed as the car did the one-way-street boogie until it was heading south now on Van Ness, then down Mission to Twenty-first Street, where it turned right and finally pulled to a stop at the curb in front of a nicely maintained, free-standing Victorian house. Hardy drove by as both men were getting out of their car. There was no paper bag, although Sephia walked with both of his hands inside the pockets of his black coat.

Hardy pulled over a couple of houses up the road. "What's this?" he asked.

"I don't know." Glitsky was writing down the address, though. "Drug drop maybe? I don't know," he said again.

It wasn't a long wait, perhaps ten minutes. When they came out of the house, this time Rez was holding a briefcase. They got back on the road and the tail continued.

By noon, when they turned back into the Diamond Center lot, they'd made four similar stops, from the Mission out to Diamond Heights and then to a palatial, gated home in St. Francis Wood. By this time, both Hardy and Glitsky had concluded that whatever the boys were up to, it wasn't kosher. But they didn't get much time to air any of their theories. They were parked in a loading zone, waiting for the two men to exit the lot again. Hardy had just turned off the motor when he looked into the rearview mirror and said, "Okay, here they come."

At the same moment, Hardy's cell phone rang. He watched Sephia and Rez, each with a briefcase now, as they crossed the street, but he stopped paying attention to them when he heard his wife's voice, crying. "Dismas," she managed to get out. "Please . . ."

"What is it, Fran? Do you hear me? Easy."

"*I can't be easy!*" she screamed. Then, "Dismas, you've got to come home."

"I will, but . . ."

"Please! Now!"

"Are you all right? Should I call nine one one?"

"No, but it's . . ." Her breathing came in ragged gasps. "Just get here."

"Okay, sure. I'm on my way, but what's . . ."

"I can't explain. You'll have to see. Oh God, I've got to call the school."

"The school? Why? Are the kids . . . ?"

"I've got to call the school," she repeated, and hung up.

"Fran? Frannie?" He stared at the dead phone.

"What is it?" Glitsky asked.

"Not good," Hardy said. A muscle twitched at the side of his jaw. "Whatever it is, it's not good. She's calling the school." He turned to his friend. "Listen, Abe, I'm done here. I've got to go now." He hit the ignition. "I can drop you someplace on the way."

"No." Glitsky was already halfway out of the car. "You go."

The car peeled out in a spray of gravel.

Holiday was alone now in the Yerba Buena Motel at the corner of Van Ness and Lombard, not even three blocks from Michelle's house. She had come back home last night traumatized and panic-stricken. She was sure that the policemen that had been at his place had followed her home. They both had to get out of there right away. So they'd walked down here, a few blocks, and Michelle had checked them both in under her name.

And now she was gone. She had a deadline for a big article on bonsais for *Sunset* and she needed to do a ton of research. She told him he should just hang out here in the room and she'd be back midafternoon with some lunch. He called Hardy's office three times and redundantly left Michelle's cell phone number each time, but it appeared that his lawyer had taken the day off. The one time he ventured a look out the window, a black-and-white police car had been parked in the lot outside. The next time he looked, it had gone, but the anxiety hadn't.

This was getting bad, he knew. He was going to have to do something. He couldn't just sit here.

When the maid knocked, he let her in and went out across the street and into the convenience store on the corner. At least his picture wasn't on the front page of the newspapers out front today. He bought a quart of milk, a quart of apple juice, six apples, a Snickers candy bar and a copy of the *Chronicle*. When he got back, the maid had finished.

He drank the milk and ate an apple and the candy bar. He read the *Chronicle*, was pleased to note on page two that they still hadn't found him, although the search continued. He tried Hardy again, but he still wasn't in.

Finally, he took a clean towel from the bathroom and used it as a tablecloth on the bedside table. He took his gun from his jacket pocket, made sure there wasn't a bullet in the chamber, nor a clip in the handle. After wiping it clean with the towel, he tried the action, sighted down the barrel, squeezed off a succession of phantom rounds. To his surprise, he found that the clip had only four rounds in it, and he opened his box and squeezed in another three, so that it was fully loaded. He worked the action to chamber a round, then dropped the clip and put another bullet in its place.

Finally, he jammed the clip into the weapon.

Loaded for bear.

Thieu didn't get much sleep, but he wasn't accustomed to more than five hours anyway, so it didn't bother him. After he and Faro had finished their dusting at Holiday's, he decided on his own that Dismas

Hardy's strategy had if not a flaw, at least a difficulty. Thieu still had to find a way that he could plausibly inject himself into a discussion with Sephia and Rez about their possible presence at Holiday's duplex. That wasn't his case. On the other hand, he had been the responding inspector to the Terry/Wills scene. Any concerns he had about the inviolability of that scene would be completely appropriate.

So at a little before two, he appeared at the Diamond Center and ten minutes later found himself in a small anteroom off the showroom floor, explaining about his problem to the private security guards Sephia and Rez. "So the basic security of the scene is still my responsibility," he lied, "and I know both you guys and" — he looked down at his pad — "and Roy Panos have been helping out Inspectors Cuneo and Russell, isn't that right?"

"Some," Sephia replied. "Mostly that's been Roy, though."

"Yeah. I already got him." Thieu passed over Roy quickly. He didn't want them to ask what he meant by saying he "got" him. "But they mentioned you, too."

Sephia looked to Rez — a question. Then he shrugged. "We just talked to them a couple of times."

"But you never went with them. You never were at Terry's and Wills's apartment?"

"Why would we?" Rez asked. "Did anybody say we were? Why don't you ask them, the other inspectors?"

Thieu played innocent. "They're out today interviewing witnesses and they asked me to clear this up. Look, we're trying to get the neighbors and other folks to tell us who had been in and out of there. It's a simple question. Have either of you guys ever been there before?"

Rez looked at Sephia. They both looked at Thieu. "No, of course not."

Now Thieu had them. He pulled out his tape recorder and they couldn't very well refuse to repeat the denial. Then, when he got to the end, he set the hook. "By the way," he said with the tape still running, "have either of you guys ever been to John Holiday's apartment?"

Glitsky wandered around downtown for over an hour, his mind jumping between Hardy's sudden emergency and the odyssey they'd witnessed with Sephia and Rez. He ended up at David's Deli, where he sat at the bar and ordered a pastrami sandwich and a Cel-Ray soda. He checked his watch. He was dying to know, but wanted to give Hardy time to work out the problem. Whatever it was, it seemed serious, but if he'd have wanted Glitsky's company or help, he would have asked in the car.

Again, he looked at his watch. If he bolted down his sandwich, he could get back to the Hall in time still to get in a half-day. He could just say he was feeling better and didn't want to be home if he wasn't really sick. It would be a good example for the troops.

"No," he said aloud. Suddenly he stood up, took off his jacket and hung it over the back of his seat to save his place. At the pay telephone, he called Treya at work, but a different woman answered at her personal number, and this brought a crease to his brow. "I'm trying to reach Treya Glitsky."

"I'm sorry, but she's not in. Is this Lieutenant Glitsky?"

"Yes it is."

"Treya's left for the day, Lieutenant. She left a message if you called that you should get home, or at least call, as fast as you could. And that you should be very careful."

"Call home?"

"That's what she said. She left here in a hurry. She said she'd try and page you."

He hung up, dug in his pocket for some coins as his pager went off, and punched in his home number. "Treya, it's me. Tell me Rachel's all right."

When Treya had her voice under this much control, she was dangerously angry. "She's fine, but I think you'd better come home."

"What is it?"

"I guess you'd say a threat. A threat to Rachel."

"What kind of threat?"

"Just a picture of her. A Polaroid, probably taken yesterday, from what Rita and she were wearing. Rita's holding her on the steps. Somebody circled Rachel in red."

Suddenly Glitsky understood the urgency of Hardy's problem, as well as Frannie's panic. She, too, had gotten a recent Polaroid of her children. The message was unequivocal, its meaning clear. We know where your children are. We can get to them anytime we want.

Back off or they die.

27

A fingerprint search is nearly always run first by a computer against a local database of known criminals. In this case, since Thieu had some specific people in mind, he'd asked Faro to hand check the prints they'd lifted from Holiday's and Terry/Wills's places directly against Rez, Panos and Sephia.

Thieu got the results at a little before 3:30 and figured he could make it back uptown easily, even with traffic, and get the news to Gerson before the lieutenant went home for the day. First he wanted to share the news and tell Glitsky, though, so he stopped by the fifth floor, only to discover that his old mentor had called in sick — astounding. Certainly Thieu had never known him to do it when he was in homicide. He had his home phone number, however, and closing the door behind him — no one seemed to be minding the store in Glitsky's absence — he borrowed the phone on the desk to make the call. "Abe? What's the matter? You don't sound so good."

"No. I'm fine, Paul. Maybe coming down the flu or something, that's all. What's going on?"

"What's going on is I got the results on the fingerprints and you were right. Hardy was right. Sephia and Rez were all over Holiday's place. And I have them on tape denying ever being there."

Glitsky sounded weary beyond imagining. Even this terrific news of Thieu's didn't seem to cheer him in the least. "That's great, Paul." He sounded as though he were almost bored by it. "So what are you going to do now?"

"Lieutenant, are you all right?"

"I don't know." A long pause. "I may not be in for a few days after all. So I assume you'll be talking to Gerson?"

"Sure, showing him the results. It's naked eye stuff, almost. Gerson was my next stop. I'm in your office now."

"Well, you want to do me one last favor?"

"Sure. Anything."

"I want you to leave Hardy and me completely out of it."

"I can't do that, Lieutenant. You were the ones who had the idea. If we get these guys from this evidence, people here, I mean in the department, have got to know it was you."

Glitsky's voice suddenly became far more familiar to Thieu — terse, biting, brooking no resistance. "Paul, I want you to hear me good. People have *not* got to know it was me. Or Hardy, for that matter. In fact, it's critical — *critical,* do you understand? — that it look like we had nothing to do with it. Nothing!"

"But . . ."

"No buts. If you get this into the system now with Gerson, you'll be the hero and you deserve to be the hero. You did all the work."

"I don't care about being the hero, Abe. I don't want to hog your credit."

"Forget my credit. I've already got way too much profile around this case as it is. You've got enough now, with this, that from here on out it's by the numbers. With any kind of hustle, these guys should be under a lot of heat. I don't want them to come back on us. So no me, no Hardy. Just good police work did these guys in. And that's all that did it, okay?"

"Okay." Thieu didn't like it. "If it were

me, though, I'd at least want to remind the people who'd accused me, make them eat a little crow."

"I don't care about that. I really don't. I'm payroll, remember?" A silence, then, "You still don't get it, do you?"

"No, sir. I'm sorry, but I don't."

"All right. I guess you've earned the real reason." Suddenly, Glitsky's tone changed again. It became nearly intimate, quietly intense. "They've threatened my family, Paul, my daughter. Same with Hardy, his kids. It's what you'd call a credible threat. So I don't want them to think we did this. In fact, I want them to think we *didn't*. After they're in prison for life plus a hundred, maybe then we can go back and gently remind some people on our side that we might have had something to say. But as far as the public needs to know, I'm done. Hardy's done. We were done before you even started thinking about fingerprints. Okay?"

"Okay."

"Just get this to Gerson direct. Don't go through Cuneo and Russell."

"That was my plan."

"It's a good one. You've still got time today, I see. Go."

Thieu looked out Glitsky's one window.

The sun had just set, but he might just get lucky and find Gerson still at the job.

"I'm gone," he said.

Behind Gerson's closed door, Thieu had been sitting now for over twenty minutes and still couldn't believe he was hearing this. The lieutenant had, at first, been reasonably enthusiastic, listening to Thieu's explanation of how his earlier suspicions at the Terry/Wills scene — the shoe, the plethora of convenient evidence — combined with the suspicion of planted evidence at Holiday's . . .

"What suspicion of planted evidence? Have you been talking to Glitsky?"

"Lieutenant Glitsky? No, sir. I haven't talked to anybody. This is just me."

"Just you?"

"Yes, sir."

"Who got these prints for you?"

"That was Len Faro, but he was just dusting. He had no idea what it was all about. And nobody at all knows about this taped statement. Not a soul."

Gerson let out a heavy breath. "All right. So. Where did you hear about this so-called planted evidence?"

Thieu fidgeted in his chair. "Remember, sir? From Sadie Silverman's statement.

Dan Cuneo didn't believe it, but I thought . . ."

"Nobody believed it, Sergeant. Nobody suspected planted evidence at Holiday's." He shook his head in profound displeasure. "But go on, you were saying."

And he did go on, but instead of Gerson's approval, Thieu sensed a growing impatience and even anger. "The point is, sir," he concluded, "that in fact these fingerprints from Sephia and Rez do prove that they were there, at Holiday's. And they flatly deny it. So they could only have been there to plant the incriminating evidence."

Gerson crossed one leg over the other, leaned an elbow back against his computer table. "I'm trying to see where you get this, Sergeant. I really am. And maybe I am slightly blinded by my anger at the fact that you took it upon yourself to go investigate these cases that I'd assigned to other inspectors. But" — he held up a hand — "of course if you did find a smoking gun, it would be a different matter. More easily overlooked anyway."

"But with respect, sir, this is pretty much a smoking gun."

"Maybe that's what I'm having trouble seeing. You have statements from both

Sephia and Rez that they hadn't been in the Terry/Wills apartment, but you don't have their fingerprints from that scene."

"I didn't really expect there would be, sir. They went there to kill these guys and either wiped the place down or, more likely, wore gloves."

"But the fact remains, no prints where they said they'd never been. I fail to understand how this can be compelling to you."

"What's compelling is that their prints were at Holiday's, where they also deny ever being. They didn't know I was going to ask that until the tape was already on, so they told a stupid lie."

Gerson drew a large and histrionic breath. "Sergeant, these men played poker together at least several times in the past year. They may have had some kind of falling out recently — I don't know about that — but they certainly shared each other's company, quite possibly at Mr. Holiday's house. So now they simply admit that they lied to you. They say they knew Holiday was a murder suspect and didn't want to be more closely associated with him." Gerson already had the tape in its case under a paperweight on his computer table.

"But sir, the bare fact . . ." Thieu

paused. "You have to admit this looks a lot like something fishy, at the very least. Sephia and Rez should be thoroughly interrogated. In my opinion," he added.

Finally the lieutenant seemed to break through some barrier. He leaned back, let out a long exhalation. "You might be right," he said. "I don't know why I'm fighting you so hard on this. Everything you're saying makes sense. It's just that this case has been nothing but a headache from day one." Gerson's hand, in fact, went to his head. He sighed again. "I've got to use the can a minute. Be right back."

Thieu came forward, his elbows on his knees, his head tucked. He had of course considered the objections that Gerson had made. Nothing was simple. Okay, so what's new? The point was, Thieu thought, that any conscientious cop would see enough questions for Sephia and Rez to at the very least jump all over them and move them up to the realm of legitimate suspects in the multiple slayings. If only to avoid the embarrassment and hassle of falsely arresting John Holiday when there were obviously so many other possible interpretations of the evidence.

But until tonight, just now, Gerson had

seemed congenitally blind to these subtleties. He had a suspect and evidence and an arrest warrant, and goddammit, why should he keep looking at all?

Now the lieutenant returned, got back in his swivel chair, made some kind of conciliatory gesture. "I apologize for being such a hard-ass about this, Paul. It's actually nice to have an inspector with this kind of initiative. It certainly wouldn't hurt to put these two guys in an interrogation room and sweat them on videotape, would it? If they broke . . ." Gerson brightened up, met Thieu's eyes. "But I would be more comfortable either way if we got Dan and Lincoln on board. Does that sit all right with you?"

Thieu remembered Glitsky's admonition that he should go directly through Gerson, without involving the two inspectors of record. But the reaction here had rendered that suggestion moot. If there was going to be any resolution to this case, there was no avoiding Cuneo and Russell now. "Sure. Your call, sir."

Gerson turned and punched numbers into the phone. "Hey, is Cuneo or Russell out there? Do you know when they . . . ? Oh. Really? Okay, thanks." He hung up.

"Evidently they're coming in by chopper

right now. Five minutes." The police helicopter, as well as others belonging to the Highway Patrol and even private companies such as Georgia AAA, often landed on the target painted on the roof of the Hall of Justice. "I don't think I've been out of this room all day, Paul. You mind if we get some exercise and meet them up there? I could use the air."

"Sure. Why not?"

Gerson grabbed his jacket from the peg by his door while Thieu went to get his off his chair. They passed out of the homicide detail and into the hallway, where Gerson turned right and Thieu followed. They went into the Inspectors Bureau, unoccupied at that time of the night, and pulled a key off a hook in a side room. This enabled the elevator to go all the way to the roof. They ascended in a companionable silence.

"Watch out," Gerson said, as he stepped over a low sill and out, "it's gotten a little dark."

And indeed it had come to full night, with a chill and biting wind.

Thieu had his hands in his pockets and shuddered against the cold. With the stiff breeze, he wasn't surprised that he couldn't yet hear the *thwack-thwack* of the helicopter's approach, but he turned a half circle and looked for it anyway.

The city was all dressed up. Thanksgiving was still a couple of weeks off, but already the Christmas lights were burning in several locations, some of the hotels, uptown. Taking in the sight, Thieu wondered why he didn't come up here more often. There was a splendid isolation, especially at this time of night, when the traffic was heavy but mostly unhearable, the stars close enough to touch. He moved a couple of steps toward the low edge of the roof, then started to turn back to ask his lieutenant if he knew from which direction the chopper might be approaching.

But he hadn't really begun the turn when a pair of strong hands hit him low in the back. With his own hands stuck deeply in his pockets, he could offer no resistance. "Wait!" was all he could think to say. "Wait!" But his feet hit the bottom of the wall almost before he realized he was being pushed, and there was nothing to stop his body from pitching over into the air.

Thieu's last whole thought, in the instant before the falling wiped his consciousness clean of anything but terror, was that Gerson had made that call to the outer office to check on the whereabouts of Cuneo and Russell. He'd talked to someone out there, and then less than a minute later they'd left the office to come up here. But no one had been in the office when Thieu had gone to retrieve his jacket. He should have remembered that, grown suspicious. He should have . . .

28

Susan Weiss, McGuire's wife, was doing her best to cope with the unexpected crisis, but it had thrown her off balance. This — the sudden arrival of her sister-in-law's family at her three-bedroom apartment in the Haight — was not something she felt equipped for, or trained to handle. She listened to their talk about fleeing from their house after the darkness had become complete, all of them making certain no one was behind them, with an air of disbelief. Was this really happening?

No one was acting as though the threat to the Hardy kids extended to the McGuire family, to her own children, Brittany and Erica. But even though Susan doubted that Panos knew that Moses and Frannie were brother and sister, she couldn't get that thought out of her mind. A cellist by profession and a true pacifist, Susan went through the motions of dinner and sleeping bags for the cousins and the fold-out couch for Dismas and Frannie with a wary, sleepwalking quality.

Susan knew the degree of protectiveness that Moses felt for Frannie. Her husband might be a good man with a pure nature, but at heart — and it had always troubled her — he was also a fighter, the veteran of dozens of bar brawls, rugby skirmishes, shillelagh altercations. Moses, like her brother-in-law Dismas, had seen action in Vietnam. Both of them had actually killed people, although she preferred to forget that most of the time.

Here, though, tonight, that was not possible.

Rebecca and Vincent wouldn't be going to their school for at least the next day and perhaps several more. Frannie wasn't going to her classes, either. After he talked to Glitsky tonight, Dismas would decide if the family needed to go into true hiding. They could get on a plane for somewhere, or at least check into a hotel out of town.

Now it was way past bedtime and still her girls sat spellbound on the floor, caught up in their cousins' fear and excitement. Suddenly, through no fault of Susan's, here was her whole family involved in a world of threats and violence, of intrigue and terror. She couldn't help herself, couldn't stop a great wave of resentment from washing over her. At her husband for insisting that they all come here, at Dismas and Frannie for agreeing. And now Dismas had gone off to discuss the situation with Glitsky, and Moses was back at the Shamrock.

Susan went to the kitchen, where poor Frannie was rinsing dishes and piling them in the dishwasher. Busing a few more dinner items from the table over to the sink, Susan fell in next to her, and shortly found she couldn't sustain any resentment toward her sister-in-law. Frannie, too, moved in a slightly robotic fashion, as though the strain of all this was just too great to contemplate, and Susan's heart went out to her.

Frannie finished rinsing a plate, then put it back down on top of the others, turned off the water and hung her head. Susan put an arm around her. "What are you thinking?" she asked.

Frannie sighed. "That maybe we're going to have to move after all."

"Where to?"

"It doesn't matter. Away from here. At least for a while. I can't imagine ever letting the kids go back to that school. Or really, to the house for that matter."

Susan understood what she was saying — she'd of course seen the Polaroid that Dismas had brought with him in a Ziploc bag. The two kids were at the gate in front of their house, knapsacks on, leaving for school, Frannie behind them a little out of focus. Whoever shot the picture couldn't have been more than thirty feet away. A red circle enclosed both of the children's torsos, smack in the crosshairs.

It was an image that would live with Susan for a long time. "Maybe," she said, "it really is just trying to get Dismas to stop working on this case."

Frannie turned the water back on, reached for the already rinsed plate. "He's already called their lawyer. But what if it's not who he thinks?" She shuddered. "I just see the man who took the picture sitting in his car *right there,* Susan. Close enough to touch. Except next time not with a camera. God." Suddenly the shuddering seemed to gather in on her and her shoulders were shaking. She brought her wet hands up to her face and covered it completely.

Susan tightened her arm around her sister-in-law. She could think of nothing to say.

Nat Glitsky's one-bedroom made Abe's duplex feel like the Taj Mahal by comparison. As the Hardys had done, Abe and Treya decided that they'd feel safer, for this night at least, somewhere other than their homes. They, too, waited until it had gotten dark. They, too, watched for following headlights on the way over, making sure there were none.

Now all the adults were in the postage-stamp living room while Rachel slept next to grandpa's bed. Abe sat hunched over, all knees and elbows, on the end of the coffee table. His face was set and expressionless, his eyes dark and forbidding. After much discussion with Treya and his father, he'd decided to call the station cops. Hearing who he was, they'd bumped it up to the station captain, who'd come over from his home, and the duty sergeant.

"All right." At this point, Hardy felt he'd take any sign of cooperation. "At least that's some action. What did they say?"

Glitsky shot him down. "Basically, they weren't too interested. Wasn't that your impression, Trey?"

"That might be overselling it," she said. Turning to Hardy. "They couldn't have cared less is more like it."

"And you showed 'em the picture? Told 'em the whole story?"

"Of course."

Hardy sat forward, using only the front two inches of a wooden chair Nat had brought in from the kitchen. "How could they not care? What's it going to take?"

"It's probably a prank," Treya said bitterly. "This kind of stuff happens all the time."

"All the time? They said that?"

"Not those exact words. They seemed to expect Abe to take it that way and were a little uncomfortable that he didn't."

"Even after I pointed out to them that I had been a cop for a while myself and really didn't run into something like this every day. Or even every year."

"What'd they say to that?"

"Nothing. They didn't care enough to argue. But more to the point," Glitsky added, "what would we like them to do? So I told them. Go rattle some cages. We know who it was."

"But let me guess. They said they'd do passing calls at the school and your house. More than that would need to come from downtown."

"You've been reading his mail," Treya said.

Nat, who'd been sitting, listening to all this at the end of the couch, suddenly piped in. "What I don't see is how they don't care. 'Nothin' happened,' they say. I go, 'Nothin'? Look at this picture. This is a threat on my granddaughter's life! Something like this happened to you, what would you do?'" He threw up his hands. "They look at me like I'm an old man, like I got nothing left up here."

"It wasn't you, Dad," Abe said. He came back to Hardy. "And it wasn't even that they didn't believe me, which was kind of a relief after the past few days. It was just, 'Hey, we can send the picture down to the lab, but after that, what?'"

"Yeah, but my favorite part," Treya said, "is the captain starts telling us about dope-sellers in the projects, who threaten the families there. 'You don't let us do our thing here, you get in our way, we're going to kill you and your kids, get it?'"

"And this teaches us what?" Hardy asked.

Treya's mouth formed a kind of smile, though she wasn't amused. "The actual message got a little lost in the telling, I think. But we should realize people get threatened all the time."

Abe picked it up. "And we of all people

ought to know that cops can't really prevent crime from happening. We can only clean up after it."

"Great. I'm thrilled to hear it," Hardy enthused. "So in the meanwhile, what do we — and by 'we,' I'm not talking society in general, I mean 'us' — what do *we* do?"

"I called Clarence," Treya said, "and the good news there is that I think he's come around to believing you both, finally. He's really worried about this."

"Good for him," Hardy snapped. "Better late than never. What's the bad news?"

"Same as usual," Glitsky said. "What's he supposed to do now? What can he do? He's not unsympathetic, but so what? He hopes whoever it is doesn't kill anybody."

"Me, too." Hardy's fuse was just about burned all the way down. "And it's not some unknown whoever. It's Panos."

"Wade?" Glitsky asked. "Or Roy? Or Sephia and Rez? Or somebody else on the payroll we don't even know about?"

Hardy knew what he was saying. He shook his head in frustration, finally raised his eyes. "I called Kroll, you know. Told him I was out of the lawsuit. It was over."

"What'd you say about Holiday?"

"Nothing. And he didn't ask. Why?"

"Because I'm not involved in your lawsuit, whatever some people might have thought. So if that was it, the lawsuit, there's no reason to threaten me." He took a long breath. "On the other hand, if either of us is still looking to get at the truth behind these murders and this finally gets homicide to rethink Holiday, who's that leave?" Glitsky nodded. "That's what they're warning us off. Both of us."

"Yeah, well, he's my client. What do they think I'm going to do, give him up?"

"I think it's crossed their minds you might."

Hardy's hard stare went around the room. "I can't do that."

"No one here is asking you to," Treya said, "but he's not Abe's client."

"What does that mean?"

Glitsky straightened his back. "I'm not trying to clear Holiday. I'm letting the law take its course from here on out."

Hardy snorted. "Our friend, the law."

"Sometimes it might be. I talked to Paul Thieu late this afternoon. I apologize. With all this madness" — he gestured around him — "I never told you. He went last night as we recommended and found some Sephia and Rez prints at Holiday's.

Then he got a statement from them saying they'd never been there."

"Son of a bitch." Hardy pumped a fist. "I knew it! So he's off?"

Glitsky temporized. "Maybe. If Gerson does the right thing. It's possible. But the point is I told Paul that no matter what, I was out of it. No credit, no blame, no nothing. I'm done."

"If they've got Sephia and Rez at John's, we both are."

"I repeat," Glitsky said, "maybe. I'd hold off on the party until I got the official word. I'd feel better if I heard that these guys were already behind bars. In any case, even if they pull our guys in, they still might be a long way from dropping any charges against Holiday. I'd be tempted to keep a low profile if I were you."

Hardy left Nat's place at 10:30. He called Frannie from there and Susan, who was still awake, told him that his emotionally drained and exhausted wife was asleep on the fold-out. Hardy, no less depleted, was nonetheless wired and would not be able to sleep even if he had a truckload of valium on board. But a black and tan or two might do the trick. He told Susan he was stopping by to see her husband and might not be home until the bar closed. Nobody should worry. Things might be looking up.

When he got to the Shamrock, the forty or fifty patrons were kicking into the kind of manic mode he'd seen hundreds of times over the years. Suddenly it was the kind of night that developed out of nowhere when a critical mass of humanity encountered just the right cosmic mix of alcohol, noise, and sexual possibilities. The juke, which had been audible down around the corner on Tenth where Hardy had parked, blared out Toby Keith's "Wanna Talk About Me" at the absolute limit of its speakers. Some football, loud, on the two TV's. The four dartboards had games going; all the stools were taken at the bar. Chairs, couches, floor space, packed.

Hardy made his way through the crowd, nodding and talking to the many familiar faces, a steady line of patter going, since he knew most of the patrons at least by sight. The Shamrock was the oldest bar in the city, now going on 110, but it wasn't big. Side to side, the public area from the bar stools to the wall was maybe twelve feet. Back at the dartboards, it widened to eighteen or so. He worked his way through the mob to the back of the bar, then hung his coat on the rack and ducked under the opening.

McGuire was tending, working hard keeping up with the orders. Hardy filled a pint glass with ice, a squeeze of lime, and gunned it full of club soda. After he drank half of it off in a gulp, he jumped in to help, and for most of an hour, didn't stop moving. It wasn't just a large crowd, but a remarkably friendly, patient and orderly one. They were mostly locals — thirsty but not belligerent. The jukebox kept cranking out the hits, although at one point Hardy realized that most of them weren't hits anymore — they were oldies. But then again, he thought, so was he, pouring his drinks, pulling his drafts, ringing up the charges, shooting the bull in five-second sound bites since it was far too busy for conversation. He and McGuire worked back into the rhythms they'd perfected back in the days twenty years before when Hardy had been the lead man behind the bar, before his marriage, before kids and his career.

Nowadays, and for a long while, all the other parts of his life had felt so different from this. Nowhere was there this simple busyness, the pleasure of doing something uncomplicated, good and well. Here, if somebody ordered a drink, he could be pretty sure that they weren't lying to him. That was the drink they wanted. He gave it to them, they paid him, he gave them their change. Maybe they tipped him. End of transaction.

When he looked up, surprised, to find that he finally had a minute, that most of the customers had left, he was sweating with the exertion and activity, but something had given inside him, the tremendous pressure, almost as though he'd taken a week's vacation on a warm beach. He realized that the ache in his back had at last subsided. He could still feel his injured hand when he squeezed it, but he'd been using it with a natural ease all night. He allowed himself to hope for a minute that with Paul Thieu's information, his enemies would be thwarted and with them, the threats to his family ended.

McGuire muted the televisions, turned the volume down on the jukebox, then came down from the other end of the bar. He put a heavy hand on Hardy's shoulder and sincerely thanked him for his work. "Where did that come from?" he asked, meaning the crowd.

"The word must have gotten out that I'd be here. Damn celebrity seekers." But

Hardy was grinning, first time in a week or so. Almost directly over his head, and behind him, Paul Thieu's picture showed up on the television for a minute, the late news, and McGuire glanced up, but he didn't know who Thieu was, so he never mentioned it.

Not that it would have made any difference.

They'd made last call a little early, shagged out the stragglers, locked up by 12:30, and restocked. They counted the money — $1,428, unheard of on a Tuesday night. Moses didn't ask, but poured Hardy a stiff Macallan to match his own and the two of them sat at the dark end of the bar, away from the windows, kitty-corner to each other. Hardy never needed to sleep again, but then again two days ago, he was never going to drink alcohol again, and here he was. The night-light above the register worked with the reflected streetlights outside to illuminate the place with about the intensity of a full moon.

While they'd been pulling bottles and rolling kegs, Hardy had been trying to convey some sense of his guarded optimism to McGuire, but now they were able to really talk and his brother-in-law wasn't buying. "Yeah," he said, "all that's great, but what if they don't get to Panos and his people soon enough, and in the meantime they decide to come after everybody anyway? You willing to take that chance?"

"I don't know what my other option would be, Mose."

"I do."

"I know. Go out and shoot them first. You've already told me. Have another drink."

"You think I'm kidding?"

Hardy took his first sip of the scotch, a small one. "No, but you're not thinking. You go out after them, you're a murderer. That's the whole story."

"I'd argue self-defense."

"How would you do that? Nobody's threatening you."

McGuire grunted. "I'm not letting anybody kill Frannie, Diz. Never, no how, no way."

"If it's any consolation, Mose, I'm not either."

"But you're not doing anything to stop it."

Hardy put his glass down slowly. "As a matter of fact, I've been doing quite a lot, which is why I now have some reason to suspect that this threat is less now than it was even three or four hours ago. They're going to bring these guys in."

"And then they're going to put them on trial, or maybe cop some lesser plea. . . ."

"This is multiple murder, Mose. That's special circumstances. Life without."

"So you're safe?"

"Right."

"They'll get them all? You're sure? And they don't have family? They don't have people who'll know you're behind it?" McGuire put his glass down. "I guess what I don't understand, Diz, is why, after you've seen all the ways the law doesn't protect you for squat — I'm talking in the past couple of weeks alone — you still think it's something you can count on."

"Maybe because that's the deal we make. We don't break the law and in return the law protects us."

"And you believe that? You got any poor, black friends, Diz? You got any cabróns?"

Hardy rolled his eyes. "Here we go."

"Here we go is right. You ever think about why there's so much more violence in the barrios, huh? Or the projects?"

"No, Mose, that's never crossed my mind. I never think about anything like that 'cause I'm a rich, white guy."

"Hey, you said it."

"Hey, yourself!" Hardy pointed a finger in McGuire's face. "It turns out you're arguing my point exactly. You know why there's so much violence in the hoods? Because the people there have lost their faith in the law. And you know why that is? Because it doesn't protect them. They feel like they've got to do it themselves."

"Right. Exactly *my* fucking point."

"But what *I'm* saying is take a look at what you get once you decide that's your position. You're taking your protection into your own hands, outside the law."

"At least you're alive."

"Actually, no. Probably not. You've got a much better chance at getting to be dead in fact. Why? 'Cause Pablo threatens to kill you if you mess with his dope business. You don't want dope around your kids, but you can't go to the law, so you decide you've got to kill Pablo. Then Pablo's brother Jose, who also doesn't think the law is going to punish you, comes and shoots your ass. So then *your* brother, or father, or mother . . . Anyway, you see where this is going. "

"Except look at you right now. Your family's driven out of your house. Where's your law there? Who's protecting you now?"

"Still, the law. Look, Mose, if Panos

wasn't worried about *somebody* doing something about it, he would have come for me long ago. He could have grabbed the kids, or shot them, when he took the picture."

"Maybe you're forgetting he did shoot some people."

"Maybe I'm not. But if I believe that the whole purpose of law is to take violence out of the hands of individuals, like you and me, and Panos for that matter, how am I supposed to justify going after him myself? As soon as I do that, I am so fundamentally like him that there's no moral distinction between us."

"Oh, no shit. He hits you, you can't hit him back? Are you giving me that?"

"I'm saying that if I go outside the law, then I can't expect anything from it anymore. And I'm not willing to give that up. It's pretty basic."

"It's pretty bullshit, you ask me."

"Oh yeah? So what happens, then, after one of the shots you fire at Panos or Sephia misses them completely, but kills the poor old lady eating her Cheerios three houses down? Or the mom pushing her baby half a mile away? You don't think that happens? You don't think that's the *main* thing that happens with every fucked-up

656

drive-by shooting you ever heard of? Once these things start, there's no controlling what happens next. People get killed who had nothing to do with it. And then, guess what? Those innocent people want to see the law punish *you*. And they've got every reason to expect that it will. Whether or not you *started* the whole thing. Once you're in it, you're the bad guy. Period."

Moses tipped up his glass, rattled the ice a little, tipped it up again. "If I knew for a fact who took that picture, I'd get real close and put a slug in the fucker's brain. I'd do it tonight, swear to God."

"And then your life, from then on, is never the same."

"I wouldn't tell anybody. And nobody would know my connection to you and Frannie. The cops would never even think to talk to me."

"Except if they did. And then what about Susan and your girls?"

McGuire was shaking his head. "Not going to happen. Listen, Diz, you got gangbangers killing each other all the time. You're telling me the cops even look real hard? So you get a known dirtball like, say, Sephia, who dies violently, and who's going to get all worked up over it? Nobody.

Probably not even his family, if he's got one."

Hardy acknowledged that truth with half a nod. "I wouldn't exactly weep and gnash my teeth myself."

"See?"

"But there's a difference between someone being dead and you making someone be dead."

"That's what you keep saying. But you and I have both pulled a trigger, Diz. Killed people we didn't even hate. We both know we could do it again if we had to. My question is how far do they have to push you before you do something on your own?"

"Pretty far, I'd guess. Where it turned into real self-defense."

"Which is pretty much after the fact, isn't it?"

"Yep. I think it has to be."

"And you're okay with that? You can live with it?" His brother-in-law's face was etched in concern that showed as though magnified by the dim light. "No, let me put it another way," he said. "I *hope* you can live with that. I hope your family can. I really do."

Hardy drained his own glass. "Me, too, Mose. Me, too."

★ ★ ★

Hardy was still dressed — jeans and a pullover — sitting on a two-person love seat in the back of the apartment, in the old laundry room that Susan had converted into a studio for her music students. It was quiet here, away from the beds, and he didn't want his own restlessness to keep anyone else up. A single, large, north-facing window revealed a smattering of lights stretching out toward the Presidio — he was up six stories — but the view, so lovely in the light, didn't captivate. He stared out, more through it than at it, aware but unthinking, or at least not thinking discrete thoughts.

Since he'd gotten into bed, then given up and come in here, his mind had returned again and again, unbidden, to David Freeman. Visions of him in his bed in the ICU. The damage they'd done to him, even should he survive it, a result about which Hardy had little confidence. A cold premonition had entered his gut along with the renewed conviction that these were very dangerous men, now perhaps made more desperate by their inability to isolate and destroy John Holiday. And without him, Hardy believed, they were surely, eventually doomed. They had to get to him, any way they could, as quickly as they could. And no mistake about it, Hardy believed that the surest route to Holiday was through him.

Another nonthought, a bother, a twinge, like a pestering insect alighting again and again on the surface of his consciousness, was that he should in fact disengage himself from Holiday, at least until things shook out here somewhat. Call Kroll and get that message delivered. As Moses had argued, he should save his family above all else, and he could do it without going outside the law. He'd never even taken a retainer from Holiday. There was no legal issue.

After all, he told himself, Holiday would probably be okay without him now. The evidence would set him free. Hardy didn't need to stay involved. The rationalizations gnawed.

"Dad?"

He started as though from a doze, but he hadn't been sleeping. "Hey, Beck."

"Are you all right?"

"Sure. Having some trouble sleeping, that's all. How's my little girl?" Sixteen years old, five foot five, 110 pounds. His little girl.

"I know you hate it," she said, "but I'm scared."

"Oh, babe." He looked up and caught the shining streak of a tear on her cheek. "Come here." He shifted to one side, patted the cushion next to him. "Have a seat next to your old man." He longed to tell her that there was nothing to be scared of — the perhaps comforting lie was almost out of his mouth — but he couldn't make himself say it. She was too old for that now; she'd feel patronized, and he didn't want that.

In a moment, her feet tucked under her, she was curled up against him, under his arm — all flannel and bathrobe, long hair and a slightly stale breath that he loved. At first, this seemed to be all she needed, and he absently stroked her hair as he had done since she'd been a baby. He felt her weight settle almost imperceptibly and she exhaled a shallow sigh, quietly but audibly. "You okay?" he asked. "A little better?"

"A little."

"But still scared?" He felt her head move up and down.

"Well." He couldn't resist the impulse to comfort her. "Maybe it's really not as bad as we thought originally. . . ."

"But those pictures, Daddy . . ."

"I know. I know what they were trying to do there, and that's make us afraid. And it worked, didn't it? But I went and saw Uncle Abe tonight and I really think there's a good chance now that the police will be able to . . . to do something."

"Like what?"

"Like maybe arrest these people. Some new stuff's come up. They're going to have to act on it. And when they do, we'll get back to normal."

"But what if they don't?"

Hardy sighed. "They probably will, Beck. You don't have to worry about that."

"And that's why you can't sleep, either? Because you're not worried anymore?"

Hardy tightened his arm around her. Sometimes she was too perceptive, he thought, for her own good. "I'm still a little worried," he conceded.

The Beck squirmed out and sat up, facing him. "It's just that I don't understand these people. Even if they wanted to hurt you, why would they want to hurt your family?"

"Because they know that nothing, really, would hurt me more."

"Okay, but then what do they think? That you'll just go away? I mean, the logical thing is that you'll just get crazier and come after their families. Doesn't that make sense?"

Hardy, again, didn't feel that he could be completely forthright. "I wouldn't do that. I couldn't do that. That wouldn't be right."

"Why not? If they came after us? I bet you would. I know you would."

"Well, luckily they haven't done anything physical to you or Vince yet, so we don't get to find out. I don't really want to find out. I'm plenty mad at them for what they've already done." This time he couldn't stop himself from lying. "But I really think this is pretty much over, Beck. Tomorrow night at this time we're back in our own beds. You'll see."

"But what if we're not?"

"Then the night after."

She frowned. "Now you're just trying to make me feel better."

"Not just now," he said. "All the time."

"But I need to know what's really happening."

"What's really happening . . ." He drew a deep breath, came out with a deeper truth. "I don't know for sure what's really happening, Beck. I don't want you to have to go through this."

"But I'm already in it, Daddy. We're here."

"I know." He gathered her back against

him. "I know." The city lights blinked in the windblown dust outside. Hardy tightened his arm around his girl. "I don't think I've been much of a help tonight, have I?"

"I'm still a little scared, if that's what you mean."

Hardy sighed. "That's what I mean."

"You can't protect me against my feelings, Daddy."

"I know," Hardy said. "And that just breaks my heart." He wondered anew whether he could protect her from anything at all, and a fresh wave of anger swept over him. All the words in the world to the contrary, he suddenly knew he would kill without mercy if anyone harmed his girl. And maybe it wouldn't hurt her to have some intimation of that, in spite of what he'd just told her to the contrary. "You know how I said I wouldn't do anything if something happened to you?"

"Yes."

"Well, if I could stop it before it could get to you, if it got to that . . ." He didn't finish. "I'm speaking hypothetically, now, Beck. But there's absolutely no way I'd let anybody hurt you."

Her tentative question nearly brought him to tears. "So what are we going to do?"

"I'm not completely sure yet, hon. But your mother and I, we're going to take care of you, no matter what. Maybe," he said, "if I can get myself to abandon John Holiday . . ."

"But you can't do that. He's your friend."

"Right." Out of the mouths of babes, Hardy thought. "I know. But maybe I can make them think I stopped." He stopped himself again. He was about to say, "Then set some kind of trap for them." "But look," he did say, "let's believe for a minute there's a really pretty decent chance that in a day or two they'll have these people in jail."

"And then they won't be after us?"

"No." He chucked her gently under her chin. "But they're probably already not after you now, not really."

She looked up at him hopefully. "Promise?"

Hardy hesitated. They had a rule about a promise being a promise, sacred and unbreakable. "I really don't think so," he finally said.

He felt a small shudder pass through her. "That's not a promise."

"No, I know," he said. "But close."

29

Hardy pushed open the street level door to the Freeman building. He crossed the foyer and got to the top of the staircase, then stood still a moment where it opened into the reception lobby. For the first time since the attack on David, he felt some sense of life here again. A half dozen people in the Solarium appeared to be taking depositions; three of the associates and a couple of paralegals stood by the coffee machine, deep in conversation; the steady whine of the copying machines filled in the background noise. Maybe he'd just happened upon a flurry, but the telephones kept Phyllis's head down and hands busy.

"Mr. Hardy. Dismas." Suddenly Norma appeared at his elbow. "We missed you yesterday. Is everything all right?"

He didn't know the answer to that. Certainly everything didn't feel all right. His family was still in hiding at McGuire's. He was going on less than four hours' sleep. Freeman was still unconscious. He hadn't heard that Sephia and Panos had been arrested.

"I mean, you never came in," she said. "Some of us were worried."

"I had some work out of the office," he said. "It hung me up all day." Smiling politely, he pointed across the lobby to the other set of stairs that led to his office. "I don't even want to look at the clutter on my desk, but I'd better get on up there."

"Of course, but I . . . I wanted to thank you."

"For what?"

"For your inspiration the other night." She gestured vaguely around the lobby, the steady hum of industry.

"Well." In truth, after Hardy had finished his little speech on Friday night, the Solarium hadn't exactly exploded into wild applause. He'd told everybody good night and gotten out of there as quickly as he could, slightly embarrassed that he'd gotten caught up in the moment and exposed himself so openly as basically uncool. He felt sure that he'd given some of the younger people, especially, but also a few of the more cynical associates and paralegals, fuel for the fires of ridicule. He could easily imagine the snickering after he left. All in all, he wished he hadn't done it at all, or failing that, that he'd thought of something light and gotten everybody laughing.

But now Norma had her hand on his arm. "You shouldn't be modest. Look what that did for everybody here."

Hardy couldn't deny that the buzz was better, but . . . "I don't really think that was me."

"Well, be that as it may," Norma said, "everybody else does. And I just wanted to thank you again, to tell you how much it meant to me. And to the firm. It was the perfect note. You can see the results for yourself. Look around."

Hardy had already seen enough, and it did gratify him. With David in the hospital, though, and so many other problems hanging fire, he wasn't quite ready to do cartwheels. Still, he gave the lobby a last glance. "Well," he said, "I'm glad I could help. And now" — he pointed again — "the grind awaits."

He crossed over to the reception area, looked a question at Phyllis, who held up a finger, asking him to wait. After an impressive trifecta of "Freeman and Associates, would you please hold," got the switchboard under control, she looked up and actually smiled as though she were happy to see him. New ground. "Lieutenant Glitsky has already called three times this morning. He says it's urgent."

Glitsky had found out about Thieu when he opened the morning paper and read about his apparent suicide. It didn't much convince him. Or rather, it finally did convince him of what he'd begun strongly to suspect. He decided on the spot that he wasn't going into his office again today. A sworn policeman with a clear duty, he was going to do some real police work at last, on his own if need be.

Hardy had already talked to Holiday, continuing in his counsel that the client should stay out of sight, don't worry, they'd found strong evidence that might clear him before too long. He should just remain patient. By the time Gina Roake called, Hardy was on the other line with his second judge of the morning, Oscar Thomasino. The first one, this week's magistrate Timothy Hill, had shot him down about quashing Holiday's arrest warrant almost before Hardy got the question out. "Surrender your client, Diz. Then we litigate. That's the process and you know it."

And Thomasino, who'd known and respected Hardy for many years, told him he didn't see what he could do. He'd be happy to put in a good word to Jackman or Batiste on Hardy's basic trustworthiness, even Glitsky's, but didn't think it would serve much purpose.

When he finally got back to Gina at her office, filling him in about her talk with Hector Blanca, specifically about the helicopter to Nevada, she was in a clear and quiet rage. The General Work inspector had told her that he'd really like to help, but that the consensus among his superiors, and he tended to agree, was that the supposed attack on Hardy and John Holiday never took place at all.

As to David Freeman, Blanca had just checked with the hospital this morning and he was very, very sorry — maybe Ms. Roake hadn't heard? — but Freeman seemed to be going into renal failure. His kidneys hadn't produced more than a teaspoon of urine overnight. Blanca liked Roake right away, and was possibly more straightforward than he would have been with someone else. Very probably, he told her, this would soon be a murder case, and hence outside of Blanca's jurisdiction. But by all means, Gina should bring her suspicions to homicide.

Hardy took her phone call as an opportunity to bring her up to date and she heard him out. She'd really been unaware of the escalations — the threats to the families, the probable murder of Paul Thieu. It seemed to galvanize her somehow, and when she heard that Glitsky would be at Hardy's office to discuss possibilities, she told him she was coming, too. Something had to be done and she wanted to be in on whatever it was. Hardy told her to come right on up.

So at a little before noon on a blustery and overcast Wednesday morning, Glitsky, Roake and Hardy had all gathered and now they sat in varying degrees of unease around the coffee table in Hardy's office. Hardy had put on a pot and two of them were drinking coffee.

Glitsky, of course, had his tea. Facing Hardy's office door, he was explaining that after he read about Thieu this morning, he had finally been driven to speak to Special Agent Bill Schuyler of the FBI, who had expressed interest in Abe's theory, but who said it would take at least a couple of days to arrange any kind of task force, and that's if he could get his field director's approval. Was

Glitsky really saying he believed the head of homicide was involved in cover-up and murder? This could be a lot of fun, Schuyler agreed, but it was going to take a degree of manpower and some time.

"Which is something we don't have."

"Isn't that a little dramatic, Diz?" Roake asked. "We get the FBI involved in a week or so, there's plenty of . . ."

But Hardy was shaking his head. "If they do anything, it will take years. Wiretaps, following people, background investigations. Maybe trying to infiltrate the gang. By then, all of our physical evidence has disappeared. That's if they do anything at all. And meanwhile, we're dead."

"Besides which," Glitsky added, "these people have just killed Paul Thieu. . . ."

"Allegedly." Roake's knee-jerk reaction.

"No, really." Glitsky's dark scowl ended that debate. "And there's every reason to think they're at this moment planning the same thing for Diz or me, or our families. Diz is right, Gina. It's not overdramatic. Drama happens. There's no time."

"So what do you propose to do?" Roake asked.

Glitsky sat quietly, looked down at his feet, said in an uncharacteristic, almost in-

672

audible voice. "I was hoping . . . I'm going to go down and make some arrests myself."

Hardy stared, looking for a sign that Glitsky was being ironic. He saw none. Which made his friend's message clear and unambiguous, at least to Hardy. And it shocked him.

First Moses, now Abe.

Glitsky raised his eyes to Hardy, then Roake, continued with the charade. "Maybe park 'em in San Mateo County overnight, get some judge to listen." This, Hardy knew, would never happen. No judge would ever listen under those circumstances. As no judge had given Hardy the time of day this morning. This wasn't what judges did and he, Glitsky and Roake all knew it. But it didn't make any difference. Glitsky was simply padding the pretense.

But Hardy didn't get to call him on it. At that moment, there was a quick knock, the door to Hardy's office opened and John Holiday introduced his lanky figure to the proceedings. "Howdy, y'all," he said, a genial grin in place. He wore a heavy sheepskin coat that reached midway down his thighs. He'd tucked his longish blond hair into an Australian shepherd's hat, one side of the brim tacked against the crown. Smiling all around with the obvious surprise he'd pulled off, he turned to close the door behind him.

By the time he turned back around to face them again, Glitsky had stood up. And now Hardy did the same, saying, "John, what in the hell are you doing here?"

Glitsky, a baleful glance at Hardy, took a step forward. He had no choice. He was a cop and here was a man wanted for murder. "I'm afraid you're under arrest," he said.

For Holiday, the surprise element suddenly and completely lost its charm. He glared with startled incomprehension at Glitsky for a beat, shot a look at Hardy, then with no hesitation half turned again, as though he were going back to the door. But when he came back around, he was holding a gun in his right hand. It was pointed down at the floor, but nobody in the room missed it or its import.

"I don't think anybody's gettin' arrested just right now," he said, the quiet tone and soft Tennessee accent taking nothing away from his resolve. "Now, Lieutenant, you just sit down, would you? I won't ask for your gun because I'm gonna assume you'll act like a gentleman. But please keep your hands out where I can see them. Then we can have a civil discussion, all four of us."

Glitsky found his chair and took it.

Hardy remained standing, folded his arms over his chest. "Jesus, John, what are you doing? How'd you get here?"

Holiday made no effort to put up the gun. "My lady dropped me by the alley in the back. I came in through the garage and up the elevator. Don't worry, nobody followed me. I'm sure."

"That's not what I was worried about. Haven't you ever heard that when you've already dug yourself into a hole, you ought to stop digging?"

Glitsky concurred. "This is a big mistake."

Holiday was all agreement. "I can see that now, Lieutenant; you're probably right. But I didn't know anybody else was going to be here."

"Why don't you put away the gun, though?" Roake asked. Then, to Hardy, "This is your client, I presume?"

Hardy made the introductions, and Holiday bowed in a courtly fashion, although without ever taking his eyes from Glitsky.

"So why did you come here?" Hardy asked again.

"Tell you the truth, Diz, part of it was

cabin fever. Mostly, though, I was thinking you and I might come up with a way to turn me in and guarantee my safety. That thing with your kids . . ." The words petered out. "Anyway, I figure if Panos thinks they got me, that ends. Am I right?"

Hardy shrugged. "Maybe not all wrong. But the kid thing. You know Abe's got the same problem?"

Holiday looked across the room at Glitsky. "Have I got to keep this gun out, Lieutenant, or could we come to an understanding for the time being?"

"As far as I'm concerned, you're still under arrest. When I leave here, you're coming with me."

"I don't think so."

Glitsky almost laughed. "You going to shoot to stop me? So you can do whatever you want with the gun. It's not helping your case, as I'm sure your lawyer will agree." He shot a glance over to Hardy, an invitation to back him up.

But Hardy had gone bolt upright in his chair, his eyes glazed and faraway.

Roake, across from him, spoke up. "Diz? Are you all right?"

He came back with them. "What? Yeah, sure. John, put the damn gun away, would you? The rule is you don't wave one around if you're not prepared to use it."

"What if I am?"

"Then you're a bigger idiot than even I think you are, which is hard to imagine. Nobody here thinks you killed anybody, okay? You're not about to start now." He didn't wait to give Holiday a chance to respond, but turned directly to the other two. "Abe and Gina, check me on something, would you? We're assuming that Gerson pushed Thieu off the roof, right?" Out of the corner of his eye, he saw Holiday moving, sticking the gun back under his belt. "The question is why? Why right then?"

Glitsky had clearly given this a great deal of thought. "Because Thieu put Sephia and Rez at Holiday's when they denied they'd ever been there."

"And, John" — Hardy turned — "have they ever, to your knowledge, been to your place?"

"Are you kidding?"

"I'll take that as a 'no.' That's what I thought. So." He came back to the others. "Doesn't this mean that Gerson must have thought Thieu was the only person with this information? Otherwise, why kill him if somebody else is going to show up tomorrow and confront him with the same problem?"

"Except by now Gerson has probably destroyed the tape," Glitsky said.

"Maybe not," Roake said. "Especially if he figures nobody else knew about it."

Hardy nodded at Glitsky. "Assume, Abe, that Gerson doesn't know that *you* know."

"I'm sure he doesn't. I specifically asked Paul to keep you and me out of it, and if anybody in the world was capable of that, it was him."

"Well, there you go." He held up his hands as though he'd proven something.

"Where, though?" Glitsky asked. "Call me slow, but I don't see where you're going."

"Okay, Slow. What exactly did Paul tell you?"

Glitsky wasn't sure where this was going, but Hardy seemed to have an idea, and at this point, anything was worth pursuing. "Just that he'd lifted Sephia's and Rez's prints from Holiday's house. He had this tape. He was going down to play it for Gerson." He lifted and dropped his shoulders. "That's about it."

Hardy looked across the room. "Gina, you see it?"

She nodded.

Back at Glitsky. "Abe, now you can go to a judge and do an affidavit, which ought to be probable cause to search Gerson's office, maybe even his home, for the tape. Odds are they'll even have a copy of Thieu's original fingerprint request and the results with the tape, showing Gerson knew its significance."

Roake had come forward to the edge of the couch. "So you're saying Abe should get a warrant for Gerson's house and office without telling anyone else in the PD?"

"That's the general idea, yeah. We've finally got some probable cause and here's our chance to use it."

Glitsky didn't buy it. "Impossible," he said. "Even if Gerson hasn't already gotten rid of the tape and every one of those reports — which I know, if I were him, I would have — if we do find them we have no real proof of anything. And my career would be completely over."

"It seems to me like our only chance. You've got to get something on Gerson and squeeze him."

Glitsky was all concentration. "Don't get me wrong. I love the idea, but it doesn't go anywhere." He looked up at Hardy. "And at best it still leaves Panos, who'll then know we — that's you and me, Diz — we haven't backed off." He shook his head. "I'm not sure I want to dare him to see how far he'll go."

Holiday, who'd been listening all this while, suddenly butted in. Quietly. "How about this, instead? You call this Gerson and tell him you've got me."

"What do you mean, got you?" Glitsky asked.

"In custody. You want to turn me over to him, but Diz here, my whizzo lawyer, doesn't trust the normal procedure. He won't give me up to anybody but you, Lieutenant. Gerson would believe that."

"And how does that help us, John? Or help you?" Hardy asked.

"I'm not exactly sure about the nuts and bolts. But if Gerson knows that you, Lieutenant, are going to be some place at some time with me . . ."

"You'd get ambushed," Hardy said. "No way is that happening."

But Glitsky liked it. "If we could in fact get them all together on some pretext . . ."

Roake went with it. "The fact that they're all there together is probable cause right there, Abe. And you arrest the lot of 'em."

Glitsky, Holiday and Hardy just looked at her.

After a moment, she turned pale, then crimson, then added in a flat tone. "There would have to be backup. I'm talking police, of course."

Glitsky went on as if she hadn't spoken. "So I call Gerson and tell him where and when, and that it's just me and you, Diz, and your client turning himself in to me. And that after I have John in custody, I will personally take him downtown for booking. I also tell him it's imperative that no one else, including him, is there to blow the deal. Especially not him. But he's going to think the three of us are out wherever it is, all alone."

"Okay," Hardy said. "Then what?"

"Then we field-test our theory, which all along has been that this ends when Holiday is dead."

"Don't sugarcoat it," Holiday said.

Glitsky ignored him. "The point is, if Gerson does show up, I know there could only be one reason."

Roake was shaking her head. "It's no good, Abe. You'd be absolutely exposed. No way would Gerson come alone."

Glitsky nodded. "That's probably right. And that would remove any doubt about his guilt and conspiracy, wouldn't it? Not that I have any. But that would be rock-solid proof."

"No question, proof is good," Hardy agreed. "Except when it leaves you outnumbered four or five to one."

"Any trace of the rest of them," Glitsky said, "and I call for backup."

Sure you will, Hardy thought to himself.

Glitsky went on. "Then I go to Batiste and let him know what happened. And then they have to listen."

Hardy got up and walked over to the window. He turned back around. "No way, Abe. This can't happen. You're talking suicide."

"Well, if they succeed in killing me, which I strongly doubt, there's three witnesses in this room can swear to what happened."

"Be that as it may, Abe, I won't allow it."

Glitsky's mouth turned up a fraction of an inch. "I know it runs counter to your worldview, Diz, but you've got nothing to say about it. This is my job."

"So get your backup there and in place first."

"On what pretext? I'm the payroll lieutenant. Remember? Besides, then it would just leak and scare everybody off." Now Glitsky stood up, full of resolve. "This is a good plan, people. It might be the only one before they can hit us again, and that I can't let them do." He was over behind Hardy's desk, reaching for the phone, punching the numbers.

The three others watched in a kind of helpless, mute panic as Glitsky's few words put things into irrevocable motion.

"Lieutenant Gerson, please. Lieutenant, Abe Glitsky here. Yeah, I heard. I know, it's awful about Paul, but that's not what I'm calling about. John Holiday. And I told them they should go to you, but as you may know his lawyer's a friend of mine, and . . ."

In under five minutes, they had it all arranged. Holiday and Hardy, Glitsky said, would be showing up to surrender at four o'clock at Pier 70, a mostly abandoned and completely deserted dock of dilapidated boathouses and razed ancient warehouses. Glitsky didn't know why they'd picked such a godforsaken place, but . . .

"Because then there's no way Gerson can argue that he just happened to be in the neighborhood."

"So how about if John and I really do show up with you?"

Glitsky looked straight-faced from one of them to the other, over to Roake. "I hope I haven't given you the impression that's an option, because it's not."

"Now wait a minute —" Holiday stood up.

Glitsky raised his voice against any interruption. "So I'm just running down the hall to the bathroom for a minute, maybe less. Diz, your client is your responsibility. I expect you as an officer of the court to keep my prisoner here under your watch until I get back. I need your word on it."

Hardy solemnly raised his right hand. "You've got it."

"All right, then." And Glitsky was gone.

Roake, Glitsky and Hardy were standing downstairs in the lobby. Upstairs in Hardy's office, Glitsky had put on a perfectly convincing display of anger and disappointment when he returned from the bathroom to find that Holiday had "escaped." Both Roake and Hardy swore he'd pulled his weapon on them again. They'd been helpless to stop him.

Now Hardy noticed Phyllis as she stood up behind her switchboard. She caught his eye as she came around her partition and motioned with her head toward Norma's office, where she stopped and stood expectantly in the doorway. Hardy reached out for Gina's arm and turned her, guiding her that way as well. Glitsky followed.

They all were there, crowding behind Phyllis, in time to see Norma put down the receiver and hang her head, her shoulders collapsing around her. When she finally looked up, tears streaked her cheeks.

Wordless, she nodded at the assemblage in her doorway. It seemed the limit of all the acknowledgment she was capable of. Phyllis, next to Hardy, put her hand over her mouth and began to sob.

30

After leaving Hardy's office, Glitsky returned to his empty home. He was tempted to stop by Nat's to see his father and his daughter, but in the end decided that this would serve no purpose. He kept trying to convince himself that today was in a fundamental way no different than any other. The situation was personal and extreme, true, but basically it wasn't too far removed from the work done by most cops every day — sometimes you had to put yourself in the line of fire. It came with the territory.

He still wasn't clear in his mind about how the logistics would play out, but this uncertainty again was, if not exactly comforting, at least familiar enough. He remembered earlier in his career, making busts in places where he had little or no knowledge of what he'd be facing after he hit the doorway, most often at or before the very first light of dawn. Would there be three small terrified children and their mother huddled in a corner? A wired junkie who might decide on the spur of the moment to take a nearby and convenient hostage? A pit bull with a bad attitude? A dark room with a desperate gunman in each corner? Or maybe just a sleepy and strung-out loser who'd just as soon wake up tomorrow in jail anyway, where it was cleaner, warmer and they had better food.

So he'd done this kind of thing before, many times. You knew the basic rules. You tried to keep your options open, stay flexible and be prepared. You wore your vest for sure, you had enough ammunition and at least a couple of loaded guns so you didn't have to reload at an inopportune moment. His experience had taught him that ejecting a spent clip and slamming in a new one wasn't as easy in the heat of the moment as it might appear on television. Even when he'd been younger, his hands tended to shake in moments of stress and danger. They still did. He could more easily imagine himself fumbling and dropping his reload to the ground at the worst possible moment than otherwise.

So he took out two guns from the safe in his bedroom. His everyday weapon was a

Glock 9mm automatic, and it was a fine gun, easy to carry and to handle. But in this case, he reached for his matching Colt .357 revolvers with custom rubber grips. The damn things bucked like horses with the kind of heavy load he'd be using — .357 ammunition, special hand-loaded hot rounds, hollow-point bullets — but if things developed the way he thought they might, he wanted a bullet that could spin a man around twice and bring him down if it nicked him on the pinky. A hit in any large muscle and the slug would flatten and pretty much take the fight out of its target, guaranteed. A body hit was a death sentence.

Sitting on his bed, Glitsky slid the bullets into the cylinder on the first gun, snapped it closed, did the same with the second. Twelve shots, less than he'd get with two automatics, but less chance of a jam or a misfire. Speed loaders for quick reloads. People disagreed with him, but he'd take a revolver every time.

Taking off his shirt, he went to his closet and pulled his vest off the nail where it had hung undisturbed for probably ten years. He realized suddenly with a pang of regret that if he'd continued wearing the darned thing to work as a matter of course, his last eighteen months of medical madness and recovery might have been avoided. He might have only had a bruised rib for a couple of days, a black-and-blue stomach instead of IVs and antibiotics, tubes and monitors, to say nothing of the pain, the guilt, the self-doubt.

He shook himself to clear those thoughts. No point in whipping himself further on that score. It was what he had done — gone into a potentially violent situation unprepared. He would not do the same thing again.

With his regular shirt back on and buttoned over the vest, he checked himself in the closet door mirror. With a jacket on, no one would be able to tell. Since he wore a shoulder holster every day, it felt natural under his left arm, even with the slightly unwieldy bulge of the rig he used for the revolver. He hadn't worn a belt holster, though, since he'd been on a beat, and he was slightly surprised at how comfortable it felt, high on his right hip.

It had been unusually cold, even for November in the city, and it would probably be worse on the pier jutting out into the Bay, so he forsook his standard leather flight jacket in favor of his old dark blue goose-down ski parka. Snapping the lower buttons, he pulled the hem down and checked the mirror again to make sure that it covered his hip weapon.

Glitsky almost never looked at himself. When he'd come to college, as a kind of private joke to himself, he started telling people that he got the scar through his lips in a knife fight with some gang kids in high school. In reality, it had been a prosaic accident on parallel bars when he was in junior high. But whatever had caused it, the scar itself didn't heal perfectly and came to be something he tended to avoid looking at. The same thing with the blue eyes in his dark face. They made him uncomfortable. Was he in fact black like his mom, or a nice Jewish boy like his dad? As a young man, all the superficial stuff was too confusing to him and, in the end, he realized, meaningless. He was who he was inside. And so was everybody else.

Now, though, he stood an extra moment before the mirror, trying to glean in the image there some hint of his essence as he was today. Why was he doing this? He had an incredible wife and a new daughter and everything to live for. Had it really gotten to the point where he had no other choice? Weren't there other cops he knew, friends and allies over the years, to whom he could turn? Or at least from whom he could request backup? What was he hoping to accomplish?

But then he ran down the numbers — Chief Rigby, no. Deputy Chief Batiste, no. Jackman, no. Lanier, impossible. The FBI, no time. Paul Thieu, dead. What was he going to do next, go to the mayor? Any man on the force who joined with him now risked his career at the very least. Beyond that, Glitsky had always been a loner on the job, a solo inspector for his entire career, and then as lieutenant, mostly a by-the-book justice freak. He'd always believed that although people might not like him, he was at least respected. Recent events called even that minimal standard into question.

Now he couldn't afford to care about that public opinion. He only had to answer to his family. These threats to them could not be allowed to stand. If he could not enlist help among those whose job it was to provide it, then it was up to him. And him alone, if need be.

He glanced one last time at the middle-aged man in the mirror. Knocking three times on the Kevlar over his heart, he drew a deep breath, then let it out heavily. "Okay," he said.

★ ★ ★

He'd chosen Pier 70 quickly and intuitively out of several possibilities that had occurred to him as he'd spoken to Gerson. The more obvious spot might have been the outer edges of the parking lots at Candlestick Point, where there would be no opportunity for his enemies to ambush him and where, frankly, if it came to a gunfight, there would be less chance of bystanders becoming victims. But to his mind, more than equally balancing out the ambush question, was the parking area's total lack of cover for himself. If Gerson came out with enough friends to surround him, Glitsky didn't want to be standing alone in the middle of a concrete field, where Gerson could see Holiday was in fact not with him, where even a mediocre shot with a rifle could take him down from outside the county.

By chance, Glitsky, along with most of the workers at the Hall of Justice, had come to know Pier 70 very well about three years ago, when it had been the major crime and finale scene in a movie one of the big-shot Hollywood directors was always shooting somewhere in town. For about three months, the tinseltown crew had worked out of the Hall of Justice,

692

and everybody had become starstruck to some degree. One of Abe's inspectors, Billy Marcusik, even got tapped for a credited speaking role in the eventually awful film, playing essentially himself. After shooting wrapped, Billy quit the force and moved to L.A., but so far he hadn't been in any more movies that Abe had seen. In any event, in the glory days, just about every cop and clerk and even a few judges in the Hall thought they might turn out to be the next big thing if they hung around the director enough. If nothing else, they might get five seconds with one of the stars. For a week or more near the end of shooting, hordes of city workers would descend upon Pier 70, either in hopes of working as an extra, or to watch the fools who entertained those hopes.

Now, not much after one o'clock, Glitsky pulled over and parked. He'd told Gerson he'd be there at 4:00, but it would be bad luck to be late. He wanted to be absolutely sure he was the first man here. He wanted to walk over every inch of the area. He stopped on an unnamed industrial street of low-rise warehouses and garages a few blocks west of a dent in the Bay's shoreline called the Central Basin. An abandoned railroad line ran down the middle of the road. When they'd been shooting the movie out on Pier 70, this street had been the glamorous, albeit slightly funky, production base — trailers for the stars, incredible catered spreads of food for everyone with a pass, lights and gurneys and hundreds of people. Now Glitsky sat behind the wheel for a short while, letting his senses take it in, warn him of anything that resembled trouble.

There was nothing but the empty street. A gust off the bay skipped some heavy dust off the car's hood; some newspapers and candy wrappers fluttered in the recessed doorway of an empty storefront across from him. Another car was parked at the end of the block, but Glitsky had already driven by it once, and it appeared empty.

He got out and walked to the corner, looked out toward the Bay on his right. Pier 70 was the last of a series of six or seven piers jutting north into the water. In front of them was a relatively large open expanse of cement — reminiscent in some ways of Candlestick Point — although in this case there were few if any individual parking spaces. The area had once been used for loading and unloading and container storage, but for the past ten years or so, the piers on this stretch of the bay had been allowed to fall into disrepair.

Hands in his pockets, head down against the dusty wind, Glitsky crossed the shortest distance to the squat, yellowish building that marked the entrance to the first pier. The next three piers were similarly constructed — a large warehouse-style building out of which protruded the actual pier and boat loading area behind it. Everything was deserted.

Pier 70 itself was nearly a quarter of a mile long, a little over sixty feet wide. It was the farthest east of the half-dozen sister piers. Although there were a few open areas leading down to docks at the water level, most of the pier's entire eastern exposure, along the Bay, had been built up into various one-story structures, many of them open to the elements, some of them railroad cars, to service its trade. This left a relatively broad asphalt roadway on Glitsky's left as he walked out along the pier, his shoulder weapon drawn now and held in his hand, mostly concealed in his jacket pocket. He looked into the various doorways and openings. There was no mystery in why the famous director had chosen this spot for his finale — with its ramshackle, low- or open-roofed, wooden buildings facing a wide thoroughfare posing as Main Street, the pier resembled nothing so much as an Old West movie set, false fronts and all.

But Glitsky wasn't in much of an aesthetic frame of mind to appreciate the art of it all. When he reached the end of the pier, water on three sides and no escape, he realized where he had to set himself — back where he'd begun, maybe a few structures in. Let whoever was coming next get in behind him and cut themselves off. With no escape.

Except past him.

He made it back in half the time he'd taken going out, but it still seemed to be one of the longest walks of his entire life. Doorway to doorway, one at a time, his gun in hand, eyes always on the head of the pier, the open expanse in front of it. Nothing and no one.

He was a hunter now, not a cop. Cops didn't draw weapons without suspects or specific situations at hand. They didn't conceal the weapon if drawn. They called for backup if even the remote chance of gunplay loomed.

A gull landed on a post across the way, studied him for a moment, then flew off with a series of derisive squawks. Somehow rattled by this natural display, Glitsky turned quickly, now impatient to find a suitable place to wait.

He found it in a low, barnlike structure maybe sixty feet from the front of the pier. It had no front door and was also open in the back, but half-height partitions within created several eight-by-four-foot spaces that might have served as horse or cattle stalls. He had looked cursorily into the place on his way out and had concluded that, because there was light from the front and back openings, and they were only four feet high, the partitions would be inadequate for hiding. He hadn't even looked behind them when he passed.

Now, for the same reasons, suddenly they looked good to him.

He put his gun back in his holster. At the back opening, he scanned along the waterline, then turned and came back to the front. Another gull, or maybe the same one, had landed on the nearest post, and now was squawking continually. Glitsky looked around in the barn and found a large rusty hinge of some kind, which he chucked at the bird. It missed and splashed into the water below with a noise that sounded to Glitsky's ears loud as a depth charge. The bird didn't so much as shift its feet, and kept on squawking.

He pushed back the sleeve of his jacket and checked his watch. It was ten minutes until two. The wind whistled through the cracks in the structures around him. Not a streak of blue showed in the dun-gray sky overhead. Somewhere in the white noise of the background, he thought he heard a *chunk*, like a car door closing. He looked at his watch again. It was the same time as before. His hands, he realized, were damp with sweat.

On the cement no-man's-land, a body appeared. A man alone, walking.

Once Glitsky was sure, he came back into view and stood in the barn's doorway where he could be seen. Surprises among armed men could turn unlucky very quickly and he had no intention to be part of one. He found that he was unprepared for the wave of relief he felt at John Holiday's appearance here. He hadn't let himself consciously acknowledge that some part of him had half expected reinforcements of some kind to show up. In any case, he was glad of it.

Glitsky motioned him to move it forward, Holiday broke into a trot, and in a moment they were together, back in the shadows of the barn, but able to look out.

"Where's Hardy?" Glitsky asked.

"I don't know. I thought he might be with you."

"No." Then, "You came down here by yourself? What for?"

"I've asked myself the same question." He shrugged. "You told Gerson you were going to turn me in. I thought it would play better if you actually had me here. Maybe give you fellows something to talk about for the first minute or so."

"He might not come at all," Glitsky said.

"And if he doesn't, you'll have to take me in. I know. We've already done that once today." Holiday pulled at his mustache, maybe to keep from breaking a smile. "Well, Lieutenant, whatever way it works out, if it comes to a fight, I figure it's mine as much as anybody's. I belong in it. These boys don't play fair."

Glitsky looked him up and down, the heavy sheepskin jacket to mid-thigh. "Are you still packing, John?"

This time Holiday did break a smile. "I don't know why you want to go and ruin a perfectly fine afternoon asking a question like that. No I am not. My lawyer advised me that it was against the law and my appearance here today points to my good faith. I'd be offended if you asked to search me."

Glitsky allowed an amused grunt. "Sounds like you've been talking to Diz, all right. Did you see anybody when you were coming in here? If not, I thought we'd wait behind these partitions and let people get by us, if anybody comes. How does that sound?"

"That's your call. I'm just here to help with the fuckin'."

Glitsky frowned at the profanity, gazed out again at the no-man's-land. "If it's Gerson alone, I want to let him walk past, come out behind him alone. You wait back in here, and listen up. If we both come back to pick you up and take you downtown, I'll pat you down and it would be smart if you didn't get yourself armed between now and then." A cold smile. "Do you understand me? If you try to escape, say out the back opening there, you've got an excellent chance of getting shot. Is that clear enough?"

"It's clearer than why Hardy thinks you're a sweet guy."

Glitsky nodded. "He's notorious for being a bad judge of character." Suddenly, he narrowed his eyes, twisted his head slightly. "Did you hear that?"

Gerson eyed the length of the pier.

He squinted out along the asphalt road-way through the midday overcast. The last structures, way out there, were blurry and indistinct; the actual end of the pier seemed to fade into the gray-green water of the bay.

He hadn't slept at all last night. The business with pushing Thieu off the roof, so suddenly conceived and hurriedly executed, might have been a mistake. Not so much that he would ever be suspected of the actual murder; that had been clean enough. But the real problem was that now and forever, any thought of getting out from under Panos was completely impossible. Because naturally Wade knew about Thieu. Wade always knew. He'd called as soon as he'd heard, said he'd figured it out and appreciated the consideration, would not forget who his friends were. The death of the woman in jail had locked him in with Wade, too, of course, but that hadn't been Gerson, personally. It had been someone in the sheriff's department and all Gerson had to do was ignore it.

But Thieu was different. Not that Gerson had ever liked the self-righteous, brilliant little shit, but when he saw the nooses tightening around Nick's and Julio's necks, he should have tried some other tack first — offered Thieu money, maybe a raise or a job at the Diamond Center. Big money for mostly doing nothing. Gradually get Thieu involved in the racket.

At least Gerson might have talked to Wade and gotten a sense of things. But instead, he'd panicked.

And now here he was at Pier 70.

"Lieutenant!"

Gerson turned around. He'd only come up the pier about seventy feet and somehow Glitsky was already here, had already gotten in behind him.

"Lieutenant," Gerson echoed. He stepped toward him.

"I thought I asked you not to come out here. That I was bringing Holiday in."

The smile faded. "I don't see him, though, do I?"

"And you might not now, if he sees you first."

"He's going to see me anyway, downtown."

Half turning to look around behind him, Glitsky intended the movement as cover while he reached in to get at the weapon in his shoulder holster. He was going to place this son of a bitch under arrest and let the chips fall.

But a movement out in the no-man's-land completely got his attention first. Two men were double-timing toward the foot of the pier while a third was already down on one knee, arm extended. A glint of metal. Someone was aiming at gun at him.

Glitsky jerked his gun from the holster and dove hard to his left just before he heard the noise of the two shots. Formal firearms training stresses the advisability of two-shot volleys, and Glitsky was still rolling as another two shots, much closer — Gerson! — exploded behind him. Still exposed on all sides, he lay flat on his stomach, his gun extended in a two-handed grip.

Gerson, still perhaps thirty feet away — the outer limit of accuracy for a pistol shot — had turned sideways and was now advancing, presenting very little target, but Glitsky took aim at his torso and squeezed off two quick rounds, then rolled again as the return fire pinged around him. He found himself wedged into a corner where a building jutted a foot farther out than its neighbor. This sheltered him slightly from Gerson, but left him wide open from the foot of the pier, where he now clearly saw Sephia, Rez and Roy Panos drawing down on him. They'd come onto the pier itself.

He couldn't forget Gerson, approaching now under the same cover Glitsky was using from his right, but he had to get off a shot at the trio on his left or he was surely dead. He got on his feet just as other shots — a volley really — exploded and a bullet smacked the stucco six inches from his head.

Reaching around the corner of the building, he took another wild shot at Gerson then whirled in time to see that part of the volley he'd heard must have come from John Holiday in the barn. The thugs had been coming at Glitsky three abreast, almost casually now that they had him cornered, but now suddenly Roy Panos was down on the ground, rolling back and forth, screaming that he'd been hit. Sephia and Rez had scattered, pressed up against the covering building facades, at the unexpected fire.

They'd just got their vests on when they heard the first shots from back on the street and now McGuire's pickup flew in a spray of gravel across the no-man's-land and skidded to a stop at the mouth of Pier 70.

Hardy was out before they'd stopped

moving, the situation clear to him at a glance. This was already a heated firefight, the smell of cordite acrid in the breeze. One man was already down, with Glitsky pinned out in the goddamned middle of nowhere. Sephia and Rez were in a couple of adjacent recessed doorways, and somebody else — Hardy didn't recognize him by sight — was beyond Glitsky, along the wall of a warehouse.

Sephia and Rez looked his way and without hesitation opened fire.

A shot ricocheted off the hood of the pickup.

McGuire, exposed on the driver's side, got down and slid across the seat, coming out with his shotgun beside Hardy, squatting behind the front tire, peering out. On the pier, another shot rang and he saw Sephia and Rez pull back.

"Who's that?" McGuire asked.

"I don't know," Hardy said. "But if he's shooting at those guys, I've got to believe he's with us."

"Yeah, but he's still shooting in our direction. What kind of shit is that?"

"That's what happens when you're all in a line."

And this, clearly, was the problem. From this angle, McGuire couldn't use his shotgun to fire at anyone this side of Glitsky, since the buckshot pattern risked hitting Glitsky beyond. By the same token, any shot of Glitsky's — or Holiday's, for that matter (though Hardy and Moses didn't know it was him) — was essentially in their direction. Somehow they needed an angle, and there was no way to get to one that wasn't immediately life-threatening.

Another couple of shots slammed into the pickup, rocking it on its wheels.

"Forty-fives," Hardy said.

"We've got to rush 'em," McGuire said. "It's the only way."

At that moment, John Holiday, perhaps coming to a similar conclusion about needing an angle, broke running from the shelter of his barn. Ten or twelve feet out into the road, he stopped abruptly, whirled, and with an almost agonizing slowness, took careful, two-handed aim at Gerson, who snapped off a shot of his own, then hit the ground himself in a continuous roll back away from Glitsky's position.

Holiday squeezed off a first shot.

"Now! Now! Now!" McGuire yelled.

More shots from the pier, but there was no time to analyze or even look at what was happening farther down there. Now it was all movement with a focus on Sephia and Rez, as McGuire, using Holiday's break as a distraction, cleared the back end of the truck. "Comin' in, Abe!" Hardy yelled and sprinted out of the truck's protection, two steps behind McGuire, both of them running full out, low to the ground.

"Go right right right!" McGuire screamed as he brought the shotgun up.

Moving out onto the pier itself now, still running, Hardy got a glimpse of Sephia hunkered down against a kind of covered doorway on the left. Moses was going to take him.

Rez was his target. He stood six feet closer toward the mouth of the pier, to Hardy's right. He raised his gun with his left hand, tried to draw a quick bead, and fired, but he hadn't reckoned on the broken bone in his hand, the immense kick of his weapon. His grip didn't have the strength it needed. The recoil knocked the gun from his grasp, sent it clattering onto the asphalt.

A deafening explosion to his left as first Sephia opened fire with everything he had, emptying his gun, while McGuire straightened up and fired first one load, then almost immediately the second. Out of the corner of his eye, Hardy saw Sephia thrown backward, glass breaking down over him as he fell slumped to the ground.

But Rez had an automatic in each hand now, both of his arms pointing straight out in front of him. He seemed to be laughing, taking aim at Hardy from no more than fifteen feet. Starting a desperate dive for his gun, Hardy was in the air when something hit him in the chest and he went down at first sideways, then over flat on his back.

John Holiday was down. He lay in a hump out in the fairway of the pier.

McGuire and Hardy were charging up from the truck.

It was Glitsky's only chance to move and he took it, pushing off from the building, turning to get a gauge of where Gerson had gotten to. Glitsky's own position, caught between Gerson and the Panos crowd, had been completely untenable, but Holiday's intervention and then the truck's arrival had given him a few seconds.

Off to his right, by the mouth of the pier, Glitsky heard the blast of a shotgun, then another, intermingled with several explosions of pistol shot in rapid succession — someone was firing an automatic with both hands. A quick glance caught Hardy going down.

Zigzagging, Glitsky broke for the cover of the barn.

McGuire, the lone man standing now out on the pier, had fired his two loads at Nick Sephia. If the man wasn't dead, McGuire figured his dancing career was over at least. McGuire had ejected his shells, had two more in his knuckles ready to insert. But it all took time. Not a lot of time, but enough for Rez, who jumped out of his doorway now and ran toward McGuire, one of his gun hands extended with the automatic in it, screaming a long wild note. He closed to three or four feet, pointed the gun at McGuire's head and pulled the trigger.

But there was no report. The automatic had misfired. Staring at it in fury for the briefest of seconds, Rez swore and threw it down onto the asphalt. Glitsky, less than twenty feet away in the door of the barn, could almost see the moment when Rez realized he still had his other gun in his other hand. McGuire was finished with his reload, though, snapping the barrel back up into place as Rez extended his other arm.

Glitsky, braced against the barn door, aimed carefully and, holding his gun with both hands, fired twice, the first bullet taking Rez under the right arm, passing through both his lungs and his heart, the second missing entirely. But the second shot wasn't needed. Firing squads had killed people more slowly — Rez was dead before he hit the ground.

But the reverberation from that shot hadn't died when another two rang simultaneously, one to Glitsky's left from the front of the pier, and the other behind him. Spinning around, his own gun in his two-handed grip, Glitsky saw Gerson not ten feet behind him slide slowly down the front of the stucco of the warehouse next door, leaving a trail of blood on the faded wall. He turned back to see that Hardy was now slowly getting up, his gun in his hand, and Moses crossing over to him.

Glitsky suddenly wasn't sure that he could move at all. In the sudden and deafening silence, he let his hands go to his sides and leaned heavily against the barn door. But there was Holiday, whose early volley had certainly saved Glitsky's life, lying without any movement on the asphalt. If he was alive, if any of them were alive, they would need to call an ambulance. And seconds could matter. Glitsky had to check.

Hardy and McGuire had something of the same thought, and the three men converged on their fallen ally. Holiday wasn't moving at all. They had gathered in a knot around him, Glitsky going down on one knee, a hand to where the pulse should be on Holiday's neck, when suddenly the silence was again defiled.

A woman's voice, harshly commanding, "Put it down! Guys, look out!" They all turned, scattering with their weapons pointed, but then immediately came one last and again nearly simultaneous round of gunfire.

Gina Roake walked slowly, ignoring them, warily approaching the body of the man who'd turned and squeezed off a shot at her when she'd called out.

Glitsky, Hardy and McGuire had all seen it, Roy Panos lying flat on his stomach, his gun extended where he'd been aiming, directly at Gina. Before she'd called out, he was obviously intending to take out at least one and maybe all of the men before they could finish him.

Gina stopped at his body and kicked at it as she might have some dead vermin, her pistol pointed the whole time at his head. Then she looked up at the three other gunmen, her shoulders fell and she walked toward them.

None of the principals could have guessed the length of the battle, although none of them would have believed it lasted less than ten minutes. But from the first shot to the last, the total time of the engagement was one minute, twenty-two seconds.

31

Len Faro stood outside the lit perimeter of the crime scene for a moment before wading in, thinking that this had been about the deadliest two weeks since he'd come on with the force. By the time he arrived at Pier 70, dusk was well advanced and the place was a madhouse of activity with three TV and a couple of local radio crews, six or seven black-and-whites, several unmarked cars, two ambulances, the coroner's van, and a limousine that he guessed would belong to one of the higher brass.

Which, now that he thought of it, made little sense if this was a gang shooting. And that's what he would normally have expected in this location. So, wondering now, making his way through the phalanx of vehicles, he showed his badge to the officer at the tape and stepped over it. The scene was lit by the television lights as well as headlights from the cars, but even without the illumination, Faro could see at a glance that there'd been significant carnage.

He passed the first body only a few feet onto the pier itself and paused by the knot of daytime CSI people attending it. "Gangbangers?" he asked Gretchen, tonight's photographer. After all, four bodies were lying in plain sight — there might be more inside any of these buildings — and Faro had up until now only seen this kind of slaughter in a drive-by or other organized retaliation environment.

But Gretchen looked shell-shocked herself, and in a woman to whom violence was literally a daily event, this was surprising. "Gerson," she said. And at first he thought she was asking him if the lieutenant had been notified to come to the scene.

"I assume," he began, then stopped. "What about him?"

She motioned with a toss of her head back down the pier another forty feet or so, where another group of men were standing around another body, propped under a thick streak of brown on a stucco wall. Was that Frank Batiste down there? The deputy chief did not come to homicide scenes unless something was radically unusual. Faro broke into a trot, was with them all in five seconds — Cuneo and Russell from homi-

714

cide, John Strout the chief medical examiner, two daytime CSI people. Everybody with hands in their pockets against the biting wind. To get to them, Faro had to pass a third corpse on the pier on his way down, and a fourth buried in a hail of broken glass in one of the doorways. Other homicide inspectors, half the lot of them — Darrel Bracco, Sarah Evans, Marcel Lanier — appeared as recognizable suddenly in the glut of faces.

Still, getting up to this victim, Faro slowed before he'd quite reached it, took a last step or two, stopped dead in his tracks. Jesus Christ, he thought.

Barry Gerson's eyes were open. He hadn't yet been moved, and so sat with his legs almost straight out, tipped a little to his right side, at the bottom of the brown line, which disappeared into his back. Faro leaned down closer, made out two small holes in the front of his jacket. He straightened up and turned to the knot of men. "How did this happen?"

"We're in the process of trying to piece that together right now, Sergeant." Batiste had come up through homicide — he'd been lieutenant before Glitsky — and so he knew the drill. "I'm hearing from these inspectors" — he indicated Cuneo and Russell — "that there's been some history among these men."

Faro, out of the loop, glanced at his dead lieutenant, came back to Batiste. But Cuneo, pointing up the pier, was the one to speak. "The first stiff back there is John Holiday, Len. Beyond him is Roy Panos. That speak to you at all?"

"John Holiday, I know," Faro said. A nod. "The name only." He paused, knowing that his next words would be a bomb, decided he had to say them. "I was at his house a couple of nights ago. With Paul Thieu."

All heads snapped toward him. Russell and Cuneo exchanged a meaningful look. "What was he doing there?" Cuneo asked. "What were you doing there?"

"Holiday was our suspect." Russell, bitching about turf.

But Batiste cut them both off. "I don't give a damn about any of that. Sergeant, you're telling me Paul Thieu was in this, too?"

"It seems like he would have had to be somehow, sir. Doesn't it?"

"And killed himself over it?"

"That might not have been over this," Cuneo said. "It might have been something else."

"Or maybe he didn't even kill himself at all," Faro said. "Maybe somebody killed him."

"What for?" Russell snapped.

"I don't know. Shut him up?"

"About what?" Cuneo.

Faro shrugged. He didn't know. He motioned back toward the other bodies. "So who are the other two?"

Batiste provided the identifications. When he heard the names, Faro nodded. "Just yesterday, sir, Inspector Thieu had me check fingerprints we found at Holiday's house against these guys. They'd been there."

"Which means what?"

"I don't know, sir." He looked around. "Holiday and these men must have been into something together, though."

The deputy chief didn't like this turn of events at all, and it showed all over him. His eyes strafed the men knotted around him, went back to Gerson, over to Holiday's body, took in the whole scene. "What the hell's going on? Anybody got any idea?"

"Y'all hold the fort here," John Strout said. "I'm going to take a walk, see some other clients. Jimmy." The medical examiner moved back up the pier with one of the other crime scene inspectors.

After he'd gone, Cuneo and Russell shared another look, and Batiste caught it. "Let's hear it, boys. You even think you got anything at all, now'd be a good time to share."

Cuneo cleared his throat, took the lead. "Lincoln and I, we've been working a little with Roy Panos." He jerked a thumb. "The first body up there."

"What do you mean, working with him?" Batiste asked.

"He was an assistant patrol special . . ."

"Related to Wade?"

"Yes, sir. His brother. He became a source."

"For what?"

"First the Silverman murder. Then Matt Creed, the other Patrol Special . . ." The admission was costing Cuneo. He cleared his throat again. ". . . and the Tenderloin multiple."

Batiste crossed his arms. "You're telling me this man Panos was a source for what, four homicide investigations?"

Russell jumped to his partner's defense. "They were all related, sir."

"I would hope to smile. Okay, so where does Paul Thieu come in?"

Again, the glance between the homicide guys, but there was no hiding it, and

Cuneo took it again. "He originally drew both Creed and the Tenderloin guys."

Batiste, trying to get it clear. "But you wound up with both of them."

"That's right." Cuneo nodded. "The lieutenant handed them off to us. There was a connection with both of them to Silverman, which was ours already. He thought it would be more efficient."

"But Thieu stuck with it anyway? Why would he do that?" Blank stares all around, and Batiste turned back to Faro. "Sergeant, I'd be interested in anything you'd like to contribute."

Faro tugged at his bug, the tuft of hair under his lower lip. "He had some questions, I guess."

"What kind of questions?"

"With the evidence at the Tenderloin scene."

"He told you that?"

"In vague terms only."

"But nothing specific?"

"Not really, sir, or if there was, he didn't share that information with me."

"So what did he tell you when you were going out to Holiday's? What was that about?"

"I told you. To lift prints." Faro turned to the inspectors. "He told me it was a favor for you guys."

"That's bullshit," Cuneo said. "We never sent anybody out there." He was angry and was making very little effort to hide it. If Batiste hadn't been there, he might have swung at Faro. "We would have made any request like that directly to CSI, Len, like we always do, and you know it. This really pisses me off," he added to no one in particular.

Batiste ignored him. "All right." He pointed at Cuneo and Russell. "Put that on your list, way up there, maybe first." Again, he surveyed the area all around. "So what the hell happened here? What got Barry out here? It had to be something with these Patrol Specials, wouldn't you think? How many of them are dead now?"

"Two," Russell said. "Roy Panos and Matt Creed."

But Cuneo couldn't let that go. "You might as well include Nick Sephia. He used to work for Panos, too. He's his nephew." He indicated the spot. "That's him in the doorway up there."

"Shit." Batiste blew out heavily. "Anybody call Wade yet? Where's Lanier?" He turned and called out. "Marcel!"

Lanier came trotting up from where Sephia had fallen. "Yes, sir?"

"You'd better get ahold of Wade Panos and get him over here ASAP. That's his brother Roy, and his nephew Nick. This has got to have something to do with him. We've got to find out what he knows."

"What are you thinking?" Lanier asked.

"I'm thinking somebody with Panos tried to broker some kind of a deal."

"Not with Holiday," Cuneo put in. "Panos and him don't get along."

"That's interesting," Batiste said. "I wonder where he was when this was going on. Well, we'll get to that. Meanwhile, Marcel, did I read somewhere you finally passed for lieutenant?"

"Yes, sir."

"All right, then congratulations, you're the point man on this." He gestured around. "All of it. The detail reports to you, you come to me. I know you'll thank me some day. Guys" — the deputy chief turned to Cuneo and Russell — "everything through Marcel, clear?" Batiste then turned around and looked down at the body of Barry Gerson. He went to a knee, shook his head with great sadness. "What the hell were you thinking, coming down here with no backup?"

Marcel Lanier had been a homicide inspector for twenty years, and during that time had formed some of the same conclusions about Wade Panos that Glitsky had reached. The last time Lanier had done anything even tangentially connected to the Patrol Special, he'd been trying to do a favor for both his new and old lieutenant, bridging the gap between them. That had backfired awkwardly.

Now he was coming to his interrogation of Wade Panos with a different, and mostly negative, set of preconceptions. Before he'd sent Cuneo and Russell off to the lab to check on Thieu's fingerprint question, Lanier had pressed the two inspectors for a brief recap of the events, and their interpretations of them, since Sam Silverman's death. The roles of both Roy and Wade Panos struck him as unusual, to say the least.

Lanier had been at Pier 70 for over three hours and hadn't been in a good mood when he'd arrived. By now, he was frozen to the bone, overwhelmed with his new and sudden responsibilities, sickened by all he'd seen. The media had, if anything, multiplied. They had set up camps at the pier, fighting for exclusive quotes and breaking bulletins. In the pools of artificial light from the department's portable lamps, all five bodies had been tagged, bagged and transported, but several teams of crime scene specialists were still doing their painstaking work up and down the pier.

Panos had arrived with his lawyer — his lawyer? — in time to see his brother and nephew packed into the coroner's van, and Lanier had asked them both, as a courtesy, if they could wait for a few minutes and have Wade answer a few questions, try to clear up some of the mystery here. He had managed to keep himself looking busy with the various teams — it wasn't terribly difficult — so that the few minutes could grow to a half hour.

Now Lanier knocked at the window to Panos's car, opened the back door and slid in. Reaching a hand over the seat, he shook hands all around, offered condolences, everybody's pal. He then took out his pocket recorder, and, getting their permission, placed it on the seatback between them. He got right to it. "So, do you have any idea what this is about?"

"Damn straight I do, and a pretty good one."

"Tell me."

"He didn't really say that, that he

thought I was actually *there?*" Glitsky shook his head in disbelief. "That man's a piece of work. Was there any physical indication that I was?"

"You didn't carve your initials into anything, did you, Abe?" Treya, calm and relaxed, making a joke. "It's an old habit he's trying to break, Marcel. Everywhere he goes, if there's a tree . . . He's worse than a dog."

Lanier smiled. "No trees there. No initials, either."

"How can I put this, Marcel? That's because I wasn't there."

Glitsky had crossed a leg and leaned back on the couch, his arm around his wife. It was close to eight o'clock, and the family, including grandfather, had finished dinner about twenty minutes before. Because Inspector Lanier had come by, Nat offered to baby-sit Rachel in her playpen while he did the dishes, and they could all hear him singing songs from *Fiddler on the Roof* to keep her entertained. Now Lanier sat across from them in the living room with a Diet Coke.

Lanier made an apologetic face. "I've got to ask, Abe. Panos didn't actually say you were, he said he thought you might have been. Then when I found you hadn't been at work . . ."

"Sure, of course, no offense. I'd ask the same thing." Glitsky came forward. "Look, I'm not making any secret of it, Marcel. Panos isn't a friend of mine. I told you about him when? A week ago? So you could warn Barry. Not that it did him any good."

"But you weren't at work."

"That's right. And I wasn't sick either. So where was I?"

"Right. That's the question."

"What time, more or less?"

"Two-ish."

Glitsky remembered right away. "I was at David Freeman's apartment with Gina Roake. You know Freeman?"

"Sure."

"Well, you may not have heard, but he died today, too. Around noon. Roake wanted to get some of Freeman's clothes picked out for the funeral and I thought she could use the company. She was a mess, Marcel. Anyway, Freeman had this one suit, but it had gotten ruined and she'd forgotten . . . anyway, long afternoon. Sorry, but she'll vouch for it. Unless Panos thinks she was there, too. Out at the pier, I mean."

"Maybe she brought a howitzer," Treya

added with scorn. "Was there any sign of a howitzer shell out there, Marcel?"

"Easy," Glitsky said to his wife. "It's just the job."

"I hate it," Treya said, and stood up abruptly. "Sorry, Marcel. I'm a little impatient lately." She went into the kitchen.

"Roake will back me up, Marcel. I was there. If she's not at her office," Glitsky said, "R-O-A-K-E, try Freeman's. They'll know where to find her. Dismas Hardy probably will have her number, too."

Lanier scribbled on his pad, let some air out. "Okay, one more, Abe, if you don't mind. If you were working with Hardy, how'd you get connected with Roake?"

Glitsky sat back again, relaxed. "She came by to check with Freeman's office, which is where Hardy works. He and I were just about finished, and Roake needed some help at Freeman's. So I went with her. Good Samaritan."

"And what were you doing at Hardy's in the first place?"

"It's why I took the two days off. We were both trying to get somebody interested in investigating these same guys who got killed today."

"Why?"

"Because somebody had threatened us,

and Hardy thought he knew who it was." The plan they'd all agreed upon — Hardy, Glitsky, McGuire, Roake — was to keep as close to the truth as possible during all the interrogations that were likely to follow. "So did I."

"So who'd you try to get interested? Management and Control?" This was the department, formerly called Internal Affairs, that investigated police misconduct.

"No. Let's just say Hardy went to some judges and I went to another law enforcement agency."

"Outside the department? You're saying you went to the FBI?"

"I went to another agency," Glitsky repeated. "It's moot anyway, Marcel. The point was I was doing some work at Hardy's office because it could have been embarrassing at the Hall." Glitsky held up his hands, palms out, all innocence. "Look, you know about Gerson calling me off Silverman right after I talked to you?"

"Yeah?"

"Well, I didn't stay all the way out." He leaned back again, matter of fact. "Sam Silverman's widow is a friend of mine. She had a question and asked me. I forwarded it on to Cuneo and Russell. Then Paul

Thieu had a bit of a moral dilemma about some evidence and he came to me about it."

"And you talked to him?"

"Briefly."

"You think any of this had to do with his death?"

"I think it's possible. I don't think he killed himself."

"Then who killed him?"

"I don't know, Marcel. I wish I did know."

Lanier grimaced. "An objective observer might say you were involved at this point, Abe."

"I never said I wasn't. After my family got threatened, I got proactive. You would have, too."

"All right. That's what Panos said today. You were trying to take these boys down. The same ones who got shot."

"And I wanted to take out Barry Gerson, too?" Glitsky allowed a trace of asperity. "And I wanted to do all of this with the help of John Holiday, who was wanted for murder? Are you saying you believe I could have been part of that, Marcel?" He leaned back, softened his tone. "I was trying to find a way to do this kosher." He sighed. "All right. I might as well tell you. You know Bill Schuyler, FBI? Talk to him."

"So what was Hardy doing?"

"Hardy thought these guys were trying to frame Holiday. He was calling judges. You can ask around on that, too. Look, Marcel, I don't know what got Barry down there to the pier, or Holiday for that matter, but these guys are bad people. I'm not surprised they got themselves killed. But if you think I was there or had anything to do with it . . ." He let the words hang in the room.

Marcel put down his empty glass and sighed heavily. "If you weren't there, you weren't there, Abe. I've just got to touch all the bases. Tell your wife I'm sorry I upset her, would you? And you, too."

When Lanier got to the door, Glitsky held it for him, stopped him for a second. "So, Panos aside, Marcel, how many people are they saying were down there?"

Lanier's eyes were drawn with fatigue. "CSI's saying at least six, maybe as many as ten. Lots of hardware, different calibers, but people might have been doubled up. At least one shotgun. Could have been seven thousand Macedonians in full battle array." He shrugged wearily. "You ask me, Abe, nobody's got a clue."

"That was Norma," Hardy said, "from the office."

Frannie was at the dining room table, studying. She looked up. "How is she?"

"Okay, considering."

She put the book down. "What?"

"She just got a call from Lieutenant Lanier, homicide. One of the associates was working late and gave him her home number. He wanted to know where I'd been all afternoon. She'd never had anyone from the police call and ask her that before. She hoped it was okay with me that she just went ahead and told them without checking with me first. I told her sure, why not? She gave him Phyllis's number, too. Wanted to know what it was all about."

"What did you tell her?"

"That I had no idea."

Frannie pushed her chair back, brushed a rogue hair from her forehead. She rested her hand over her heart. "And what did she tell him? Lanier."

"That I'd been in my office."

"The whole afternoon?"

"Until a little after three. Working."

Hardy had changed out of the Kevlar in the truck and asked McGuire, on his way to Ghirardelli Square and the Municipal

Pier where he was going to ditch the guns and, if he could, the vests, to drop him back at Sutter Street. He had come in through the garage, up the inside elevator all the way to the third floor. In his office, he changed into the business suit he kept hanging in his closet. Then — it had been just three o'clock — he'd walked back by the staircase into the lobby, carrying his old clothes, hiking boots and all, in a laundry bag that he'd dropped at St. Vincent de Paul on the way home. In the lobby, he'd said hello to Phyllis and shared a moment of commiseration. After that, he looked in on Norma and said he wasn't able to concentrate at all after the news about David. He'd been trying for a couple of hours to do some simple admin stuff but he really couldn't work at all and was going home. Maybe she should do the same. Tomorrow they could start picking up the pieces if they could. She'd gotten up and hugged him again. He'd nearly passed out from the pain where the bullet had smashed into the vest, but she probably thought the tears were for Freeman. And in some sense, maybe they were.

"She was positive. I was there all day. She hoped that was the right thing to say."

"What did you tell her?"

"That it was the truth. How could it be wrong?"

Overtime was being had by all.

At 10:30, Lanier was out at his desk in the detail. He might have just been named the provisional and nominal head of the unit, but he wasn't going into Gerson's office for a good long while, even if it got announced officially. Cuneo and Russell both wore hangdog looks as they sat there, and Lanier couldn't say he blamed them. Something about their investigations must have gotten seriously out of whack early on, and now in the wake of today's slaughter they both seemed lost and confused.

Cuneo had it all going tonight, playing the whole invisible drum kit — snare and kick drum, riding the high hat, the occasional crash of cymbal. Lanier wondered what track he was using in his brain, because part of him obviously had no idea that any of this percussion was going on. "What I can't figure out is why Thieu would have even thought to look at Holiday's. I mean, what did he know that we didn't know?"

"The question is, Dan, what do we know now?"

"About what?"

"About the fingerprints at Holiday's house, for example. What do they mean? Were these guys friends, or what?"

"They played poker together at Silverman's," Cuneo said. "But otherwise, did they hang out together? No, I'd say not."

"But they'd both been to Holiday's place."

"I doubt it." Cuneo was upping the tempo. "No. I can't see that."

"Wait a minute, Dan, wait a minute," Lanier said. "I wasn't asking if they'd been to Holiday's. We *know* they went there. The prints were there. The question is why."

"Maybe they played poker there, too, once or twice."

"But why, if they weren't friends?" Lanier focused on each of them in turn. "I don't know anything more than you do, okay? In fact, I know way less on these cases. I'm asking you both to think why these fingerprints might have been enough to get Paul killed, if somebody killed him. What they might mean."

Blanks, until Cuneo suddenly stopped all his frenetic movement. It was like a vacuum in the room. When he first spoke, it was almost inaudible.

"What's that, Dan?" Lanier asked.

Cuneo looked up, let out a long sigh. "It means they did plant the evidence," he said. "It's like Mrs. Silverman thought . . . if they did plant . . ." He stopped again, stared across Lanier's desk.

"If they did plant what, Dan?" Marcel said.

"The evidence at Holiday's," Cuneo said. He gripped his temples and squeezed so that his fingers went white. "Man oh man oh man."

Michelle sat in the big chair by her picture window that afforded no view of the black night outside. The reading light glared next to her and reflected the room back at her, her own pitiful image in the glass of the window. She'd cocooned herself into a comforter that offered little comfort, huddled into as small a position as she could get herself. Next to her on the light table there was an untouched glass of white wine and an envelope. In her hand, she held what had been the contents of the envelope, two pages of her own personal stationery — no letterhead, no border, just five-by-seven heavy rag, not quite white, bits of pulp throughout.

She'd been sitting, empty now, unmoving, for the twenty minutes since she'd finished reading the letter for the second time, and now her eyes had cleared enough to read it yet again.

Dear Michelle: (she read)

As you know better than anyone, it's been my tendency to want to come across as the world's most easygoing guy. It keeps the expectations low, both mine for myself, and my friends' for me. I don't ever promise anything other than perhaps a good time in the here and now, and since I don't pretend to have any depth or seriousness, no one can be disappointed in me when I don't deliver, when I flake out, when I get drunk or loaded and do any one of the many stupid and embarrassing things that have cost me friends and self-esteem.

When I think back on the time that I was married to Emma, especially the few months after we had Jolie, I sometimes wonder what happened to the person I was then. Where suddenly for that short time it was okay to feel like things mattered.

Like everything mattered, in fact.

It was strange, but I found I actually wanted Em and Jolie to have expectations for me, to want the best out of me. When before I'd always run from that, telling myself that I was just a clown, deep as a dinner plate. Maybe also, though, because I was afraid that if I tried to be more, I'd fail. It's a true fact that if you don't try, you can never fail. Foolproof.

But a funny thing happened. I found out with my girls that the more I acknowledged how much I cared about them, the better my life became. I started trying all the time in a hundred different ways and stunned myself by succeeding. I was faithful, for example, and wanted to be. Suddenly I didn't need women on the side as a backup position if Em dumped me because I didn't deserve her. Or if she cheated on me. I just knew that wouldn't happen, ever. I believed in all of us, pathetic though that may sound. Some of my core bedrock had shifted and settled and now I could take down my guard and breathe. And enjoy.

I don't know what it was about my hardwiring that had made me fear commitment so much before that, but gradually the life I was living with them became the only thing I really wanted.

Me and Em and Jolie. The whole world.

Which of course ended.

And then what a massively gullible fool I'd been, huh? To believe in all that? To think it could last? Talk about pathetic. Talk about stupid.

Well, none of that was ever going to happen to me again, ever. The goal was get a nice buzz, keep it going, risk your money and your job and everything else because then you really could fail completely. You could get to zero hope, rock bottom, which was pure freedom. And none of it mattered anyway, right? Take every single opportunity for physical pleasure and make sure it was purely physical, nothing more. Happiness was a moment and that was all it was. Any thought that a life could take on a shape and be fulfilling was out of the question.

So why am I writing this now?

Because something has shifted inside me again. Knowing you has changed me. Once and for all, I really feel as though I've laid those awful ghosts to rest. I don't know where you and I are going exactly, but I wanted you to know that suddenly I want you to have expectations of me; I want to find my best self, and be that person. I want to try and try and keep trying even if sometimes I do fail. It's all in the trying.

Does this make any sense?

Now, this afternoon, there's something else I've got to do. Another commitment, a matter of honor if that's not too overblown a word. It seems all of a piece, somehow. Expectations and responsibilities. And suddenly I'm okay with them. I even welcome them.

If you're reading this, I didn't come back. This time, it's because I can't, not because I didn't try. But whatever happens to me, I want you to know that life is good and that I left this apartment today as happy and filled with hope for the future as I have ever been in my life.

I love you with all my heart.

Epilogue

Epilogue

32

In late November, a high-pressure front settled in off the coast, and the last three days set records for the cold, with highs in the low forties. Newscasters were saying that with the windchill it was equivalent to the mid-twenties.

Vincent Hardy was the first one up on the holiday morning. They'd used the living room fireplace the past few nights, and all he had to do was crumple up yesterday's *Chronicle* and blow on the embers to get a flame. By the time his father came downstairs at a little after eight, three oak logs crackled. Vincent sat Indian style on the floor four feet or so in front of the blaze, staring into it.

His father, barefoot, wore jeans and an old gray sweatshirt. He had his coffee in a mug and put it on the floor when he sat down.

"Good fire. Nice job."

"Thanks."

"Happy Thanksgiving."

Silence.

"The Beck sleeping?"

"I think so."

"On the floor in your room again?"

"Yeah." Then, "It's okay. I don't mind."

"No. I know. You're a good guy."

Hardy picked up his mug, stared at the flames. Vincent moved over a few inches. Hardy put an arm around him, drew him in for a minute.

"She's just afraid, you know. She keeps seeing that picture. . . ."

"How about you?" Hardy asked.

He felt his son's shoulders lift, then drop. "I don't think about it."

"Really?"

"Yeah."

With a sharp crack, the fire spit, flared, settled. Hardy stole a sideways glance at his boy. His hands were clasped. He appeared mesmerized by the fire.

" 'Cause if you do," Hardy finally said, "if you're worried about anything . . ."

Vincent shuddered, then shook himself away, was suddenly on his feet. *I just don't think about it! Okay?"*

"Okay, Vin. Okay."

His son looked down at him, eyes threatening to tear. He started to walk away, out of the room.

Hardy stood, turning after him. "Hey, Vin! Wait. Don't go running away, please. It's okay. C'mere. It's all right." Vincent stopped and turned to him. "Come on back over here. Please. Give your old man a hug."

The boy sighed deeply, eventually came forward. He was soon going to be fourteen years old. His dad still had a foot of height on him. When he got close enough, Hardy reached out and put an arm around his shoulders, quickly kissed the top of his head. "It's okay," he said, one last time.

Then he let go of his son and walked out the door and over the frost on the lawn to get the morning paper.

Dinner was the classic turkey and stuffing, mashed potatoes, cranberry sauce and brussels sprouts. Treya brought her famous marshmallow candied yams, green beans with almonds; Susan her spinach salad with mandarin oranges; Abe some macaroons for those who didn't like pumpkin pie. Even Nat chipped in with creamed onions, a surprise hit. They'd extended the table out with all its leaves so that it took up the whole dining room and half the living room and could accommodate fifteen people.

McGuire was there with Susan and the girls. The Glitsky contingent included not only Abe, Treya and the baby, but also Nat and the older kids home for Thanksgiving — Orel and Raney from their respective colleges, and even Abe's eldest, Isaac, made it up from Los Angeles where he'd gotten on — temporarily, he said — with a construction crew. The only missing Glitsky was Jacob the opera singer — he was touring, perennially, somewhere in Europe.

After dinner they'd closed the table back up. The older kids had pitched in on the hundred and fifty dishes while the adults had more coffee or, for some, drinks in the living room. Now almost everybody had gathered at the front of the house, and they were playing games.

Games, Hardy thought, were good. Talking — the stories and jokes the whole time they ate — that was good, too. Throwing the football around all afternoon out in the street — great idea. As was the communal cooking. The daily things, the simple things.

No reason to mention Wade Panos, or the fact that he was still very much alive, possibly even more of a threat than he'd been. Everyone was aware of that every waking minute, sometimes during sleep. Hardy, drenched in sweat and gasping for breath, had jolted himself awake more than once. Frannie and the kids cried out, between them, every night the first week, a couple of times since.

Although now, a couple of weeks into it, Hardy had privately begun to consider that maybe their show of force had made Panos, at least, cautious. At best, they'd scared him off. But Hardy wasn't going to say that out loud. Not yet.

After dinner, the games had started with several rounds of St. Peter/St. Paul, and now they had moved on to charades. Abe was trying to pantomime "Peter, Paul & Mary" and it wasn't going very well. Unless he was lucky, it would be a while before he was through.

Hardy took the opportunity to get up and walk back to the empty kitchen. The high-energy laughter from the game in the living room still rang through the house, and Hardy found he'd run out of tolerance for it. He opened the kitchen's back door, which led to his tool and workroom, and was surprised to find Moses there, sitting alone on the countertop, nursing a drink.

"Hey," Hardy said, "you're missing a great show — Abe's trying to emote. It's something to see."

Moses raised his eyes. "You're missing it yourself, I notice."

Hardy closed the door behind him, took a hit from McGuire's glass, handed it back to him. "How you holding up?"

A shrug. "Good."

"You sound like my son. One syllable per sentence. 'Good.' 'Fine.' 'Great.' "

"Okay, maybe I'm not so good." He drank an inch of scotch. "I worry about it, and don't say, 'about what?' "

"I worry, too. Is Panos done? Are the cops going to put us there?"

McGuire nodded. "There you go."

"Okay, so the answers are one, maybe he isn't, and two, maybe they will. So what?"

"So I'm having some issues with it."

"Guilt?"

This seemed to bring McGuire up short. "No," he said, "no guilt."

"Me, neither. It had to be done."

"No question. But all this having to pretend nothing happened . . ."

"Who's pretending that?"

"Oh, nobody," McGuire said. "Just everybody at dinner here today. Every day at home."

"So what do you want?"

"I don't know. I wish it had never started, that's all."

"You mean you wish there wasn't evil in the world?"

McGuire drained his glass, brought his bloodshot eyes up to Hardy's. "Yeah, maybe that."

"Well, there is," Hardy said. He rested a hand on McGuire's shoulder. "I guess we're going to have to get used to it."

33

CityTalk

BY JEFFREY ELLIOT

Shock waves are still rippling through the various Halls of the city over the raids yesterday by local police and federal marshals on several upscale homes in various San Francisco neighborhoods as well as on downtown's Georgia AAA Diamond Center, and the disappearance of its chief executive officer. Dmitri Solon, the young Russian immigrant with a penchant for fine clothes and a luxurious lifestyle, had in a very few years become just as well-known as an art aficionado and political contributor. He had well-documented and close ties with many highly ranked (and now plenty embarrassed) city officials, including the mayor and District Attorney, and his Russian-built helicopter had become a familiar, albeit annoying, presence over the city's skyline as it ferried jewelry and gemstones to and from the airport.

This reporter has learned that yesterday's raid, which netted over $1.5 million in cash and nearly thirty pounds of cocaine and heroin, followed a six-month investigation into alleged money laundering and drug trafficking activities occurring out of several homes in the Mission, Diamond Heights and St. Francis Wood neighborhoods, activities financed by diamonds from Georgia AAA, which in turn had been smuggled out of the Russian treasury by that country's own minister of Precious Gems and Metals, and delivered here to San Francisco in diplomatic pouches carried by commercial airliners.

Also implicated in the scheme, and arrested in yesterday's raids, was Wade Panos, another influential political donor, whose company, WGP Enterprises, Inc., provided formal security for Georgia AAA, as well as the pool from which the Diamond Center selected its drivers. Mr. Panos's drivers allegedly coordinated and executed the actual deliveries of contraband among the various drop houses.

Sources with the police and FBI confirm that the initial investigation into irregularities at Georgia AAA commenced last November when Lieutenant Abraham Glitsky inadvertently stumbled upon two of Mr. Panos's drivers acting in a suspicious manner. On a hunch, he followed them to several addresses. When local authorities, many the recipients of Panos's political contributions, declined to act, Glitsky forwarded the information to federal authorities.

On a related front as the story grows, and in light of the principals involved, Lieutenant Marcel Lanier of homicide expressed concern and interest in reopening the investigation into the so-called Dockside Massacre of last November. Two of the victims in that gunfight, Nick Sephia and Julio Rez, had been couriers for Georgia AAA and a third, Roy Panos, was employed by his brother at WGP. Speaking on condition of anonymity, highly placed police sources have opined that these two men, Sephia and Rez, were the security guards who originally attracted the suspicion of Lieutenant Glitsky. Additionally, Sephia was a nephew to Wade Panos.

The FBI believes that several of the

employees of Georgia AAA may in fact have been recruits from organized crime syndicates within Russia, and that the intimate and perhaps conflicting connections between the Panos group and these people may have played a significant role in the Pier 70 gunfight where five men, including homicide's Lieutenant Barry Gerson, were killed. Police have theorized that as many as seven more people, besides the five victims, took part in the battle. None have been arrested to date, and Lanier does not dispute the possibility that they may have used some sort of diplomatic immunity — and the Diamond Center's helicopter — to perpetrate the slaughter and then leave the country.

Finally, lawyer Dismas Hardy has asked that the police reopen the investigation into the death of Sam Silverman that led to a warrant for the arrest of John Holiday, who was a client of Hardy's and one of the men killed at Pier 70. Hardy is confident that the evidence upon which his client's murder warrant was issued was planted by Sephia and Rez. Hardy could not explain Holiday's presence at Pier 70, but noted that Lieutenant Gerson's presence has been equally confounding to authorities. Hardy offered the possibility that, in possession of evidence linking Rez and Sephia to the crimes for which Holiday had been charged, Holiday had arranged his surrender to Gerson, and that the Panos group had somehow been tipped to the plan, and ambushed them.

"He was a great guy," Hardy said. "I'd like to see his name cleared."

Often, in early June, snow remains in the high passes on the John Muir Trail.

Michelle Maier and her companion had packed out of Tuolumne Meadows in Yosemite yesterday, camping last night at Lyell Fork. Though the rangers going out had warned them that the way would be snow-blocked, today's goal was to get over Donohue Pass, elevation 11,056 and then descend a thousand or so feet down the other side. This early in the season, the sight of other campers up here wasn't always a daily event, and neither Michelle nor her companion had seen a soul all day.

Michelle was planning to spend four more days in the back country, then get to San Francisco in time to catch her flight to Barcelona, where she'd enrolled in a gourmet cooking class for the entire summer.

This had entailed giving up the apartment she'd kept since college. Possibly she could have sublet the thing, but she didn't want to be bound to return to the Bay Area when the class was complete. What if she got offered a sous-chef job somewhere? Or just wanted to stay overseas?

Her companion was a new friend. Gina was the first new friend, although not the only one, she'd made since John Holiday's death. Michelle had thought it was probable she'd be the only person at John's burial in Colma; certainly she expected to be the only woman there. But Gina Roake had been at the gravesite with some men, one of whom had been John's lawyer.

After the interment, they'd invited her to an Irish bar. Thinking Roake must have been another of John's girlfriends, Michelle didn't want to go at first, but then Gina's situation had become clear — she had lost her own fiancé, also to violence, and evidently on the same day John had died. So all of them from the gravesite sat and talked until it got dark and the men had to go home. She and Gina had stayed on at the bar. Gotten smashed.

The next day, both of them dying of alcohol poisoning, she had accompanied Gina to her fiancé's funeral, attended by the same three men who'd been at John's, as well as about six hundred other close personal friends and acquaintances of David Freeman's, who had evidently been somebody important, although Michelle had never heard of him.

But the connection between the two grieving women had become strong. They'd gone on their first hike together — a couple of miles around Tilden Park in Oakland — last January. A few weeks ago they'd walked the Bay to Breakers race. Getting in shape. Having some fun. At least once every two weeks they went out to dinner, usually at someplace Michelle would recommend.

The first time, they'd gone to Jeanty at Jack's. Michelle had shown up in her usual camo gear and afterward felt like a bit of a fool. Gradually, she rethought her style, or lack of. Recently, both women had taken to dressing up for these dinners. Even in San Francisco, where the odds did not favor single women, to say the least, they would almost always have the clear opportunity to meet men. Offers to buy drinks. None of these advances had gone anywhere, but they were flattering nonetheless. Nonthreatening.

Michelle wondered what in the world

she had been so afraid of.

And knew the answer, of course. Everything. Her funky, stupid hide-me clothes. Hiding out in the corners of restaurants and libraries. Communicating by email. The small, familiar world of her small, familiar apartment.

Now, well into early evening, the two women had been hiking in long shadows for an hour or more when they came around a bend in the path and found themselves suddenly squinting into the sunlight that reflected off a field of ice that covered the entire trail.

"At least now we know why we haven't seen anybody coming the other way," Roake said. She unshouldered her pack and took a long drink of water. Grimaced. "This iodine pill thing. I don't think I'm getting very used to the taste."

"I stopped using it," Michelle said.

Roake stopped in mid-drink. "Then why am I still gagging on this stuff? I thought there was giardia" — a particularly unpleasant intestinal parasite — "everywhere up here."

"There is, I suppose. But my dad used to hike up here all the time and he never used it, either. And never got sick." She shrugged. "If I've learned anything the past year, Gina, it's that the world's a dangerous place. It's never really been safe, although it's comforting to pretend it is. But really there's risk everywhere. Might as well embrace it and enjoy the days. So I'm going to drink the goddamned good-tasting, noniodized water."

Roake took another pull at her canteen, made another face. "Will you think I'm a wimp if I don't?"

"Absolutely." A big grin. "But who cares what I think? You do it your way; I'll still like you."

Michelle stood up, brushed off her bottom, stared at the ice shelf looming up ahead of them. "Talk about risk," she said. "Do you want to go for this? Maybe we should give it up?"

Roake, too, was on her feet. "And miss the best view in the Sierra? I'd rather die trying."

"So we go?"

"Lead on, girlfriend, lead on."

The employees of Thorndike Press hope you have enjoyed this Large Print book. All our Thorndike and Wheeler Large Print titles are designed for easy reading, and all our books are made to last. Other Thorndike Press Large Print books are available at your library, through selected bookstores, or directly from us.

For information about titles, please call:

(800) 223-1244

or visit our Web site at:

www.gale.com/thorndike
www.gale.com/wheeler

To share your comments, please write:

Publisher
Thorndike Press
295 Kennedy Memorial Drive
Waterville, ME   04901